Message From Baghdad

W0007328

CW00692469

Message From Baghdad

Bob Langley

PIATKUS

First published in Great Britain in 1993 by
Judy Piatkus (Publishers) Ltd of
5 Windmill Street, London W1

**The moral right of the author
has been asserted**

*A catalogue record for this book is available
from the British Library*

ISBN 0 7499 0197 7

Phototypeset in 11/12pt Compugraphic Times by
Action Typesetting Limited, Gloucester
Printed and bound in Great Britain by
Biddles Ltd, Guildford and Kings Lynn

Chapter One

Tension knotted Nuri's stomach as he moved along the deserted corridor. The humming of the air conditioner emphasized the beating of his heart and his fingers clutching the food tray felt damp and slippery. The building was hushed, the floor carpeted. There were no windows, and the only light came from a series of wire-bracketed lamps tracing the centre of the ceiling. He was acutely conscious of how unlikely it was he would escape.

Nuri was lean and slender, with a deceptive suppleness to his meagre frame. His passport listed his profession as student, and to some extent the description was true for Nuri was indeed registered in theological studies at Baghdad University, but in the Rub al Najar where he had spent his boyhood, he had pursued a different kind of learning from the time he was six years old. He had studied how to fire an Armalite, assemble a machine-gun, construct a homemade bomb from ordinary household materials, how ultimately to sacrifice his life with neither protest nor hesitation if the occasion demanded it. Nuri was a devout Moslem who believed that Paradise awaited the man who accepted martyrdom in the name of Allah; he was prepared to die tonight if necessary.

He drew to a halt at the sealed doors leading to the Israeli security office, and spoke into the accoustic grill: 'Suppertime.'

There was a brief pause as the two guards studied him on their internal video screen, then with a muffled click the doors slid gently open.

1

The room was large, and filled with surveillance equipment covering every approach route to the top-secret research laboratory. Seated behind the command desk, the duty guards, Kefim and Leiber, examined Nuri with surprise. 'I thought this was your night off,' Kefim said. 'What happened to Yakov?'

'He got sick. Some kind of stomach bug, the supervisor says.'

'Yakov's always sick,' Leiber grunted with disdain.

Nuri had worked at the plant for barely four months, and knew the two guards only vaguely; Leiber he liked – the man was friendly and courteous – but Kefim had a tendency toward arrogance. Nevertheless, Nuri felt sorry for what he had to do tonight.

He placed the food tray on the office table and watched Kefim and Leiber unwrapping the foil-covered containers. His breath made little rasping noises in his throat as he reached into his jumpsuit and drew out his Sauer and Sohn .38. He saw the shock on the security guards' faces.

'Nuri, what in the hell are you playing at?'

'Shut up.'

Nuri was keeping calm with an effort. It was not the danger which unnerved him – for Nuri, the prospect of sacrifice carried an intoxicating allure – but being alone was a different matter. He was a gregarious young man. He needed people.

Keeping his voice low, he said: 'I want the laboratory doors opened. Please type the necessary command on to the computer keyboard.'

The two guards looked at him defiantly, regaining their composure. Now that the initial surprise had passed, Nuri could see their minds beginning to work, calculating timing, opportunity. Their features hardened into baleful masks. 'Go screw yourself,' Kefim answered.

Nuri took a deep breath, and with compressed lips, gently squeezed the trigger. The shot made a noise like a snapping twig, its resonance muted by the chamber's insulation. There was something innocuous in the sound, but Kefim hit the floor like a falling log and rolled over in agony, clutching his left thigh.

'I shall continue firing,' Nuri said calmly, 'until one of you obeys me.'

Leiber glanced down at his wounded companion, then without a word, stepped to the instrument panel and punched out the required code. The sealed doors slid open with a muffled hum.

Nuri glanced quickly around the room. On the opposite wall was an unmarked door. 'What's in there?'

'Cleaning stuff,' Leiber answered.

Nuri backed toward it and glanced inside. Brooms stood propped in the corner and cans of floor polish lined the shelves. He gestured with his head. 'Get in.'

Leiber hesitated.

'Get in,' Nuri shouted, his voice trembling.

'Kefim's bleeding badly. He needs medical attention.'

'He'll get it faster if you do as I say.'

Scowling but intimidated, Leiber dragged his wounded colleague into the tiny cupboard and Nuri locked the door behind them. He stood for a moment, resting his head against the cool formica surface, his heart beating wildly, then he sucked in his breath and walked through the laboratory entrance.

The room was large – larger than Nuri had expected. Its walls were coated with thermal protection panels, and the only light came from the overhead striplamps. A narrow ventilator carried air and heating from the main construction plant.

There were pipes everywhere, twisting and trailing from unit to unit. The metal condensers looked like miniature grain elevators, bulky at the top, slender at the bottom. Steam hissed out of hidden apertures, imbuing the chamber with an eerie, almost futuristic air.

Nuri paused to savour the moment, then took out a tiny camera and began photographing. He knelt and crouched, directing his shots from every angle, pausing from time to time to concentrate on special appliances. In the training camp on the Euphrates River, they had warned him that clarity would be important. The click of his shutter made a sibilant hissing sound on the musty air.

So absorbed was Nuri in his task that only when he heard

the clamour of a distant alarm bell did he realize that he had unwittingly triggered an electronic sensor device. He felt no panic, merely a tightness in his stomach and genitals as tension enhanced his senses.

He removed the film from the camera and slipped it into a tiny phial. He was sweating copiously now, the perspiration streaming down his cheeks and drenching his cotton jumpsuit. He saw a ventilation grille on the wall above and climbed towards it. It was an easy haul, for the central-heating pipes provided excellent hand and footholds, and he was still breathing normally when he reached the tiny aperture. Behind the grille was a window, just large enough to permit the intake of air. Nuri tugged away the wire mesh and pushed back the pane as far as it would go. He could see the high-wire perimeter fence directly below, and a faint ribbon of orange light formed by the floodlamps on Watch-towers two and three.

He took out his flashlight and began to signal into the darkness; after a moment a series of answering flashes winked back at him. Nuri fumbled down the front of his jumpsuit and produced a small metal catapult with a rubber sling. Slipping the film phial into the pouch, he aimed it through the open window and let the elastic go. He watched the phial curve through the air, sailing in a perfect arc over the fence rim, its metal surface picking up slivers of refracted light before it landed with a muffled thud on the waste ground beyond. Almost instantly, a figure darted out of the darkness and snatched it up. The figure paused for a moment to wave at Nuri before vanishing back the way it had come.

Nuri sucked in a mouthful of cool night air. Now that his task had been accomplished, he was filled with an extra-ordinary sense of peace. He leapt from the wall pipes, landing on the floor with a noisy clatter as two Israeli soldiers emerged through the open doorway. They wore no caps, and their khaki tunics were open to the waist. Nuri pulled out his pistol, and the soldiers froze in their tracks, startled by the scrawny figure confronting them. Nuri laughed out loud. He felt joyously light-hearted.

'I take refuge in the Lord of the worlds,' he said, and

placing the pistol barrel between his lips, gently squeezed the trigger.

'We've got something strange on the downlink, sir,' said the duty operator at the US Satellite Tracking station in Sunnyvale, California.

Major Harry Stanton frowned as he leaned forward to examine the fractured images being beamed in from the satellite in geosynchronous orbit twenty-three thousand miles above the earth. A series of dark blotches showed in the video screen's left-hand corner. 'What do you make of it?'

'Looks like troop movements, sir.'

'An army?'

'Yes, sir. A big one, I'd say.'

'What's the location?'

'Tajura in the Iraqi Desert. Musallim al Shisur's territory. Of course ...' The operator hesitated. 'It could be an exercise, military manoeuvres.'

'That's no exercise sergeant. It looks more like an invasion force to me. Can we get this enlarged?'

'It'll take time. Three or four hours.'

'Do what you can. Then get the pictures up to R and A for immediate analysis.' Stanton picked up the telephone. 'I'd better call Washington right away.'

US President Lawrence Clayman was standing in the White House lobby when Emmett Rone entered the marbled portico. An urbane man, Clayman was doing his best to appear fascinated as a lady in a fur hat several sizes too large for her expounded passionately on the latest moves to cut the budget deficit. Rone smiled to himself. President Clayman might appear elegant and sophisticated on the surface, but he hadn't yet mastered the art of enduring fools gracefully. Anyone with half an eye could see he was bored out of his wits.

An SS man stepped forward as Rone approached, and Rone flashed his ID card for the umpteenth time. 'Secretary of State's Office,' he said. 'I have to speak to the President urgently.'

'The President is engaged at the moment, sir,' the guard

said. 'Perhaps you should have a word with his secretary.'

At that moment, Clayman himself spotted Rone above the sea of bobbing heads, and he saw a flicker of relief come into the President's eyes. He spoke quickly to the lady who was barracking him then, taking Rone's arm, led him along the White House corridor, moaning under his breath: 'Thank God you've arrived, Emmett. That woman was driving me scatty. Do you know she can jump from one subject to another without even drawing breath?'

'What excuse did you give her?' Rone asked.

'I said we had a matter of supreme importance to discuss.'

'You must be psychic, Mr President.'

Clayman glanced at him, frowning, his sharp eyes noting the strain on his associate's face. He peered over his shoulder, then without a word, ushered Rone into an empty office and leaned against the door, folding his arms. 'Something wrong, Emmett?'

Rone said: 'We've just had word from our satellite tracking station in Sunnyvale that they've spotted evidence of major troop movements in the Iraqi Desert.'

'Musallim al Shisur's territory?'

'Yes, sir.'

Clayman pursed his lips, absorbing the information thoughtfully. 'Could be some kind of elaborate war game. Al Shisur's always playing at toy soldiers. He's a classic example of arrested development.'

'The movements are too big for that. We think he has something a lot more sinister in mind.'

'Israel?'

'Israel would be the most obvious target.'

Clayman moved to the window and stood gazing across the White House lawn. 'God-*damn*! I thought we'd put an end to Middle East instability.'

'With respect, sir, I'd call that an impossible dream. We know for a fact that despite the arms sanctions, most of the Mid-East countries have been secretly building up their arsenals, smuggling in weapons through unscrupulous foreign dealers. Even our old ally Israel has been flouting the agreements, and it's an accepted fact that Musallim al

6

Shisur is a past master at promising one thing and doing another.'

'Al Shisur is a tyrant with a tyrant's mind,' Clayman said. 'He sees himself as a second Sadaam Hussein.'

Rone agreed. Iraq's president, Musallim al Shisur, had bludgeoned his way into power by eliminating anyone he saw as a potential rival. Ruthless and tyrannical, he maintained his position by a shrewd blend of clever politics and old-fashioned brutality. 'Al Shisur was little more than a boy when the Iraqi army was defeated in Kuwait,' Rone said, 'but I guess he never forgot the anger and humiliation. Now he wants to fulfil Sadaam Hussein's most cherished dream − unite the Arab nations and turn himself into some kind of Islamic supremo.'

Clayman gently massaged his cheek. Seen in the brilliant sunlight, his skin was covered with tiny wrinkles; it was the first time Rone had noticed the weariness beneath his leader's dignified pose. 'The question is − and it's one we have to address seriously − is he a harmless nut or a genuine threat to Middle Eastern peace?'

'No one as unpredictable as al Shisur can be comfortably regarded as harmless, Mr President. Most of the fortune he makes on oil is funnelled into military sources. At our last count, he was spending four billion dollars annually. He has at his disposal almost eighty thousand troops, making up ten divisions. He has nearly a thousand tanks, more than a thousand artillery pieces and God knows how many missiles. His air force consists of nearly three hundred attack aircraft, including MIG 23s, SU-20 Fitter Hs, Python B-5s, and US-built F-19s. Al Shisur's made no secret of the fact that despite the diplomatic settlements, he still dreams of driving Israel into the sea. We have to consider the possibility that he's about to do something catastrophic.'

'He also has nuclear capability, Emmett, which makes him a very dangerous protagonist indeed.'

Rone looked dubious. He was unimpressed by reports of Iraq's atomic arsenal; according to intelligence sources, their weapons were extremely low-grade and primitive − certainly no match for Israel's. 'I guess it was obvious Iraq would get its hands on nuclear weapons sooner or later, despite the arms limitation agreements, but al Shisur sees himself as the saviour of the Holy Land, not its destroyer. My bet is he'll want to operate along conventional lines as much as possible.'

'That's something to be thankful for, at least, but backed into a corner, who knows what the idiot might be capable of?' The President paused for a moment, considering thoughtfully. 'If al Shisur's planning to destabilize the Mid-East, we'll need to be kept informed. I'd like an executive committee to monitor the situation, Emmett. Ask the Secretary of State to head it. Tell him to include the Secretary of Defence, the Chairman of the Joint Chiefs of Staff and the Director of Central Intelligence. The minute things look like getting out of hand, they're to notify me immediately.'

'I'll see to it at once, Mr President,' Rone answered.

The Californian sun cast vivid shadows across the kidney-shaped pool where Leon B. Snyder was swimming. He had just completed his thirtieth length when Soames, his English butler, appeared on the patio and placed a padded envelope on the table beneath the sun-umbrella. 'Mr Snyder, sir. Special delivery.'

Snyder climbed from the pool, shaking the water from his silvery hair. Despite his age – he was in his mid-fifties – Snyder's physique was muscular and supple, his face tanned and hawk-like in appearance. He might have been an attractive man – handsome even, in the Hollywood sense – if it hadn't been for the avarice in his eyes and the feral hunger in his features. This quality was evident in the way he moved, for his body carried an assurance that was almost overwhelming as he walked to the table, slit open the envelope and examined its contents, whistling softly. 'So it's finally arrived?'

'It would seem so, sir.'

Snyder rubbed his hair with the towel. 'Give Kliban a call for me, will you, Soames? Tell him I'll be at his office at four o'clock. Then fetch the limo and park it in front of the house.'

'As you wish, sir,' the butler said, and hurried off.

8

The headquarters of Napier Oil Incorporated stood on the outskirts of Muna City, a large, palatial-looking building surrounded by the squat storage tanks of the local oil refinery. Snyder left his car on the forecourt and, clutching the package under his arm, took the elevator to the seventh floor.

Napier's President, Miles Kliban, looked nervous as Snyder entered his office. Kliban was a slim man with long artistic fingers who had been running Napier for seventeen years, and running the cartel to which Napier belonged . for a further three. Though Snyder was his subordinate, the man's dynamic personality always made the oil president feel uneasy. Snyder made decisions at a moment's notice and followed them through with the imperviousness of a battering ram, crushing anyone who stood in his way.

As usual, he wasted little time in getting down to business. He opened the package, scattered its contents across the desktop, and waited in silence as Kliban read the letter and examined the photographs. 'When were these taken?' Kliban asked.

'Two days ago. The Iraqis managed to plant a man among the Mazar administrative staff.'

'Enterprising,' Kliban said.

'Terminal, from the intruder's viewpoint. He committed suicide. No doubt he'll find salvation in Paradise.'

Kliban winced — Snyder's callousness often unnerved him — and to hide his discomfort, ruffled through the pictures again. 'Have al Shisur's experts examined these?'

'Yes. And they now believe Tel Aviv is about to launch its latest assault, not on the military but on the economic front. Iraq is convinced that unless drastic steps are taken, the Israelis, without firing a shot, will soon dominate the whole Middle East. They're ready to take those steps. The question is, are we in or out?'

Kliban looked unhappy. He picked up a pencil and rolled it between his fingers. 'It's a dangerous game we're playing, Leon.'

'No more dangerous than the one we played in 1991.'

'That's what I mean. If our association with the late Sadaam Hussein had leaked, even the slightest hint ...'

9

'But it didn't,' Snyder pointed out mildly.

'Nevertheless, things are different now. The peace treaties, the arms limitation agreements − it's a whole new ballpark, Leon. If we stir things up out there, who knows where the road might lead?'

'You're saying you want to walk, is that it?'

'No, no, of course not.'

Kliban rose to his feet and stood looking out of the window, nervously twisting his fingers. The sunlight cast shadows across his cheekbones. 'How confident do the Iraqis feel?'

'They're ready to go for broke. I've been dealing with the head of their armed forces in Baghdad, General Abu Bakhit. He's Musallim al Shisur's right-hand man. I get the feeling that he doesn't entirely approve of his country's president, but he's a loyal Iraqi and he'll do whatever's necessary to protect their economic future.'

'Including war?'

'Hell, yes,' Snyder said. 'How else can the Israelis be halted?'

'War's a terrible thing, Leon. Thousands of people will be killed. Maybe millions. That's an awesome responsibility.'

'Speaking frankly, when you consider the alternative, I believe we have no option. And if I may say so, Mr Kliban, that is also the opinion of our executive committee.'

Kliban nodded, struggling to maintain his composure, and returned to his desk. He thumbed through the photographs for a second time. 'We've got the muscle to make this operation work,' he said, 'but what about the Iraqi end? Whoever handles it will have to be very special. We need a man who can think not like an Arab, but like a westerner.'

'The Iraqis have such a man. His name is Joktan.'

'Joktan?'

'Salih Joktan. He was raised as a Bedouin tribesman until General Bakhit adopted him as his son and sent him to Oxford University in England. Joktan understands the western way of thinking. He's also a Christian, which makes him more amenable to western concepts and traditions.'

'What about experience?'

10

Snyder said: 'For years, Joktan carried out a one-man war of attrition against Israeli interests in Europe and the Middle East. He trained in Libya and made his debut in Paris where he shot dead the Israeli ambassador. Later, he executed four members of the French DST. He carried out the Lumdt Massacre, the Damascus hijacking, and the kidnapping of the Israeli Minister of State. He's noted not only for his savagery, but also for his planning ability. He became something of a hero in Iraq, where they made him an honorary colonel in the Republican Guard. He now tops Mossad's "most-wanted" lists.'

'Where is this Joktan now?'

Snyder hesitated, brushing absently at a dust speck on his trouser leg. 'Somewhere in the Iraqi desert.'

'The desert?'

'Uh-huh.' Snyder looked embarrassed. 'Seems our notorious terrorist had a change of heart. After the peace treaties of the nineties, he renounced his life of violence and returned to the Bedouin. He's been with them ever since.'

'What are you telling me, Leon? That the man on whom we're about to gamble our future has lost the will to fight?'

'I wouldn't put it quite like that. I guess he's encountered the kind of dilemma which confronts many men in the fullness of time: not the whisper of mortality or decay, but the transfiguring catalysts of doubt and change.'

'Will he be ruthless enough, I wonder.'

'Only one way to find out,' Snyder said. 'I'll fly to Baghdad and talk to him first thing in the morning.'

Chapter Two

The wind picked up spirals of spindrift, hurling them into Joktan's face. He watched the sand blending into an orange blur as Umbarack came slithering towards them through the storm, his pale robes billowing.

'They are resting in the hollow ahead,' Umbarack said, his voice hoarse with tension. 'Men of the Bait Kebir.'

'How many?'

'Four. All armed.'

Crouched in the darkness, the seven tribesmen looked like blocks of granite, their slitted eyes feathered with dust.

'Did you see the camels?' Rashid asked.

'I saw bin Ghabaisha's gelding, and the albino Sadr brought back from Salala.'

Rashid pulled back his *keffiyah* to spit on the ground. 'Their guilt is proven then. We must send them to Satan where they belong.'

Joktan said mildly: 'Would you take a man's life for the price of a few miserable pack-beasts?'

Rashid looked at him with surprise. 'But the Bait Kebir are thieves, Salih. They are a pestilence upon the earth. There can be only one punishment for such men.'

'Is it not holier to regain our possessions without the spilling of blood?'

Joktan's reasoning bewildered Umbarack. 'When a man sins, you must smite him down. How else can justice and order be maintained?'

'Sometimes it may be enough to point out the error of his ways.'

'How you've changed, Salih,' Umbarack said, squatting back on his haunches and frowning.

Joktan was silent as his eyes swept the line of sand dunes in front. His cheeks, caked with dust, appeared empty of expression. 'Take Rashid and approach the encampment from the east,' he ordered. 'Under no circumstances open fire unless the Bait Kebir do so first.'

'Where will you be?' Rashid demanded.

'Negotiating.'

'Umbarack snorted. 'You can't negotiate with the Bait Kebir. They've been suckled by hyenas.'

'We will see. Go swiftly, and remember – no shooting, unless it becomes absolutely necessary.'

They faded into the storm, moving like wraiths among the tendrils of whipped-up sand, and Joktan fastened his *keffiyah* across his mouth. Tiny pellets of sand peppered his eyes, forming a filmy curtain along his brow. He felt no emotion as he reached down to strip the covering from his rifle; he had tucked emotion into some convenient corner of his head so that his mind and body were functioning in perfect harmony.

Joktan was a big man with strong dark features. His eyes were deep, his hands large and corded. A fierce moustache adorned his upper lip. At first glance, he looked like a wrestler – the long arms and powerful shoulders carried an air of sturdy tenacity – but something in his face suggested refinement. It was not a sensitive face – the brow was heavy, the cheekbones blunt – but it carried a degree of perceptiveness that was difficult to ignore. When he moved, his motions were fluid and controlled, and the wind tore at his *ghutra* as he rose to his feet and strode purposefully through the storm.

The dunes parted and he saw the stolen camels tethered beneath a clump of acacia trees. Several feet away sat the Bait Kebir. They were huddled motionless beneath their robes with the stoicism of men who knew the desert in all its variable moods. When they spotted Joktan, however, they sprang to their feet, reaching for their weapons.

'Who are you?' one of the men demanded, his voice distorted by the gale.

He wore a pair of spectacles beneath his turban, and carried an ancient rifle with pieces of cloth tied around its stock.

Joktan drew to a halt. 'I am Salih Joktan,' he answered.

the Bait Kebir looked at each other, their robes fluttering audibly.

'You lie,' a man said. 'Everyone knows that Joktan is dead.'

'Not dead,' he told him. 'Merely sleeping.'

The man spat on the ground. 'If you really are Joktan, then why are we still alive?'

'Praise God and rejoice for His mercy and goodness, and in the name of the Prophet, show your gratitude by returning the camels you have stolen.'

'You either have great courage or great stupidity,' another tribesman said. 'You come into our camp demanding camels, yet you make no mention of payment.'

'Why should we pay for something which is rightfully ours?'

'The camels were stolen honestly. It is not the way of the Bait Kebir to give up possessions without a fight.'

'You have no choice, brother. Your encampment is surrounded.'

The four tribesmen glanced nervously into the darkness. 'He is lying,' one of them growled.

'In all the stories you have heard about me, did anyone say that Joktan lied? In the name of Allah the Merciful, do not force us to take back our possessions in blood.'

The warrior who had spoken slid back his rifle bolt with a muffled click. His face carried not the traditional elegance of the desert Bedu, but the Mongolian features of the Kurdish people to the north. 'Godless pig, do you imagine that we are afraid of you? You must be cast into darkness like the whispering devil.'

With a sinking heart, Joktan realized the man was going to make a fight of it. It was the Bedu way. No compromise.

The warrior raised his rifle, and without hesitation Joktan shot him through the chest. The man catapulted backwards, his arms and legs flailing, and almost simultaneously,

14

a fusillade of gunfire erupted around the camp perimeter. Joktan heard the lethal swish-swish of bullets ripping the air above his head. A second tribesman dropped, writhing, into the sand.

A third man leapt at Joktan, swinging his rifle like a club, and Joktan parried it easily aside, twisting to the left. He saw a glint of steel and realized the Arab had drawn his sword. The blade came streaking in toward him, its curved edge bearing down on his unprotected neck, and Joktan felt the icy slipstream as the weapon grazed his skull. He drove his rifle butt hard into the man's crotch, hearing him grunt in pain, then pivoting on his heel, brought the weapon down savagely on the Arab's cowled head. The man dropped senseless into the dust.

Galloping out of the darkness, Rashid took aim at the last fleeing survivor, but Joktan jerked his barrel to one side, allowing the fugitive to vanish over the dune crests.

'You let him get away,' Rashid accused.

'We've got what we came for,' Joktan said.

Rashid's eyes blazed with indignation. 'Umbarack was right – you *have* changed,' he said.

Joktan made no comment as he knelt to examine the wounded man.

The storm eased off as morning approached, and the rising dawn sent a flush of pink across the open *badiya*. Joktan rode in silence, lost in a reverie of his own making. The killing of the Bait Kebir had disturbed him deeply. The wounded camel thieves would face no judgement, Joktan knew – the recaptured animals would be regarded as *zakat*, a traditional offering to Joktan's tribal chieftain, and after medical treatment, the prisoners would be returned to their people unharmed – but it seemed a futile exercise, and Joktan hated the senseless waste of human life.

Salving his conscience had never been easy, he thought. Penitence, contrition, absolution – the words were meaningless against the blinding reality of death itself. If he lived to be a hundred, he could never exorcise the enormity of his guilt – though he hadn't done badly, all things considered. He had blotted the past from his mind as a man might expunge an unpleasant memory, concentrating instead on living his life in the simplest and most virtuous fashion. Could that atone for his sins? he wondered. He didn't think so. A man created guilt as he created offspring, in the hot-blooded passion of the moment, but it ill befitted him to complain afterwards. If sin was his heritage, then he had learned to endure it, and would go on doing so as long as there was breath in his body, though it pained him to discover that some things could never change. Like a secret affliction, he carried violence inside him wherever he went.

The storm faded as the party approached the Bedu camp. Joktan saw the *beth shar*, or goatskin tents, heard the yodelling of the women welcoming them home. A group of small boys stood filling jars at the communal waterhole, and when the riders appeared, ran forward excitedly to greet them.

The Bedouin settlement was not so much a village as a *humulah*, a gathering of friendly and related families. Few Bedouin still followed their traditional way of life. Most had been enticed into the cities; others worked for the oil companies, riding pick-up trucks instead of camels. Though Joktan lamented the change, he was a realist, and recognized the need for his people to blend into the modern world.

He frowned as he spotted a helicopter parked at the encampment edge. It was a Bell HSL-1, originally designed for anti-submarine warfare and purchased from the British Royal Navy by the Iraqi government. The pilot, a major in a dust-grimed beret, jumped to the ground and saluted as Joktan approached. 'Welcome home, colonel.'

'Do not call me "colonel",' Joktan said. 'I am Bedu now.'

'Forgive me.' The man gave a little bow. 'General Bakhit would like to see you as quickly as possible. He asked me to stress that the matter is most urgent. I am to convey you at once to the Presidential Palace in Baghdad.'

Joktan was silent at the news. Under normal circumstances, nothing would have cheered Joktan more than the prospect of seeing his beloved guardian again, but he

16

realized the summons could mean only one thing. He was being called back into service and the idea depressed him. 'Wait here,' he ordered. 'I will bathe and change.'

Joktan spoke little during the noisy journey to Baghdad. He had the Arab gift for fatalism and rarely speculated on the future, accepting it, even though he was a Christian, as the will of Allah. Clad in an ordinary business suit, he sat strapped into a bucket seat, gazing down at the moving countryside. Soon, he saw the turquoise-tiled domes of the nineteenth-century Hadar Khanah lining the bank of the winding Tigris, and beyond it, the high-rise apartment blocks of the modern city. At the Presidential Palace, the pilot brought his machine to a hover and descended into the central courtyard. A small man in white robes stood waiting to greet them. Joktan recognized Moktar, General Bakhit's personal servant. Moktar bowed, giving the traditional Arab greeting. 'As-salaam alaikum.'

'Wa alaikum as-salaam wa rabmat Allah wa barakatu,' Joktan said. 'Why have I been summoned so imperiously?

'The general does not honour me with his thoughts.' Moktar smiled. 'It is enough that he desires your company. Have you forgotten your code of nakwa?'

Nakwa was an ancient Bedouin word meaning 'honour' and 'chivalry'. Joktan knew its use had been deliberately calculated. He said: 'Where is the general now?'

'Entertaining visitors, but he will see you, colonel, I feel sure. Please come with me.'

Moktar led Joktan through a labyrinth of corridors filled with the fragrance of burning incense. The Palace was part of the old Baghdad, but much of it had been rebuilt after the 1991 Gulf War, presenting a fascinating blend of architectural distinction and slightly dubious taste.

Moktar motioned Joktan into an airy chamber where French windows opened onto a stone balcony overlooking the Palace grounds. There was no furniture apart from a huge four-poster bed, completely encircled by gaily-coloured drapes.

The sound of giggling reached Joktan. Frowning, he thrust the drapes brusquely aside. Three naked girls lay

17

huddled on the mattress, gazing at him nervously. Joktan looked at Moktar, who smiled.

Joktan let the veils fall back into place. 'The general is generous,' he said, 'but I no longer have time for such frivolous pleasures.'

Moktar made an eloquent gesture, and this time led the way to a spacious modern office. A mahogany desk stood in front of the open window.

Moktar withdrew, bowing, and after a moment Joktan saw General Bakhit entering from the ante-room outside. Abu Bakhit was a small man with olive skin and soulful brown eyes. During the 1991 Gulf War, he had commanded a brigade of Sadaam Hussein's Republican Guard which had held its position under blistering fire; largely because of this, he was regarded as a hero by a large proportion of the Iraqi people.

The general hugged Joktan warmly, then stepped back to examine him in the light from the window. 'You look well,' he said. 'The desert air must agree with you.'

'I am anxious to return to it as quickly as possible.'

Bakhit ignored the remark, glancing up at the President's portrait on the office wall. His lips twisted in distaste as he studied the man's indulgent features. Bakhit had a capacity, one Joktan admired, for ridiculing the most sacred institutions whilst maintaining an air of respectful innocence. 'I see you've been looking at our beloved leader, son of God the Prophet, messenger of the religious and scourge of the infidel.'

'How is the little goat?' Joktan asked.

'Crazier than ever. He now claims he's hearing voices urging him to liberate the Holy Land.'

'It's time somebody silenced the idiot for good.'

'Many men have tried, Salih. Unfortunately, no one has ever succeeded. However, let us forget al Shisur.' Bakhit's eyes twinkled mischeivously. 'I gather from Moktar that you refused my present? They told me you'd changed, but I didn't believe them.'

A servant appeared, placing a tray of coffee on the writing desk. Bakhit waved at the tiny cups. 'It's *mocca*. Knowing how you desert barbarians feel about western

18

coffee, I had it ordered specially. However ...' Pulling
open a drawer, he took out a bottle of Scotch. 'I do have
a little something to liven up the taste.'

'What will the immans say?'

'What do they always say? That it is sinful to poison the
body with impurities, but since − in public, at least − I am
never less than a pious man, and since everyone knows that
your Christian upbringing has led you into unsavoury prac-
tices, who will pass judgement?'

'I may be a Christian,' Joktan said as Bakhit poured the
coffee, 'but I am still an Arab.'

'Indeed you are. And a Bedu Arab at that.'

There was between them this source of unspoken dis-
sension; Bakhit disapproved of Joktan's nomadic existence.
He was plagued by the thought that his adopted son was
squandering his life senselessly.

'You are still happy living with those desert hooligans?'

'It is preferable to killing men.'

'You were killing Jews, Salih. There is a difference.'

'Killing is killing,' Joktan said flatly.

Bakhit's eyes filled with sadness. 'It's true then. You *have*
changed.'

Never, even in his wildest moments, had Bakhit sought to
impose his beliefs upon his family. He had raised his sons
in an atmosphere of open-mindedness, extolling the virtues
of logic and reason, but Joktan knew that he himself had
proved a bitter disappointment.

'Killing for a cause is not a dishonourable thing, Salih.
The Junuba bombing at Tel Aviv was a *tour-de-force*. The
shooting of the Israeli Minister of Justice, the TWA hijack
at Damascus − they were brilliant attacks carried out with
audacity and daring. Now you skulk in the wilderness,
turning your back on everything that is holy. Of course,
all men have a right to live their lives as they choose,
according to the word of the Koran, even Christian Arabs
like yourself.' He permitted himself a fleeting smile. 'But
then, you have only your conscience to appease. It is that
conscience I am calling on now. You owe me this, Salih.
It is a debt of honour.'

The general walked to the desk, holding his body erect,

19

as if anxious to utilise every inch of height his frame could muster. His hair, greased with coconut oil, looked very sleek against his dome-like skull. 'Have you ever contemplated the ironies of history? What would the British have said, I wonder, when they traded off our barren little country in the early part of the twentieth century if they'd realized that beneath its topsoil lay one of the greatest riches known to man?'

'Oil?'

'Naturally, oil. It was oil which transformed us from a modest sheikdom into the nation we are today. But consider what would happen, Salih, if oil were to lose its place as the premier source of world energy. Once again, we would be relegated to the Middle Ages.'

'How could such a thing happen?'

Bakit opened a desk drawer and took out a sheaf of photographs. He handed them to Joktan who examined them in puzzlement. The pictures showed pieces of machinery and industrial equipment. He identified several large tank-like objects, but there was nothing to indicate their function or purpose.

Bakhit said: 'Those were taken two nights ago by one of our agents who infiltrated the Israeli experimental plant at Mazar. They confirm what we already feared: that the Israelis have managed to produced a revolutionary new source of power, inexpensive, and virtually inexhaustible.'

'What kind of power?' Joktan asked.

'Bio-gas. It's a substance similar to petroleum, produced from chemical and industrial waste.'

Joktan looked unconvinced. 'I have read about bio-gas. The Indians have been experimenting with it for years. It's impractical. It takes two hundred and twenty five cubic feet to equal one gallon of gasoline.'

'True, but with this new process the Israelis can turn out billions of cubic feet a day at a fraction of the cost. They claim − with some justification − that what they are doing will benefit mankind, but within a year, two years at the outside, they will be in a position to destroy our principle source of revenue. Of course, no one is saying that bio-gas will fully take the place of oil, but in such

20

a competitive atmosphere, the commodity on which we have depended for generations, the deposits which have underpinned our economy, could soon prove to be virtually worthless.'

Joktan was silent for a moment. Abu Bakhit was not given to flights of fancy. If he said the new bio-gas process was a threat, then a threat it undoubtedly was. 'You could always try sabotaging the plant.'

'The Israelis would simply rebuild. Our President feels the situation calls for a more permanent solution.'

'War?'

Bakhit nodded.

'What about the peace agreements?'

'Did the Jews consider the peace agreements when they started these experiments?'

'This is madness, general.'

Bakhit sighed. 'I am merely a soldier, Salih, and soldiers have to obey orders. It's the nature of things.'

'You could change that, if you wanted to. You're popular among the people.'

'Dangerous talk.'

'Israel's a dangerous opponent.'

'True, but on this occasion, we will not be acting alone.'

Bakhit motioned toward the door and, puzzled, Joktan followed him into a neighbouring chamber. Two men seated at a small coffee table rose to their feet as the general entered. They were both dressed in western business suits. The first was medium-sized and unremarkable in appearance, but the second carried the bulky musculature of a professional athlete, and despite his age – Joktan estimated him to be somewhere in his mid-fifties – looked trim and fit. His hair was completely white and brushed back Stalin-style to emphasize his prominent features. His face was ruddy and displayed the predatory air of a basking shark.

Bakhit smiled, switching easily to English. 'Allow me to introduce Mr Leon Snyder and Mr Samuel Gronk from the United States.'

Snyder exuded charm as they shook hands, but his eyes remained as cold as chipped glass. 'We've been told a great

21

deal about you, Mr Joktan. You have quite a pedigree, it seems.'

'One I deeply regret,' Joktan replied.

'Nonsense, a man should never belittle his achievements. I understand from the general that you live the life of a recluse these days?'

'I have returned to my people,' Joktan said.

'Well, I hope we can persuade you to get back into harness, sir.' Snyder took out a cigar and lit it carefully, blowing a stream of smoke at the ceiling. His eyes shone with an elusive humour, as if he derived some curious entertainment from his role. Rarely in his life had Joktan encountered a man he felt less disposed to trust.

'It isn't often that American and Arab interests coincide, Mr Joktan. Tragically, in the past, we've often been on opposite sides of the fence.'

'Indeed, that is true.'

'However, I consider myself a practical man, and when the occasion demands it, I'll shake hands with the devil himself if it becomes necessary.'

'I take it you are referring to me?'

'No offence, Mr Joktan. In 1991, our company formed a liaison with your late president, Sadaam Hussein − a relationship which, sad to say, proved somewhat belated. This time, by acting swiftly, we hope to nip the threat in the bud before it gets out of all proportion.'

'You must understand,' Samuel Gronk interjected, 'that if these Israeli experiments work, Washington is planning to funnel millions of dollars into the Mazar project. Mr Snyder and I represent a group of people who are deeply unhappy about American plans for bio-gas energy.'

'What kind of people?'

'Oil people,' Snyder told him. 'Companies which stand to lose fortunes if Mazar goes into full production. We are not without influence, sir − influence at the highest level, I may say − but since the process has been kept a closely guarded secret, and since President Clayman himself is personally committed to its pursuance, blocking its progress hasn't been easy. We have people lobbying Congressmen

22

to staunch the flow of funds, but the matter is too serious to rely on diplomacy alone.'

'What Mr Snyder means,' Gronk explained, 'is that if the bio-gas program goes ahead, our clients − together with your country's prosperity − will simply cease to exist.'

'I see.' Joktan tried to look suitably concerned. He did not care for his new associates, but resolved to hide his distaste for General Bakhit's sake.

'Stifling this threat will not be easy.' Snyder fixed Joktan with his vulpine eyes. 'It will be a complex and delicate operation, but with your help and the grace of God, together we will alter history.'

It was cold in Paris, despite the softness of the April sky. Most of the cafes still had glass canopies protecting their terraces from the evening chill.

Seated at the table, Leila Assad saw stars gleaming along the Rue du Mont Canis. Traffic formed an unbroken line, heading toward the Place du Tetre and the Sacre Coeur.

She was an attractive girl with short-cropped hair and angular features. She had been born in Cleveland, Ohio, but at the age of fourteen had emigrated with her family to Israel. Her four brothers had returned to the United States as soon as they'd reached the age of consent, but Leila had gone to university in Jerusalem and at the age of twenty-four had joined the Israeli security forces. Now, she worked for Mossad, tracking down the small groups of Arab fanatics who, despite the new international order, still engaged in anti-Jewish activities.

The young man who had brought her here, an Arab agent named Harun Uzbak, examined her shrewdly across the table. 'You look sad tonight. I haven't said anything to upset you?'

'I'm not sad, really.'

'Then why are you so quiet?'

'It's my nature to be quiet. I'm always quiet.'

He leaned forward, taking her hand. 'I know so little about you, and yet in a strange kind of way, I feel as if I've known you all my life. Meeting you tonight was like a miracle.'

'I don't believe in miracles,' Leila said. 'I believe in fate.'

He hesitated, moistening his lips with his tongue. 'Would you care for more wine?'

'No, thanks. I've had enough.'

'Something to eat perhaps?'

'I'm not hungry.'

'Then why don't we leave?'

'So soon?' Leila was surprised. 'It's barely eight o'clock.'

His mouth twisted into a suggestive smile. 'I just thought we'd be a lot more comfortable if we went back to my place.'

Under the table, his free hand moved beneath her skirt, and Leila sucked in her breath as she felt his fingers massaging the inside of her thigh. 'But I hardly know you.'

'What is there to know? We are kindred spirits – two people alone in Paris. Why indulge in time-wasting formalities for the sake of some outdated convention?'

A shiver ran through Leila as, beneath the table, Harun's fingers grew bolder and more intimate. She reached for her purse. 'I have to freshen my lipstick first. I'll be back in a minute.'

She rose to her feet and hurried to the cafe rear, her nubile body moving with an explicitness that was difficult to ignore. She saw Eitan and Ivri waiting outside the ladies room. They straightened as Leila walked toward them.

'He's ready to leave now,' she told them in a low voice. 'He's taking me to his apartment.'

'It's not eight o'clock yet,' Eitan grunted.

'Our Arab friend is a fast worker.'

'You don't think he suspects anything?'

'He hasn't the brain. Biology's motivating him, not common sense.'

'Just the same,' Ivri said, 'if he shows any sign of uneasiness, get out fast. Make sure the outside door is unlocked.'

'What do you take me for, an amateur?'

The prospect of the coming encounter presented few

24

qualms for Leila. Though outwardly she seemed an intelligent, personable and sensual young lady, she experienced no empathy toward the opposite sex. The act of physical union gave her little pleasure, but she had learned over the years to seal off her mind, so that while she was aware of the curious and sometimes shocking things which happened to her body, they rarely penetrated her consciousness.

In the taxi home, Harun took her into his arms with a low moan, and she smelled his shaving soap as he fumbled inside her blouse. His hard hands fondled her tiny breasts, and she responded dutifully, kissing his throat and ear, but the breathless flurry scarcely affected her. Simulating passion was easier than experiencing it.

At the apartment building, she let Harun go first up the rackety stairway, and reaching behind her, deftly slipped the door catch. She did the same as they entered the room itself.

Harun made no attempt to switch on the light. He seized her roughly, pushed her against the wall and kissed her hard on the mouth, sliding his hand under the waistbelt of her skirt. She saw lights from the street casting fractured patterns across the untidy apartment.

In the semi-darkness, Harun's face looked almost demented as he began to undress her. So engrossed was he in fumbling with the straps and fastenings that he did not notice the door creaking softly open. The first intimation he had that something was wrong was when a pistol was thrust against his neck, and a voice said: 'One wrong move and you'll never breathe again.'

A terrible sickness came over Harun, and his eyes filled with defeat as he raised his hands resignedly.

Samuel Bernstein had lived in Paris for almost a year, working as Mossad's section head, controlling agents in all the major European capitals. He had started his career during the 'Year of Decision' – 1971 – when Egypt's President Sadat had planned a surprise attack by fifty bombers on Sharf El-Sheikh. The attack had later been cancelled because of the Indo-Pakistan war, but it had been Bernstein who had recognized the significance of the general mobilization. A year later, when a second mobilization had taken place, Bernstein, working behind the lines, had managed to send back details of Egyptian troop concentrations along the Suez Canal. In the Yom Kippur War which followed, he had remained at his post, flashing messages to Israeli positions, and had been personally credited with the relief of the unit defending the Bar-Lev Line. In recognition of this enterprise, Bernstein had been made head of Section 11, *Modi'in*, the military branch of the secret service, later transferring to Section 1 under the auspices of the Director of Intelligence. Now, unmarried, and with few interests outside his job, he ran Mossad's European network from one of the world's most glamorous cities.

The section of Paris Bernstein had come to was known locally as 'the Arab Quarter'. Here, the vast bulk of the city's Islamic residents lived. The buildings were seedy and rundown, but the cafes offered an exotic selection of North African and Middle Eastern dishes.

He got out of his taxi and followed a stairway to an underground basement where he knocked three times, paused, and knocked again. The door was opened a moment later by Leila Assad, who peered through the aperture, then stepped back to let him into the room.

The basement was almost cavernous in appearance, covering as it did the entire lower floor of the multi-storey office block above. Central heating boilers took up most of the empty space and in the centre, tied to a chair, Harun sat staring listlessly at the wall. His grubby shirt was open at the throat, and he looked weary and dispirited after the long hours of interrogation. Standing behind him were Eitan and Ivri.

'How did it go?' Bernstein asked.

Leila said: 'We gave him an injection of DX-3 every fifteen minutes for the first two hours, then every thirty minutes afterwards. He didn't want to talk, but in the end he had little choice.'

Bernstein nodded approvingly. Leila was a beautiful girl, he reflected; if the strain of ensnaring Harun had shaken her composure, she gave little sign. Bernstein had no conception of Leila's coldness in matters relating to the opposite sex.

'Did he explain what he's doing here in Paris?'

'Waiting, he claims. He's been ordered to prepare a dossier of possible French terrorist targets.'

'For what purpose?'

'If France backs any UN resolution against Iraq, Harun is to start bombing the city. Harun says that al Shisur is calling for an Arab *Jihad* against the state of Israel. He dreams of turning himself into a Middle East Godfather figure, and believes that if he proves, by a series of dramatic victories, that Israel *can* be defeated, the other Arab countries will fall in behind him.'

'Al Shisur's a tinpot dictator. He has an impressive army, it's true, but he'll be committing diplomatic suicide if he attempts to take on Israel.'

Leila paused. It was her prize revelation and she timed it beautifully. 'Harun claims he has a new secret weapon − a weapon even more devastating than nuclear missiles.'

Bernstein frowned. 'What kind of weapon?'

'Harun doesn't know. But it's something innovative, revolutionary. Using it, a relatively modest force can defeat an army many times its number.'

For the first time, Bernstein looked interested. He fumbled in his pocket, and took out a packet of cigarettes. 'Do we know the name of this new weapon?'

'It's called Talon Blue,' Leila said.

Chapter Three

Ellen Conway picked up the bandit on her radar, coming in high at eleven o'clock. She glanced at the instrument panel, and increased her speed to 400 knots, keeping the throttle in afterburn. Setting the data processor on her radar scanner, she switched the selector from 'ripple' to 'single-shot' and the surveillance system processed its information to the missile launcher, flashing out the words: 'Target Acquired'.

Ellen's limbs felt shivery as she went through the circuit check, flicking the relay switches. The screen bleeped out the message: 'Firing solution go'.

Sucking in her breath, she punched the little button marked 'Fire', and peeled off to starboard as the missile streaked into the air. There was a fractional pause, then Ellen felt a surge of savage elation as the incoming aircraft erupted in a sheet of flame.

Her rapture proved short-lived however, for almost immediately, a second bandit appeared on the scanner, forcing her into a steep dive. Streaking over the desert floor, she called up another SAM, watching the optics sensor for a missile lock indication. This time, when she let the warhead go, the SAM nose-dived, spinning and twisting earthwards. A dud.

Panic started in Ellen's chest. The bandit was closing fast, and she nursed the jet into a steep turn, watching the desert skimming by beneath her. Suddenly, the cockpit filled with the ear-splitting shriek of the stall-alarm, and she saw the ground expanding until the screen erupted

28

in a dissolving flash and she slumped back, panting, in her chair.

A light switched on as Wally Gordimer stepped into the room. 'You stalled again,' he said with a grin.

'I was trying to keep the fight tight,' Ellen moaned as she rose to her feet. 'The second missile turned out to be a bummer.'

'That's how the simulator keeps you on your toes.'

'God, Wal, I almost fainted there.'

'Don't worry, every pilot has an off-day. Just be thankful yours happened on solid ground.'

Wally escorted her from the aerial-combat hut into the blinding sunlight of Moffat Field Air Station, and Ellen gazed longingly at a line of Python B-5s standing motionless on the runway in front. 'I think flying fighters is what I was born for.'

Wally laughed, steering her toward the main gate. 'Just remember, there's a hell of a difference between sitting in a cockpit and operating a simulator.' He looked handsome and debonair in his officer's uniform, his skin tanned, his features chiselled and evenly planed.

'I still say I'd have made a terrific pilot,' Ellen insisted. 'Sometimes, I find flying even better than sex.'

'That's because you've been making love to the wrong guy.'

'Now don't start that old chestnut again,' Ellen chuckled.

Wally Gordimer belonged to the never-give-up school of American courtship. Though their relationship was strictly a platonic one, he made little secret of the fact that he would like to alter its status. Ellen had resisted his advances, largely because she had been living for the past two years with a brilliant young designer from the company for which she worked, Mackhead Engineering. His name was Paul McKlelland.

'I keep hoping that sooner or later I'll wear you down,' Wally said.

'On Paul? No way.'

'How I detest virtuous women.'

'Virtue, nix. Loyalty, that's different.'

'I'm not trying to belittle Paul, but the guy lives and

breathes aeronautical space design, for Pete's sake. You need somebody who belongs in the real world.'

'If Paul seems a little absent-minded at times, it's because he's sensitive. You should read some of the poetry he writes.'

'I hate poetry,' Wally said.

'Philistine. Anyhow, you're engaged.'

'All lies. My interest in Joanna Swaney is strictly fraternal.'

'You couldn't even spell that word.'

They reached the main gate, and Ellen squeezed his hand. 'Thanks for the flying lesson,' she said.

'Say the word, and one of these days I'll fly you to the moon and back.'

'Promises, promises,' she laughed, and set off through the leafy streets of Sunnyvale. Ellen Conway was twenty-nine years old, and for the past seven years had worked for Mackhead Engineering as a senior designer, specializing in electromagnetic impulses. She was slim and elegant, with the supple grace of a trained ballet dancer. Her hair was blonde and hung in a tangle almost to her shoulders, and though she seldom wore make-up, the symmetry of her features made a lasting impression on everyone she met.

The laboratory where she worked occupied an extensive site on the Moffat Field perimeter; it was a sprawling complex of three-storey buildings and warehouses of corrugated metal. When she reached her desk, Ellen found a note from her supervisor, Dick Pybus, asking her to report immediately to his office. Mystified, she took the elevator to the second floor.

Pybus was a thickset man with heavy jowls who always looked at though he had forgotten to shave. He regarded her dourly as he waved her to a seat. 'I'll bet you've been up at that damned naval base again. If you wanted to be a pilot, why didn't you join the air force?'

'Maybe I will,' she answered. 'I'm still under recruiting age.'

Ellen knew Pybus's truculence was nothing more than an act, for he was a gentle and considerate man by nature, but on this occasion he seemed unusually tense and, to Ellen's surprise, wasted little time in getting down to business. 'How much do you know about impulse emissions?'

'Only what I picked up in training. Most of my work has been in energy and optics.'

'According to your record, you worked on the Ballard Program. Is that correct?'

'You know it is.'

'Ever heard of Talon Blue?'

Ellen thought for a moment. 'Some kind of new secret weapon designed to make modern warfare obsolete.'

'"Conventional" warfare,' Pybus corrected. 'Talon Blue makes "conventional" warfare obsolete. Nuclear warfare's something else again.'

'Doesn't Talon Blue carry a "black" rating?'

'You bet. That's why you'll never read about it in the training brochures. However, they're planning to assemble a prototype at Stand Hill Air Base in Arizona, and they've specifically asked for you.'

Ellen felt her senses quicken. 'Me? Are you sure?'

'I have the requisition form right here. They want you by Saturday next at the latest.'

'Saturday? That's crazy. There must be at least a dozen designers who are better qualified.'

'But no one with practical experience. It's a VIP job, Ellen. They're laying on a private jet.'

'You're kidding me.'

He pushed the letter toward her. 'Read it for yourself. By the time you've finished this program, you'll be able to write your own ticket to any part of the company you choose.' He watched her shrewdly as she scanned the document. He liked Ellen and took an avuncular interest in her welfare. 'You'll be away for three to four months,' he said. 'How will Paul take it?'

Ellen felt her excitement waning. 'He won't like it much. Apart from the separation, he's against weapon design on principle.'

'He's a scientist, isn't he? He knows it's a scientist's job to explore new territory. If we hadn't developed the atomic bomb, we wouldn't have discovered nuclear power.

31

Who knows? One day Talon Blue could benefit the whole of mankind.'

Ellen was pensive as she picked up the requisition letter. 'I'll have to try a little feminine persuasion,' she said.

The lights were on as Ellen pulled into the drive of the bungalow she shared with Paul on Santa Clara's Capitola Way. Paul's car was already in the garage, which surprised her; as a rule she arrived home at least an hour earlier.

A delicious aroma reached her as she let herself in at the front door. In the dining room, she could see the table set with coloured napkins and lighted candles. Music drifted from the tape machine.

Paul stepped from the kitchen, wearing an apron around his waist. He was carrying a gaily-wrapped package with a large bow on the front. 'Happy birthday to yoooouuuu . . .' he crooned tunelessly.

Ellen stopped in her tracks. 'My God, I completely forgot. I'm twenty-nine today.'

He seized her in his arms, kissing her fiercely on the mouth. 'Like camembert,' he said, 'you get better as you grow older.'

'I can't believe it. I can't believe I forgot my own birthday.'

'Here.' Paul pushed the package into her hands. 'Open it.'

She tugged loose the bow and tore away the wrapping. Inside was a cardboard box. Ellen lifted the lid. 'Shoes,' she breathed.

'They're the ones you liked in San Francisco. You tried them on and they fitted like a glove, remember? I got the store assistant to keep them for me.'

Ellen took out the shoes and examined them under the light. 'Paul, the reason I didn't buy these is because I thought they were too expensive.'

'What's the point of money if it can't get you what you want?'

She kissed him lightly on the lips. 'I love them. They're beautiful, and you're a darling. But you're much too extravagant.' She sniffed the air. 'What are you cooking?'

'Your favourite. *Arni psito.*'

'I thought we'd decided to phone in a pizza tonight.'

'Are you nuts? How many times in her life does a girl get to be twenty-nine? I may be a trifle immodest, but I don't mind telling you this is probably the finest *arni psito* ever baked by man. Why don't you open the wine and let it breathe for a few minutes? Dinner will be served at seven-thirty sharp.'

Ellen watched him bustle back to the kitchen, whistling softly under his breath. Paul McKlelland always reminded her of a young John Denver. His features were delicate, and he wore a pair of wire-rimmed spectacles which gave him a faintly intellectual air. He kept himself fit by regular jogging, and wrote volumes of poetry which nobody except Ellen ever troubled to read. There were times she felt he was everything she'd ever wanted in a man, but something was missing in their relationship and she'd be a fool to deny that. She needed excitement. Uncertainty. Paul was sensitive and loving, it was true, but sometimes his devotion almost drove her crazy. She felt smothered and suffocated by their comfortable, well-ordered existence, and her sense of unrest seemed to grow stronger with each passing day. After all, where in the manual of human emotions did it say she had to be satisfied with one man for the rest of her life? Or was she being selfish and cold-hearted? She did love Paul in a way. She couldn't stick a thermometer into her heart and measure the level of her emotions, but if love meant caring for someome – well, she cared for Paul. Implicitly. So why was she filled with such a burning discontent?

Dinner proved a difficult meal. Ellen racked her brain for some way of breaking her news diplomatically, and in the end decided to tackle the problem head-on. 'Paul, I have to go away for a while.'

He looked at her, taking a sip of wine. 'Where?'

'Arizona. I'm being transferred. It's a new program. They're assembling a prototype.'

Paul put down his fork, dabbing at his mouth with his napkin. 'When did this happen?'

'Just after lunch. Pybus called me up to his office. It's an Operation Immediate. I have to leave by Saturday.'

33

'Saturday? That's crazy. They wouldn't transfer you without warning. You must have applied for the post months ago.'

'I didn't apply. They're requisitioning me. It's a "black" program. It's . . .' she hesitated ' . . . Talon Blue.'

The music tape came to an end and Ellen heard the clock ticking loudly on the mantelpiece.

'Talon Blue is a weapons program,' Paul said.

'I know that. It's also the latest thing in electromagnetic technology. It's a major step in my career, Paul. If I can handle this, I'll be on my way to the top.'

'How long will you be gone?'

'Three to four months, Pybus says.'

'Three to four months? My God.'

'It isn't the end of the world. What about that time you went on the spectrometry course? It passed like a shot, you said so yourself.'

'The spectrometry course was only twenty-one days. Besides, how are we ever going to change this world if we go on building bigger and better weapons all the time?'

Ellen was exasperated. 'Don't start moralizing with me. Nobody's going to use the damn' thing, for Pete's sake. It's a prototype, nothing more. Besides, it's my one chance to break out of Energy and Optics, and I'm not going to louse it up just because of your "love-thy-neighbour" philosophy.'

Paul threw down his napkin on the table. She could see the anger in his eyes, but he had a capacity, one she greatly admired, for always seeing the other person's point of view, and though he was truculent at first, he relented eventually, just as she'd known he would.

But that night, as they made love, she reflected that it was Paul's very reasonableness which exasperated her most. Anger, she could understand. Passion, fury – even jealousy. But moderation drove her almost insane. He was so predictable, she thought. If only once in his life he could really surprise her.

The concourse was flooded with people when Joktan arrived at San Francisco Airport. He joined the passengers flooding

34

through Passport Control, his dark eyes registering the uniformed officials and the long trestle tables. Why were airports always so clinical? he wondered.

He felt testy after the long trans-Atlantic flight; not tired exactly – he had stopped off in Paris to rest and recuperate – yet his body was filled with a curious languor. He scarcely knew what he was doing here. He had no enthusiasm for the operation ahead, but he'd owed General Bakhit too much to refuse. How could he tell Bakhit that the man he was seeking no longer existed? Joktan had tried to turn his back on the past, but he should have realized that the past, like destiny, was implacable.

He walked across the concourse and saw Bechar Rasul waiting in the entrance hall. Bechar was a dark-haired young man with cherubic features and a constantly cheerful expression.

'Welcome to the United States, colonel,' he said, smiling. 'Did you have a good flight?'

'Excellent,' Joktan told him drily. 'I slept through the movie, which was a blessed relief. I hate Jewish comedies.'

Bechar laughed as they headed toward the parking lot. The morning was bright, and heat-waves shimmered off the concrete roadway. After the starkness of the Iraqi desert, the foliage bordering the highway seemed too luxuriant to be believed.

'Tell me about the war,' Bechar said. 'Are there many victories?'

"The war" was a euphemism for the endless struggle against Israel. Though, officially at least, the conflict had ended, "the war", in the hearts of many Arabs, still went on.

'There are no victories,' Joktan said. 'And I no longer care if we are winning or not.'

'If it was still your war, man, then you would care.'

'No, I would not care.'

Sometimes Joktan felt he wasn't a man any more, merely a crucible in which all the fears of his life had simmered and distilled. It had left him confused, empty, bitter and disgusted.

He watched the flood of traffic rolling toward the exit gates, the little shuttle buses nipping deftly in and out of the loading bays. A party of nuns strolled by, shepherded by a uniformed guide with a harassed expression.

'Where are we staying?' Joktan asked.

'The Americans have rented a house near Carmel. Easy to guard, easy to defend. It's about two hours' drive away.'

'Neighbours?'

'None within viewing distance. The nearest building is a Coastguard station. Most of the time, it appears deserted. We've been in touch with some of Snyder's people, and it does seem he has considerable influence here.'

Their car stood at the edge of the parking lot, and Joktan saw Tahi seated behind the wheel. Tahi was small and wiry, with thick dark hair tied in a pony tail. His left eye was made of glass, and it gave his face a faintly lopsided appearance.

As Joktan approached, he climbed out of the car and, smiling, opened the rear door.

'*As-salaam alaikum*,' he said.

'*Wa alaikum as-salaam*,' Joktan answered. 'Are you well?'

'Very well, colonel. How is the war?'

'Like all wars. Bad.'

'Well, there is no war here,' Tahi smiled, his tanned face flushed and healthy.

'No,' Joktan said as he climbed into the car. 'I am bringing the war with me.'

At the age of twenty-four, Amos Landau had emigrated to the United States from Tel Aviv, and now worked as a parking lot attendant at San Francisco airport. When he saw the three Arabs standing around their automobile, he frowned in puzzlement for something about the powerful-looking man with the muscular shoulders seemed hauntingly familiar. Then, in a flash of inspiration, the answer came to him. During his national service in the Israeli army, Landau had seen the stranger's face staring down at him daily from 'wanted' posters on the barrack-room walls. It was Joktan. Salih Joktan.

36

Landau could scarcely believe his eyes. Joktan was a notorious terrorist with unnumerable outrages to his name. What was he doing in the United States?

Landau stepped, trembling, into his cubicle and examined the visitors through the customer grille, trying to force himself to think. Should he notify the airport authorities? What good would it do if Joktan had broken no laws on American soil? Immigration then? Hardly. Joktan wouldn't be foolish enough to travel on a phony passport. The Press? No, if Joktan's documentation was in order, and Landau had to assume that it must be, then his only hope was to get word to Tel Aviv. Mossad had been after Joktan for years.

Beneath the counter, Landau kept a tiny camera. He used it to take pictures of famous celebrities arriving at San Francisco airport. He took it out, checked the film roll, then with his heart beating wildly, aimed the lens through the customer grille and gently pressed the trigger. He went on photographing as the car pulled out of the parking lot and vanished along the road ahead.

Still trembling, he scribbled a long explanatory note and slipped it, together with the film, into a padded envelope. Then he made his way to the Flight Crew Briefing Room and flashed his ID at the security guard on duty.

Only a handful of pilots sat relaxing in the padded armchairs, waiting for their flight numbers to be called. Landau saw Eli Kedmi, the El Al captain, standing beside the coffee machine. As Landau approached, Kedmi looked at him with amusement.

'Amos, what's up? You look like you've seen a ghost.'

Landau said: 'Eli, I've got something I want you to deliver for me.'

Kedmi's face clouded. 'You know I can't do that, kid. It's illegal, sneaking stuff through Customs without a declaration form.'

'It's not a gift, it's a message. I wouldn't ask if it wasn't important.'

Kedmi sensed the urgency in Landau's tone and glanced at the other crew members, then taking the package from Landau's hand, he slipped it into his tunic pocket. 'I'll do it this once,' he promised, 'but that's it, understand? No more favours, not even for old time's sake. I don't want to lose my job.'

Thirty-two hours' later, the package was delivered by hand to Mossad headquarters in Tel Aviv.

The soft purr of the air conditioner was little more than a cosmetic exercise since it was woefully inadequate for the blistering heat of the Israeli noon. The six men who sat at the conference table had loosened their ties and rolled up their shirtsleeves. They were members of the ruling council which governed the most secretive branch of the Israeli secret service. Scattered in front of them lay the photographs Landau had taken in San Francisco two days before.

'It's Joktan all right,' said Jacob Jabari, a large man, fifty-two years old, with muscular arms and crinkly black hair. 'He's older now, his face is thicker, but he's been identified by three different sources.'

'I thought Joktan had been assassinated in Beirut over two years ago,' Chaim Elohin remarked.

'There was no official confirmation of that. The man disappeared, that's all. It looks as though, in the words of Mark Twain, reports of his death were greatly exaggerated.'

'What's he doing in the United States?' Sabah Yadin asked.

'My guess is, it has something to do with Musallim al Shisur's new secret weapon.'

'Think we should warn the US authorities?'

Jabari picked up a pencil and toyed with it absently. 'As far as we know, Joktan has committed no crime on American soil. If the US Immigration people deport him, he'll still be free to carry out terrorist attacks in the Middle East.'

The six men looked at each other, their faces tensing in the midday heat. They knew Jabari's capacity for ruthlessness. He was intuitive, imaginative, and if the occasion demanded it, totally merciless in dealing with Israel's enemies.

'What are you suggesting, Jacob?' Yadin demanded.

'This is the first time in two years we've known where Joktan is. Amos Landau, the man who took the photographs, checked his address with the car rental company.'

'So?'

'We'll never get another opportunity like it. Christ, Yadin, do I have to spell it out?'

'Jacob, we can't send an assassination team into the United States. There'll be hell to pay.'

'There'll be hell to pay anyhow if we let Joktan escape. You think he's in San Francisco for his health?'

Jabari leaned forward in his chair. There were dark sweat stains on his olive-green shirt. His eyes were cold, his features as impressionable as stamped steel. 'I say we send this murderous bastard to hell where he belongs.'

Late on the afternoon of Thursday, 17 April four young men flew into San Francisco on the El Al flight from Tel Aviv, members of a crack Israeli killer squad. Their leader was Matti Hirsch, a veteran of numerous anti-terrorist campaigns. Hirsch was noted both for his analytical approach and his coolness under fire. The four arrivals were met at the terminal gate by Amos Landau, who shook their hands and led them out to his battered old Renault. Never in his life had Landau been the centre of so much attention. Since photographing Joktan, he had been caught in a welter of activity. He had talked daily by telephone with Israeli officials in Tel Aviv, and had kept a close watch on the Arab headquarters near Carmel. He loved the limelight, and was filled with excitement at the thought that he was striking a blow for his former homeland.

Driving south, the Israeli leader, Matti Hirsch, inquired if Landau had managed to get the handguns they had asked for. Landau told him they were in the glove compartment.

Hirsch took out the weapons and examined them closely as they sped through Palo Alto. There was a Starfire .380, a Blackhawk Rueger and two .38 Special Colt Cobras. 'Ammunition?'

'In the trunk.'

'You've done well, Mr Landau. What about the boat?'

'I rented a motor cruiser for a month. Pretty pricey.'

'Don't worry. You will be reimbursed.'

Landau said: 'What the hell do you need a boat for, anyhow? We know where the guy's hiding. I've got the house earmarked. You move in fast, do the hit, catch the next flight out.'

'Joktan is not to be killed on American soil,' Hirsch said.

'Why not?'

'Mossad's orders.'

'Then how d'you plan to eliminate him?'

Smiling thinly, Hirsch slipped a handgun into his jacket pocket. His face was calm, his eyes impassive. 'We'll take him out beyond the ten-mile limit and feed his body to the sharks.'

The London sun was pale and misty as Morris Dobkin trotted down the steps of the US Embassy and kissed Leila Assad lightly on the cheek. Dobkin was a big man in his mid-forties. His hair was greying, and he wore a thin moustache to hide the network of tiny lines which had begun to form along his upper lip. He had been in the Diplomatic Service for almost twenty years, and twelve months earlier, while serving at the US Embassy in Tel Aviv, Dobkin, a married man, had embarked on a passionate affair with Leila that had almost cost him his career. What he had been unaware of at the time was that Leila had seduced him on the direct orders of her intelligence bosses, setting up a liaison which had provided Mossad with a wealth of useful and interesting information.

'I got your message,' he said. 'What on earth are you doing in London?'

'It's Harrods spring sale. I wouldn't miss it for the world.'

He chuckled. 'That's a fine attitude, coming from a Jew. Don't you know Harrods is owned by Arabs now?'

'Have you ever met a Jew who let sentiment stand in the way of a good bargain?'

Laughing, Dobkin slipped his arm around Leila's waist and led her to the network of bustling streets which formed the heart of London's Mayfair. They found a little pub tucked in a narrow alleyway, and Leila sat in the corner while Dobkin ordered drinks.

'It's wonderful to see you again,' he said, joining her at the table. 'The last twelve months haven't changed you a bit.'

'Likewise,' Leila smiled. 'And I approve of the moustache. It makes you look like Ronald Colman.'

'You're too young to remember Ronald Colman,' he teased.

'Wrong. I've seen all his movies on TV.'

She wriggled out of her coat, laying it beside her on the seat. She experienced no emotion at seeing Dobkin again. Though she'd liked the man, admired him even, their relationship – in Leila's mind at least – had been strictly a professional one. She was incapable of anything else. She had learned over the years to simulate her feelings, and she had to admit that Dobkin had been easy to fool, probably because he had believed himself in love with her.

Leila opened her purse and took out a pack of cigarettes. 'How's Mildred?' she asked, her voice losing its jaunty tone.

Dobkin's face sobered. 'She's fine. She likes London – the shops, the atmosphere. She says she wants to retire here.'

'And the kids?'

'They're fine also. Robbie's at university now. We're sending him to Yale in the fall.'

'That's marvellous, Morris.'

Leila lit her cigarette, and Dobkin's sharp eyes noted the signs of tension in her face. Leila excited him, always had. It wasn't merely her looks – though he had few quibbles in that department – it was the air of sensuality that she exuded like a physical force. Even now, after more than a year, he could barely keep his hands off her. 'Is this a nostalgic meeting?' he asked. 'Or did you have something more practical in mind?'

Leila blew smoke toward the raftered ceiling. 'It's business, Morris. It's true I wanted to see you again, but this is far more important than renewing old acquaintance. I hope your sentiments are still in the same place?'

'My sentiments?'

'I mean you're still a loyal Jew, I take it?'

Dobkin's face grew wary. 'Now hold on a minute, Leila. I must warn you that no matter how sympathetic I may feel towards Israel and its people, I have no intention of betraying my trust as a member of the US Diplomatic Corps.'

'And I wouldn't ask you to,' Leila said quickly. 'Have I ever compromised you, ever? But something is happening, Morris, which could pose a threat to Israel's very existence, and unless we can identify and evaluate that threat, the Middle East may be thrown into a turmoil that'll make 1991 look like a country hoedown. Can you tell me anything, anything at all, about a weapon system called Talon Blue?'

Dobkin looked as if she had slapped him in the face. 'Where did you hear that name?'

'We picked it up from an Arab terrorist during a routine interrogation.'

'That's impossible.' Dobkin glanced nervously around the bar. 'Talon Blue is a top secret weapon program. Nobody knows about it, nobody.'

'So it's true – it *is* American in origin?'

'Of course it's American.'

'And hush-hush?'

'Like ice. I just happened to hear a rumour – and believe me, it was only a rumour – during a White House briefing session last October.'

'Did the rumour tell you how lethal Talon Blue might be?'

'For Christ's sake, Leila, I may be a Jew but I'm also a US government official. I'm not supposed to divulge information to anyone, not even my wife.'

'I thought you said it was only a rumour? If that's the case, what harm can there be in a little idle gossip?'

Dobkin said: 'Leila, you have no right to put me on the spot this way.'

'My country may be facing annihilation. That gives me the right.'

'You're talking nonsense. No Arab nation could even have heard of Talon Blue.'

'What is it, Morris? Some kind of nuclear device?'

'No, not nuclear. It's innovative, a whole new concept in modern warfare, but at this point in time, it's still in the development stage.'

'How do you know? If it was last October when you heard about it, maybe they've got a prototype by now?'

Dobkin looked unhappy. 'Leila, I have to stop the conversation right here. If the State Department knew I was discussing this, I'd be subjected to an immediate full-field FBI investigation.'

Leila's gaze was unrelenting. 'What does it *do*, Morris? At least you can tell me that.'

'I don't know, for Chrissake! It's being constructed by Mackhead's Missile and Space Company. It was originally intended as part of the Strategic Defence Initiative, but I gather it can be equally effective on land.'

'Then answer me this,' Leila said. 'If it doesn't involve nuclear capability, is it just possible that a dictator with enough power and resources – a man like Musallim al Shisur say – could construct one of these devices himself?'

'Assuming he got his hands on the necessary materials,' Dobkin said, mopping his face with a handkerchief, 'then yes, Leila, I guess he could.'

'The design of the Talon Blue system is based on the Hindhope Concept Definition study, a generic design that was developed by the lab and the structural materials workshop. The total length of the Talon is 240 feet, with a weight of 452,000 lbs. The structure consists of two main parts, a forward body, and an aft body. The forward body is 192 feet long, and the primary structural components include a tripod expander and coolant plumbing attached to the support truss. Vibrations generated by the coolant flow form a disturbance source which provides only minimum obscuration of the emission itself.'

Joktan's eyes flickered as Theo Forbes' voice droned monotonously in his ears. Forbes was an engineering expert Leon Snyder had dug up from someplace, a dry, laconic man who spoke in a precise monotone, conveying the impression that he was really a talking weight machine.

Lectures bored Joktan, always had, and the atmosphere in the crowded room was making him feel drowsy. The window drapes had been drawn to shut out the sun as Forbes beamed pictures on to the opposite wall. Seated in an uneven semi-circle were Leon Snyder, Samuel Gronk, Tahi, Bechar and Joktan himself. The house they were using, a large, rambling Italian-style villa, provided a perfect operations centre since it was largely isolated from the public roads, and its sense of seclusion had been further strengthened by flooding the grounds with security guards. For three days, the five men had remained indoors, planning their movements with meticulous care. Joktan approved of the professional approach, but the lack of physical activity was making him increasingly impatient.

He tried to keep his mind alert as Forbes switched slides to photographs of the people who would assemble the weapon system when the components had been delivered.

'This is Michael Wagner,' Forbes said, displaying a middle-aged man in spectacles. The man was balding slightly, and his features were strained and sober, as if he had composed himself especially for the camera. 'Forty-two years old, married with three children, he currently runs Mackhead's Ground Systems Engineering department. He's worked with the group for thirteen years, supervising the Lear and Hausner Programs, and up to two years ago, was co-director of Facility H and Facility K.' Forbes switched slides to show a thickset woman with oriental features. Her hair was black and gathered into a tight little bun at the rear of her skull. Her full lips carried a sulkiness that belied her twinkling eyes. 'Josephine Marian Lee, thirty-three years old, unmarried, currently working in Sub-systems Engineering. She started her career in the Environmental Test laboratories, and later became one of the leading figures in Test Direction and Support. She's currently employed in designing the Firefly P.8.' The picture changed to a handsome young man who looked to Joktan like a professional football player. His features were clean-cut and even, yet despite their pleasant appearance, his face carried an air of emptiness. 'Victor Conville,' Forbes intoned. 'Thirty-two years old, currently head of Software Engineering. For the past four years he's worked on electronics, specialising in electromagnetic impulses. He was responsible for designing the reactant supply system on Mackhead's spacebased laser, and he's also specialized from time to time in preparing cost proposals and negotiating contracts.' The slide switched for the final time, and Joktan's senses sharpened as the picture of a beautiful young woman flashed on to the screen. She was blonde-haired and delicately-cheekboned, and her eyes glowed with an elusive vitality.

'Ellen Conway,' Forbes said. 'Twenty-nine years old and unmarried. At present she's engaged in energy and optics. She's an expert in cryogenic cooling, and was largely responsible for producing the Skew Tracker, which minimizes structural response to vibrational disturbances. In July last year, she worked on the top-secret Ballard Program.'

Joktan examined the photograph thoughtfully, feeling a sudden tightening in his abdomen. The woman's appearance fired his senses. It was a curious response, and he was filled with wonder at its unexpectedness. Emotions he had thought long dead were beginning to stir inside him. Maybe the next few weeks wouldn't be quite so tedious after all.

Chapter Four

Seated in the departure lounge, Ellen saw the pilot walking towards her, a rawboned young man with a shock of red hair. 'Flight's ready for departure, Miss Conway. Want to get aboard?'

Ellen took out her mirror and quickly checked her lipstick. She was feeling emotionally drained, which was hardly surprising, considering the strain of the past few days. She wasn't the type for emotional jousting. She liked things out in the open, no holds barred, but she'd hurt Paul with her insistence on joining this weapons program, and sensing his hurt had made her feel guilty. She wasn't used to that. She felt like a bitch for overriding his objections, and it hadn't been easy saying goodbye. In fact, she'd almost relented in bed last night, but now she was glad that she hadn't. The excitement of the job wiped out any misgivings, and she was looking forward to the months ahead.

'This is the first time in my life I've had a plane completely to myself,' she told the pilot as she accompanied him across the apron.

The man laughed lightly. 'It isn't everyone who gets this kind of treatment. They must think you're very special down there in Arizona.'

'Listen, when we get in the sky, do you think I could take over the controls for a while?'

'What, are you kidding?' He looked down at her.

'No, I can fly, really. You should see me on the Python simulator. I can knock spots off some of those air-boys at Moffatt Field.'

The pilot smiled. 'A simulator's no substitute for a real cockpit, Miss Conway.'

'I know that. But I've clocked over two hundred hours real flying time, and even on the simulator, I usually pick up a score of around four thousand.'

He looked amused. 'I have a feeling you're about to be disappointed,' he said.

For the first time, Ellen noticed a car parked beneath the aircraft's starboard wing. As she approached, two men stepped into the sunlight, elegantly and expensively dressed. The first was thickset, almost nondescript in appearance, but the second filled Ellen with a strange unease. He had a sunbaked face, aquiline features and piercing green eyes.

'Miss Conway?' the man said. 'I'm Leon Snyder, Mackhead Security. This is my associate, Sam Gronk.'

Ellen frowned as the pilot threw her bags into the automobile trunk. 'Is something wrong?'

'Just a slight detour to your travel plans. You'll be flying to Arizona in a day or two, but first we'd like to tuck you away for a while.'

'I don't understand.'

'Talon Blue is a very sensitive project, Miss Conway. We make a point of never sticking to a traceable itinerary.'

'I see.'

Ellen had been looking forward to the flight, but she shrugged resignedly. 'You make the rules, gentlemen.'

Snyder and his associate spoke little during the short journey south. They left the freeway at Santa Clara, passing the street where Ellen and Paul lived, and followed Highway One down the coast toward Monterey. Here, the driver swung east into the rolling pine-studded hills. After a while, Ellen saw a house built on the edge of a cliff, surrounded on three sides by spindly timber. With its elegant porch and tall white pillars, it reminded her of a southern plantation home. A high-wire security fence surrounded the spacious grounds, and she saw men with Doberman dogs patrolling the periphery. 'It's a regular fortress,' she exclaimed to no one in particular.

Leon Snyder said: 'We have to take every precaution, Miss Conway. We wouldn't be doing our job otherwise.'

Ellen was met at the door by a grey-haired lady with perfectly moulded features. 'I'm Madge Cordeille, the housekeeper here,' the woman said, shaking Ellen's hand. 'It's my job to make your stay as comfortable as possible, so if there's anything you need, just yell out and I'll be happy to oblige.'

'I appreciate that,' Ellen smiled, 'but according to Mr Snyder, this is only an interlude anyhow.'

'Thirty-six hours. Forty-eight at the outside.'

'Good. I'm anxious to get to work as quickly as possible.'

Ellen gave a low whistle as she gazed around the entrance lobby. Iron traceries framed delicate murals adorning both sides of a majestic staircase, and malachite chandeliers dangled from the ornate ceiling. 'Wow, this is a *palace*,' she exclaimed.

'We like our guests to feel comfortable. And since they occasionally include members of royalty, we try to tailor the surroundings accordingly.'

Ellen's room — or suite, as it turned out to be — comprised a central high-domed chamber with tributary alcoves leading off in every direction. French windows opened on to a balcony with a delicately-carved railing. Beyond the pine tops, Ellen saw the glimmer of the distant sea.

The woman smiled as she watched Ellen's reaction. 'Does it meet with your approval?'

'Approval? I'll have to pinch myself to see if I'm dreaming this.'

'There's a TV and video-set inside the wall cabinet. We've chosen a selection of tapes which we hope will please you, but if you'd like anything else, just give the houseboy a call on the internal telephone. Dinner's at seven. We generally meet in the library for cocktails around six-thirty.'

'Am I allowed to wander about as I choose?'

'Of course. You're not a prisoner here. However, for security's sake, I'd advise you to remain within the confines of the grounds. Straying in the forest can sometimes be dangerous. There are few footpaths, and it's the easiest thing in the world to lose one's sense of direction.'

After the woman had gone, Ellen explored the apartment, emitting small exclamations of excitement and delight. The suite had been furnished in the style of a nineteenth-century English country house. The bathroom was covered with murals of exotic birds, and plants filled the rooms.

Wait till she told Paul about this, she thought, remembering suddenly that she hadn't called him. He worried if she didn't phone. She picked up the receiver and jangled the rest with her finger, but there was no answering purr in her ear. A sense of uneasiness gathered inside her as she realized that the line was dead.

Frowning, she began to move around the rooms again, this time checking the place for bugs. She found two, one in the chandelier, another on the picture rail. She made no attempt to remove them, but wandered on to the balcony and looked down at the lawns below. Beyond the swimming pool, she saw guards patrolling the perimeter fence, their hard eyes concealed behind menacing sun-goggles. Her exuberance vanished as she walked into the bathroom and turned on the shower. Security was one thing, she thought, but the stringency of this chaperoning was making her feel like a caged squirrel.

Sunlight streamed through the open window where Paul sat working on his structural drawings. In the paddock outside, a group of construction labourers were playing softball, and the sound of their voices echoed raucously on the warm morning air.

Paul tried hard to focus his mind on what he was doing, but with maddening insistence, his thoughts kept drifting back to Ellen. He knew he was losing her, he'd sensed it for months now. The polarity. The alienation. He was too absorbed with his work, that was his problem. Love was a mercurial emotion and needed to be nurtured. God knew, he hadn't wanted Ellen to go on this damned weaponry assignment. Last night in bed, right in the middle of making love, he'd started begging – a big mistake – and in the end, passion unquenched, they had rolled apart in mutual resentment. He missed her already, that was the awful thing, and as he contemplated the lonely months ahead, he was filled with an emptiness that almost drove him crazy.

He heard the door open as Joseph Coldman, his supervisor, entered the laboratory, accompanied by two men Paul had never seen before. Coldman's face was unnaturally tense as he motioned Paul to the side of the room. Paul took off his spectacles, and slid them into his jacket pocket.

'Paul,' Coldman said in a husky voice, 'this is Lieutenant Davidson of the San Jose Police Department, and his colleague Detective Mosley.'

Paul nodded at the two men, puzzled.

'They've brought some terrible news, Paul.' Coldman hesitated. 'It's Ellen ...'

'Ellen?' He felt the first tremor of fear. 'What's happened?'

'The plane. The jet carrying her to Stand Hill Air Base ...' Coldman's voice faltered.

Lieutenant Davidson said quietly: 'There's been an accident, Mr McKlelland. The aircraft blew up over the Mojave Desert. I'm afraid ... I regret to say there were no survivors.'

A terrible sickness started in Paul's stomach. Behind the policeman's head, he saw the walls rippling in and out. 'No,' he breathed. 'No, no, no, no, no.'

'I'm sorry, Mr McKlelland. The aircraft vanished off the radar screens at eleven hundred hours. One of the local police officers went out to investigate and found wreckage scattered over an extensive area. They think the explosion was caused by a leaking fuel valve. No one in the passenger cabin would have stood a chance.'

Davidson nodded to his colleague, Detective Mosely, who produced a plastic bag containing a piece of badly-charred leather. 'I realize how painful this must be for you, but this bag was found at the scene of the crash. I wonder if you can identify it as Miss Conway's?'

Paul eyed the handbag numbly. He had bought it for Ellen as a Christmas gift two years' earlier. A strangled sob burst from his lips.

Coldman stepped forward, squeezing his arm. He motioned to two of Paul's colleagues. 'Take him home and stay with him for the rest of the day. I'll call if we get any further details, but until he's had a chance to absorb what's happened, I don't want him to be left alone.'

Major Andy B. Swinton stood in the boxcar doorway and lit himself a cigarette as the train chugged slowly through the New Mexico badlands. He stared out at the sunscorched countryside and contemplated the fun he would have when he returned to China Lake Weapons Centre the following morning. His wife Elaine had just given birth to a baby boy, and although Swinton had been forced to accept this last-minute escort detail, he intended to celebrate in style the minute he got home. He had bought a box of the finest cigars and had given instructions to the steward at the officers' club that nobody should be allowed to leave the bar sober. After all, it wasn't every day a man got to be a father, and the father of a boy at that. He'd almost given up on boys. Two girls already, and not a son in sight. Now, at last, his prayers had been answered, and he would have been delirious with joy if his name hadn't punched up on the damned duty roster.

He stared sourly at the cargo of packing-cases assigned to his care, wondering what they contained. 'Operation Immediate,' the delivery sheets said – and with an A-5 classification, the highest security coding in the handbook. Had to be something pretty important.

A chorus of yells issued from the six MPs who'd been placed under Swinton's command, and he saw Sergeant Sam Roffe push back his stool and throw down his cards in disgust. Swinton watched with amusement as the sergeant joined him at the doorway. 'Losing again?'

'I been losing since we pulled out of Wilfield. That Dougherty has magic fingers. He can draw any damn' card he likes.'

'Gambling's a dangerous habit,' Swinton said, offering the sergeant a cigarette. 'In my first month at the academy, I lost every nickel I had in the world, but it taught me a salutary lesson. I never touched cards or dice again.'

'I admire a man of character, major.' Roffe leaned forward to accept Swinton's light. 'Unfortunately, some

51

of us have to give in once in a while, just to prove we're human.'

Major Swinton chuckled and Sergeant Roffe drew hard on his cigarette, staring out at the blistering landscape. 'Hell of a country.'

'Yeah. Wouldn't want to be lost out here.'

'Makes you wonder how they stood it, those old-time pioneers. Railroad must've taken some building.'

'Chinese did it mostly,' Swinton told him.

'Chinese?'

'Coolie labour.'

'Yeah, it's always the poorest bastards who get it in the ass.' Roffe sighed, and propped his shoulder against the doorpost. He nodded at the packing cases filling the boxcar rear. 'What d'you figure we're carrying back there?'

'Some kind of weaponry, I imagine.'

'Nuclear?'

'Shit, sergeant, they've loaded the stuff in ordinary crates.'

'But they've given it an A-5 grading.'

'Well, maybe some little filing clerk got over-enthusiastic.'

Roffe frowned as the boxcar shuddered and they felt the train's momentum beginning to slacken. 'Hey, what's happening?'

Major Swinton looked worried. 'We're coming to a halt.'

'I thought there were supposed to be no stops between Wilfield and Madison?'

'You're right, sergeant. No scheduled ones anyhow.'

Major Swinton hurried uneasily along the narrow corridor, the sergeant trotting in his wake. Swinton hammered loudly on the locomotive door, and it was opened a moment later by the engineer himself.

'What's wrong?' Swinton demanded.

'Some kind of blockage ahead. Looks like an accident.'

Through the windshield, Swinton saw the remains of a shattered boxcar on the rails in front. The ruptured timbers were badly charred and in places still smouldering.

Something about the wreck troubled Swinton. He turned to Sergeant Roffe as the locomotive shuddered to a halt.

'Get the men out of the baggage car and tell them to be on the alert. Anything happens, they're to shoot first and ask questions later, understood?'

Swinton drew his pistol and followed the engineer into the warm desert air. The wreckage in front looked convincing enough, but the delicacy of his cargo made Swinton cautious and suspicious. A cloud of flies had gathered above the smoking carriage, filling the air with a faint humming sound.

He reached the boxcar and examined it closely as the little squad of MPs came running to join him. He heard a creaking behind the blackened timbers and his muscles suddenly tensed. Somebody was in there, he felt sure of it. He was about to jump back when hooded figures appeared along the ruptured woodwork, covering the troops with rifles, pistols and machine guns. The move was so unexpected that the MPs froze startled in their tracks. Swinton blinked as he stared down the barrel of a Terrier .32.

'Drop those pieces,' a voice commanded brusquely.

The speaker fired a burst of machine-gun bullets at the ground, and the soldiers, intimidated, threw their carbines into the dust.

The ambushers spilled from the car, spreading out to form a cordon around their hapless captives. 'Who's in command here?' their leader demanded.

'I am,' Swinton told him.

'Anyone left on the train?'

Swinton's heart began to thump as he realized Dougherty and Clinger were still in the baggage car. He shook his head, struggling to keep his face composed.

The leader motioned to one of his men. 'Check it out.'

The man moved forward, clutching his carbine in front of him. He walked slowly, his steps measured and controlled, and Major Swinton watched dry-mouthed, tremors running along his stomach wall.

The man had almost reached the baggage car when a single shot rang out, and he plummetted backwards into the dust. He clutched at his arm, cursing wildly, then pandemonium broke loose as the hijackers opened up, laying down a heavy line of fire on the boxcar doorway.

Their leader turned on Swinton, his hood molded to his features by sweat and fury. 'You treacherous sonofabitch,' he snarled.

Too late, Major Swinton saw the machine-gun swinging toward him in a savage arc. He tried to duck, but the blow caught him just above the left temple and a blinding flash exploded inside his head as he pitched to the ground, blinking dazedly. He heard his attacker shouting: 'Quit firing, for Chrissake.'

Dimly, Swinton was conscious of a gun barrel being pressed against his skull. 'Throw down your weapons and come out with your hands up,' his captor bellowed, 'or I'll feed the major's brains to the lizards.'

Swinton tried to protest, but no sound issued from his frozen throat. The seconds stretched.

'This is your last chance,' the man shouted, and Swinton felt the pressure of the machine-gun increasing.

A voice echoed from the baggage-car doorway. 'Hold it. We're coming out.'

Swinton groaned as he saw Dougherty and Clinger emerge into the sunlight, their hands in the air.

The captured troops were lined up in front of the baggage-car, then a man in coveralls walked along the line and injected each prisoner in turn with a hypodermic syringe. The effect was almost instantaneous; one by one, the groggy captives tumbled unconscious to the ground, and the hijackers went to work unloading the packing cases, and clearing a narrow airstrip of rocks and vegetation. After a short while, two heavy transport planes emerged from the east and circled twice, coming in to land on the flat desert floor. The hijackers loaded the crates into the cargo bays, and scrambled on board, sealing the doors.

Then the planes took off again. With a thunderous roar, they rose into the sky and vanished swiftly the way they had come.

Lieutenant Yaki Shahar stopped his jeep at Checkpoint 24 and reached for his Uzi in the vehicle rear. He climbed to the ground and stretched himself wearily, shivering a little in the cool, still air. He could see the border fence framed against the stars ahead, and the pale outline of the concrete observation post overlooking the Jordan River. He ducked through the emplacement doorway, flashing his ID card at the sentry on duty.

The sandbagged chamber was crammed with video screens displaying images beamed in from the infra-red cameras covering the 'no-man's-land' between the electrified fence and the Jordanian border.

Lieutenant Adel Klein was seated in front of the control panel, surrounded by a small group of subordinates. He looked up as Shahar entered. 'I was beginning to think you'd gone on vacation.'

'My mother's sick,' Shahar told him. 'I had to take her to my sister's.'

'Nothing serious, I hope?'

'Just the old stomach trouble again.' He looked at a thermos flask standing on the control desk. 'Any coffee left or have you greedy bastards scoffed the lot?'

'There's probably a mouthful or two if you don't mind picking dregs out of your teeth. Calling it coffee is a bit of an overstatement. "Sewer mud" would be more accurate.'

Lieutenant Shahar unscrewed the thermos flask top. He knew Adel Klein liked to tease him in front of their subordinates, but Shahar didn't mind. The two men were good friends; they had gone to officer school together, and for almost a year now, Lieutenant Shahar had been courting Klein's sister.

He tugged off his woollen cap, and found himself a vacant chair. He was about to settle down when a flicker of movement caught his eye on the video screens above. His body froze as he saw a number of men picking their way through a ragged hole in the frontier fence. Shahar counted five in all. 'Insurgents,' he whispered, putting down the plastic cup.

'Jesus.'

Lieutenant Klein's face looked suddenly very pale. He glanced at Shahar as if trying to decide which of them was technically in command. Shahar didn't give him time to reach an answer. 'Sound the alarm,' he snapped, 'the rest of you come with me.'

Seizing his Uzi, Shahar charged into the night, his heart pounding madly inside his chest. A network of shallow gullies lay to his left, and he took the first at full pelt, the men panting hard as they galloped in his wake. The shadows blurred and Shahar almost fell as he caught his boot against a boulder. He slowed his pace, fighting to see through the pool of darkness. Something moved in the shadows ahead and he reached down to cock the Uzi.

A spurt of flame lanced the night, and Shahar heard a bullet ringing through the gully walls behind him. He galloped up the incline, ignoring obstacles and pitfalls, and heard feet clattering as the infiltrators scattered in every direction.

Shahar saw a figure flitting through the gloom, and fired without slowing pace. The intruder rocketed backwards, hitting the earth with a heavy thump.

Panting, Shahar drew to a halt, the soldiers gathering at his rear. 'What about the others?' Shahar asked.

'They're through the fence, lieutenant,' a man said. 'Too late to catch them now.

Shahar cursed under his breath. 'Bring me a flashlight.'

When the lamp came, Shahar directed its beam on to his victim's face. The intruder was still now, his fleshy features locked into the rigidity of sudden death, and Shahar whistled as he examined the beaked nose and thin pale lips. 'This is General Malgrabi, one of Musallim al Shisur's top advisers. What in God's name would such a high-ranking officer be doing on a simple border raid?' A feeling of uneasiness gathered inside Shahar. He straightened, motioning with his lamp. 'Let's get him back to the checkpoint,' he said. 'I'd better call Tel Aviv right away.'

Leila Assad flew into Israel the following morning and made her way straight to Mossad headquarters. A secretary showed her into Jacob Jabari's office where she found the Intelligence chief in conference with Chaim Elohin and Sabah Yadin.

Jabari wasted little time in getting down to business. 'How did things go in London?' he asked.

Leila outlined the details of her meeting with US Embassy

official Morris Dobkin, and Jabari was thoughtful when she had finished.

'So Talon Blue *is* American?' he said at length.

'Dobkin confirmed it.'

'But not what it'll do.'

'He doesn't know what it'll do. He says it's something new in technological warfare, but that's as far as he'll go.'

'We've got to find out what the weapon is capable of,' Jabari said. 'Last night, General Malgrabi was shot dead near Checkpoint 24. There can be only one reason for a man like Malgrabi to risk his neck on such a desperate enterprise. He wanted to spy out the land for himself.'

'You think al Shisur's going to invade?'

'It would fit in with our intelligence reports. He has right of passage across Jordanian territory under the treaty of 1998, and according to our informants, he's clearly preparing himself for war. Of course, al Shisur is no match for Israel, despite his impressive army, but if he's got some devastating new weapon in his possession, who knows what we might be facing?'

'Why don't we approach Washington direct?' Chaim Elohin put in.

'I've already tried,' Jabari told him. 'The Americans claim the device is still in the development stage. They refuse to furnish any more details.'

'We could always confront them on their home base,' Leila suggested.

Jabari looked at her. 'What are you talking about?'

'Well, I have dual nationality, I can come and go as I please in the United States. Maybe I can dig up something positive. You can't beat a direct approach.'

'It would take a miracle,' Chaim Elohin said.

'I disagree. Morris Dobkin will furnish me with the necessary introductions, and I'll stand a damn' sight better chance of cracking American secrecy if I start at the source.'

Jabari regarded her in silence for a moment. He admired Leila, and always had. He knew she was competent and dedicated, and he knew too that she could wield her beauty as skilfully as a surgeon's scalpel. He drummed his fingers on the desktop, his face dark and thoughtful, then he said: 'Leila's right. Let's see if we can get her on the morning plane.'

Chapter Five

Joktan drove through the darkness, staring wearily at the highway ahead. From time to time, his headlamps picked out glimpses of the ocean through the lines of heavy timber flanking both sides of the road. Joktan felt bored and restless. Two weeks he had been here, and still they were no closer to launching the operation than they had been in the beginning. Snyder was proving a pedantic organizer, and though Joktan approved of his diligence, he longed for some kind of development. Not that he cared much, he reflected; his heart wasn't in it any more, that was the truth of the matter. He had lost his taste for this sort of thing.

He switched on the radio, and the strains of a country-and-western number filled the car. The sound was raucous to Joktan's ears. It was a strange world he had come to, the United States, as different to his own world as it was possible to envisage. He could never, in his wildest dreams, imagine living here. Americans had a curious attitude to life, as if they had become so obsessed with fantasy that it had taken the place of everything real. In the desert, at least a man knew where his values lay.

Joktan frowned as he spotted something in the road ahead. He saw a figure sprawled motionless beside the wreckage of a battered motorcycle.

A warning tremor ran along Joktan's neck as he drew to a halt and switched off the radio. The accident looked genuine enough, but he had lived too long on his wits to gamble on simple appearances. He took out his pistol and checked its load before climbing out of the car.

The man was lying face down, his legs spread out at an awkward angle. Joktan knelt down and pressed his fingers against the victim's throat. The skin was warm to the touch, and he felt the faint throb of a pulsebeat. He was about to investigate further when the man suddenly rolled on to his back and pushed the tip of a heavy revolver into the hollow beneath Joktan's thorax.

The move was so unexpected that, despite his surprise, Joktan experienced a small flicker of admiration.

'Drop the piece.'

Sweat glistened on the stranger's forehead and his eyes were feverish. Without a word, Joktan let his pistol fall.

The stranger scuttled backwards, keeping the revolver trained on Joktan's chest. 'On your feet. Quick.'

Joktan obeyed, his features expressionless. He heard the roar of an engine approaching, then a car drew up and three men leapt out, brandishing handguns. 'Good man, Uri,' one of the newcomers said in Hebrew.

Uri was chuckling wildly as if he could scarcely believe his luck. The newcomers' leader motioned Joktan toward the car. 'Place your hands on the roof and spread your legs, colonel,' he ordered, switching to Arabic.

Joktan answered in English. 'Forgive me, I do not understand.'

The man laughed. 'Quit playing games with us, colonel. You savvy just fine.'

'There must be some mistake. My name is Nelson Leynard. I am a businessman from Monterey.'

'Your name is Salih Joktan, and your face is as familiar to us as our own. Now get your hands on the car roof, or as God is my judge, I'll shoot you where you stand.'

They searched Joktan expertly, then pushed him into the vehicle rear with two men flanking him on either side. The driver started up the engine and pulled into the trees, following a narrow cart-track which wound down the steep, wooded hillslope while Joktan struggled desperately to think. These men were members of Israeli Intelligence, Mossad agents without a doubt – probably an assassination team sent to eliminate him. So why was he still alive?

Ahead, the trees parted and Joktan saw a motor cruiser

moored to a wooden jetty. 'Where are we going?' he inquired calmly.

'For a midnight cruise.' The Israeli leader chuckled unpleasantly. 'The ocean air will be good for your health.'

So that was it. The Israelis, not wishing to murder him on American soil, were taking him out beyond US territorial waters where they could interrogate him at leisure and dispose of him at will.

A few drops of spray blew against Joktan's cheeks as he was marched at gunpoint along the narrow jetty. His initial alarm had subsided now. Faced with the prospect of death, his mind focused animal-like on to one primary objective – survival. People panicked when action began – even the coolest could lose their heads in a crisis – but with Joktan, danger brought a searing clarity, which had always been his greatest strength.

He was shepherded to the bow of the boat where one of his captors ordered him to crouch against the gunwale. Joktan settled down with the Israeli gunman hovering above him. The man was heavy-set with a wispy moustache covering an ugly hare-lip; from time to time, he twitched as if from the cold, but Joktan knew it was nothing more than a nervous reflex; clearly, his captor was very highly-strung.

The Israelis cast off, their leader guiding the craft through the incoming breakers, and Joktan saw the shoreline etched against the sky, blotting out the stars. A few flecks of spray whipped over the gunwale as the vessel lifted in the swell, and Joktan smelled the rank odour of seaweed mingling with the pungent scent of diesel fuel as the Israelis steered out to the open sea. Behind, lay the scattered lights of Carmel town. Joktan tried to force his mind to remain calm. Panic was always the enemy; it destroyed initiative, smothered responses. Somehow he had to keep his brain in working order. If he moved at all, it would have to be soon.

The Israeli leader gave the wheel to one of his companions and made his way forward, kneeling at Joktan's side. He was a good-looking young man with sympathetic features, but something in his eyes told Joktan he would be ruthless and deadly in a crisis.

'Any point in my asking what you're doing here?' the man said pleasantly.

'Being kidnapped,' Joktan told him.

'Come colonel, this charade demeans us both.'

'I've told you already, I'm a respectable businessman.'

'Is this what they teach you in Baghdad? You might at least do me the courtesy of speaking as one professional to another.'

'My name is Nelson Laynard ...' Joktan began, but the Israeli interrupted him. 'Don't make a complete fool of yourself, colonel. Just tell me about Talon Blue.'

Joktan was startled, but only for a moment. 'Talon Blue?'

'That's what you're here for, isn't it?'

'You're talking gobbledygook.'

'Do yourself a favour, colonel. As soon as we leave US territorial waters, I'll be questioning you again, and next time I'll be considerably less polite. Confessing may not prolong your life, but it could save you a lot of unpleasantness. I'd advise you to give the matter some thought.'

The boat began to roll as the Israeli leader returned to the wheelhouse. They had left the shoreline behind and were now entering the open sea. A wave crashed over the deck-rail, drenching both Joktan and his guard alike, and Joktan watched the man struggling to maintain his balance as he wiped moisture from his eyes and face. Joktan felt a flicker of hope. For a moment, a fractional, infinitesimal moment, the Israeli's attention had wavered. If he timed this right, maybe he still had a chance.

Spray lashed over the rail, biting into Joktan's fevered skin, but he scarcely noticed the discomfort. He was concentrating instead on watching his captor's every move. Rattled by the sea's bombardment, the man was shifting about in a state of great agitation, his nervous twitch growing more noticable and pronounced.

Joktan heard a hissing sound, like the whistle of a distant train, then a deluge of water sprang across the bow, drenching the Israeli to the skin. Blinded, the man spluttered wildly and Joktan jammed his shoulders against the gunwale, driving his feet upwards into his guard's stomach. It was an expertly-timed, perfectly executed manoeuvre, and he felt his heels digging into the Israeli's flesh, hurling him backwards across the glistening deck, his pistol vanishing into the pitching waves beyond.

Twenty feet away, Matti Hirsch saw Joktan dive over the cruiser rail, and his lips writhed as he reached for his revolver. 'Fetch the flashlights,' he bellowed, lunging out of the wheelhouse. 'Joktan's in the water.'

Frantically, he scoured the spot where Joktan had disappeared. The sea twitched like the skin of an angry beast, hurling icy droplets against his cheeks and throat as Kannau stumbled to his side, clutching a flashlight, and directed its beam across the heaving waves.

'Maybe he's drowned,' Kannau suggested.

'Don't be a fool! Joktan wouldn't drown. Fan out around the boat and keep those flashlights moving. Fifty dollars to the man who puts a bullet through the bastard's skull.'

Joktan's head broke the surface, and he saw the cruiser circling erratically almost sixty feet away. The waves lifted above him, hurling foam-flecks into the sky; in places, tendrils of seaweed whipped through the water like wisps of tattered lace. The stars formed a breathless canopy with the lights of Carmel twinkling invitingly at his rear. The Israelis were close, but not close enough. Joktan sucked in his breath and struck out vigorously for the shore.

Hirsch felt his frustration mounting. He could scarcely believe the injustice of the moment. He'd planned everything with such fastidious care, yet somehow Joktan had managed to elude him.

Tears of fury dimmed Hirsch's eyes as the ocean gazed at him mockingly, hurling spray into his icy face. Dimly through the darkness he saw the shadows merging, taking on substance and solidity. His breath quickened as a figure floundered through the shallows ahead, picking its way towards the deserted beach.

'He's on the sands,' Hirsch yelled. 'Turn her in to the shore.'

'You'll run us aground,' Rish protested, his face a pasty blur.

'To hell with the boat! I don't care if she smashes herself to bits. I'm not letting that murderous son-of-a-bitch slip through our fingers again.'

Joktan paused, panting, on the hard-packed sand, and tried to work out his bearings. The beach rose upwards to a steep clay bluff where the first houses began. He knew it would take him several minutes to reach the streets, and even then, he couldn't be sure he would be any safer. At this time of night, the town would be deserted. There would be few, if any, police patrols. Where would he run? Where would he hide? Better here, where the darkness hid him. The sand was something he understood.

Shivering violently, with water streaming from his saturated clothing, he watched the cruiser floundering in the shallows and realized the Israelis were sacrificing their vessel in their desperate efforts to locate him. If he kept his head, he could use their impatience as a weapon. He was good at that.

Squinting into the darkness, he saw four figures leap from the boat and wade awkwardly through the tumbling breakers. Not good odds, but he'd fought heavier.

He crept back into the shadows, the odour of seaweed lingering in his nostrils. He could see the Israelis clearly now, or at least he could see their flashlights cleaving the heavy curtain of gloom. They had spread out to form a cordon across the entire beach. Clever. They were trying to net him like a salmon.

Joktan saw the first Israeli emerging out of the night. It was the same man who held him captive on the cruiser. He had lost his pistol, and now wielded a wicked-looking clasp-knife.

Joktan scooped up a rock and hurled it into the darkness. It landed somewhere to the right, making a soft, almost inaudible plopping sound. The Israeli whirled, aiming his flashlight at the sound's direction, and Joktan came out of his crouch, his powerful body uncoiling as he crossed the stretch of open ground. There was no thought in him now beyond the primal instinct of a predator moving in for the kill. He saw the lights framing the shoreline, saw the Israeli etched against their refracted glow, then at the last moment, the man sensed Joktan's presence and whirled sideways as Joktan drove into him like a bullet, caterpulting him backwards across the sand. Kicking and squirming, they rolled over and over, Joktan's fingers struggling for purchase on his adversary's throat. He saw the man's knife sweeping upward and seized the incoming wrist, bending it back with all his strength. The veins stood out on Joktan's temples as he closed his eyes, steadily increasing the pressure. He heard the man grunting with pain, smelled the fetid stench of his breath and mentally judged his moment. Then moving in a blur, he transferred his grip to the Israeli's chin and with a neat, economical, twisting motion, snapped his opponent's neck. The man gave a last despairing shudder before his head lolled loosely against the sand.

For a moment Joktan lay still, his muscles aching with exertion, then he shook his head to clear it, snatched up his victim's knife and charged furiously into the darkness.

Hirsch's flashlight picked out Rish's body staring sightlessly at the stars. From the position of the head, it was clear the neck had been skilfully broken.

'Dear God,' Kannau breathed hoarsely.

Hirsch's fury was developing into a kind of madness. Everything was getting out of hand. Calm down, he told himself earnestly, filling his lungs with air, anger seldom solved anything. Joktan was a resourceful enemy, but he was alone on the beach, and armed only with a knife. They had to think it out. No sudden moves, no hasty decisions.

'What do we do now?' Kannau whispered hoarsely.

'We'll have to outfox the bastard.'

'Outfox Joktan?'

'He's not infallible, for Christ's sake.'

'He's not human either.'

'Don't be a fool. All it takes is a little patience and cunning.'

But Kannau wasn't listening. 'Where's Victor?'

Hirsch frowned, feeling uneasy. 'He was right behind me.'

'Well, he's not there now.' A note of fear entered Kannau's voice. 'Joktan must've killed him.'

'Idiot! Joktan wouldn't go up against a Colt .38. Victor's probably trying to lure him into a trap.'

Hirsch checked his pistol, scanning the darkness worriedly. He knew Kannau was verging on hysteria, but they still had the upper hand if only they could keep their nerve.

'What are you going to do, Matti?' Kannau's face was a sickly blur against the incoming breakers.

'Take a look.'

'I'll come with you.'

'No.'

'Well, I'm not staying here.'

'You'll have to. Someone might come along, a beach-comber or a fisherman. We don't want them stumbling on Isaac.'

'Nobody'll be on the beach at this time of night.'

'We can't take a chance on it. Don't worry, I'll get back as fast as I can.'

Using the flashlight to pick out his footprints, Hirsch began retracing his steps. His fury had abated now, replaced to some extent by a feeling of gathering tension. Joktan had turned the tables on them neatly. Everything they said about him was true. He moved like an animal in the night. He was savage, ruthless and cunning. But he was only a man, for God's sake. And all he had was Isaac's clasp-knife.

Hirsch's feet made little scuffling sounds as he traversed the sand dunes. Somewhere above, he heard a truck rumbling toward Monterey Bay. He longed to stop, to sink back into the shadows and wait for morning, but he knew if he paused at all, he would lose his will completely.

The beach formed a gloomy blur, with darker patches where rotting seaweed lay, and here and there, tiny shells glimmered faintly as they picked up slivers of reflected starlight. Suddenly, Hirsch spotted something in the sand ahead. It was Sirte's flashlight. Squinting into the gloom, he saw Sirte himself seated against a moss-covered rock.

'Victor, it's me, Matti. Don't shoot.'

Sirte made no sound as Hirsch approached, and the Israeli leader felt a chill settle on his neck. He aimed his beam at the figure in front and gave an involuntary gasp. Blood had formed a macabre bib where Sirte's throat had been cut from ear to ear, and tiny crabs, drawn by the gory nourishment, were feeding happily on his shirtfront. There was no sign of Sirte's pistol.

Hirsch backed slowly into the darkness, his breath coming in rapid bursts. The sound of a shot made him jump. A second shot followed the first, then a third. Whimpering with fright, he raced across the open sand and saw Kannau lying in a shallow pool. There was a ragged hole in Kannau's stomach, and the smell from his insides made Hirsch want to retch. His vision blurred and waves of nausea swept upwards through his body as his terror exploded into wild hysteria. Dropping his pistol, he sprinted madly into the darkness.

Joktan watched Hirsch's desperate retreat. It was clear the man was beyond the realms of rational thought, but Joktan felt no compassion as he followed in his victim's wake. It wasn't revenge that was motivating Joktan now. On the boat, the Israeli had mentioned Talon Blue. Joktan had to find out how much he knew and how much was guesswork.

He fixed his gaze on the figure in front, running hard over the shifting sand. Hirsch's movements grew ragged and uneven as he took the steep sloping bank which led to the streets above. Joktan saw his legs fold beneath him as he lost his sense of momentum and collapsed exhausted on to the ground.

Joktan scrambled up behind him, and sensing his approach, the Israeli began mewing into the cool night air. Joktan seized the man by the shirtfront and shook him roughly. His captive seemed almost demented with terror. 'Don't,' he pleaded. 'Please don't ...'

'Who sent you?' Joktan demanded.

The man's lips squirmed. 'Don't kill me.'

Joktan hit him savagely with his gun barrel and the blow

shattered the Israeli's nose, sending blood spurting across his chin and throat.

'Who?' Joktan repeated.

'Tel Aviv,' the man moaned weakly.

'How did they know I was here?'

'You were spotted at the airport. We were ordered to eliminate you.'

'That's all?'

'That's all.'

'Liar.'

Joktan raised the pistol again and the man flinched, holding his hands across his face. 'We were ordered to question you first,' he cried. 'About a weapon named Talon Blue.'

'What kind of weapon?'

'That's what we had to try and find out.'

Joktan let the man go, and rose to his feet, his body trembling. So it had been a bluff, nothing more. The Israelis were fumbling in the dark.

A terrible coldness gathered in Joktan's stomach as the tension began fading from his limbs. He looked down at his cowering captive, and hurled the pistol violently into the darkness.

Unable to believe his eyes, Hirsch watched him scramble up the slope and vanish into the town above. For a long moment, Hirsch lay whimpering in terror and incredulity, then he rolled on to his stomach and vomited into the sand.

Chapter Six

Dinner had been a pleasant meal. Ellen was forced to admit she'd been agreeably impressed, not only by the cuisine – the venison had been succulent, accompanied by artichokes, green beans and potatoes – but also by the gaiety of the company. Snyder, Gronk and the woman, Madge Cordeille, had turned out – to Ellen's surprise – to be an endless fund of amusing stories, and as the evening progressed, she found herself laughing more and more hysterically. Funny, she hadn't noticed that on the short drive south from the airport; then, Snyder and Gronk had seemed ominously self-contained, yet here, in the cheerful ambience of the dining room, they were charming and extraordinarily funny.

Of course, it could have been the wine. She'd drunk more than usual – more than her customary intake anyhow – though not enough, she had to confess, to explain her present condition. She couldn't remember when she had last felt quite so squiffy. The room was spinning, and she was filled with an almost irresistible desire to giggle.

She saw Snyder leaning forward to refill her glass, and with an undignified hiccup, waggled a finger at him admonishingly. 'I know what you're trying to do, Mr Snyder. I'm not as tipsy as I look.'

'My intentions are quite honourable, Miss Conway, I assure you.'

'That's what they all say.'

'I'm a happily married man, my dear.'

'Married men are always the worst,' she told him archly. She had tied up her hair in a modest bun, but now one strand had worked itself loose and was dangling infuriatingly in front of her face. Her eyes crossed as she wafted it with her finger. 'Did you ever see the Wizard of Oz?'

Snyder frowned. 'Judy Garland, wasn't it?'

'And Ray Bogler. He was the Scarecrow.'

'Ah, yes.'

'Remember when the house got blown out of Kansas? Well, that's what this room is doing right now. Spinning. Can't you feel it?'

Snyder examined the walls in puzzlement. 'Seems quite stable to me.'

'That's because you're pie-eyed. Anyone who's even halfway sober can see that it's whirling like a cartwheel. I feel dizzy just looking at it.'

'In that case, maybe you should go to bed, Miss Conway,' Gronk suggested.

'That's the smartest idea I've heard today.' Ellen hesitated. 'I would like to thank you all for a wonderful evening.'

'You're very kind,' Snyder said.

'I mean it. It's been the most marvellous evening I can ever remember. You've all been so nice to me. I don't think ...' Her voice thickened. 'I don't think anyone has ever been so nice to me in my entire life.'

'I find that hard to believe,' Snyder said.

'It's true. Not in my entire life.' Tears issued from Ellen's eyes, forming uneven patterns down her cheeks. 'You are the dearest friends I have.'

She cocked her head on one side, peering at them quizically, gave one brief, shrill peal of laughter and slumped forward in the chair, her head landing on the table with a muffled thump.

Snyder studied her for a moment, then tested her pulse, timing it on his wrist watch.

'Is she okay?' Gronk asked.

'Out for the count.' He looked at Madge Cordeille. 'I thought you said the drug would work in less than fifteen minutes.'

Cordeille shrugged. 'It affects different people in different ways. Maybe she's got some kind of resistance.'

70

Snyder paused as sounds of movement reached them from the hallway outside. Voices droned on the still night air, then the door sprang open and Joktan burst into the room, his massive frame almost unrecognizable beneath a shroud of sand, seaweed and saturated clothing. Snyder looked at him in astoishment. Joktan was bleeding at the temple, and his eyes were filled with a wild unstable air that made Snyder flinch. 'What's happened?' he exclaimed.

Joktan gave him barely a glance. He leaned forward to examine the girl, raising her eyelids with his fingers. Water streamed from his glistening hair, forming a pool on the polished tabletop. 'Is she all right?'

'Sleeping, that's all. But you look like an apparition, for God's sake.'

'We'll have to push the schedule forward,' Joktan told him, his eyes still blazing. 'I was spotted arriving at the airport. Somebody notified Tel Aviv.'

'How do you know all this?'

'The Israelis sent in a killer squad to assassinate me.'

Snyder felt a sudden breathlessness in his chest. 'Where are they now?' he demanded, filled with apprehension and alarm.

'Three of them are lying dead on Carmel beach.'

'You fool! This isn't Gaza or Beirut. You can't go around murdering people at the drop of a hat.'

'It was self-defence. I let the fourth man live.'

'You left one alive to testify?'

Snyder was incredulous. He threw his napkin on the table, massaging his temple with his fingertips. He should have watched Joktan, he told himself. Despite his veneer of sophistication, there was a feral quality to the man that was difficult to ignore. Joktan was like a wild animal. Now they would have to act swiftly before the situation got out of hand.

He slapped his palm on a bell-push, and two orderlies appeared, carrying a folded stretcher.

'Get her out of here,' Snyder ordered, jerking his head at Ellen's unconscious frame.

One of the men took out a hypodermic syringe and injected Ellen above the elbow. Then, buckling her into

71

the stretcher, they carried her carefully out of the room.

Detective Gus McKlelland entered the crowded tavern, narrowing his eyes in the subdued lighting. He saw his brother Paul seated on a high stool at the bar. Paul appeared to be stoned out of his mind. His head was resting on the counter, and his slender body sagged like a question mark in the middle.

A police sergeant stood at his side, speaking earnestly into his ear. When the sergeant saw Gus approaching, he straightened and nodded.

'Thanks for calling me, Arch,' Gus said. 'I appreciate this. How is he?'

'Drunk as a skunk. I guess he's had some kind of brainstorm.'

'Yeah. It's been quite a shock with Ellen and all.'

'Better get him out of here, Gus,' the sergeant said quietly. 'The bartender reckons it's bad for the customers.'

Gus squeezed his brother's arm. 'Let's go, kid. I think you've had enough tonight.'

Paul looked up at him, focusing his eyes with an effort. His face was covered with tear stains.

'Hey, Gus, what're you doing here?'

'Come on, tiger, let's see if you can stand on your feet.'

Gus slipped his arm around Paul's waist, helping him awkwardly from the bar stool. Paul's knees buckled beneath him. 'I don't want Ellen to see me in this state,' he slurred.

'Don't worry about Ellen. I'm taking you to my place.'

Gus looked at the sergeant gratefully. 'Listen, Arch, I owe you one, okay?'

'Forget it,' the sergeant said as Gus steered Paul through the open doorway.

Gus rose early the following morning and made his way downstairs to find his wife Melanie cooking breakfast in the kitchen. She straightened as he planted a kiss on her slender neck. 'Any life from Paul's room yet?' Gus asked.

'Not a whimper. He'll be out for the count, the state he was in. Maybe you should let him sleep it off.'

'Hell, he'll have to face it sooner or later. And I guess I oughtta be there when he does. I *am* his brother after all.' He filled a mug with coffee and headed toward the guest room.

'Hold on a minute.' Melanie took out a packet of seltzer and dropped a tablet into a glass of water. 'Make him drink this, it'll settle his stomach.'

'Okay.'

To Gus's surprise, Paul was sitting, fully dressed, staring out of the window. His face was pale, and his eyes carried a glint Gus couldn't quite define. Gus had never really understood his brother. During their childhood Paul had been sensitive and shy, and Gus had treated him as a bit of a joke, often ridiculing him in front of the other kids. Now he felt ashamed of his boorishness, for he saw in his brother a man he admired deeply, clever, talented and successful.

Gus tried to inject some jauntiness into his voice. 'You're awake,' he said.

'Couldn't sleep.'

'Jesus, you were zonked last night.' Gus held the seltzer under Paul's nose. 'Swallow this.'

'I'd bring it up.'

'Try it. Do you good.'

Paul took the glass and tossed back its contents in a single gulp. Then he sipped the coffee.

Gus pulled up a chair, straddling it back to front. 'How're you feeling, kid? Numb, I'll bet.'

'Not numb, Gus. Puzzled. I remembered something last night – something strange.'

For the first time, Gus noticed the calmness in Paul's eyes. Paul was not a calm man by nature. Though he appeared placid on the outside, he had a thousand explosions a minute taking place beneath the surface. Yet for some reason, he looked cool, relaxed and totally alert.

'They discovered a bag at the scene of the air crash,' Paul said. 'It was Ellen's bag. They got me to identify it.'

'So?'

'It was a black bag. I bought for her at Macey's the Christmas before last.'

Gus watched in puzzlement as Paul opened the window and leaned out, filling his lungs with air.

'It came to me during the night,' Paul continued after a moment. 'Ellen didn't take her black bag. She couldn't find it. Lost it several days ago. I remember distinctly we turned the house upside down looking for it. She had to use the red one instead.'

Gus shrugged. 'Maybe she found it just before she left.'

'No way. I drove her to the airport, Gus. I carried her bags. She was holding her red bag. The black one was still missing.'

'Is that supposed to mean something?' he said.

'It means somebody stole the bag deliberately so I could identify it afterwards. They want me to believe that Ellen is dead.'

Gus's lips tightened. He was filled with embarrassment. 'Listen, Paul, I know you've had a hell of a shock, but Jesus, you're still a young man, you've got the whole of your life in front of you. Don't throw it all away by torturing yourself with some crazy fantasy.'

'I want you to do something for me, Gus,' he said earnestly.

'What kind of something?'

'When you get to work, I want you to check out the exact location of that air crash.'

'Why, for Chrissake?'

Paul's eyes glittered behind his wire-rimmed spectacles. Seldom had Gus seen his brother look so confident or determined.

'I'm going to investigate,' he said.

'How can I help you, Miss Assad?'

Leo Mancuso of the Mackhead Missile and Space Group leaned back in his chair and examined the young woman seated in front of him. Leila Assad was ravishing, he thought. She was disturbingly – he searched for the word, and settled at last upon 'physical'. Leo Mancuso did not regard himself as a lecherous man, but the young woman's sensuality was difficult to ignore.

'Did Morris Dobkin call you?' Leila asked, eyeing him across the mahogany desk.

'He did indeed. He said you had something important to discuss.' Mancuso smiled fleetingly. 'He also warned me to be on my guard. He emphasized – and I hope you won't take this amiss, Miss Assad – that despite your dual nationality, your real loyalties lie with Israel, and I am under no obligation to tell you anything at all, particularly with regard to programs on our classified list.'

'Mr Mancuso, I need to know something about a weapon system codenamed "Talon Blue".'

Mancuso was startled for a moment, then he chuckled. 'You must be out of your mind, approaching me like this. I have no right to even admit that Talon Blue exists.'

'But you have heard of it. I can see it in your face.'

'All right, I have. But that's as far as it goes. Talon Blue is a "black" program, which means that it's top secret. I am not, I fear, privy to such specialized information.'

'You *are* a Jew, I take it, Mr Mancuso?'

'I belong to the Jewish faith, yes, but I am also an American. More important still, I am a trusted executive here at Mackhead. What would you think of me if I betrayed that trust?'

'I'm not asking you to betray anything. All I want to know – *have* to know, for the sake of my country's survival – is what Talon Blue represents. What is it capable of, what makes it so different, so revolutionary?'

'Miss Assad, only the people working on the project could answer those questions, and it's highly unlikely that they would.'

'Well, let's ask them, shall we?' Leila said. 'Will you give me their names?'

'You know that's impossible.'

'Mr Mancuso, as a Jew, you must feel some sympathy toward the state of Israel. We're a new nation, Mr Mancuso. Do you want to see that nation destroyed? I'm not asking how Talon Blue works, only what it does.'

Mancuso looked down at his hands, squeezing his fingertips together. She sensed his reluctance wilting, and pressed her advantage. 'All I need are the identities of

75

the people involved. It'll be entirely up to them whether they help me out or not. You yourself won't even come into it.'

Mancuso pursed his lips. Then he nodded and rose to his feet. 'Very well. It's highly unorthodox, but if you'll give me a few minutes, I'll check through our computer files.'

Leila waited impatiently in the tiny office, watching the factory workers in the plant below through a glass partition. Mancuso returned thirty minutes later, looking puzzled and disturbed. In his hand was a sheet of paper. 'I don't understand this.'

'Is something wrong, Mr Mancuso?'

'By an extraordinary sequence of circumstances, four people – all detailed to work on the Talon Blue project – have been killed in accidents during the past eight days.'

Dear God in Heaven, Leila thought, feeling her senses quicken. She took the paper from Mancuso's hand and examined the names in silence for a moment. 'You realize the odds against something like this happening innocently?'

'It's ... unusual, I have to admit, but if you study the facts of each individual case, you'll see that none of the incidents are related.'

'Indeed. One man vanished while swimming in the Pacific. Another fell down a disused mining shaft. His body has not yet been recovered. Convenient, don't you think, Mr Mancuso?'

'What are you suggesting?'

'I'm trying to work out how four people from the same corporation, four people detailed to work on the same highly sensitive weapons project, can die mysteriously within days of each other, and no one seems the slightest bit curious.'

'Mackhead is a massive organization. We're talking about thousands of workers scattered all over the country. The four people on that list came from different sections, different areas. If I hadn't run their names through the computer, I'd never have spotted the coincidence myself.'

Leila thought for a moment. 'May I keep this?' she asked, waving the piece of paper.

'That's confidential information, Miss Assad.'

'May I keep it?' she repeated stubbornly.

Mancuso hesitated, then sighed. 'Very well.'

Leila folded the paper and tucked it into her purse. 'There's one more thing I'd like you to do for me.'

'Miss Assad, I've already done more than enough.'

'This is something a little more delicate.'

Mancuso looked unhappy. 'What is it you want?' he asked.

'I want you to furnish me with a Mackhead identity card.'

The bungalow was tucked discreetly along a leafy little boulevard. Leila parked her car in the drive and rang the front doorbell. It was opened a moment later by Gus's wife, Melanie.

'Is Mr McKlelland in?'

'He's gone to work.' Melanie examined Leila suspiciously, noting the thin lips, the sensuous eyes, the small firm breasts. 'Anything I can do?"

Leila flashed the ID card Mancuso had given her. 'Mackhead Personnel Department, Mrs McKlelland. We've run into a snag on one of our projects and I need to locate your husband's brother rather urgently. His neighbour told me he might be staying at this address.'

'Oh.' Melanie relaxed when she realized it was Paul, not Gus, her visitor was looking for. 'Paul *was* here,' she admitted, 'but he left this morning. He's gone to Lomstoun in the Mojave Desert.'

'You've no idea where he's likely to be staying? I may have to drive there personally.'

'He's at the Maple Creek Motel. That's the name he gave Gus. I can get you the phone number if you like.'

'That's kind of you, Mrs McKlelland.' Leila forced a smile to her lips, keeping her voice light and casual as she said: 'I don't suppose you have a photograph of Paul lying around by any chance? I know this sounds kind've silly, but I haven't the faintest idea of what Mr McKlelland looks like.'

The police officer slid his jeep to a halt, and Paul climbed stiffly to the ground. Sunlight cast shadows across clumps of scrub dotting the desert floor in front. A few pieces of wreckage lay scattered around a shallow crater – a fractured wing-tip, a charred section of fuselage, a piece of unidentifiable machinery.

'This is where she came down,' Patrolman Lenny Driscoll said. 'She was still burning when I got to her, but there wasn't much left to identify.'

Paul examined the blackened remains. He had steeled himself mentally, expecting to experience some kind of emotional reaction, but there was no feeling inside him at all as he stared down at the pieces of crumpled metal. That's because I know she's not dead, he thought. If she really *was* dead, I'd sure as hell realize it. But she isn't, so I don't. 'You saw no sign of bodies?'

'Hell, no. The way she blew, everything inside the cockpit would have incinerated. I never seen anything like it in my life.'

'But there should've been pieces of flesh, even scorched clothing.'

'Burnt to a frazzle, I'd say. That's what heat does sometimes, makes everything vaporize.'

'What about the bag? Where did you find it?'

'Over west about fifty feet. I guess the bang must've blown it clear.'

Paul was silent for a moment as he walked around the scattered wreckage. He kicked aimlessly at a piece of twisted fuselage. It was painfully clear that these meagre remains would throw little light on what had really happened. If the plane crash had been phony, whoever was responsible would have made damned sure there'd be plenty of evidence to back up the police report. The question was – and he had to face it sooner or later – was Ellen's death really a fake, or was he making a futile attempt to find a way out of his anguish and grief?

'What d'you figure on finding here?' the policeman asked.

'Nothing,' Paul said. 'I just wanted to see for myself. Sort of a pilgrimage, if you like.'

He hesitated as something caught his eye across the desert

floor. A cloud of dust came swirling toward them, rising eerily into the blazing sky. It looked like a twister, except that it was moving in a straight and even line.

The police officer followed his gaze and chuckled, wiping his lips with the back of his hand. 'That's Arch Millbrook,' he said. 'He lives in a shack out by Mimbreno Wash. He's kind of a local eccentric − doesn't believe in electricity, stuff like that. Prefers to live the way the old pioneers lived.'

As the cloud approached, the vehicle began to take on definition. It was some kind of buggy, driven not by an internal combustion engine, but by a billowing sail which propelled it across the flatlands at a stupefying rate. A man sitting in the front seat took off his cap and waved it at them as he passed, whooping and yippeeing wildly.

The policeman grinned as the dust began to settle. 'He's crazier than a coon, is old Arch, but he can cross this desert faster than I can, and it don't cost him a cent for gas.'

Paul was thoughtful as they climbed into the jeep and headed back the way they had come.

Paul slid to a halt at the side of the track, and switched off his engine. Through the windshield, he saw the lights of Arch Millbrook's shack gleaming by the dried-up riverbed. Stars formed a dazzling backdrop above the desert floor. A faint uneasiness started up inside him. He must be crazy for doing this, he thought. If he had any choice in the matter, he'd be sound asleep in Santa Clara − he wasn't cut out for the heroic stuff − but if Ellen was still alive, and he truly believed she was, then he, Paul McKlelland, was the only hope she had.

He opened the glove compartment, took out a tiny flashlight, and slipped it into his jacket pocket. Then he reached for the bag of meat he had bought at the local supermarket, and climbed quietly out of the car.

The air was cool against his cheeks as he picked his way down the crumbling hillside. Somewhere nearby, he heard a night jar wailing. There was no sign of movement from the cabin in front. A faint column of smoke rose from its cooking stove, but the windows were shaded and devoid of life.

He had to be out of his mind, chasing phantoms in the middle of the night, he thought. He was a brain man, strictly cerebral. And he had no illusions about Arch Millbrook's temperament. A man who turned his back on the modern world was hardly operating on all cylinders. If he got this wrong, he'd end up with a backside full of buckshot.

The cabin took on shape and substance as Paul approached. He saw a tiny shack situated to one side, a workshop or storage hut of some kind, and turned toward it. He heard a snarling in the darkness, and his heart froze as he saw two figures crouching directly in his path. Dobermans. Jesus Christ, the guy had to be crazy to have such monsters roaming around unleashed.

Pursing his lips, Paul emitted a low musical humming sound and fumbled with the package in his other hand. Still humming soothingly, he tossed the meat scraps on the ground. Snivelling and grunting, the two dogs gobbled them up.

Paul took advantage of the diversion to duck into the outhouse, and close the door gently behind him. For a moment, he stood panting in the darkness, then he pulled out his flashlight and began exploring the interior.

Arch Millbrook's buggy stood in the centre of the floor, its crude wheels heavily caked with dust. Its sail had been furled along the cross-tie of its solitary mainmast.

Paul rubbed the material between his fingers, examining it carefully. He heard a scraping sound in the yard outside and his stomach muscles tightened as he realized somebody was coming. Then the door burst suddenly open and Millbrook himself stood framed against the stars, covering Paul with a heavy pump-action shotgun. He was a short man with a straggly grey beard. 'Hold it right there,' he snapped. Behind him, Paul could hear the Dobermans snarling in the dark.

'Take it easy, Mr Millbrook. I'm not trying to rob you, if that's what you're thinking.'

'Then what the hell are you doing in my shack?'

'I wanted to examine your wind buggy,' Paul explained.

'What in Christ's name for?' Millbrook looked like a man to whom any affront, real or imagined, would be an automatic declaration of war. 'I don't like snoopers and I don't like trespassers.'

'The police officer told me you'd be difficult. That's why I didn't approach you direct.'

Millbrook frowned. 'You're the guy I saw with Lenny Driscoll this morning?'

'That's right. Something about your sail intrigued me and I wanted to check it out.' Paul touched the material again, rubbing it gently. 'Parachute silk, and brand new, I'd say.'

'So what?'

'Just curious. I was wondering where you got it.'

'I didn't steal it,' Millbrook snapped defensively.

'No, Mr Millbrook, I guess you probably found it. The desert can be a regular treasure-house for a man like you. A man who knows where to look, who knows what to look for.'

'What the hell kind of game are you playing here?' Millbrook brandished the shotgun menacingly.

'Mr Millbrook, bear with me for a moment, please. How long ago did you find the parachute this sail was made from?'

'Yesterday. It was buried under a heap of rocks.'

'Buried?' Paul took a deep breath. He felt almost dizzy with excitement. 'Mr Millbrook, I'll give you fifty dollars if you'll show me exactly where.'

Dawn was breaking when Paul arrived back at his motel room. Though he had been awake all night, his body felt vital and alert. Any doubts he might have harboured about Ellen's death had finally disappeared. He was sure now she was still alive, and the realization was like emerging from a long and debilitating illness. Suddenly, the world, which had looked so bleak, had begun to take on new shape and meaning.

He picked up the telephone and punched out Gus's number. The line rang for a moment, then Gus's voice answered, heavy with sleep. 'Yeah?'

81

'Gus, it's me. Paul.'

'Jesus, it's five o'clock in the morning, for Chrissake!'

'Calm down and listen. I've found something. Something important.'

Quickly, Paul outlined the details of his encounter with Arch Millbrook. When he had finished, Gus said: 'So he found a parachute buried in the desert? It could've been there for the past fifty years. They used to train pilots in the Mojave during World War Two.'

'This was no World War Two chute, Gus. The silk was brand new. I think the pilot deliberately wired his aircraft with some kind of explosive device, then bailed out just before it went off. My guess is, Ellen never got on that plane at all.'

There was a pause at the end of the line, then Gus said: 'Paul, you'd better come back to Santa Clara right away. I think Ellen's death has rattled you more than you realize.'

Paul ignored the remark. 'Do something for me, will you, Gus? At work this morning, check the aircraft's number and the name of the pilot on the central computer.'

'Why, for Chrissake?'

'Because I'm your brother, that's why. You owe me this, at least.'

Gus sighed. 'Okay, give me your number, and I'll call back as soon as I can.'

Gus phoned just before eleven. His voice had lost its exasperated tone. Now he sounded tense and alert. 'Get this,' he said. 'That aircraft wasn't owned by Mackhead at all. It was registered to the Napier Oil Corporation of Muna City. The pilot's name was Roger Becker. He operated partly on charter, partly on contract to Napier itself. His job was ferrying oil executives to business conferences around the country. He was also personal air chauffeur to Napier's president, Miles Kliban.'

Paul felt his pulses quickening. 'Does Kliban live in Muna City?'

'No. Most of the time he operates out of Palm Springs.'

'Got his address?'

'Listen Paul, I shouldn't be giving you this.'

'For Christ's sake, Gus, it's Ellen's life we're talking

about here. I know in my heart she didn't die in that phony air crash, and one way or another, I'm going to prove it.'

Sighing, Gus spelled out the address, and Paul scribbled it down.

'Don't do anything stupid,' Gus warned. 'Miles Kliban is a powerful man.'

'He's going to to be a very sorry man if he's got anything to do with Ellen's disappearance,' Paul said.

His pulses were racing as he put down the telephone.

The roar of the aircraft created a resonance in Snyder's ears as he watched the hospital orderlies loading Ellen's unconscious body into the empty passenger cabin. Her face looked glacial in repose, and just for a moment Snyder experienced a small twinge of regret. She really was a beautiful woman, he thought. But he knew where his duty lay. He had never shrunk from unpleasant decisions before, and he was damned if he would do so now.

An airport official called him from the transit lounge. 'Phone call, Mr Snyder.'

Snyder followed him into the office and picked up the receiver. 'Yes?'

'It's Gibskof,' a voice said breathlessly. 'We got trouble.'

Snyder glanced at the two receptionists and cupped his palm around the receiver, lowering his voice. 'What kind of trouble?'

'It's the Conway woman. The man she lives with, Paul McKlelland, he's been snooping around.'

'How d'you know?'

'Somebody checked out the aircraft number on the San Jose police computer. The signature on the authorization form was Detective Angus McKlelland. It's too much of a coincidence, Leon. They've got to be related.'

Snyder sighed. He knew Gibskof was right. 'Any idea where the boyfriend is now?'

'He's at the crash site in the Mojave. Vince checked with the police officer who drove him out there. He's staying at the Maple Creek Motel.'

Snyder massaged his forehead with his fingertips, and

lowered his voice still further. 'I want McKlelland taken care of, understand?'

'Terminally?' Gibskof asked.

'Of course, terminally. What do you think this is, a forfeit game? And Gibbo?'

'Yes, Leon?'

Snyder's eyes were cold and hard. 'Make it look accidental.'

Chapter Seven

A faint breeze stirred the air as Paul emerged from his motel room and paused for a moment to savour the faint, slightly metallic odour that came from the desert floor. He felt better than he'd felt for days, he decided. The realization that Ellen was still alive had filled him with a new sense of purpose.

He spotted a police car on the motel forecourt and frowned uneasily as he saw two uniformed officers examining his Dodge convertible. 'Is something wrong?' he asked, walking toward them.

The men looked at him and glanced at each other. 'This your car?' one asked.

'Yes, it is.'

'Your name Paul McKlelland?'

'That's right.'

'Then I'm sorry, Mr McKlelland, but you're under arrest.'

Paul blinked. 'On what charge?'

'No charge. We've been ordered to bring you in, that's all.'

'Hold on a minute, this doesn't make sense. I have a right to know what I'm being arrested for.'

'I guess you do, Mr McKlelland,' the second officer said. 'It's probably nothing more than some kind of misunderstanding, but until we get it straightened out, I'm afraid you'll have to accompany us to the station, that's the law. Got any keys for this thing?'

Paul gave him the Dodge keys, and he tossed them to

his companion. 'Mick'll bring your car. You can ride with me.' He smiled apologetically. 'I'll have to frisk you first though, it's routine.'

It seemed a humiliating ritual, but Paul placed his palms on the car roof while the policeman carried out a brisk body search. When the man produced a pair of handcuffs, however, Paul protested. 'You can't put those things on me. I'm no criminal.'

'If it was up to me, Mr McKlelland, I'd say let's forget it, but no civilians are allowed to ride in a patrol car unrestrained. Police policy.'

Terrific, Paul thought. Suddenly I'm public enemy number one. Shrugging resignedly he turned his back while the patrolman slipped the handcuffs into place. 'Comfortable?'

Paul nodded.

'This way, Mr McKlelland.'

Paul climbed into the vehicle's rear.

Seated in her Chevrolet Blazer, Leila Assad watched the proceedings from the opposite side of the road. She had driven south during the night, arriving at the motel in the early hours of the morning, and had been on the point of approaching Paul McKlelland's room when the two policemen had made their appearance. According to Leila's information, Paul McKlelland was a highly respectable businessman, yet here he was being arrested. The incident was puzzling, to say the least. However, McKlelland was the only real lead she had. She had travelled so far in the hope of securing his co-operation. She couldn't afford to abandon him now.

Switching on her engine, she followed cautiously in the patrol car's wake.

The road bobbed and dipped, picking its way through a line of arid foothills. Paul gazed out at the parched countryside, his body shuddering with the motions of the car. He could scarcely believe the indignity of the moment. It was the first time in his life he had ever been arrested and he found the experience mortifying. Soon, however, his embarrassment

86

gave way to a sense of uneasiness. Something was wrong here. The hills seemed endless, a baffling sprawl of rock and thorn-studded arroyos with no sign of human habitation. 'I thought we were going to Lomstoun,' he said at length.

The patrolman examined him with amusement in the rearview mirror, his eyes twinkling malevolently. 'Who said we ain't?'

'You've been driving for almost forty minutes. We should have arrived there ages ago.'

'I'm taking the scenic route. We do that sometimes with strangers to the neighbourhood.'

Paul looked out at the surrounding terrain. The hills were growing higher, wilder. His uneasiness developed into sudden alarm. He wasn't being arrested. He was being kidnapped.

Jesus, Paul thought wildly, he'd walked right into a trap. Whoever these characters were, there could be only one explanation for what they were doing. They were trying to prevent him from finding Ellen.

'Where are we going?' he snapped.

'Sightseeing. Just sit back and enjoy the ride.'

Perspiration trickled between Paul's shoulder-blades as the patrolman pulled off the road and slid to a halt on a jagged clifftop. With a muffled purr, his companion drew up alongside, driving Paul's Dodge. In front, Paul could see a precipitous drop of two to three thousand feet. Below, the desert formed a hazy ghostline, blending into the distant sky. The sense of perspective was breathtaking.

'Quite a sight, ain't it?' the man said pleasantly. 'This is my favourite look-out point.'

'What are we doing here?' Paul demanded.

'Communing with nature. Don't you like nature, Mr McKlelland?'

'This has gone far enough. Kindly remove these handcuffs and give me back my car.'

The rear door opened as the second patrolman slithered in beside him. He was smaller than his companion and his features were faintly rat-like in appearance, giving his face a crumpled look. A great shock of dark hair sprang from beneath his police cap.

'Mick, Mr McKlelland would like his keys back,' the first officer said.

'Why, sure, Mr McKlelland, I wasn't trying to steal the vehicle, if that's what you're thinking.' The man pushed the keys into Paul's jacket pocket. 'How d'you like the view?'

Paul tried to conceal his fear as he glared angrily at his two captors. 'I don't know what kind of game you're playing, but when I get out of this, somebody's going to look pretty damned sick.'

The patrolman called Mick grinned at his companion. His face was slightly lopsided, as if at some time in the past one of his cheekbones had been badly broken. 'I don't think Mr McKlelland approves of us, Vince.'

'Maybe Mr McKlelland is thirsty,' Vince suggested.

'You think so?'

'He has a thirsty look to me.'

'Would you care for a drink, Mr McKlelland?' The man called Mick eyed Paul queryingly.

'Just get these damned handcuffs off,' Paul growled.

'I think he really would appreciate a drink, Vince.'

Opening the glove compartment, the first patrolman took out a whisky bottle and pulled out the stopper with his teeth. Paul watched him. 'What are you doing?'

'Being convivial, Mr McKlelland.'

The man nodded to his companion who seized Paul by the throat. He tried to pull back, but the man held him brutally in position, and with his free hand nipped Paul's nostrils, shutting off his air supply. Paul held his breath as long as he could, but in the end he was forced to suck oxygen into his chest and lungs. When he did so, the first patrolman tilted the bottle between his lips, and Paul gagged and spluttered as the fiery liquid poured down his throat.

Leila sat at the bend of the road, studying events through a pair of high-powered binoculars. Her initial puzzlement had given way to a feeling of alarm. The two policemen — if indeed policemen they were — clearly had some sinister intention in mind. This was no ordinary arrest she was witnessing, but a coldblooded murder attempt. Whatever Paul McKlelland had done – or knew – somebody had decided he couldn't be allowed to live.

Leila took a pistol from her purse and placed it on the passenger seat beside her.

'I can't swallow any more,' Paul slurred, slumping forward. 'I'm going to be sick.'

'Not in my car, good buddy. Just sit back and fill your lungs with air.'

Someone forced him upright, slapping him several times across the face. He felt no pain, that was the curious thing. Pain, along with everything else, had receded amid the dim complexities of his brain. His head was spinning and a terrible nausea had started in his stomach. He was scared, he thought, more scared than he'd ever been in his life, and what made it worse – almost unbearable, in fact – was the realization that he'd screwed up completely, which was the story of his whole stupid existence, only this time it looked at though the screw up was going to prove permanent. Whoever these characters were, they were making sure his investigations got no further.

The policemen grinned as they thrust the whisky bottle against his lips, causing him to splutter and choke. 'No more,' Paul protested weakly.

'What's wrong with this guy?' the second patrolman grunted. 'He don't seem to be in the party spirit.'

His companion shook Paul roughly. 'Hey, Mr McKlelland, you see this precipice here? You wouldn't believe the number of people who've committed suicide driving over this cliff.'

Paul struggled to focus his gaze. Through the windshield he saw the dreadful emptiness waiting below, and amid the alcohol clouding his senses, a terrible fear started.

The policeman was smiling at him now. It was not a pleasant smile; his jovial features contrasted strangely with the callous cruelty in his eyes. 'Some guys do it because they can't stand their wives any more. Others because their businessess are folding up. A man like you now – stricken with grief — what could be more understandable than a one-way ticket to oblivion? A tiny squeeze on the gas pedal, and — splat — all your troubles will be over. You'll be going out in good company, Mr McKlelland.'

Paul slumped, panting, in the chair.

'I think he's loaded enough, Vince,' the second patrolman said.

The first officer seized Paul's chin, tilting back his head. 'I guess you're right. Let's get him into the other car.'

'What about the cuffs?'

'Leave them on until we're ready. He might start struggling, and I don't want to hit him any more than I have to. Bruises raise question marks on the coroner's report.'

Fifty yards away, Leila watched the patrolmen wrestle Paul into the sunlight. His knees sagged and his head lolled as they manoeuvred him toward the empty car. It was chillingly clear what they intended to do. Unless she moved quickly, her inquiries would come to a shuddering halt.

She reached for the ignition switch and started up the engine. She stabbed her foot on the gas pedal, and the patrolmen froze in astonishment as she swung on to the lookout point and screeched to a halt in a thick cloud of dust. 'Excuse me, officer,' she smiled, sliding down the window. 'I appear to have taken a wrong turning. Can you tell me the way to Lomstoun?'

The patrolmen looked at each other. 'You should have looped left about eight miles back,' the first officer said.

'Can't I detour somewhere ahead?'

'No, ma'am. This road peters out beyond Furness Point.'

'Damn. I guess it'll teach me to be a little more careful in future.' She looked at Paul, crinkling her eyes. 'Looks like you've got your hands full, officer.'

The first patrolman gave Paul a playful hoist. 'Yes, ma'am, we found him perched on the clifftop, high as a kite. Probably getting up his nerve to drive over. Folks do it all the time. This is a suicide black spot.'

'Poor man, he looks so level-headed too.'

'They're the ones you have to watch.'

90

Leila breathed deeply, and her muscles tensed as her fingers closed on the pistol butt. Now, she thought.

In one fluid motion, she threw open the door and sprang to the ground, holding the pistol at arm's length with its barrel pointing at the two patrolmen. They stared at her in astonishment.

'Put him in the truck,' she snapped.

For a moment they remained quite still, the suddenness of Leila's move paralysing their senses. Then one of the officers began to grin.

'Smile at me, you bastard, and I'll give you a second asshole right between the eyes.'

The patrolman froze, and Leila motioned with the handgun. 'Inside.'

They shepherded Paul to the Blazer and bundled him roughly into the rear.

'Throw your handguns over the cliff,' Leila ordered.

Wordlessly, they obeyed, their faces livid.

'Now, bellies in the dirt.'

'Who are you, lady?' The first patrolman demanded.

Leila sent a shot whistling past his ear. 'Do it,' she shouted.

The two patrolmen dove into the dust and Leila scrambled behind the Blazer wheel, swinging the vehicle swiftly into reverse. She rammed Paul's car, forcing it over the precipice edge. With an ear-splitting screech, it crashed onto the rocks below.

Leila stabbed the pedal again. This time, she struck the police car, and in stony silence, the two patrolmen watched their vehicle sliding into the empty void.

They were still staring at the clifftop as Leila roared off furiously around the bend.

Ellen opened her eyes, moaning softly. She was in a Quonset hut, she saw, the floor lined with narrow bunks. Sunlight gleamed through the open windows, and the wall clock stood at 7 am. A woman sat watching her with amusement. The woman was small and thickset, with oriental features. 'Hi,' she said as Ellen stirred.

'Who are you?' Ellen asked.

91

'Jo Marian Lee. Welcome to Stand Hill air base. How's the head?'

'Splitting in two. What happened?'

'They brought you in last night on a stretcher. You were out cold.'

'My God, I must've been slewed.'

The woman handed her a glass. 'Drink this. It's soluble aspirin.'

Ellen tossed back the contents in a single gulp, grimacing as the bitter liquid flowed down her throat. 'I'll never touch alcohol again,' she vowed. 'Never.'

'I take it you're Ellen Conway.'

'Correction. *Was* Ellen Conway. I can't believe I can feel this bad without being dead.'

Jo Marian Lee smiled as she shook Ellen's hand. Her face carried a peasant sturdiness, but her eyes were humorous and intelligent, and her thick dark hair had been tied into a braid which hung over her shoulder like a length of rope.

'We the only ones in here?' Ellen asked, looking around.

'Hell, we're the only females on the block. You feeling strong enough to get up yet, or are you one of those people who nurse a hangover like the Bubonic Plague?'

Ellen swung her feet to the floor, and instantly, a wave of dizziness engulfed her. She groaned softly as she held into the bed for support. 'My God, I'm coming apart at the seams.'

Jo Marian Lee watched her critically. 'What you need is some breakfast.'

'I'd bring it up. Besides, I have to call home. My boy-friend will be having a fit.'

'Sorry. Against the rules.'

'What rules?'

'First Commandment. Phoning's taboo.'

'You're kidding me.'

'The personnel people get in touch with our families three times a month. You can send messages through them if you like, but everything has to be censored.'

'I can't believe this,' Ellen said.

'You'll get used to it. Just think of Stand Hill as like being marooned on the moon.' Jo motioned toward the hut rear.

'There's a shower in the back if you want to freshen up, but don't be too long. Work starts at eight am and I have a slow digestive system.'

Ellen felt better after she'd bathed. She changed her things and followed Jo through the empty air-base in the cool softness of the desert morning. Mountains formed an arid backdrop against the distant horizon. Close, white-washed fences divided the barrack-hut echelons, giving them an orderly, well-kept appearance. The buildings seemed almost too perfectly proportioned to be real, as if they formed part of some giant museum piece, like Disneyworld. 'It's awfully quiet,' Ellen commented, noting the absence of people.

'Well, we're not fully operational yet. Most of the personnel here are Hispanic, pilots from Mexico and Central America. They speak little or no English, which is probably deliberate. If they can't talk to the guests, they can't tittle-tattle either.'

'What part of Mackhead did you spring from?' Ellen asked.

'Systems Testing up in Washington state. How about you?'

'Energy and Optics.'

'Sunnyvale?'

'Right. The Stand Hill offer came out of the blue. I thought it was my passport to fortune and glory. Now I'm beginning to wonder.'

'Well, look at it this way. If things can't get worse, they're bound to get better.'

'Are you married, Jo?'

'My old man took off about eight years ago, and never came back. It wasn't much of a relationship anyhow. How about that boyfriend you wanted to telephone? I guess he must be somebody pretty special.'

'He is,' Ellen agreed, then hesitated. 'Well, if you want the truth, I'm not really sure any more. I'm hoping this little assignment will give me a chance to think things out.'

Jo laughed drily. 'That's something you can count on. Time is the one thing there's no shortage of around here.'

The mess hall was practically deserted when they got there.

Only a handful of Hispanic officers sat drinking coffee in the corner, the sound of their voices echoing beneath the raftered ceiling. Cooks in white aprons served breakfast from an insulated hotplate at the head of the hall. A large sign said: EAT ALL YOU WANT, BUT NO WASTE.

Ellen's head was at last beginning to clear as she joined Jo at one of the tables, and toyed absently with her scrambled eggs. She knew Paul would be going crazy by now – he got agitated if she didn't call at least once a day from work – but how could she help it when they'd put her in virtual quarantine? Why did life have to be so damned difficult? she thought.

She noticed a man seated alone at the far end of the dining room, and examined him curiously. He was powerfully built, with smoldering eyes and a fierce moustache. His features were strong and totally composed, but she had the feeling that he could erupt like a volcano at a moment's notice. Something about him made Ellen's breath quicken.

'Who's that?' she whispered.

Jo followed her gaze. 'Salih Joktan. Head of security.'

'Mexican?'

'Arab. According to Colonel Chivers, his parents emigrated from the Middle East when he was fourteen years old.'

'He looks kind of dangerous,' Ellen said.

Jo's eyes twinkled. 'Interested?'

'Of course not. I just said he looked dangerous, that's all. Like a South American bandit.'

'Speaking of bandits,' Jo whispered as a shadow fell across their table.

Ellen looked up to see a young man in coveralls smiling down at them, holding a breakfast tray. He looked like a model from a Wheaties commercial, with tanned skin, crewcut-blond hair and evenly planed features. 'Morning, ladies,' he said breezily. 'How're you folks today?'

'Terrific till you showed up,' Jo told him.

The young man showed no sign of annoyance at this rudeness, but placed his tray on the table and leaned forward to shake Ellen's hand. 'Hi, I'm Vic Conville. You must be the new pro from Sunnyvale.'

94

'That's right. Ellen Conway.'

'Don't pay any attention to Jo here. Most folks find I'm kind of endearing after they get to know me.'

Conville began to unload his scrambled eggs, his movements measured and precise, as if he had practised them in front of a mirror. Ellen had the feeling that Conville was a natural actor who found it difficult to define where reality ended and illusion began. 'Get in last night?' he asked.

'So they tell me. I wasn't exactly in a state of compos mentis at the time.'

'She means she was pie-eyed,' Jo explained.

'Ah. I like a lady who knows how to make an entrance. Drinking's about the only thing there is to do around here. Of course ... ' He smiled. 'I do have certain virtues when it comes to relieving boredom.'

'It's probably your modesty,' Jo said.

When breakfast was over, they made their way to the construction complex, a huge converted aircraft hanger where Ellen was introduced to her colleagues by the program director. Most of them appeared to be Hispanic, apart from the four supervisors who came from the United States.

Ellen was given a written brief and a team of manual workers who, puzzlingly, seemed incapable of understanding not only English but Spanish too. It was explained that for security reasons, each supervisor would operate independently of the other three; that way, no one could divulge sensitive details of Talon Blue's function or operation, even by accident.

To Ellen's relief, the instructions covered fairly familiar territory and for the rest of the morning, she busied herself with work.

She was in the process of checking the inventory list when, to her astonishment, she felt fingers exploring the contours of her buttocks and turned, startled, to find Victor Conville smiling down at her. 'Just getting acquainted,' he said.

'Mr Conville ... '

'Vic,' he corrected.

Ellen moved so fast that her hand was a blur. She seized him between the legs and squeezed with all her strength. Conville collapsed against the lathe machine, his eyes bulging, his lips sucking desperately at the air. 'Touch me again and you'll be singing soprano in the Stand Hill choir,' Ellen told him angrily as she went back to work.

'Conville's an asshole,' Jo said. 'He can't believe there might be women in this world who don't get orgasmic every time he crooks his little finger.'

'Has he made a pass at you?' Ellen asked.

'Do I look the kind of girl men make passes at? Let's face it, I'm homely. I was born homely, and I guess I'll die homely. No, Vic Conville never made a pass at me. Maybe that's why I'm so sore.'

Ellen lay back on her bunk and stared listlessly through the open window. Apart from her confrontation with Victor Conville, her first day had gone smoothly enough, she had to admit, but the idea of spending the next three months here filled her with desolation. Ambition was one thing, but turning herself into a virtual nun wasn't exactly her idea of a meaningful existence.

She frowned as she noticed a glow in the desert sky. 'What's that?' she asked.

Jo followed her gaze. 'City of Phoenix. It's only thirty miles away.'

'Thirty miles? My God, it seems like a different universe.'

Ellen was thoughtful for a moment. Something about the air-base disturbed her, though she couldn't say why. Everything seemed too authentic − too meticulous − to be real. 'Jo?'

'Yeah?'

'Think this place is genuine?'

'Genuine?'

'I mean, Stand Hill. Those people out there?'

Jo looked at a bunch of airmen strolling past the row of Quonset huts. 'Well, let's face it, they're not exactly Uncle Sam's finest but training Hispanic pilots is part of the government program.'

'What makes you so sure they're Hispanic? They can't even speak Spanish, for Pete's sake.'

'Maybe it's your accent. Some of these characters are

mountain people. They have their own dialect, their own way of saying things.'

'Look at it logically for a moment,' Ellen said. 'If Talon Blue really is so sensitive, would Washington allow us anywhere near non-US personnel?'

'Why not? It means fewer gossip-mongers.'

'Come on, Jo. Did you try that meat loaf at dinner tonight? It looked like the real thing, it smelled like the real thing, but there was something weird about the taste. Everything here is slightly off centre. Even the TV programs have a dated feel to them, as if they'd been carefully pre-recorded.'

'You're nuts.'

Ellen said: 'I was unconscious when they brought me here. What about you?'

Jo hesitated. 'Dunno.'

'What do you mean, dunno?'

'I arrived in the early hours. It was dark outside.'

'Where you awake?'

'Not exactly. I opened my eyes just after we landed.'

'So you slept through the entire flight?'

'I guess so.'

'How long?'

'I don't know. I ...' Jo shook her head, puzzled. 'I know this sounds kind of strange, but I can't remember the take-off.'

'Is it possible we were both drugged?'

'They wouldn't dare.'

'Why wouldn't they? I think they're prepared to do anything to keep Talon Blue under wraps.'

A sudden movement caught Ellen's eye and through the window she saw Salih Joktan walking among the Quonset huts, clad in a rumpled sweatsuit. His hair was fluttering in the wind and his dark moustache seemed to emphasize the muscular features and thin pale mouth. Something in the way Joktan moved made Ellen's senses quiver.

'Our neanderthal man's out late tonight,' Jo remarked.

'What's he doing?'

'Security patrol. He likes to run a last-minute check before the night guards take over.'

Suddenly, Joktan looked up and his eyes met Ellen's. He made no attempt to look away, but stared at her, calmly and insinuatingly. The breath caught in Ellen's throat, and her stomach muscles tightened. She felt a wave of relief when he finally walked away.

Jo whistled under her breath. 'Now that's what I call "chemical attraction", ' she said. 'Or are you going to tell me I only imagined it, along with everything else in this Godforsaken hole?'

Chapter Eight

Jacob Jabari, director of Mossad, the Israeli intelligence service, sat in his office, examining the photographs in front of him. They had been taken at night from a low-flying spy plane, and the infra-red vision lens had coated the black-and-white images with a slightly greenish hue. They showed a network of buildings and aircraft runways. 'Were there any lights?' Jabari asked. 'Signs of life, movement?'

'The pilot saw nothing,' Chaim Elohin told him. 'He caught a flash of headlamps, which started him photographing, but apart from that he thought he was taking snapshots of the desert floor.'

Jabari was silent for a moment. 'This airfield wasn't here eight weeks ago. We covered the entire area by satellite.'

'Maybe our approach was slightly off-angle.'

'No. I know this desert like the back of my hand. I can pinpoint every missile base, every tank emplacement Musallim al Shisur ever built. This is new, and it's big, impressively big.'

'You want me to get another plane over?'

'It's not conclusive enough. We have to know the truth.'

'A recce team then?'

Jabari nodded. 'It'll be dangerous. If al Shisur really is preparing for war, we'll be giving him just the kind of ammunition he needs. Could we put a helicopter in, flying low under al Shisur's radar?'

'It'd mean violating Jordanian air space.'

'To hell with Jordan. Can we do it, Chaim?'

Elohin said: 'If we use two helicopters, one carrying our

infiltration team, the other stacked with extra fuel, we might just be able to make it there and back, but we'll be taking a hell of a risk.'

'We're taking a risk anyhow,' Jabari grunted. 'I say let's give it a go.'

US President Lawrence Clayman sat at the conference table, wearily rubbing his face with his fingertips. It had been an exhausting meeting; the visual information provided by the US Satellite Tracking Service had proved complex and difficult to absorb, and after several hours of discussion with his cabinet members, President Clayman was certain of only one thing: Musallim al Shisur was indeed set on a confrontation with Israel. 'He's making a mockery of everything we've worked for,' Clayman said. 'The Palestinian territories, the arms limitation agreements − our entire program will be thrown into jeopardy.'

'Well, he'll be playing Russian Roulette with all the chambers loaded,' replied the Secretary of Defence. 'Israel has made no secret of the fact that she'll strike back with everything she's got.'

'Including nuclear missiles?'

'If the fight gets rough enough.'

'Don't worry, Mr President,' the CIA Director said. 'In nuclear terms, al Shisur doesn't stand a chance against Israel.'

'For God's sake,' Clayman exclaimed, 'any nuclear involvement is a potential disaster area. Once this thing starts, it could easily get out of hand.'

'Al Shisur won't use atomic weapons if he can possibly avoid it,' General Lewis Carman pointed out. 'He may have something else up his sleeve, something so devastating it could humble even Israel's military might.'

'Is that possible?'

'Anything's possible, Mr President.'

'We could do what we did with Sadaam Hussein,' the Secretary of Defence suggested. 'Send in troops. Under the UN banner, of course.'

'Arab opinion wouldn't stand for it. They think we're already too dominant in Islamic affairs.'

'The Arabs have little love for Musallim al Shisur. If we made our force international as we did in 1991, I'm sure they'd be more than willing to co-operate.'

'What about the Iraqi people?' the Secretary of Defence asked. 'Can't they stop this lunatic?'

'There've been at least eight uprisings in the past two years,' General Carman said, 'but al Shisur's secret police have crushed them all. I'm afraid the ball's in our court on this one.'

'Well, according to yesterday's *Washington Post* survey, the American people are strongly opposed to military intervention,' the Chairman of the Joint Chiefs of Staff put in. 'They don't want American troops risking their lives in a conflict eight thousand miles away.'

'And yet, what kind of president would I be,' Clayman said softly, 'if I watched the fires of war igniting and didn't raise a finger to put them out?'

'You can't ignore the feelings of the people, Larry.'

'Negotiate, that's all I'm saying. Make a direct approach, and let's see if we can walk this kitty back. Anything's better than watching the Mid-East disintegrate.' He turned to the Secretary of State. 'Think you can handle that, Frank?'

The Secretary of State looked sombre as all eyes turned in his direction. He understood more than anyone the enormity of the task. Nevertheless, it was clear some kind of initiative had to be made. 'I'll do my best, Mr President,' he promised.

The giant aircraft hangar echoed with noise. Boots clattered on the concrete floor as the little group of ancillary workers struggled to fit the weapon system together. They moved slowly, almost apprehensively, as if the structure's lethal nature intimidated them in some peculiar way.

Ellen watched in silence, fuming with impatience. Talon Blue's assembly was taking an interminable time to complete. Much of the problem lay in the inexperience of the Hispanic construction crews − since they spoke little English, every order Ellen delivered had to be repeated over and over, and sometimes even demonstrated visually − but a lot of the blame, she knew, belonged to the ludicrous compartment system. None of the supervisors knew what the other three were doing, or even how the weapon would eventually function. Nevertheless, something was at last beginning to materialize beneath the hangar's high arched ceiling. The structure looked grotesque, Ellen had to admit; it reminded her of a space satellite, its aluminum sphere and omni-directional electronic antennae forming a weird protoplasm which dwarfed the entire area. When she looked at it, she felt her stomach tingle. Hard to believe she was partly responsible for this monstrosity; harder still to accept that despite her contribution, she knew even less about it than she had in the beginning. Which raised the inevitable question – from a personal view, had there been any real point to this exercise? She had abandoned Paul and probably screwed up their relationship for good, yet in career terms she had made no appreciable forward progress. It was a demoralizing thought.

'How's it going?' Victor Conville asked, leaning against the workbench behind her.

Ellen glanced at him coolly. Her relationship with Conville had been icily polite since the day of her arrival, but it was clear that they had to work together so she softened her voice. 'Not good. I don't know where these boys got their technical knowledge, but they belong in the Ark.'

'My bunch too. It's like operating with chimpanzees.'

'I can't understand why they won't give us American construction crews?'

'Security. They figure this lot can't talk afterwards.'

'That's the craziest logic I ever heard.'

A violent creaking sound echoed above her and Ellen looked up, startled, as shouts of alarm rose from the construction workers. Part of the weapon structure had begun to sag. Ellen held her breath, watching the framework buckle and shudder. Suddenly, the high shunt accelerator which towered above them like an electric pylon disintegrated in front of her eyes and clattered to the ground with a resounding crash. The assembly crews leapt for safety, yelling in consternation. The din was deafening.

'Dear God,' Ellen exclaimed, and ran forward, pushing her way through the milling throng.

102

Splintered metal lay scattered about in a welter of devastation. There were shattered piston rods, fractured guidance sensors, ruptured stabilizers and blunted antennae. The electronic cones and high-pressure nitrogen tanks had been crushed beyond repair, and Ellen realized at a glance that the damage would set back their schedule by at least a week.

She saw Joktan approaching from the hangar entrance, attracted by the noise. He stared at the wreckage, his dark eyes expressionless. 'What happened here?'

Ellen felt her anger rising. The tension of the last few weeks was reaching a crisis point inside her. Flustered, she brushed back her hair. 'As you've probably gathered, we've been having a few problems.'

'What kind of problems?'

'Communication for a start.'

'Communication?'

'It's really quite simple. How can we work efficiently with all four supervisors operating in the dark?'

'What about the assembly brochures?'

'The brochures tell us how to build the thing, yes, but we need some kind of co-ordinated policy. We're not machines, for God's sake, we're experienced pros.'

Joktan frowned. 'Why did you never mention this before?'

'Because nobody asked us before. If they had, maybe this accident wouldn't have happened.'

'I see.'

Joktan examined her in silence for a moment, puzzled by the intensity of her outburst, and she felt her anger draining away. 'Listen, I'm sorry. I'm not laying blame. Just looking for answers, that's all.'

'I understand.'

She hesitated, feeling her cheeks beginning to flush. 'Maybe we should talk it over,' she suggested.

He looked surprised. 'Together?'

'Why not? That way, we could iron out the main areas of difficulty.'

What am I doing? she thought wildly. I'm throwing myself at him, for Pete's sake.

But Joktan was nodding in agreement. 'You are quite right,' he said.

Ellen took a deep breath and moistened her lips with her tongue. 'Shall we make the officers' club at eight o'clock?'

Jo watched Ellen with amusement as she bustled around the Quonset hut, getting ready.

'How does this look?' Ellen asked, examining her dress in the full-length mirror.

'That's the fourth outfit you've tried on tonight. Who do you think this guy is, for pete's sake?'

'I'm just trying to make a good impression.'

'I'll bet.'

'It's important, Jo. Joktan's the only one who can get the camp authorities to see any sense.'

'Oh, so that's why you're meeting him, is it?'

'Of course it's why. What else?'

'It wouldn't have anything to do with the fact that Salih Joktan's an extremely attractive man, I don't suppose?'

'Don't tease me, Jo. I'd hate to screw things up by wearing the wrong outfit or choosing the wrong lipstick. You know how sensitive these Arabs can be.'

'I've heard Joktan called many things,' Jo admitted, 'but "sensitive" was never one of them.'

'You wouldn't say that if you'd ever looked into his eyes.'

'Wow, he's really got to you, this guy.'

'I like him, is that a crime?'

'How about whatsisname – Old Faithful – back home?'

'Well, Paul's got nothing to worry about,' Ellen said irritably. 'This is a business meeting, that's all.' She turned to face Jo smoothing the dress around her. 'How do I look?'

'Like a million bucks.'

'Think Joktan'll like it?'

Jo emitted a low wolf whistle, and smiled roguishly. 'If this guy isn't knocked out by that, he must be made of ice.'

Joktan sat in his office, examining a map of the surrounding area. He had gone over it a thousand times and knew the features blindfolded. Tonight however, he seemed reluctant to put it down. What had he been thinking of, agreeing to meet the American, Ellen Conway? It was a stupid idea, whichever way he looked at it. He had no time for unnecessary distractions. Of course, he could tell himself it was all in the line of duty, but something about the woman fired his senses, penetrated his natural reserve. It wasn't simply her beauty – that he recognized and tried to disregard – but Ellen Conway had something else, something he found difficult to define. Character, he decided at last. She displayed an independent streak that was rare among Arab women, and Joktan had to admit that he found it attractive. Nevertheless, he had come here for a purpose, and until his debt was paid, it was his sacred duty to devote himself body and soul to the demands of the operation ahead.

There was a knock at the door, and Joktan glanced up as Hamdu Kitab entered the room.

'The sensors have picked up a series of signatures near the south-east turret,' Hamdu said.

'Intruders?'

'Human, definitely. A party of about six strong, the operator says.'

Joktan reached for his pistol belt and strapped it around his waist. His reverie was forgotten as he followed Kitab across the darkened compound. A thin veil of cloud had crept in from the west, shutting out the stars, and dimly, against the sky, he saw the skeletal outlines of watchtowers 11 and 111. A party of troops stood waiting at the gate, their faces smeared to blend easily into the night. The young officer saluted as Joktan approached.

'See anything?' Joktan demanded.

'Only sand, colonel. Whoever they are, they're very professional.'

'Israelis?'

'That's what it looks like. About fifty yards this side of the south-east tower.'

Motioning with his hand, Joktan moved off into the darkness, the men trailing behind him in a ragged line. The density of the night made it impossible to tell where the sand ended and the sky began, and despite the coolness of the air, he was conscious of an almost suffocating warmth, as if he had a fever starting. Nerves, he thought, struggling to see through the curtain of gloom.

Something moved in the shadows ahead; it wasn't much, a slight shift in density, but suddenly, the night flared into brilliant day as a fusilade of gun fire erupted. Joktan saw the sand dunes lit by demonic flashes, and threw himself into the dirt, laying down a line of frenzied return fire. He heard a distant roaring sound as he ejected cartridges and inserted new ones. The noise intensified, growing louder, and Joktan felt his pulses quickening in unison. A helicopter.

Jumping to his feet, he waved at his men and charged blindly into the night.

Ellen sat in the officers' club, nursing a small martini. The clock on the wall stood at ten-fifteen. Her initial disappointment had given way first to puzzlement, then dismay. She'd hung on as long as she could — longer, she realized, than she had ever waited for a man before — but she realized now that Joktan wasn't coming. What a fool she'd been. She'd thrown herself at him with all the brazenness of a Las Vegas hooker, and he'd reacted by treating her with contempt. Arabs didn't think like western men. Their attitude to life was diametrically different. Just the same, a little compassion wouldn't have come amiss. He could at least have sent a message, a note, a phone-call, anything. Now she felt angry and humiliated. Well, to hell with him, she thought. To hell with you, Salih Joktan. You're not the only fish in the pool, not by a long shot.

Ellan drained her drink, and quietly left the bar.

Leila Assad woke slowly, shading her eyes from the sunlight filtering through the Blazer's windshield. She was lying across the passenger seat, her body curled into the fetal position. A soft moaning reached her from the vehicle rear, and rolling over, she saw Paul McKlelland.

Leila sat up, brushing her clothing. There was a cold nip to the air, and for the first time she noticed that Paul was shivering. 'You okay?'

His teeth chattered. 'Freezing.'

'Why didn't you use the car rug?'

'I can't. My wrists are still handcuffed.'

Reaching over, Leila drew the rug carefully around him. 'You look like death,' she said.

She scarcely knew why she'd rescued the man; not out of the goodness of her heart, she felt sure. It had been a spur-of-the-moment thing, nothing weighed, nothing planned. He looked strangely innocent beneath his air of surface composure. His hair was long, and his face, studious in the sunlight, was not handsome exactly, but attractive enough to pass muster.

Leila opened the glove compartment and took out a vacuum flask. 'I made this yesterday, so it's probably cold by now, but it's the only breakfast we're likely to get.'

Filling the plastic cup with coffee, she handed it to Paul.

'My wrists are still manacled behind my back,' he told her helplessly.

Great, she thought, so now I have to play nursemaid as well. 'I'd better warn you, I am not and never have been the motherly type,' she said, raising the mug to his mouth.

When Paul had finished, she dabbed his lips with a tissue and topped up the coffee for herself. He sat watching her in puzzlement.

'Who are you?' he asked at last.

'My name's Leila Assad. I work for Mackhead Personnel. You're Paul McKlelland, right?'

'Right.'

'Why were those two policemen trying to murder you?'

'Christ knows.'

'They must have had a reason.'

'I didn't wait around to ask.'

'Could it involve your fiancee, Ellen Conway?'

His eyes sharpened. 'How do you know about Ellen?'

'Well, I know she was working on the Talon Blue program.' Leila tried to look nonchalant. 'Did she ever discuss it with you, by any chance?'

'Talon Blue? In what sense?'

'Well, did she ever tell you what it consisted of, for example?'

'How could she? She'd only just started.' A flicker of suspicion entered his eyes. 'If you really were from Mackhead, you'd know that already.'

Splat, Leila thought. She'd walked right into that one. Should she brazen it out and hope for the best, or confess everything and beg for McKlelland's help? There was just a chance he might feel grateful after having been snatched from the jaws of death. He looked the type. 'Okay,' she admitted, 'I'm not really from Mackhead at all.'

'Who are you then?'

'Better hold on to your hat. This'll probably blow your mind.'

As calmly as she could, she told Paul the entire story and when she had finished, he looked at her in astonishment. 'You expect me to believe that stuff?'

'Would I risk my neck to save your hide if it wasn't true?'

'You're from Jerusalem?'

'That's correct.'

'And you want to find out about Talon Blue?'

'Not "want to",' she corrected. '"Have to." I have to know what the system is capable of.'

'Well, you've come to the wrong department,' Paul said, 'The person you need to talk to is Ellen herself.'

'Your fiancee? But she's dead.'

'Wrong.' Paul's eyes flashed fiercely. 'That's what they'd like you to think. That's what they'd like everyone to think.'

Quickly, he outlined the events of the past two days, and Leila listened in silence, digesting the story thoughtfully. It seemed grotesque, but she had learned from experience never to dismiss even the unlikeliest circumstance. 'So you think the plane crash was nothing more than a smoke-screen?'

'I'll bet my life on it.'

'But why would the US authorities deliberately fabricate the deaths of four of its key scientists?'

'Security reasons, I guess.'

'Won't there be some very embarrassing explaining to do when they return to the normal world?'

Paul's cheeks blanched as he absorbed the implications of her statement. 'You mean, they might try to eliminate her?'

'They tried to eliminate you, didn't they?'

'But they wouldn't kill one of their own people.'

'What makes you so sure they *are* your own people? Maybe this has nothing to do with the United States at all. Where was Ellen flying when the plane crash happened?'

'Stand Hill air base in Arizona.'

'Stand Hill.' Leila considered the information thoughtfully. Not much to go on, but she'd started out with less. The question was, what should she do with her protégé? He looked a pleasant young man – attractive even, in a boyish kind of way – but she was accustomed to working alone, she preferred it that way. Still, he could prove an invaluable asset if he was Ellen Conway's fiancee. And there was little doubt that in a situation like this, two heads were better than one. 'Listen,' she said, 'I'd like to find Ellen just as much as you would. Why don't we drive down to Arizona and take ourselves a look?'

She paused as a strained expression came into his face.

'There's something you'll have to do for me first,' he said hoarsely.

'What's that?'

'It's the coffee. It's gone right through my system.' His cheeks flushed with embarrassment as he rattled the hand-cuffs behind his back.

'I need to pee.'

The atmosphere in the conference room was tense. General Abu Bakhit sensed it the moment he popped his head through the open doorway. He could see the US Secretary of State surrounded by his subordinates. No one was speaking.

Bakhit looked at his aide, Hamad Jabrin. 'How long have they been like this?'

The man shrugged. 'Almost four-and-a-half hours. The President refuses to see them. The Americans seem to think he is going through some kind of elaborate charade.'

General Bakhit frowned. Musallim al Shisur could be difficult at times, but snubbing the US Secretary of State seemed a foolish and indelicate gesture.

'He's got to meet the Americans halfway. In the eyes of the world, he is branding us the aggressors.'

'No one can talk to him,' Jabrin said. 'He busys himself in his palace, plotting out strategies and troop movements. He'll let nothing get in the way of his confrontation with Israel.'

'Let's hope he doesn't overreach himself. Remember what happened to Sadaam Hussein.'

'I think he is gambling everything on the success of Talon Blue.'

'In my experience,' General Bakhit said, 'gamblers seldom ever win.'

He paused as the door opened, and the US Secretary of State emerged, accompanied by his entourage. The diplomat's face was pale with anger.

'You have my sympathies, Mr Secretary,' General Bakhit told him softly.

'Let's hope it will be enough to save your people,' the American replied.

Bakhit watched the delegation storming off along the corridor. His eyes looked sombre and reflective. 'I have a feeling,' he said, 'that we've just closed the door on our last chance for peace.'

President Clayman sat in the Oval Office with CIA Director, Phil Bowan, and the Chairman of the Joint Chiefs of Staff, Major General Nathan Kincaid. 'Frank called me this afternoon,' Clayman told them. 'Al Shisur failed to turn up for their meeting.'

'Failed to turn up?' Bowan echoed.

'It was a calculated snub. He kept our people waiting more than four-and-a-half hours.

'And offered no explanation?'

'Al Shisur doesn't care about explanations. His mind is already set on war.'

'He hasn't the firepower to defeat Israel in a free-for-all,' General Kincaid stated.

'That's why we have to decide what the bastard's up to.'

'Well,' Phil Bowan said, 'according to reports, the forces he's amassing are strictly conventional. There's no sign of nuclear weaponry.'

'But what happens if he's backed into a corner? Al Shisur's perfectly capable of cutting loose with everything he's got.'

'Maybe he won't need to, Mr President,' Kincaid said. 'There's a rumour he has some new kind of prototype which could bring Israel to its knees in a matter of hours.'

'What prototype?'

'That isn't clear at the moment.'

'Well, we can't stand by and watch war breaking out without doing something to prevent it.'

'Careful, Larry. The Arabs are already paranoid about what they see as US interference. And the American people won't like it much either. Remember this is election year.'

'I know, Nat, I know.'

The President took out a pocket inhaler and thrust it into his nostril, breathing deeply several times. 'Phil,' he said at last. 'Let's call an emergency session of the UN Security Council, and see if we can find a way of settling this affair without involving American troops.'

'Mr President, that's the best idea I've heard in months,' Bowan replied with a smile.

Ellen lay on her bed, staring out moodily at the stars. She felt tired and depressed. For some reason she couldn't define, the job that had started out so promisingly now seemed to be turning into a debilitating burden. It wasn't simply Joktan's snub, although that had hurt, she had to admit. She'd liked Joktan, it was true, and she wasn't accustomed to such a cavalier attitude, but she'd endured rejection before – it wasn't the end of the world, and she could learn to live with such things, a woman of her age. No, the thing which bothered her most was the sheer monotony of Stand Hill routine. Never in her life had she felt so constricted. It was like being locked up in a prison, she thought. She wasn't a machine, for God's sake. She needed a break.

Though the window, she saw the lights of the distant city and studied them wistfully. A city meant life, movement, people.

'Jo, how far did you say Phoenix was?'

'Thirty miles,' Jo told her.

'How 'bout taking a drive tonight?'

Jo frowned. 'What kind of drive?'

'Let's grab one of the trucks and head into town.'

'You're screwballed. We're not supposed to leave the air base.'

'Maybe they'll never notice.'

Jo raised her head from the pillow, examining Ellen critically. 'And the guards at the security gate?'

'They can't hold us against our will, can they? I mean, we do have some rights, after all.'

For a moment, Jo studied Ellen in silence, then her face broke into a grin. 'Well, if you really think we can get away with it, let's give it a try, goddamnit!'

Ellen laughed out loud, her melancholy forgotten. They scuttled around the Quonset hut, brushing their teeth, combing their hair, fixing their make-up, and thirty minutes later, tingling with excitement, crept furtively through the darkened Garrison Echelon.

The sound of motor vehicles reached them from the M/T Section, and Ellen pulled Jo behind a cluster of garbage cans. They saw a truck convoy rumbling toward the open gateway.

'Where on earth are they going at this time of night?' Jo whispered.

'Who cares? They could be our passport out of here.'

An abandoned jeep stood parked against the high-wire fence, and they ran toward it, scrambling inside. Jo reached down and checked the dashboard. 'No key,' she exclaimed, disappointed.

'To hell with the key.' Ellen leaned forward, fumbling with the electrical leads. The engine gave a muffled cough and burst into life.

'You're a marvel,' Jo said, looking at Ellen admiringly.

'Put it down to my misspent youth.'

She engaged the gear and swung into line behind the

112

slow-moving convoy, her body trembling with anticipation. The vehicle in front was a militarised Saviem TP3 with massive sand tyres designed to absorb the vibrations of the desert floor. A sheet of camouflaged canvas had been drawn across its rear, and its back lights were crusted with dust.

Ellen kept her face expressionless as the cavalcade rattled through the main gate but the sentries scarcely gave her a glance. The vehicles spread out across the desert floor, and she slapped the driving wheel in triumph. 'We've done it,' she breathed. 'I never believed it could be this easy.'

'Remember we still have to get in again.'

'Let's worry about that when the time comes.'

The convoy set out across the open landscape and Ellen nudged her foot on the brake, allowing their jeep to drop further and further behind. She waited until the trucks were many yards in front, then swung the wheel into a tight U-turn. 'Phoenix fleshpots, here we come,' she yelled.

Whooping and yelling, they steered the jeep into the awesome blackness of the desert night, their blinkered headlamps picking out the rutted track ahead. The air was cool, and the slipstream bit through their flimsy clothing. Occasionally, small animals scampered from their path, making little scuffling sounds in the murky darkness.

Ellen's feeling of exhiliration began to fade as the desert unfolded. Maybe it had been a crazy idea, flouting the security system. She'd endangered not only her own career but Jo's too. Boredom was one thing, but stupidity was something else entirely. They'd throw the book at her if the security people found out. There'd be no glittering prizes then, no promotion, no advancement. It would be back to Santa Clara in disgrace, and everything she'd worked for during these past few weeks would have been for nothing.

Soon Ellen began to worry in earnest. Though the city lights were drawing closer, there was still no sign of human habitation. Moreover, the route itself remained ragged and unpaved. 'Jo,' she said at last, 'how long have we been driving now?'

Jo glanced at her luminous wrist-watch. 'An hour and fifteen minutes.'

'Even allowing for the bumps, we should have reached Phoenix ages ago.'

'I was thinking the same thing myself.'

'Something funny's going on here. What happened to the highways and the people?'

Ellen nursed the jeep up a ragged hill, her sense of pre-monition deepening, and as she topped the rise, both girls gave an involuntary gasp. Directly in front, floodlamps had been erected to form a gigantic starburst and for as far as they could see, the plain was blanketed by a vast armada of tanks and artillery pieces. Never in her life had Ellen seen so many vehicles in one place. They covered the land like a metallic skin, their caterpillar treads giving them the appeance of multitudinous insects. Troops moved between the rows, singly or in groups, carrying weapons, fuel and equipment. Even at the distance, Ellen heard the wail of radios playing. 'Look at this,' she breathed.

'Soldiers.'

'Not just soldiers. An army.'

'What happened to the city, for Pete's sake?'

'There is no city, Never was.'

'But if we're not in Arizona, then where the hell are we?'

Ellen didn't answer. She was wondering the same thing herself. They heard the roar of an engine, and saw a helicopter weaving toward them, hosing the ground with a powerful searchbeam.

'They're checking for intruders,' Jo whispered.

'What in Heaven's name is going on here?' Ellen exclaimed as she swung the vehicle into reverse and headed back the way they had come.

Chapter Nine

Leila stopped the truck and checked the map on the dashboard in front of her. A narrow track drifted obliquely across the desert floor.

'Where are we?' Paul asked, seated in the rear with his wrists still manacled behind him.

'En route to Meteor Springs. That's the nearest town to Stand Hill Air Base.'

'What happened to the paved road?'

'There *is* no paved road. Just thirty-two miles of sand.'

'That's screwballed. They wouldn't build an air base without a proper highway.'

'Maybe there *was* a highway once. Maybe it crumbled away with age. Anyhow, see for yourself.' Leila showed him the map. 'Nothing around here but empty space.'

She sent the Chevrolet Blazer lurching along the rutted cart-track, kicking up clouds of choking thick dust, and Paul groaned as the vehicle's shuddering pitched him about in the rear. 'Thirty-two miles of this, did you say?'

'Just think of it as being good for the liver.'

At times, the track became so bad Leila had to slow almost to a standstill, picking her way through twisted rock formations, the country growing wilder by the minute.

Paul said little, allowing her to concentrate on the driving. He was not a garrulous man, she reflected. Kept pretty much to himself, and she approved of that. Compulsive talkers bored her. Paul was unassuming and self-contained, but he made an unlikely ally, she had to admit. He was decent, slightly naive and wholly unsuited to the violent world in which he found himself. Well, she had no time at all for shorn lambs. She still had a job to do. She would ditch him the minute his usefulness was over.

They drove for almost two hours before the badlands levelled into a thorn-studded plain, and Leila spotted a cluster of ramshackle buildings ahead. A sign said: 'Meteor Springs Mercantile and Motel. Elevation 800 feet, population 3'. 'Looks like we made it.'

There seemed little left of the settlement itself. Oblong patches in the sand showed where dwellings had once stood, but the shacks which remained were delapitated and falling to bits. Paul looked at the tin roofs and sagging porches. 'It's a ghost town.'

'Not even that.' She pulled to a halt and sat staring out at the tumbledown shanties. Something was wrong, she knew it; if there really *was* an air-base nearby, Meteor Springs should have been a bustling community.

'Let's see if we can get those bracelets off,' she said. 'Wait in the car until I get back.'

The motel building was low-beamed and musty, a combination of supermarket, post office and reception lobby. The floor descended into an elongated annex where high stools lined a stained coffee bar. In the store itself, a bristling array of shelves offered goods which looked as if they had been lying there for at least a decade. Photographs of air-crews adorned the walls.

'Anyone at home?' Leila called.

A man entered, wiping his hands on a ragged towel. He was tall and cadaverous-looking with a razor-scraped adam's apple. 'Howdy, didn't hear ya come in.'

'Open for business?'

'Never close, ma'am. Can't afford to out here.'

'Got such a thing as a screwdriver?'

The man gestured toward a shelf. 'Try the bottom box on the left.'

Leila paid the proprietor, and made her way back to the car.

'Find anything?' Paul asked.

'One step at a time. First, let's get your wrists free. Put your hands on the seat-rest.'

For several minutes, she tinkered with his handcuffs, working the screwdriver backwards and forwards until at last the lock gave a muffled click and sprang abruptly open. Paul trossed the manacles aside, rubbing his wrists in gratitude and relief.

'How does it feel?' she asked.

'Like being reborn.'

She examined her handiwork approvingly. 'Okay, let's rent ourselves a couple of rooms and see if we can find that air-base.'

Still massaging his chafed skin, Paul climbed out of the Blazer and followed her across the rackety porch. He gazed around the interior with an expression of disbelief. 'Wow, it's like stepping back in time,' he whispered.

The old man was still behind the counter when they entered. He watched them curiously, his beady eyes slightly out of alignment.

Leila nodded at the pictures of air-crews on the wall above. 'Those taken at Stand Hill?'

'Sure were,' the man said, slipping on his spectacles. 'Back in the seventies, they used the base to train pilots for Vietnam. You should've seen Meteor Springs then. We had a library and a schoolhouse and a water-works – even had our own fire station. Three hundred people lived here, and the skies were humming day and night. You never saw activity like it. Some days, you could scarcely hear yourself think for the roar of jets over the town.'

'What happened?' Paul asked.

'After 'Nam ended, the air chiefs decided the base was too remote, so they closed it down, and the town fell to bits. Martha and me, we stayed on. I got arthritis in my knee, and the desert air keeps the old bones from aching. I know it ain't exactly the Ritz, but we get a few tourists from time to time, and hunters drift in during the shooting season. We make enough to get by, I guess.'

Paul and Leila glanced at each other with dismay.

'Stand Hill is derelict?' Leila said.

'Sure. Has been for years.'

'But that's impossible.'

'No, ma'am. A battered old shell is all that's left.'

'There's nothing out there at all?' Paul echoed.

'Ghosts,' the man chuckled. 'Stand Hill's haunted. Sometimes at night, Martha and me, we hear the planes coming in just like the old days. Everyone thinks we're crazy, but funny things happen out here in the desert.'

Paul and Leila rented adjoining motel rooms, gulped a quick cup of coffee in the diner and set off across the desert, following the proprietor's crudely-drawn route-map. They said little during the bumpy, uncomfortable journey, for the realization that the air base no longer existed had depressed them both.

The land lay baking in the heat, the coarse desert sand flanked by ragged defiles where streams would flow when the winter rains came. The plain was bordered to the east by a line of foothills which looked faintly blue in the afternoon haze. After a while, they spotted a collection of buildings ahead. From a distance, they looked like sugar cubes scattered across the desert floor, and Leila recognized the haggard skeleton of an ancient control tower, its empty window frames gaping like the eye sockets in a human skull. Scattered around it were all that remained of Stand Hill's living quarters. Roofless and crumbling, they looked like relics from some bygone age.

Leila pulled to a halt, staring across the scene of desolation. 'It's like a graveyard,' she whispered.

'It *is* a graveyard,' Paul said moodily.

They wandered through the decaying remains, examining building after building. A few of the rooms still had posters fluttering from their walls, like the tattered banners of retreating armies.

Paul nudged a piece of masonary with his toe. 'It was a scam, right from the beginning. They never intended Ellen to arrive at Stand Hill at all.'

His voice was weary, filled with discouragement, and Leila patted him soothingly on the arm. 'She's got to be somewhere,' she said, 'and wherever she is, we're going to find her. So let's head back to the motel and figure out our next move.'

Leila was sitting on her bed watching TV, when Paul came

in from the adjacent room, brushing his teeth. 'I've made up my mind – I'm going to the authorities.'

'Think they'll listen?'

'I've got a brother in the San Jose police department who should be able to shake things up a bit.'

'Without evidence, they'll laugh in your face.'

'Ellen's in danger, I know she is.'

'Maybe not. Maybe they'll keep her alive as long as she's useful.'

'Who are we talking about, for God's sake? The CIA? The Pentagon? The godamned telephone company?'

Paul flopped into the armchair and Leila examined him in silence for a moment. Then getting up, she switched off the TV set and returned to her bed. 'You want my opinion?'

He nodded, his eyes sober.

Leila said: 'Musallim al Shisur is preparing to attack Israel, and we believe that somehow or other he's managed to get his hands on the Talon Blue weapon system. Ellen Conway suddenly disappears together with three other Mackhead colleagues. Doesn't that tell you something?'

'You're saying she's somewhere in the Middle East?'

'That's my guess. However, what really worries me is that al Shisur isn't sophisticated enough to pull off an operation like this alone. He'd need help, someone who's part of the US administration, someone powerful enough to make things happen at the highest level.'

'We need help too,' Paul said earnestly. 'We can't tackle this alone. We've got to tell somebody.'

'We don't even know who the enemy is, for God's sake.'

'Then let's go to the press. They'll be able to dig out the bottom dirt.'

'You'll be playing right into the opposition's hands. They've tried to kill you once. The minute you show your face . . .' Leila brought down her fist on the side of the bed.

Paul looked so miserable and disconsolate that Leila felt her senses melt. She was filled with an almost irresistible urge to take him into her arms and hug him. He was a nice man, Paul McKlelland, she thought.

'She must mean a lot to you, this Ellen Conway.'

'I love her,' he told her simply, and something in his voice sent a pang through Leila's chest. She had never in her life felt so strongly about another human being.

'I really envy you,' she said.

'Envy me?'

'Caring. Must be wonderful to be like that.'

He laughed drily. 'It isn't quite the way it looks. Our relationship is kind've one-sided.'

'In what respect?'

'In every respect. Let's face it, I'm not exactly the romantic type.'

'You seem pretty personable to me. Good-looking even.'

Paul waved his hand dismissively. 'I'm not talking about the way I look. I'm talking about the way I am. I live for my work.'

'And Ellen?'

'She's the same.'

'So what's the problem?'

'That's the point. There *is* no problem. It's too intangible to put a name to.'

'Maybe it's all in your head,' Leila suggested.

'No, I've known for a long time that it's over between us. Ellen wants something I don't seem able to give her. But that doesn't stop the way I feel. If she's in trouble, I've got to help. Whatever it takes, whatever it costs.' He looked at Leila. 'Does that sound crazy?'

'No,' Leila said. 'I don't think it's crazy at all. As a matter of fact ...' She leaned back against the pillows, her dark eyes glowing with an unusual lustre. 'I think Ellen Conway's an extremely lucky girl.'

The roar of an aircraft brought Leila to her senses. She opened her eyes, blinking in the darkness. The motel shuddered as a plane thundered overhead, heading in the direction of the air-base.

Leila threw back the blankets and tugged open the window shade. She saw lights glowing in the distant sky.

Pulling on her clothes, she hurried into Paul's room, shaking him vigorously. He sat up, his cheeks still puffy with sleep.

'Get dressed,' she told him. 'Something's happening at Stand Hill.'

Without a word, Paul scrambled out of bed and began wriggling into his things. The night air was cool as they set off across the desert floor, Leila steering the truck along the tortuous twists and bends. She kept the headlamps dipped to avoid betraying their presence, and they watched the distant lights growing steadily brighter. 'What the hell is going on out there?' Paul breathed.

'Can't be ghosts,' Leila grunted. 'They're making too much bloody noise.'

She saw the control tower outlined against the stars and pulled to a halt, switching off the headlamps. On the derelict runway stood a heavy transport plane with its cargo bay open. A line of vehicles framed the apron edge, their headlamps creating a barrage of light which shimmered fiercely on the aircraft's fuselage. Men were carrying packing cases from the nearby trucks, and loading them carefully into the hold. They were clad in boiler suits and several wore padded jackets to protect them from the cool desert night. At least two carried rifles.

Leila whistled under her breath. 'How about this?'

'Drug smugglers?' Paul suggested.

'What makes you think they're drug smugglers?'

'It would explain why our motel proprietor thinks the air base is haunted.'

'Idiot, they're not bringing stuff in, they're carrying stuff out.'

'So?'

'It's got to be something else.'

She opened the Blazer door.

'Where are you going?' Paul asked.

'I want a closer look. Coming?'

They made their way cautiously along a narrow draw, and Leila smelled the dry, slightly metallic odour of the desert night. Something scampered through the dust to her left – a rat or a vole, she couldn't tell which – and

121

vanished into a narrow crevice. Her body felt taut, every nerve ending vibrant and alive. Patches of thorn cluttered their path, and she steered a course around them, moving as deftly as she dared.

The draw ended at the runway edge, and Leila slithered to a halt behind a cactus clump. They could see the men clearly now, panting hard as they transferred their mysterious cargo. Two of the faces Leila recognized – they were the same patrolmen who had tried to murder Paul. She nudged him with her elbow, and he nodded.

Slightly to one side stood a limousine with its doors open. Leila saw a briefcase lying untended on the vehicle's rear seat. She signalled Paul to remain where he was, and began inching cautiously toward it. The car radio was still playing, and the drone of heavy rock music echoed in Leila's ears.

A man moved in her direction, and she froze in her tracks as he unzipped his pants and began to urinate in a narrow ditch. When he had finished, he spat on the ground and wandered back to join his companions.

Leila snatched the briefcase against her chest, and hurried back the way she had come.

Snyder watched the loading process with a bored expression. He lit a cigarette and breathed deeply in the desert night. Transferring the cargo was taking an interminable time, longer than he'd anticipated, so it was just as well they'd chosen an isolated transfer spot; he'd hate to have to worry about snoopers or intruders.

All things considered, Snyder was pleased with the way things were going. They'd just had word from the construction site that the two American women had made a night-time sortie into the neighbouring desert, but apart from that everything was proceeding on schedule, which was something to be thankful for. In an operation as complex as this, Snyder had learned to allow for the unexpected. Things went wrong, even on the most scrupulously planned itinerary, and experience had taught him to stay loose and be ready to improvise.

Rock music reached him on the still night air, and he glanced back at the empty limousine. That idiot Gronk had left the vehicle doors open. Snyder threw away his cigarette and walked toward it, humming softly under his breath. As he approached the car, his features creased in puzzlement. 'Sam?' he called.

Gronk came up. 'What's wrong?'

'Your briefcase has disappeared.'

Gronk stared down at the empty seat. 'It was here a minute ago.'

'You're sure?'

'Of course I'm sure.'

Kneeling, Snyder examined the ground in the headlamps' glow. He saw a set of footprints vanishing into the gloom. 'We've had a visitor.'

Gronk followed the tracks with his eyes. A second set mingled with the first, emerging from behind a thatch of prickly cactus. 'Two visitors,' he corrected.

Snyder swore under his breath. He'd been premature in thinking the operation was going smoothly. Calling to his men, he followed the footprints into the darkness.

Leila scrambled into the truck and switched on the overhead lamp. Her fingers were trembling as she tore open the briefcase and began studying the contents eagerly:

US ARMY
STRATEGIC DEFENCE COMMAND
MODEL STATEMENT OF WORK
SW-L73-82
TALON BLUE ELECTROMAGNETIC GENERATOR
(FLGIB TEE)
PULSE CONTROL SYSTEM
March 3rd, 1996

GEN SUBSYSTEM	PULSE CONTROL SUBSYSTEM	INTEGRATION DIAGNOSTIC
11-33-04-00-457	11-33-65-00-2531	11-33-78 11-33-0

CONTRACT DATE REQUIREMENTS LIST
(2 Data Items)

To Contract	Category N/A	System/Item
F2215-90-C-34	Ref: DON 5050 ALN	T:7348

Technical Operating Report (TOR) Distribution and
Addresses: WRBT/FIBG
Remarks: Tailored to allow contractor format. To be
submitted 25 days after time specified in Block 11.
Weapon Parts and Source Selection List attached. The
contractor will require access to classified source
data up to and including TOP SECRET in support
of this work effort.
This work effort is governed by the SDI Security Classification Guide dated August 1986.
General Intelligence Material/Foreign disclosure
applies. (see Page 3.)
Data RFP received: 11.30. Bid intent deadline: N + A.
Customer contact: Miles Kliban. Respective offer:
Electromagnetic emission laboratory has undertaken
the advanced material applications for Talon Blue
Program to demonstrate systems application confidence in structures technologies by designing,
fabricating and conducting tests on a full-scale
weapon structure.
The attached RFP is for a four-phase program. Phase
One is structural evaluation. Phase Two: Structural fabrication. Phase Three: Structural tests and
analysis, and Phase Four: Structural reproduction.
The basis for awarding the contract is specified in
Section L (evaluation criteria of the RFP). A cost plus
fixed B-type contract is anticipated.'

'What is this stuff?' Leila exclaimed, mystified.

'It's the original bid for the Talon Blue contract,' Paul
told her excitedly.

'You mean, you can understand this garbage?'

'Bits of it.'

'Does it tell you what the system does?'

'Nope. But it tells us something else. See this name?'
Paul pointed to the signature at the top of the contract bid. 'Miles Kliban is chairman of Napier Oil Incorporated.'

'So?'

'Napier Oil was the registered owner of the plane carrying

Ellen to Stand Hill air-base. The pilot was Kliban's personal air-chauffeur.'

Leila's eyes sharpened. 'How come you didn't tell me this before?'

'It didn't seem important before.'

'Maybe we should pay this Kliban a visit.'

'I was thinking the same thing myself.'

Paul paused as footsteps reached them from the darkness. The sound was muffled and indistinct, but they heard the rasp of laboured breathing. 'Somebody's coming.'

Leila stuffed the papers back into the briefcase, and slid behind the driving wheel. 'Hang on to your underpants,' she snapped.

Forty yards away, Snyder quickened his pace as he heard the engine burst into life, but with a deafening roar, the truck thundered into the darkness, vanishing in a thick cloud of dust. He slithered to a halt, leaning forward to press his hands against his knees. He was sucking desperately at the air as his followers came running up and gathered around him in a disorderly group.

Snyder glanced at a man cradling a Uzi submachine gun. 'Arch, didn't you say the woman who rescued the McKlelland man was driving a Chevrolet Blazer?'

'That's right,' Arch confirmed, and Snyder nodded.

'Well, I think we can guess who our intruders were.'

'And after they look inside that briefcase,' Gronk said, 'I think we can also guess where they'll be heading.'

Talon Blue looked like a giant erector set, its structure bristling with transmitters, orientation sensors and electro-magnetic conductors. Lower, its chassis was supported on a skeletal framework which bore a faint resemblance to the Eiffel Tower.

'Some sight,' Victor Conville said.

Ellen agreed. 'What do you think it does?'

Conville grinned. 'I have it on excellent authority. It leaps into the air and writes "God Bless America" in green sparks across the sky.'

'Seriously, Victor.'

'Seriously? We'll know tomorrow. The secrecy ends at

1100 hours. Chivers is holding a test run, and everyone's invited.'

'So they've decided to trust us at last.'

'Had to happen sooner or later. After all, they can't operate the thing without some kind of maintenance back-up, and how can we fix it if we don't know what its function is? Mackhead may have its faults, but stupidity isn't one of them.'

Ellen was silent for a moment. She wondered how far she could trust Conville. He seemed a dope, despite his handsome looks, but she needed some kind of support if she hoped to make any sense of this mess.

The memory of what she and Jo had discovered on their night-time sortie still loomed vividly in Ellen's mind. It had been no simple exercise, of that she felt certain, but a well-oiled military machine, ready at any moment to spring into action. Worse, after their return, they had been hauled before Colonel Chivers and severely reprimanded. Ellen had expected suspension at least. Instead, they'd been sent back to their sections with a warning to reveal nothing about what they had seen and heard. Something unorthodox was taking place here, and with no one to confide in, Ellen felt isolated and vulnerable.

She said gently: 'These people aren't from Mackhead, Victor.'

'What are you talking about?'

'I mean, they're outsiders.'

'Where from?'

'I don't know. I wish I did, but I don't. All I can tell you is, we're being used.'

'You can't be serious?'

Quickly, she outlined the details of their discovery in the desert. She told him about sneaking out of camp, about driving toward Phoenix and spotting the tanks, artillery and armoured personnel carriers. When she had finished, Conville seemed strangely unimpressed. 'So what? This is a restricted area, isn't it? They're bound to use it for all sorts of things, including military training.'

'This wasn't training. Believe me, I can tell when an army's preparing for war.'

126

'Maybe the flying saucers have finally landed,' he said with a grin.

Ellen sighed. Of all the people to choose, she had to pick on Conville. What a clown. In looks he might resemble a Greek statue, but in terms of IQ he had the brains of a rabbit. 'Just forget I said anything, Victor, okay?'

She went back to work, trying to focus her attention on the complicated structures she was assembling, but with maddening persistence her mind kept drifting to the mysterious army hiding in the desert. To whom did it belong, and what was its purpose? In the beginning, her phobias had seemed too outrageous to be taken seriously, but something was happening, something she couldn't put a name to. Unknowingly and unwittingly, she had become part of some complex and elaborate charade.

She saw Joktan approaching across the hangar floor and felt her muscles suddenly tighten. She hadn't spoken to him since the episode at the officers' club and her resentment had deepened, rather than abated. She wasn't accustomed to such callous treatment, and she had no intention of appearing friendly.

Joktan drew to a halt at her side. His eyes were earnest and contrite. 'I believe I owe you an explanation,' he said.

She shrugged. 'Forget it.'

'I couldn't help what happened the other evening. There was an emergency.'

'Yeah? What kind?'

'Security alert. Poachers hunting without a licence. They got too close to our sensor equipment, and I had to check them out.'

'Why didn't you send a message?'

'In the heat of the moment, I forgot. I know it's a flimsy excuse, but it happens to be the truth.' He hesitated. 'If there's anything I can do to put things right ...'

Ellen thought quickly. Maybe Joktan could give her the answers she was seeking? If anyone knew what was going on here, surely it had to be Joktan? Properly handled, he could tell her everything.

Keeping her voice casual, she said: 'If you really mean that, why don't you take me for a drive?'

'A drive?' He looked surprised. 'Where?'

'Anywhere. I'm going crazy stuck in this miserable pesthole.'

'But it's the middle of the desert.'

'I love driving in the desert, don't you?' She pressed the point. 'We *are* allowed to, aren't we? I mean, it's not breaking the rules or anything?'

'Well, strictly speaking, you're not supposed to leave the area. Security.'

Ellen rolled her eyes in exasperation. 'Security! That's all you people ever think about. You're top gun around here, am I right?'

'In a manner of speaking.'

'So what's the problem? I'm free for the rest of the afternoon, and you'll be with me every inch of the way. Maybe we'll be bending the rules a little, but we're not zombies, after all.'

Joktan hesitated, then shrugged. 'Why not? I don't see how it can do any harm. I'll meet you at the gate in twenty minutes.'

Ellen's heart was thumping as she returned to her quarters and changed her things. She'd handled him well, a clever professional job, but Joktan was no fool. Everything would now depend on how skilfully she dangled the bait.

She found him placing a wicker basket into the rear of a battered Land Rover. 'What's that?' she asked.

'Even in the desert, we have to eat.'

'You think of everything,' she smiled.

'I live longer that way.'

He helped her into the passenger seat, started up the engine and rumbled through the barbed-wire gate, nodding casually at the sentries.

As they headed across the desert floor, Ellen contemplated the nature of her dilemma. She liked Joktan, it was true, but she had no time for romantic dalliances. There were far more important things at stake. First, she had to win her quarry's confidence and trust, learn all she possibly could about him. 'How long have you lived in the United States?' she asked, keeping her voice casual and pleasant.

'On and off, for almost fifteen years.'

'And before that?'

'England. I studied at Oxford University. However ...'
He smiled. 'Most of my childhood was spent among the
Bedouin.'

'All that desert?' She grimaced.

'I thought you liked the desert.'

'Only in small doses.'

He said: 'The desert is the only place I really feel alive.
It's so wild and clean.'

'Clean?'

'Well, it's not like Antarctica, for example, where nothing
rots in the endless ice. Throw out your garbage, and it'll still
be there in a thousand years. Here, the local scavengers will
gobble it up in a matter of hours. The desert always takes
back its own.'

'It's lonely though, all this emptiness.'

'Quiet too. Sometimes, when the wind stops blowing,
there's a silence so perfect it's almost painful to listen to.'

'Don't you like people, music, conversation? All the
things that make life worthwhile?'

'You're thinking like a westerner,' he said. 'To you, the
desert is something to be feared. To the Bedu, man and the
desert are one and the same.'

She chuckled, 'You talk about the Bedouin as if they
were some kind of chosen people, but where would the
human race be if we'd all wandered around like nomads
for the past two thousand years?'

'You see things too simplistically. Civilization has nothing
to do with western culture. In Baghdad, we had astronomers
studying the stars while western man was still worshipping
pagan images. The Moslems understood the world was
round long before Columbus. It was the Islamic empire
which sowed the seeds for the European Renaissance,
Islamic writings, Islamic ideas, Islamic art and architecture
which fired the souls of your medieval scholars. Most of
the advances in modern thinking can be traced back to the
Moslem influence.'

'I didn't realize you were a Moslem.'

'I'm not. But I was born among an Islamic people. I
understand their ways. I sympathize with their beliefs.'

129

Joktan talked easily and articulately, with none of the restraint she had noticed earlier. He was a strange man, she realized, a curious mixture of the primal and the sophisticated, as different to Paul as it was possible to imagine. And yet, she felt drawn to him in some indefinable way.

After a while, they saw a line of palm trees tracing a shallow stream; foliage bordered the water's edge, and even from a distance, Ellen could smell the redolence of moisture on the air. 'A watering place,' she exclaimed. 'Why don't we stop there and eat?'

'If you like.'

Joktan drew to a halt and a jackal, startled by their arrival, bolted furiously for cover. Ellen laughed as she opened the Land Rover door. She stepped barefoot into the shallow river, curling her toes in the icy current. 'This is delightful,' she said.

Suddenly, her features froze as she saw, watching her from the opposite bank, their pale robes fluttering in the wind, a group of Arab tribesmen. At their rear, veiled women were pouring water into earthenware jars. It was like a scene from the Old Testament, and for a moment, Ellen was shaken by a sense of unreality and astonishment.

Then she turned to face Joktan, her expression hardening. 'This has gone far enough,' she said, and she could see by his eyes that she had him trapped neatly in her sights. 'I want to know exactly where we are, and what, in God's name, we are doing here.'

130

Chapter Ten

The house had been built into the cliff, its terrace jutting over the town like the prow of some incredible galleon. Through her fieldglasses, Leila studied the entrance drive which was blocked by a heavily barred gate. Plainclothed security guards patrolled the grounds, their faces masked by sinister sun-goggles.

She whistled softly. 'It's like Fort Knox in there. Kliban's got himself a regular army.'

'No hope of going through the front door then,' Paul said.

Not with all that muscle around.'

'What's he hiding, I wonder?'

'Why should he be hiding anything? He's a big-time oil executive, isn't he? That makes him juicy kidnap material.' She slipped the fieldglasses back into their leather case. 'Let's drive into town and think this over.'

Palm Springs looked peaceful in the late afternoon. A handful of tourists picked their way along the tree-lined boulevards, pausing from time to time to gaze in the windows of the elegant boutiques.

Leila pulled into a shopping mall and they sat in a tiny deli and ordered coffee. 'Think Kliban's expecting us?' Paul said.

'He'd be crazy not to. He knows we've got the Mackhead dossier, and he knows his name's on the front cover.'

'If he's dealing under the counter, he'll want that dossier back.'

'Not just the dossier. He'll want us too.'

'Maybe we can use ourselves as bait. Lure him out of his hidey-hole.'

'How about his commandos?'

'We could choose a public place.'

'And after the meeting's over?'

'I haven't figured that out yet,' Paul said.

He stared at a poster on the deli wall. It was an advertisement for the Palm Springs cablecar which carried tourists to the summit of San Jacinto mountain. "Ride the Aerial Tramway to the skies," it said. "Cars depart every half hour from 8 am onwards. Ride'n'Dine combination includes round-trip fare and dinner at the top."

Paul grinned at Leila mischievously. 'How's your head for heights?' he asked.

Miles Kliban heard the telephone ringing as he stepped out of the shower. He wrapped a towel around his waist, and still dripping, wandered into the sitting room to pick up the receiver. A voice said: 'Mr Kliban?'

'Who is this?'

'My name's McKlelland. Paul McKlelland.'

Kliban felt his stomach tighten. He pulled up a corner of the towel, quickly mopping his cheeks and forehead. 'Hold on a minute, Mr McKlelland.' Cupping the receiver against his chest, Kliban leaned forward to stab the intercom. 'Edith, get this call traced, will you? And ask Mr Snyder to step in here immediately.'

'Yes, sir.'

Kliban straightened, filling his lungs with air. He tried to keep his voice calm as he raised the receiver to his lips. 'Now, what is this all about?'

Paul said: 'Mr Kliban, I believe we have something belonging to you. It's an RFP on the Talon Blue weapons program, solicitation number S7721-R3-400.'

'You're speaking in riddles, Mr McKlelland. I know nothing about any such weapons program.'

'That's strange. The covering form carries your name.'

Kliban tightened his lips. Glancing through the window, he said evenly: 'What is it you want? Money?'

'Information,' Paul told him. 'Meet me, and I'll return the dossier.'

'Fine. Why don't you come on up to the house?'

Paul chuckled. 'That wouldn't be very clever of me, Mr Kliban. I know the place is bristling with armed guards.'

'Okay, any place you say.'

'You know the San Jacinto cablecar? Be on the first ride tomorrow. Eight o'clock. Come alone.'

'Mr McKlelland ...'

'Don't be late, Mr Kliban.'

There was a click in Kliban's ear as the line went dead. He replaced the receiver, and stood looking down at it, his creased faced lined with thought.

The door opened and Leon Snyder came in. Snyder was dressed in a blue business suit, with a neat grey-flecked shirt. Even in the hottest weather, Snyder believed in observing the proprieties. 'Who was it?' he asked, noting the strain in Kliban's eyes.

'McKlelland. He's here in Palm Springs.'

Snyder whistled. 'He's cleverer than I thought.'

'Cleverer? Leon, this man is after my hide. The whole project's falling to pieces around our ears.'

'Don't over-dramatize. McKlelland's a nuisance, nothing more. His luck can't last for ever.'

'If this leaks out,' Kliban said, 'if it becomes public, I'm finished, you realize that?'

'Have I ever let you down? Ever?'

Snyder gently squeezed his arm, like a benevolent uncle calming an unruly nephew. He said, 'Now what was it McKlelland wanted?'

'He's got the Talon Blue dossier, the one he stole from Gronk's limousine. He's asking for a trade.'

'Money?'

'Talk. If I tell him all I know, he'll return the dossier as a sign of good faith.'

'I see.' Snyder walked to the window and stood gazing out. His skull looked sculpted against the light, his fiercely brushed hair accentuating his rugged features.

Kliban watched him worriedly. He knew Snyder could turn on the charm at the drop of a hat, but his ruthlessness filled

133

the oil executive with apprehension and alarm. 'I'm supposed to meet him on the first cablecar in the morning,' Kliban said.

'Nice touch. Lots of privacy.'

'Except that I won't be going.'

'Of course you'll be going. How else are we supposed to nail this bastard?'

'It's out of the question, Leon.'

'Nobody else can make it work, Mr Kliban.'

Kliban massaged his cheekbone with his fingertip. He wasn't built for this, he thought, the pressure, the tension. The doctor had told him to take things easy. He had a heart condition.

'I just can't do it,' he protested.

'Don't worry. I'll have that cablecar so bristling with armed men that not even a caterpillar could work its way through. The minute McKlelland shows his face ...'

Snyder turned from the window smiling, and snapped his fingers in an eloquent gesture.

Paul moved through the camping store, humming softly under his breath, while Leila followed him in puzzlement. Ever since the phone call, he had been acting very strangely. He'd lost his indecisive air, had taken over the initiative.

Paul never failed to surprise her. Just when she thought she had him figured out, some new facet to his personality would emerge. She liked him, she realized. She liked him for his loyalty to Ellen Conway. Though he knew their relationship was over, he was willing to risk his life to save her. No hesitation, no compromise. A man in a million, was Paul McKlelland, even if he *was* sometimes incomprehensible.

'What are you doing?' she asked at last.

'Browsing,' he told her cheerfully.

The store assistant approached them. 'Can I help you folks, or are you just pottering around?'

'Do you carry emergency equipment?' Paul asked.

'That we do. Any particular kind in mind?'

'We're thinking of going into the desert for a few days. I have a horror of breaking down and being stranded out there.'

'You're right. It can be a nasty situation if you're not properly prepared. However, we have just the thing you need.' He led them to the opposite end of the store and pulled open a cupboard, taking out a box of small cylindrical cartridges. 'Smoke bombs,' he explained. 'Your truck craps out, you set fire to one of these and it sends a fifty-foot smoke column belching into the air. They make a perfect position-marker. Guaranteed to burn for an hour without stopping.'

'Give me a dozen,' Paul said.

The assistant looked surprised. 'You must be figuring on staying in that desert an awful long time.'

'How about distress flares?'

'We've got the new magnesium brand, complete with firing tube.'

'Sounds ideal. I need fifty feet of insulating wire too, plus eight Ducheneaux solid-state batteries, a jar of nitric acid and three or four electronic timers, the kind you use to switch on the lights when you're away from home.'

'I can supply the timers, the wire and the batteries,' the assistant told him. 'The acid you'll get at the DIY store on the opposite side of the boulevard.'

Leila watched Paul paying for his purchases at the check-out counter, her mind in a turmoil. Paul appeared to have some sort of plan in mind and she supposed she ought to feel grateful for that since her own brain had gone into neutral, but why all the secrecy, for Pete's sake? She wasn't exactly a stranger, after all.

As he drove through the early evening traffic, she said: 'Aren't you going to tell me what this is all about?'

'Simple,' he explained. 'When we reach that cablecar tomorrow, Kliban's going to have the place staked out. We need something to give us an edge.'

'What kind of edge?'

'Professional secret.' He smiled. 'I haven't spent my entire life as a research engineer without picking up a trick or two.'

Leila frowned as they drove along Palm Canyon Drive, leaving the buildings gradually behind. Trees lined both sides of the highway, forming a luxuriant culvert which contrasted strangely with the desert beyond. 'Where are we going now?'

'To the cablecar, of course.'

'At this time of night?'

Paul laughed. He sounded as if he hadn't a care in the world. 'Where's your joie de vivre? They say there's nothing to beat a romantic dinner on San Jacinto summit.'

The morning sun was dazzling as Leon Snyder pulled to a halt at the Aerial Tramway. Only a handful of vehicles stood scattered about the parking lot, most belonging to the cablecar staff; it was still too early for the daily tourists.

As Snyder and Kliban climbed from the limousine, their little group of bodyguards formed a cordon around them. Kliban felt depressed; he had slept badly during the night, and put it down to his natural reticence, coupled with fear. Businesswise, he could handle any situation, but when it came to the physical stuff, he was − and always had been − an extremely fearful man.

Snyder examined him critically. 'Feeling okay?'

'Lousy.'

'You've got nothing to worry about. Nothing.'

'Easy for you to talk.'

'You'll be covered from every angle.'

'Leon, I don't want to do this.'

Snyder sighed. It was the first time in their association that the oil executive had had to submit himself to physical danger, and Snyder knew that Kliban's brain was rebelling at the thought. 'You have to, Mr Kliban. Nobody else can.'

'But I'm a desk man, for God's sake. I sit in offices. I write reports. I can't handle the rough-house stuff, never could.'

'You won't need to handle a thing. The minute McKlelland appears − geronimo!'

'You promise, Leon?'

'I give you my word.'

Kliban saw Snyder's security guards watching him, their eyes inscrutable behind their sinister sunglasses. 'Okay, I'll give it a go.'

Snyder slapped him on the shoulder. 'Good man.'

The guards escorted Kliban to the edge of the parking lot, but he felt miserably alone as he made his way to the tramway office and bought a ticket on the first car up. He hated violence, always had, even as a boy when the very thought of physical confrontation had utterly unnerved him. At school, he'd been bullied unmercifully – and still was, he reflected, by Snyder in particular. If it hadn't been for Snyder, he would never, in a million years, have ventured into this mess.

A handful of tourists stood waiting at the boarding gate, but a tramway official waved Kliban on board.

'Sorry, folks,' the man said as the tourists tried to follow. 'This is a test run. Next car'll be down in a couple of minutes.'

The only other passenger was a young woman dressed in jeans and a mackinaw jacket. Kliban felt a slight bump as they pulled away from the boarding platform and ascended rapidly into the craggy ramparts of San Jacinto peak. Below, the breathtaking sprawl of Palm Springs sprang into view, but Kliban scarcely noticed the spectacular scenery. He was staring at the cablecar attendant, his face tight with tension.

The attendant turned to look at him. 'I think we might have that little talk now, Mr Kliban,' Paul said amiably.

Charlie Machschalko stood in the summit control room and stared through the observation window at the chasm below. There was no sign of the approaching passenger car – at eight thousand feet, it was impossible to detect against the bedrock of the canyon floor – but he knew it must be rising because he could hear the cables humming. Heat shimmered off the plain which lay in a panoramic sprawl for far as Machschalko could see. He felt light-headed and breathed deeply, filling his lungs with air. Altitude, he thought. He'd come up too quickly. He needed time to readjust.

Machschalko's associates were watching the ascending car on a video screen when the telehphone rang. Machschalko picked up the receiver.

'It's Snyder,' a voice said. 'How's it looking?'

'Fine, Leon. We've picked up the car on the TV console. It should be arriving in two or three minutes.'

'Got your men in position?'

'Three in the control room, and two covering the platform outside.'

'Good.' There was a pause, and Machschalko heard Snyder's breathing at the other end of the line. 'Charlie?'

'Yes, Leon?'

'This is a delicate situation. I don't want Kliban hurt if we can avoid it, but McKlelland and the girl have to be silenced, that's the important thing.'

'I understand, Leon.'

'Use your judgement. If you can spare Kliban, do it. If not ...' Snyder left the statement unfinished.

'Don't worry about McKlelland,' Machschalko said, loosening his necktie. 'There's no way that bastard can get out of here, unless he sprouts wings and learns to fly.'

As Kliban stared at the couple confronting him, he struggled to maintain — outwardly at least — some semblance of dignity and composure, but beneath the facade he felt sick with fright. Snyder's plan had gone seriously awry. Despite the security cordon, McKlelland had managed to isolate him with devastating ease, and now he was defenceless and totally alone. The realization made Kilban's insides quiver.

He examined his captor nervously. The man was no taller than Kliban himself; younger, of course, but his musculature could hardly be described as athletic. Kliban would have labelled him 'intellectual' rather than 'physical'. The girl, on the other hand, was sensuous and lithe, but Kliban sensed that she was a thousand times more dangerous than McKlelland himself.

There was little hostility in McKlelland's manner; he looked mild — even to some extent affable as he examined his prisoner intently. 'What's going on, Mr Kliban?'

'I don't understand.'

'You understand all right. What's Napier Oil up to?'

'I can't discuss business affairs with outsiders.'

'You'll discuss anything I ask if you want this dossier back.'

'You've brought it with you?'

'Talk first, trade later.'

'I can't talk. It's a national security matter.'

'Bullshit.'

'I mean it, Mr McKlelland. I'm ...' Kliban hesitated. 'I'm sworn to secrecy.'

'By whom?'

'That's the secret.'

'Okay, answer me this. What's the link between a respectable American oil company and a tin-pot dictator like Musallim al Shisur?'

'You're talking in riddles.'

'Don't bother denying it, Mr Kliban. We know all about your unsavoury friends.'

'I may be many things,' Kliban said, trying to summon an element of dignity, 'but I am not, and never have been, a traitor.'

'Then what's your connection with Talon Blue?'

'Talon Blue?'

'Don't try to deny it. Your name's on the front of the program form.'

Kliban reached for his handkerchief. He knew his fingers were trembling, but he couldn't help himself. 'Mr McKlelland, you are in serious trouble. You've blundered into something you simply don't understand.'

'So enlighten me.'

'Please don't joke. This is no trivial matter. You are a miniscule pawn in a very ambitious game. We have powerful friends – senators, congressmen, members of the Joint Secret Services Committee.'

'You're scaring me to death.'

'I mean it, Mr Klelland. You'll find Leon Snyder a dangerous man to cross.

'Who's Leon Snyder?'

'He's the one whose toes you're crushing. He has a very ruthless disposition.'

'What happened to my fiancee?' Paul asked savagely.

'Your fiancee?'

'Ellen Conway?'

Kliban looked confused. 'Why, nothing. Nothing at all.'

'Is she dead?'

'Of course not.'

'Then where is she?'

'I really can't say.'

Paul seized Kliban by the shirtfront, shaking him violently. 'We had a deal, Kliban, and now you're stalling.'

'We had no deal,' he exclaimed, sinking back against the car wall. 'They forced me to come here, Snyder and his friends. They're waiting for you on the landing stage above. You're trapped, you fool. It'll take a miracle to save you now.'

In the shimmering sunlight, Paul's face looked hard and intransigent. 'I've already arranged a miracle,' he said.

'Here it comes.'

Charlie Machschalko and his three associates took out their .38s as the cablecar approached. The control operator glanced at the sudden display of weaponry and nervously moistened his lips. 'You said there'd be no shooting.'

'That's up to the suspect, Mr McClusky. We're hoping he'll give himself up without a fight.'

'Nobody mentioned handguns,' the man protested. 'I'm always ready to help the FBI, but if there's going to be shooting, count me out.'

'Relax,' Machschalko told him. 'Everything's under control.'

He picked up the telephone. There was a faint buzzing, then Snyder's voice came on the line.

'We've got him in our sights, Leon.'

'Any sign of life?'

'Nothing at the moment. Maybe he's lying on the cabin floor.'

Snyder said: 'Charlie, if you can plant a handpiece on McKlelland, it'll help with the modus operandi report. Self-defence, and all that.'

'It'll be clean as a whistle, Leon. Count on it.'

Machschalko put down the telephone. Through the observation window, he saw the great sprawl of the desert floor, then for no reason he could clearly explain, he found himself sitting on the ground with the telephone in his lap. A tremendous explosion echoed in his ears, and clouds of thick coloured smoke belched through the control room, churning

140

around him in a smothering shroud. Behind, he heard the others coughing and retching as they battled for oxygen. Booby-trap, he thought.

The operator jammed his fist on the emergency button, and they stumbled, choking, into the open air.

Paul and Leila fell to the floor as the cablecar jerked to a halt, swinging wildly above the canyon. Only Kliban managed to maintain his balance. He was leaning against the wall with both arms outspread. For a moment he stood there, his eyes rolling in a paroxysm of hysteria, then he tore open the door and without looking down, seized the metal bar above his head and dragged himself, wriggling and kicking, on to the cablecar roof. Jesus, Paul thought, watching his legs disappear past the window, what's the idiot doing?

'You okay?' he snapped at Leila.

'I think so.'

'Sit tight.'

Paul rose to his feet and moved to the open doorway. A glimpse of the rocky floor below made his stomach quiver, but he leaned out and peered upwards, ignoring the air-waves ruffling his hair and throat. There was nothing to see but the gleaming curve of the roof rim. 'Kliban?' he yelled.

No answer.

'Kliban?'

Silence.

'Come back, dummy. You want to kill yourself?'

Paul leaned out further, stealing himself against the void yawning at his feet. He saw Kliban directly above, climbing dementedly towards the overhead cable. Brilliant, Paul thought. Somebody would have to bring the poor bastard back. He seemed almost beside himself with terror.

Paul's stomach felt hollow as he grabbed hold of the metal rail. He had never liked heights at the best of times, got dizzy on the stairs, for Chrissake, but if anything happened to Kliban, he would have to live with the memory for the rest of his life.

A terrible lightness gathered in his head as he eased himself upward, jamming his feet against both sides of the metal doorway. He paused for a moment, the mountains wheeling beneath him, then groped higher, feeling the cablecar tilt as his fingers clutched the network of girders supporting the base of the suspension rod. I'm not built for this, he thought. Aerial heroics were never my style. I'm strictly a gravity man. It would serve Kliban right if the idiot broke his stupid neck.

Paul's fingers gripped the metal supports and he felt the chill surface biting into his flesh as he dragged himself awkwardly onto the cablecar roof. For a moment he lay still, sweat tracing spidery patterns down his ashen cheeks. The car was swaying from side to side, and he saw Kliban holding onto the cable like a man hugging his last tentative link with life. 'Kliban, I'm not going to harm you, idiot. Come back before you fall.'

'Stay away from me.'

Spittle dribbling from his lips, Kliban inched his way further along the slender wire, and with a groan of resignation, Paul began to follow.

In the valley control room, Snyder bellowed into the telephone. 'Charlie, Charlie, what's going on up there?'

His assistant, standing at the observation window, called over his shoulder. 'Better take a look at this, Leon.'

Snyder trained his field-glasses on the cablecar above. The car was see-sawing dangerously above the canyon and he saw two figures struggling for balance on its narrow roof.

'What are the idiots *doing*?' he exclaimed, whistling softly under his breath.

'Where are you going, Kliban?' Paul shouted.

Kliban ignored him, dragging himself along the metal cable. It was clear he had neither the strength nor the agility to sustain his ragged momentum.

Paul gritted his teeth, holding on hard to his slender purchase. The wire was slick with grease, and his fingers kept slipping as he worked his way gingerly along the precarious filament. The wind bit through his jacket, molding his shirt against his sweaty skin. Below, the valley swayed and blurred.

Suddenly's Kliban's resolution wilted and Paul flinched

impulsively as he watched the oil man topple from his perch and, still holding the metal hauser, swing wildly in mid-air, his legs kicking and thrashing. Kliban seemed demented with terror, and his eyes bulged as he clung to his hold with a desperate tenacity. Paul quickened his pace, hauling himself monkey-like along the shuddering wire. He knew that if he paused even for a moment, his nerve would snap and he'd be on a one-way ticket to oblivion.

Kliban was still dangling from the cable, his knuckles white with strain, when Paul reached down and grasped his collar, clutching the flimsy material with his fist. 'I can't pull you up alone,' Paul gasped. 'You'll have to do it from below.'

'I can't,' Kliban wheezed.

'Try, godamnit.'

Paul saw the chords standing out on Kliban's throat as he struggled to bend his arms. Sweat was pouring down the oil man's face and his eyes were glassy with fear.

'Harder,' Paul urged. 'Pull harder.'

'I'm coming off,' Kliban exclaimed in panic.

Paul braced himself for the strain as Kliban lost his grip. The weight of his falling body almost ripped Paul's arm from its socket, but Paul gritted his teeth, clinging hard to the wire as Kliban swayed and spun beneath him.

'Grab ... my ... wrist,' Paul panted.

Kliban seemed incapable of responding. Suspended above the canyon, he looked like a man whose last vestiges of strength had finally deserted him. Frenzied mewing sounds issued from his throat as he began to slide out of his flimsy jacket.

'Hang on, you fool,' Paul gasped.

There was a terrible rending sound as the jacket began to disintegrate. 'It's tearing,' Kliban cried.

'Give me your hand. Quick.'

Kliban clawed desperately at Paul's wrist, but with a final rip the garment burst asunder, and chilled with horror, Paul watched his hostage plummeting into the abyss below.

Through his field glasses, Snyder saw Kliban arc outwards with slow athletic grace. He seemed to be executing a macabre aerial ballet, his body gathering speed as he rocketed earthwards, turning a perfect somersault before landing among the bedrock with a sickening thud.

Snyder winced and snapped at the cablecar operator: 'Bring them down, godamnit.'

Without a word, the man began to manipulate the controls.

Paul was panting as he dropped on to the cablecar roof. His right arm felt stiff, and a terrible sickness had gathered in his stomach. The vision of Kliban falling seemed imprinted into his brain. Maybe if he hadn't pushed the man so hard, Kliban wouldn't have panicked. He was at least partially responsible for what had happened.

Suddenly, he realized he was still clutching Kliban's jacket. He ran his fingers through the pockets, took out the wallet and stuffed it into his shirt. What now? he wondered. They were still dangling from the wire, and unless he could figure a way out of here, Leon Snyder, the man Kliban had told him about, had them neatly trapped.

The screech of the cable-wheel made Paul look up sharply. They were starting to move again, he realized. The operator had reversed their momentum, and was guiding them back to the valley floor.

Paul leaned over the rim. 'Leila, grab my hand. You've got to get on to the roof.'

'Are you crazy? What for?'

'It's our only way out of here.'

He saw her face, pale with fright, watching him from the open doorway. 'How can we get off a moving cablecar?' she demanded.

'Easy,' he told her, winking encouragingly. 'We'll parachute.'

Snyder watched the woman scrambling up to join her companion and an exclamation of astonishment burst from his lips as he saw the car approaching the skeletal outline of Tower Three. 'Sonofabitch,' he breathed in disbelief. 'They're going to make a jump for it.'

Holding on to Paul's hand, Leila fixed her eyes on the tower gliding up toward them and tried to shut her mind to the awesome emptiness below. Her mouth felt dry and sticky, and despite the breeze, sweat streamed over her entire body. A terrible shivering started in her limbs as the great amphitheatre of cliffs slid implacably by. In her mind, she could still see Kliban plummeting earthwards on his last fateful plunge. He'd looked so elegant turning and wheeling during those final moments of life that the horror had seemed diluted somehow. Well, she wouldn't let such a thing happen to her. Her gazed locked fixedly on the approaching tower. Concentrate, she thought. Mind steady, muscles loose. She could see the girders glinting in the sunlight.

Paul's fingers tightened on her wrist. 'Ready?'

She nodded.

'Now.'

Sucking in her breath, she leapt desperately outwards, conscious of a curious buoyancy, as if her body was floating on air. The valley blurred in her vision, rocks and scrub blending into a chaotic sprawl with neither depth nor density. Then the tower came hurtling toward her and the breath exploded from her lungs as she drove into the lattice-like framework and clung to it fiercely in a flurry of panic, hysteria and blessed relief.

Snyder shook his head as he watched the minuscule figures picking their way down the shuddering girders. Who would have believed it? He'd covered every angle, blocked every conceivable escape route, yet astonishing as it seemed, McKlelland and his girlfriend were getting away.

Snyder chuckled wryly as he lowered the binoculars. Despite his anger, he was filled with a sense of grudging admiration.

Chapter Eleven

Joktan regarded the American mercenaries with distaste. They had been hired by Napier Oil, and in Joktan's view looked like cut-throats to a man. In the crowded security office, they stood chewing gum while their leader, Major Arnold 'Pappy' Chesney, heavy-set and blunt-featured, confronted Joktan angrily. 'You told her what?'

Joktan did not care for Chesney and made little attempt to disguise the fact. 'I told her everything.'

A small observation window separated Chesney's office from the ante-room beyond. Here, Ellen sat under the watchful eye of an American guard. She seemed nervous, and from time to time brushed at a strand of hair which had fallen loose across her forehead.

Sahail Dhuailan, the Arab commandant, looked at Joktan sympathetically. 'Was it necessary to do that, Salih?'

'I could see little point in lying. She was going to find out soooner or later.'

'What were you doing in the desert anyhow?' Chesney demanded. 'You knew damn well all US personnel were confined to base.'

'That was a mistake. I thought it would be safe. Unfortunately, we ran into a group of nomadic tribesmen.'

'I blame you for this,' Chesney told Sahail Dhuailan. 'As commandant, you're responsible for the actions of your subordinates.'

'No one is responsible for Salih but Salih,' Dhuailan answered mildly.

Chesney examined Ellen through the glass partition.

Everything he did seemed exaggerated, as if he was constantly performing for some imaginary audience. He wore combat fatigues and a military forage cap which gave him a faintly intimidating air, but Joktan was unimpressed by the American's bravura. He regarded Chesney as a swaggerer and a braggart.

'What time is that weapon demonstration tomorrow?' Chesney asked.

'Eleven hundred hours,' Dhuailan told him.

'Supposing something happened to Miss Conway, would the others be able to compensate?'

Dhuailan's eyes flickered, but he said mildly: 'I'm sure they could.'

'In that case, we'll take care of this problem right away.'

'How?' Joktan demanded, frowning.

'Drive her to the desert. They'll never find her among all that sand.'

'But she's one of your own people.'

'What the hell? She was scheduled to die anyhow. It's only a question of timing.'

Joktan paused. He looked at Dhuailan. 'What's he talking about, scheduled?'

Dhuailan's eyes filled with guilt. 'It was always recognized, Salih, that none of the Americans could be allowed to return home again. This operation must appear to be Arab-orientated. There can be no evidence of US collusion.'

Joktan hadn't prepared himself for the final denouement. The callousness of the exercise shocked him.

Chesney said: 'I don't see what you're getting so touchy about. From what I gather, you're not exactly reticent in the assassination department yourself.'

'That's right.' Joktan looked at him coolly. 'And since I'm the one responsible for this mess, it is up to me to take care of it.'

'Think you're capable?'

'I will do whatever is necessary.'

'Okay.' A hint of contempt entered Chesney's eyes. 'You've got the talk, let's see if you've got the walk.'

He looked strangely exhilarated as Joktan moved into the other room, as if the prospect of violent death stimulated him in some curious way. 'Can you give me a guide who knows the territory hereabouts?' he said to Dhuailan.

The Iraqi was surprised. 'For what reason?'

'I don't trust that Joktan friend of yours. If he suffers a change of heart, we may have to finish the job ourselves.'

Ellen felt nauseous with terror as Joktan drove madly across the desert floor. He's going to kill me, she thought. It wasn't simply her imagination. She knew it as surely as she'd ever known anything in her life. Joktan had changed. Since leaving the air base, the scowl had never left his face and it didn't take a genius to figure out what was in his mind. Joktan's confession had stunned her, and she knew that she had now become a dangerous liability.

She tried to hide the tremor in her voice as she said: 'Where are we going?'

'Somewhere quiet. I need to escape for a while.'

'Have you been ordered to silence me?'

'Don't be a fool.' But something in his tone told her he was lying.

She had little doubt that Joktan was capable of carrying out his task. Something about the man, his air of utter certainty, convinced her he could kill at the drop of a hat. Moreover, the game in which she had become embroiled was being played for the highest stakes of all, and the fate of one individual would be meaningless in the face of that.

Her terror was making it difficult to speak as they steered into a narrow gully and Joktan brought the Land Rover to a halt. 'Get out,' he ordered.

She found her voice with an effort. 'Why?'

'Just do it.'

Her legs felt wobbly as she climbed to the ground. Joktan took out a pump-action shotgun and loaded it methodically, holding the weapon across one arm. 'Turn around.'

Stomach cringing, Ellen faced the line of sand dunes. She felt drained by a paralysing fear that made her body weak and shivery, but she was angry too, angry that she was being disposed of in such a casual and desultory manner. She hoped it would be quick. She was no stoic, God knew. She couldn't bear the thought of pain.

148

A soft wind fanned her cheeks, gently ruffling her hair. Somewhere above, a plane droned. The seconds stretched and Ellen's nerves tightened. What was the damned man doing, waiting to see her squirm, for God's sake?

She heard a scuffling noise and glanced over her shoulder to see Joktan tossing the shotgun into the Land Rover's rear. 'Get in,' he said, and Ellen felt a tremor of hope. She was still alive.

'I said get in,' he repeated irritably.

Whimpering under her breath, she scrambled into the passenger seat as Joktan backed out of the narrow draw.

'I knew the sonofabitch wouldn't do it.'

Standing on his vehicle roof, Chesney experienced a curious satisfaction as he watched Joktan through a pair of high-powered binoculars. He'd been right in his assessment of the man. Chesney had little regard for Iraqis. He had fought in the 1991 Gulf War and his opinion of the Iraqi fighting machine was one of open contempt. His view of the Arab character was even lower still.

Grouped around the Land Rover, the mercenaries watched him expectantly. 'What's happening, Pap?' Will Cronin asked.

'He's crapping out. I can see the girl in the passenger seat.'

Chesney jumped to the ground – despite his bulk, he was a graceful man in motion – and waved the mercenaries into a circle. He stood with his hands on his hips, his small eyes blazing with mingled excitement and exasperation. 'Looks like we'll have to handle this ourselves.'

Will Cronin spat on the ground, his features impassive beneath his khaki forage cap. 'Does that include the ay-rab too?'

'Of course it includes the ay-rab too.'

Duru, their Arab guide, looked uneasy. 'You are planning to eliminate Joktan?'

'The man's a traitor. He deserves to die like a traitor.'

'Then we will need more men,' Duru said.

'Are you nuts? There's eight of us, including you.'

'Eight is not enough.'

149

'Who is this guy, for Chrissake, Superman?'

'Eight is not enough,' Duru repeated stubbornly, his dark face creased with worry. 'This is Joktan's country. He knows it like the back of his hand.'

'This is our country too. Every one of my boys is ex-Special Forces, trained to survive in desert terrain. We're operating in a familiar ballpark, nephew.'

'You do not understand. Joktan is a very resourceful man.'

Chesney laughed. His face carried the intractibility of a battering ram. 'The cemeteries are full of resourceful men,' he said.

Paul and Leila sat on the cafe terrace, gazing out over San Francisco Bay. Paul felt jaded after the long haul north from Palm Springs. The memory of Kliban's death still hung vividly in his senses, and though he knew he wasn't responsible, a terrible guilt had taken hold of him. Kliban hadn't deserved to die like that; wouldn't have if he, Paul McKlelland, hadn't pressured him into meeting on the cablecar. He should have realized the man was emotionally unstable. The incident had depressed Paul so much he might have given up the search completely and gone straight to the police if it hadn't been for Leila.

He didn't quite know what to make of Leila. From the beginning he had sensed a certain ruthlessness in her, but now he was becoming conscious of something else; she was tough and relentless, it was true, but she was also brave and loyal and kind, and he knew in his heart he would never have gotten through the last few days without her.

He examined her curiously as she sipped her coffee. She was very attractive, he reflected. Not the way Ellen was attractive, but in terms of simple sex-appeal, Leila Assad, though he hadn't noticed it before, was an undeniable knock-out.

Paul was so absorbed in his reverie that for a moment he didn't notice Tom Gower walking across the road toward them. Tom was a research chemist, a tall young man with the impeccable features of a Madison Avenue model. He and Paul had been at college together and had continued their

150

friendship through the Claymont Sailing Club to which they both belonged.

Tom was smiling as he came up to their table. 'What are you doing in town on a Thursday?' he said. 'I thought wild horses wouldn't drag you away from that research bench.'

'I'm on vacation,' Paul told him. 'What you might call compassionate leave.'

'Yeah? How come?'

'Ellen's missing.'

'You're kidding me.'

'Nope. She's vanished − pouf − into thin air.'

'My God.' Tom's face sobered as he pulled up a chair. 'Have you been to the police?'

'The police think she's dead.'

'Jesus, Paul, that's awful.'

'Don't worry, I happen to know they're wrong. Unfortunately, because of the circumstances, I can't tell you why. It could endanger Ellen's life, and it might even endanger yours.'

Tom sat back in his chair, his brow puckering as he absorbed the implications of Paul's statement. 'I thought you sounded a little strained on the telephone,' he said, glancing at Leila curiously.

'This is my friend,' Paul told him. 'She's helping me look for Ellen. Her name's Leila.'

'What do you want from me?'

Paul fumbled in his pocket and took out a document he had found inside Kliban's wallet. 'This is an excerpt from some kind of report sponsored by the Napier Oil company. Don't ask me how I got it. Just read the section at the bottom of page three.'

Tom scanned the paper briefly. Most of it, written in scientific jargon, had proved incomprehensible to Paul and Leila.

'What does it mean?' Paul asked when Tom had finished.

'Some kind of progress report, that's all. I assume it's to do with the Danilo Experiment.'

'You've heard of the Danilo Experiment?'

'Sure. It's been pretty well documented in the science magazines. It started in India back in the early sixties, an attempt

151

to find a new energy source by converting waste products into bio-gas.'

'Bio-gas?' Leila echoed.

'It's a form of methane. Sometimes it comes in liquid form. The Indians were only partially successful. Unfortunately, the stuff they produced proved nowhere near as efficient as oil. More recently, the Israelis have been carrying out their own research. Nobody knows the results because they're keeping them strictly under wraps.'

'I've heard about it,' Leila exclaimed excitedly. 'It's taking place at the Mossberg Plant near Mazar.'

Paul said: 'Why would a company like Napier suddenly become interested in bio-gas experiments?'

Tom shrugged. 'Maybe they're looking for a new energy source. They know oil can't last for ever. They'd be pretty foolish not to consider the future.'

'Have you heard of Napier, Tom?'

'I believe we've had dealings with them at one time or another. If not Napier itself, at least the cartel to which they belong.'

'Cartel?' Paul said.

'Yeah. A group of small American oil companies amalgamated into a syndicate about six or seven years ago. Individually, their assets are relatively modest, but together they're worth several billion dollars. That's a lot of juice.'

'I don't suppose you happen to know the names of these companies?'

'I can find out, if you like. Give me five minutes and I'll pop up to the office and check them out on the computer.'

'Good man. It would be an enormous help, Tom.'

Paul was thoughtful as Tom hurried away. 'At last we're beginning to get somewhere,' he said.

'How's that?' Leila asked.

'Let's speculate for a moment. What's the worst thing that can happen to a man like Musallim al Shisur?'

'Death?'

'Wrong. Humiliation. And what's the one thing in the world that would really rub his nose in the dirt?'

'Poverty?'

'Exactly. Take away his oil, and he's just an impoverished desert sheikh. Supposing Israel found a way of making the Danilo Experiment work. Supposing they discovered a process which made bio-gas a viable alternative energy source. Think of the position they'd be in. They'd destroy at a stroke all economic opposition in the Middle East. Maybe al Shisur's trying to prevent that happening. Maybe that's the real reason he's preparing himself for war.'

Leila considered the thought for a moment, nudging her coffee cup around the saucer. 'And where do the Americans come into it?'

Paul said: 'Well, it isn't only the Arabs who'll suffer if oil becomes obsolete. You heard what Tom said. That US cartel is worth billions. We're not talking about businesses any longer, Leila. With that kind of bankroll, you can buy and sell countries, organize wars and revolutions. You can play God.'

'Are you saying American oil men are behind the military build-up in Iraq?'

'Maybe not behind it, but involved certainly. Isn't it possible that since their interests coincide, they've decided to join forces?'

'But the US would never turn against Israel.'

'Not the US Leila. Individuals inside the US. Very rich and powerful individuals, I might add, who have the means and influence to penetrate the security services at the topmost level. Isn't it conceivable that through high-powered bribery and the corruption of sensitively placed officials, this oil syndicate could smuggle out components of a top-secret weapon and transport it to the Middle East?'

Leila frowned. 'And Ellen?'

'Someone has to assemble the thing. They'll need experts, people with the skill and knowledge to make the device work. The question is – how lethal is Talon Blue? Is it powerful enough to allow a modest army like al Shisur's to overthrow a modern nuclear power like Israel?'

Paul felt sure he was right, but knowing it and proving it were two different things. As he considered the enormity of their problem, his initial excitement gave way to a feeling of dismay. 'We're running out of time,' he said. Unless we can put the finger on Napier, the bastards will plunge the Mid-East into war and Ellen will be right in the middle of it.'

Leila gently squeezed his hand. 'Don't worry,' she whispered. 'If the evidence is there, we'll find it.'

Tom returned twenty minutes later, carrying a slip of paper on which he had scribbled a list of names. 'Took me longer'n I figured,' he said, flopping into his chair. 'The office secretary kept hanging around, and I thought you'd want me to be discreet.'

'This is great, Tom,' Paul said, examining the information.

'There are eleven companies altogether. I didn't bother with the addresses, you can get those from the phone book. Most of them are in Texas, but Napier itself is in California and there are two more in Louisiana.'

Paul folded the paper and slipped it into his jacket pocket. 'Tom, you're a real prince.'

'Want me to make further enquiries?'

'No, forget the whole thing.' Paul and Leila rose to their feet. 'I know this sounds kind of crazy, but there are people trying to kill me. They might try to kill you too if they discover you're involved. I'll call you after it's over, and explain everything from A to Z. You have my word on that.'

'Well, good luck with Ellen.'

'Don't worry, we'll find her,' Paul said, and steered Leila into the jostling crowd.

The point at which Joktan had parked faced west toward a line of distant mountains. From the passenger seat, Ellen could see the buildings of a nearby village. For a long time she'd scarcely spoken, reasoning that Joktan, having spared her life, would hardly be in the mood to have his intentions questioned, but in the end she could restrain herself no longer. 'Why are we sitting here?' she asked.

'We need fuel and water. It's a long trek across the desert.'

'Well, isn't that a settlement over there?'

'Yes.'

'So what's the problem? Why don't we simply drive in and stock up on everything we want?'

154

Joktan's eyes were pensive, as if he was still struggling to come to terms with the recklessness of his behaviour. For eight hours, he had driven across the endless sand, refusing even to speak. Now, to Ellen's relief, she sensed his anger weakening.

'My colleagues will have already radioed most of the army posts in the area,' he explained. 'If we enter the village, we will run a serious risk of being arrested.'

She said: 'You were going to kill me back there, weren't you? You drove me into the desert for only one purpose, to leave my body for the jackals.'

'I am not going to kill you,' Joktan told her wearily. 'I am taking you to Jordan.'

'Jordan?'

'I want you to fly to the United States as quickly as possible. You are in great danger here.'

'What about you? If you return to the air base, they'll execute you.'

'Perhaps not. In any event, my *nakwa* demands it.'

'*Nakwa?*'

'My honour,' he said.

Now that Ellen's fear of dying had subsided, she was at last beginning to think again. She felt grateful to Joktan for sparing her life, deeply grateful, but she had a new commitment now. She had to get word to the outside world, broadcast it from the rooftops if possible.

'How far is it to the border?' she asked.

'About a hundred miles.'

'We should make it easily by nightfall then.'

'On paved roads perhaps, but in this terrain it will take two days at least.'

A cloud of dust rose from the direction of the village. Ellen watched it lift into the air and drift across the landscape like the vapor trail of a distant locomotive.

Joktan's eyes flashed as he reached for the shotgun. 'Get out and open the hood. Pretend that you've broken down.

'And you?'

'Don't worry about me. Just keep your head low, and try to look helpless. Nothing puts a man off his guard more than the sight of a helpless woman.'

Ellen's heart thumped as she pulled up the hood. She heard the roar of the vehicle's engine as it steadily approached. It was a giant truck with massive sand-tyres protecting it against the desert terrain.

The driver drew to a halt and pushed his head through the open window. He spoke briefly in Arabic, and Ellen tried to look flustered. 'I don't suppose you speak English, by any chance?'

The driver said something to his companion, and both men jumped to the ground. They were clad in dusty coveralls and woolly skullcaps.

'You are in trouble?' the first man asked.

Ellen smiled in relief. 'Thank God somebody understands me. I was beginning to think I'd be stuck here for ever.'

The man moved to her side and peered down at the engine parts. 'What happened?'

'It won't start, that's all.'

'Have you checked the fuel?'

'I've checked everything. I thought it might be the distributor head. It's been giving me trouble ever since I left Baghdad.'

As the two Arabs leaned forward to examine the engine, Joktan's voice cut through the air like a whiplash. 'Stand back and raise your hands.'

The men looked up and Joktan fired the shotgun, sending a brace of birds fluttering from the adjacent camel thorn. The drivers backed away in fright.

'I need all the gasoline you're carrying,' Joktan explained. 'You can keep whatever's in the fuel tank, but the rest — the spare jerry cans stacked in the rear — I want loaded into the Land Rover trunk. I also need your water supplies.'

'You would leave us in the desert without water?' the first driver said.

'The village is only a few miles up the road. You can go back and re-stock. Now get moving. My time and patience are both at a premium.'

It took the men, panting and grunting, almost fifteen minutes to transfer the fuel and water to the waiting Land Rover, and by the time they had finished, they were sweating copiously. Still holding the shotgun, Joktan took

156

out a large roll of banknotes and pushed some bills into the nearest man's coverall. 'That's to pay for the supplies.'

'It is too much.' The man looked puzzled.

'Consider the rest a reward for your silence and discretion.'

The drivers broke into delighted grins and Joktan watched them back up the truck and set off toward the distant village. As they vanished into the distance, Ellen saw a second column of dust approaching from the opposite direction. 'We've got visitors,' she said.

Joktan raised his binoculars, and she heard him whistle softly.

'What is it?' she asked.

'Land Rovers. Two.'

'Military or civilian?'

'Impossible to say. Probably Chesney.'

'Who's Chesney?'

'An American mercenary working for Napier.'

'Is he the one who wanted me dead?'

'You might say he's set his heart on it.'

Ellen examined the dust cloud worriedly. 'He's very close.'

'But not close enough.' Joktan pushed the binoculars into their leather case. 'He'll have to go to the village and stock up his supplies, and by that time we'll be well on our way to the Jordanian frontier.'

Chapter Twelve

The street looked deserted as Leila brought the Blazer to a halt. Paul peered out at the rows of little suburban houses. 'Seems quiet enough.'

'It's like a churchyard.' Leila whispered.

Most of the buildings had their shades drawn, and through the darkness, they heard the muffled murmur of TV sets. There was no visible sign of life.

'Let's chance it,' Paul said.

Seated in the rear of a parked delivery van, two men watched them climb from their truck through a tiny grille in the vehicle's hull. 'It's him,' the first man said, stubbing out his cigarette.

'You can't tell in this light.'

'Who else can it be, for Christ's sake? He's got the woman with him, and they're driving a Chevy Blazer.'

The second man whistled under his breath. 'That house belongs to his brother, Charlie, and his brother is a cop. I don't know about you, but I ain't too anxious to muscle in on a cop without being sure I've got the right party.'

'You're right,' Charlie said. He reached for the car phone. 'Let's get Snyder to make the decision.'

Twenty yards in front, Paul rang the house bell and waited patiently in the drive as footsteps echoed from the passageway inside. He winked at Leila who was peering anxiously along the street, her face pale and tense in the lamp-glow. It was Melanie who opened the door. She stared at them for a moment, then her eyes widened with surprise. 'Paul. I thought you'd gone to Palm Springs.'

'Can we come in, Melanie? I have to talk to Gus for a moment.'

She led him into the sitting room where Gus sat sprawled on the sofa, watching TV. He rose to his feet as the visitors entered, tossing a crumpled newspaper into a basket at the rear. When he saw Leila, he hurriedly buttoned his shirtfront, tucking the flaps into the waistband of his pants. 'Hey, it's nearly midnight, for Christ's sake.'

'I figured you wouldn't be in bed,' Paul said.

Gus eyed Leila admiringly. 'Things must be looking up in the Mojave. Found yourself a friend, I see.'

Paul couldn't suppress a note of pride as he introduced his new campanion. 'This is Leila. She's helping me search for Ellen.'

Gus said: 'Paul, Ellen's dead. Sooner or later, you'll have to come to terms with that.'

'Ellen's alive, Gus. Miles Kliban admitted as much.'

'You saw Kliban?'

'This morning, at Palm Springs.'

Paul hesitated. He knew it made an unlikely story and no cop in his right mind would accept it at face value, but Gus was his brother, for God's sake. Briefly, he outlined the events of the previous day while Gus listened in silence, his face expressionless.

When Paul had finished, Leila spoke for the first time. 'Kliban wasn't alone, Mr McKlelland. He had a small army spread around that cable car, and their target was your brother. Somebody's out to kill him.'

Gus shook his head in bewilderment. 'Woweeee, what've we got here?'

Paul hesitated. He glanced at the two women then said: 'Can I have a word with you in private, Gus?'

'Sure. Come on into the kitchen.'

Gus led Paul into the adjacent room and opened the refrigerator. 'Feel like a beer?'

'I think I could use one.'

Gus handed a can to Paul and leaned back against the kitchen table, opening his own with a muffled pop. His face was filled with worry and concern. 'Now what's this all about, chief?'

159

'Gus, I found some papers in Kliban's pocket. Among them was this.'

Paul handed Gus a typewritten letter. Gus put on a pair of spectacles and held it to the light. '"Miles,"' he read aloud. '"As long as the McKlelland man remains at large, there's a slight risk that he might find out about Mo Grazzini. Let's face it, San Quentin was built to keep convicts in, not respectable citizens out. Do you want me to take precautionary measures? Phone soonest, Snyder."'

'Who's Snyder?' Gus asked.

'He was the guy controlling the hoods at the cablecar.'

'Okay, but this letter doesn't tell us a damn' thing. Officially, I can't make a move, not without evidence.'

'I realize that. I plan to get you that evidence.'

'How?'

'Gus, I have to get into San Quentin. If Snyder wants this man Grazzini muzzled, he must know something pretty important.'

'You're nuts. You're not even a member of Grazzini's family.'

'Gus, Ellen's life — my life — may depend upon it.'

Gus's eyes were sober as he folded the letter and handed it back. He picked up his beer can and rolled it thoughtfully between his palms. 'There's a guy out there who owes me a favour,' he said. 'I'll give him a call in the morning and see if I can fix something.'

'Thanks, Gus. I knew I could depend on you.'

The traffic was light as Paul drove over the Golden Gate Bridge. Below, mist cradled Alcatraz Island like an ermine stole. He felt exhilarated, he realized; somebody was trying to prevent him finding Ellen, but with Gus and Leila in his corner, he knew nothing in the world could stand in his way.

Leila watched him curiously. She did not appear to share Paul's early morning exhuberance. 'How do you know this Grazzini will talk to us?' she asked.

'Instinct. The man's serving a life sentence for first degree murder, isn't he? That puts him in a very vulnerable position. If Snyder's out to silence him, Grazzini's going to need all

160

the friends he can get. He can't hide in the woodwork like you and me.'

'You plan on showing him Snyder's letter?'

'Sure.'

'Is that wise?'

'I'm gambling. I figure Grazzini will know better than anybody what his friends are capable of. If I was in his shoes, I'd be blabbing my heart out to anyone prepared to listen.'

Paul pulled off the freeway, failing to notice the unmarked delivery can which followed smoothly in his wake. For over an hour, the van had been trailing his Chevrolet through Palo Alto, San Carlos and Burlingame. Now the two men inside were filled with sudden consternation. 'This is the San Quentin road,' one of them exclaimed.

'Shit,' his companion said as the implication settled into his consciousness. He reached for the car phone. 'I'd better give Snyder the glad tidings.'

Snyder was shaving when he heard the telephone ringing.

'It's Andella,' a voice said. 'We've just crossed the Golden Gate Bridge and we're heading west toward San Quentin.'

'What about McKlelland?' Snyder asked.

'He's fifty feet in front. He's got the woman with him. It looks like they're on their way to see Grazzini.'

Snyder chuckled under his breath. 'Sonofabitch, they're a damn sight cleverer than I figured.'

'What do you want us to go, Leon?'

'Nothing. Just keep them under surveillance. I'm catching the next flight up to San Francisco.' Snyder's eyes glittered fiercely as he added: 'This time, I'll take care of McKlelland myself.'

The prison officer showed Paul and Leila into the interview room. 'They get pretty sticky about callers outside official hours,' he said, 'but you being Gus's brother, I figured it would be okay.'

Paul glanced around. He felt strangely subdued at finding himself inside one of the world's most notorious penitentiaries. The chamber was empty, except for a small table and a number of hardbacked chairs. 'No chickenwire?' he said.

161

The man shrugged. 'I can't let you into the visitors' section. I'm putting my neck on the line as it is.'

He paused as a door opened and a man entered, followed by a prison guard. The man was burly, with a blunt, dome-like skull. His wrists were handcuffed.

'Sit,' the prison officer told him.

Grazzini seated himself at the table, examining Paul and Leila suspiciously. His head was almost completely bald, and what little hair was left had been cropped close to the skin. Despite his pugilistic appearance, his eyes carried a sensitive air.

The prison officer said: 'You folks talk all you want, but my friend and I will have to remain inside the door.'

'That's okay,' Paul said, 'only can't you take the bracelets off?'

The officer hesitated, then leaned forward to unlock the handcuffs on Grazzini's wrists. The convict watched Paul and Leila warily as they drew up chairs. His face exuded a sullen defiance.

'My name's Paul McKlelland,' Paul said. 'This is Leila Assad.'

'So?'

'If you don't mind, we'd like to ask you a few questions.'

'Go screw yourself,' Grazzini said.

Paul sighed. 'Mr Grazzini, I appreciate that you've never seen us before, but for reasons which are too complicated to go into, our interests at the moment happen to coincide.'

'I don't have any interests. You think I give a shit what happens in the outside world?'

'I believe you'll care about this.'

Paul took out Snyder's letter and waved it at the prison officer standing by the door. The man nodded and Paul passed it to Grazzini. The convict's hands were large, the backs covered with thick red hair. The nails had been broken in places, and the tips were rimmed with dirt. Grazzini read the letter quickly, and Paul saw a glimmer of uneasiness appear in his eyes. 'Where did you get this?'

'Never mind where I got it. Just tell me what it means.'

'Go to hell.'

162

'Your life could depend upon it, Grazzini. I think Snyder, whoever he is, intends having you murdered. If that's true − if you know it's true − you're going to need protection, and we're the only people who can provide that.'

Grazzini re-read the letter carefully, molding the syllables with his lips. 'The bastard,' he said at last.

'Snyder?'

'Yeah.'

'Why does he want you killed?'

'Same reason he put me in here.'

Paul frowned. 'Snyder put you in San Quentin?'

'Sure. Even Snyder doesn't like murdering people unless he has to. I guess he figured this'd be the next best thing. I had too many unsavoury connections, and he wanted me out of the way.'

A slight softening in Grazzini's attitude told Paul the man was ready to unburden. He said casually: 'Who *is* Snyder, Mr Grazzini?'

'A professional troubleshooter. He does all the dirty jobs for Napier Oil. I worked with him nearly four years.'

'Doing what?'

'Anything the man asked. Legal or illegal, depending on the circumstances.'

Paul hesitated. He wasn't used to interrogation, didn't know how to phrase the questions, how to watch for the tell-tale signals which indicated lies or deception. All he understood was the simple, straightforward approach, but at least he had something to bargain with.

'Mr Grazzini, I'd like you to tell us everything you can remember about this Mr Snyder.'

Grazzini ran his fingers over his balding skull. 'Okay, fire away.'

'Let's start with how you met, shall we?'

'That was in Iraq,' Grazzini said.

'Iraq?' Paul was surprised.

'Saudi Arabia, to be exact. A little town named Khafji, right on the frontier. It was back in 1991. January 31st.'

'The Gulf War?'

'Right. I was a sergeant in the marine corps at the time. We'd been sent to the Mid-East to kick the Iraqis out of

Kuwait, and for damn near a month, we sat on our butts in the Saudi Arabian desert while our air force hammered the enemy to a standstill. Then one night, without warning, Iraqi tanks came thundering over the border and captured Khafji. Eleven marines were killed in that action – four blasted by our own side. They were the first real American casualties of the war.'

'I remember,' Paul said. 'It made quite an impact at the time.'

'For political reasons, the job of liberating the town was left mostly to the Saudis. We were ordered to remain at the rear and act as military observers. The fighting went on for most of the day, and when night fell, we lay about two miles out of town and listened to the clatter of machine guns as the Saudi troops moved in.'

Grazzini's former reticence had completely vanished; now he looked anxious, even eager to co-operate. His face glowed with a strange intensity as his eyes turned inward, recalling the past.

Seated behind his Humvee, Platoon Sergeant Mo Grazzini heard the roar of the scout car approaching and rose to his feet, brushing dust from his pants and raincoat. The driver skidded to a halt, and a Saudi captain poked his head through the side window, his olive skin gleaming in the starlight. 'Do you have a radio here, sergeant?' he asked, speaking English with a slightly sing-song accent.

'A radio, sir? Yes, sir.'

'We need an air strike on the central square. There's a T-55 blocking our route, and Iraqi infantry are holed up in the buildings behind.'

'Did you get a grid co-ordinate?' Platoon Sergeant Grazzini asked.

'No time,' the captain said. 'Just tell your people to pulverize the entire area. I'm going back to rejoin my men.'

Pfc Williams, snub-nosed and boyish, joined Grazzini as the Saudi scout clattered back toward the beleaguered town. 'Shall I call up comms?'

'No,' Grazzini told him. 'I'm not requesting an air strike

164

without a grid reference. It'll be like trying to hit a weevil in a cotton bale.'

'Sarge, if that T-55's blocking the way, those Saudis'll never get the town cleared.'

'Gary, how do you feel about taking a little ride?'

Williams' eyes sharpened in the darkness. A sudden excitement showed in his youthful features. 'Are you thinking what I think you're thinking?'

'I'm tired of sitting around. I think it's time we did something for a change.'

'We're supposed to be observers – that's the order, man.'

'Observe, hell. Call the platoon and tell them we're moving in.'

Burnt-out tanks littered the roadside as they drove into town. Khafji, once a prosperous holiday resort, lay almost completely in ruins. Most of the houses had been decimated by artillery fire, and a heavy pall of dust hung in the air, carrying with it the acrid odour of cordite. Stray dogs wandered among the rubble, scavenging for food. To Grazzini's surprise, several of the streetlamps were still flickering.

He pulled to a halt and turned to address his men. 'Webb and Landau bring the Redeye. The rest of you, follow me.'

They moved in formation through the shattered buildings, Grazzini in the lead. It was a manoeuver they had practised a thousand times before at their training camp in South Carolina, and each man knew the procedure blindfolded. Despite the cold, Grazzini was sweating heavily as he paused, panting, behind the charred skeleton of a burnt-out car. The men gathered around him in a breathless huddle. They could see the enemy tank in the square ahead, its turret swiveling as its crew examined the house-fronts for any signs of life.

'Woweeee,' Williams muttered under his breath. 'He's an ugly bastard all right.'

Grazzini snapped his fingers. 'Bring me the Redeye.'

His hands were slippery as he rose to his feet and balanced the missile tube over his left shoulder, eyeing the T-55 through the cross-hairs on the firing sight. It was the first time in his life he had gone through the procedure outside the training ground, and he knew there would be no second try if he missed.

He flicked the battery-coolant switch with his thumb, and heard a faint buzzing sound as the homer engaged. Keeping the tube level, he slipped his fist around the firing grip. Weapon steady, sight focused, he sucked in his stomach, holding his breath. Now, he thought.

There was a violent whooshing sound as he gently squeezed the trigger and the tube tilted upwards. A second later, the missle, already in flight, ignited in a shower of flame. Dry-mouthed, Grazzini watched it commence its awesome trajectory. White-hot air fanned his cheeks as the tank erupted in a violent explosion, hurling pieces of twisted metal in every direction. He saw the crew leap from the turret, and snatched up his carbine, firing a burst into the air. 'Over here, you sons-of-bitches.'

The tank crew turned toward him, raising their arms in surrender. They moved unwillingly, their slender bodies bent in attitudes of submission, some of their uniforms still smouldering visibly. Grazzini's men fanned out to form a semi-circle, their carbines at the ready. Then a fusilade of shots echoed from the buildings opposite, and bullets pinged into the wall at their rear. Williams said: 'Iraqis. They're laying down fire from across the square.'

'Move back,' Grazzini shouted.

The Americans took refuge in a nearby house, shepherding the terrified prisoners in front of them. The main room was largely intact, but its furniture had been splintered by pieces of flying shrapnel.

Grazzini ordered his men to search the Iraqi hostages, and crouching in the doorway, took stock of the situation. In his eagerness to engage the enemy, he had forgotten the back-up troops occupying the buildings behind. Now he realized that he and his men were effectively cut off. 'Get me comms,' he snapped.

The radio operator set up his equipment on the battered table and spoke into the microphone. 'Oscar Four, Bravo, this is China Zero, Tango. Do you read?'

A voice crackled through the static. 'We've got contact, sarge,' the operator said.

Grazzini picked up the microphone. 'Oscar Four, we need air spot at the following grid co-ordinates.' Taking the street map from his pocket, he spread it out on the table and located the square with his finger. Quickly, he reeled off the Iraqi positions. His hand was trembling as he switched off the transceiver. 'Nothing to do but wait,' he announced. 'The air boys'll be along in a minute.'

'Hey, sarge,' Pfc Williams said.

'What's up, soldier?'

Williams had been supervising the searching of the Iraqi prisoners. Now he looked puzzled. 'One of these characters claims to be an American. Says his name's Snyder, Leon Snyder. CIA.'

'Who's he kidding?'

'That's not all. Look at this.' Williams tossed a moneybelt on the table-top, undid one of the pouches and pulled out a wad of crisp new bills. 'Those are thousand dollar notes, sarge. Must be a million bucks inside this thing.'

Grazzini sucked in his breath and reached down, running his fingers over the banknotes. Never in his life had he seen so much money in one place.

'What should I do with him?' Williams asked.

Grazzini moistened his lips. 'Bring him over here.'

The prisoner was an athletic-looking man with a windbaked face and aquiline features. He was dressed in the uniform of an Iraqi major, and Grazzini was struck by the vitality in the stranger's eyes. Even without speaking, he exuded a powerful and dangerous magnetism.

'Your name Snyder?'

'That's right.'

'You claim to be an American?'

'I don't claim to be an American, sergeant. I *am* an American.'

'Then how come you're fighting for the other side?'

'I was riding, not fighting,' the man said patiently. 'The tank commander agreed to give me a lift across the Saudi frontier.'

'And this?' Grazzini indicated the Iraqi uniform.

'A simple disguise.' Snyder glanced at Pfc Williams. 'May I speak with you alone, sergeant?'

167

Grazzini motioned Williams to withdraw, and again ran his fingers lightly over the money belt. Snyder's expression was mocking as he said: 'Please don't imagine, sergeant, that what you are handling constitutes the spoils of the war. I am the legal owner of that property, a fact I shall be happy to authenticate in any US court of law.'

Grazzini grunted. 'Williams says you're CIA.'

'Williams is young and impressionable. I thought he might respond to the patriotic approach.'

'And me?'

'You, sergeant, are a different kind of animal.'

'I'm not sure how to take that.'

'Well, let me put it this way. How would you like to make ten thousand dollars?'

Grazzini heard bullets making little thudding noises against the outside wall. 'Give me that again?'

'Ten thousand, sergeant. No questions asked. For reasons too complicated to go into, it would be extremely embarrassing for my name to appear in any US military report. Now if you could see your way to describing me as, say, a radio correspondent escaping from Baghdad, it would make life much simpler from my point of view, and a good deal richer from yours.'

Grazzini said: 'If you're not CIA, then who in the hell are you?'

'In a sense, we are each of us soldiers — you on the military front and I on the monetary.'

Grazzini was thoughtful for a moment, studying Snyder reflectively. The man was like an alligator, dangerous and unpredictable, but the money was tempting, Grazzini had to admit. God knew, he was no plaster saint, had never professed to be. He lived by his wits, grabbing what he could, and an opportunity like this only happened once in a lifetime.

He paused as the roar of aircraft reached them from above.

'It's the Thunderbolts,' Williams exclaimed.

The troops began to cheer, pounding their carbine butts on the floor, and Grazzini glanced at the money belt, his resistance wilting. 'You got a deal,' he whispered.

Snyder took out ten one-thousand dollar bills and pushed them down the front of Grazzini's tunic. He was smiling as he followed the banknotes with a business card. 'Give me a call when you get out of the army,' he said. 'I can always find use for a man who's corruptable.'

'Snyder was with the Iraqis?' Paul said when Grazzini finished his story.

'Snyder was *leading* the Iraqis. The attack on Khafji was carried out on Snyder's instructions.'

'That's crazy.'

'It's the way it happened.'

'So why did you take his money?' Leila demanded.

'I figured, what the hell, maybe the guy really was a spook.'

'And you falsified the reports?'

'Sure. As it happened, Snyder hadn't been lying altogether. He'd been with CIA for nearly fourteen years before they paid him off. It made him pretty bitter.'

'How did you get together again?' Paul inquired.

'When I got my discharge papers in April 1995, Snyder took me on as part of his outfit. It was kind of a security organization allied to Napier and the Texas oil cartel.'

'Involving what?'

'Mostly routine stuff – acting as bodyguard to the big executives, checking out conference rooms, that sort of thing. Then Snyder started sending me on specialized assignments. Sometimes I had to deliver money. I never knew the exact amounts.'

'And the destinations?'

'Dissident groups in Central and South America, sometimes government ministers behind the Eastern Block. Occasionally, the rulers of Third World countries.'

'Didn't it strike you as odd – an American oil company dealing in international politics?'

'Napier was like that. They bought and sold nations the way some organizations buy and sell people. Anything which threatened the price of oil was regarded as a potential target. Revolutions were organized, opposition parties given financial, sometimes military backing. Snyder had ways of getting his hands on defence material and moving it around the world. He set up such a confusing array of front companies, it was impossible to trace where the weapons came from.'

'Have you ever heard of a system called Talon Blue?' Leila asked.

'Nope.'

'You're sure? think hard, Mr Grazzini. Could the name have been mentioned at any of Napier's meetings?'

'Grazzini shrugged. 'Not in my presence. It's a new one on me.'

Paul said: 'What else did Snyder specialize in?'

'On a smaller scale, he blackmailed politicans, ruined the reputations of people he regarded as dangerous. If the evidence didn't exist, Snyder had it fabricated. He was good at that. Said he'd learned it at the CIA.'

'Can you tell us what Snyder looks like, Mr Grazzini?'

Grazzini paused for a moment, then fumbled in his pocket and took out a battered wallet. 'I reckon I can do better than that,' he said.

He waved the wallet at the guard and when the man nodded, Grazzini slid out a faded photograph. The photograph showed a group of businessmen seated around a swimming pool. Grazzini himself figured prominently, though it was clear that his role was a strictly subordinate one. The other members of the group looked prosperous and expensively dressed.

Grazzini pointed to a powerfully built figure with pointed features. 'That's Snyder.'

Paul examined the man carefully. Snyder was not someone who would melt into a crowd, he thought. 'Mr Grazzini, would you mind if we held on to this for a while?'

'Help yourself.'

'I can get it photo-copied, if you like, and send the original back.'

'Forget it,' Grazzini said. 'I don't know why I keep the thing anyhow. It gives me bad memories.'

'How did your relationship with Snyder turn sour?' Leila asked.

For an infinitesimal moment Grazzini's eyes glistened, and Paul looked at him, frowning.

'It happened because of a girl,' Grazzini said. 'Her name was Anne Holmes. I met her at a political convention in Washington DC. She was a journalist covering the event for the local TV station, and we got involved. It went on for almost eleven months before Snyder found out. He said she could create serious problems for Napier and ordered me to give her up.'

'What happened?'

'I tried, God help me, I tried, but I just couldn't do it.'

'So you went on meeting in secret?'

Grazzini nodded, and nipped the bridge of his nose. 'Snyder got word eventually. He always does. We had a place we used to go to, an apartment belonging to a friend. One night, after dinner, I passed out on the couch. Next thing I know, somebody's slapping my cheek and the place is crawling with cops. Anne . . .' He paused, and closing his eyes, took a deep breath. Beads of sweat showed among the sparse red hairs coating the dome of his skull. 'She was hanging by her wrists from the central heating pipe, her skin covered with blood. She'd been beaten to death. There was blood on my knuckles which matched Anne's in the laboratory tests. They nailed me on murder one, and I've been here ever since.'

Paul sat back in his chair, examining the convict thoughtfully. It seemed an unlikely story, but something in Grazzini's manner convinced him the man was telling the truth.

Grazzini's muscles were rippling furiously along his forearms. 'I didn't do it,' he insisted, his voice faltering. 'It was Snyder. He must have put something in the wine.'

'And you told no one any of this?' Leila said.

'You think it would have done any good? Half the guys in here claim they've been deliberately framed.'

Paul slipped the photograph into his pocket, his mind suddenly made up. Grazzini was too intense to be play-acting. At last, the pieces were beginning to fit into place. 'Mr Grazzini, we're not exactly people of influence, but my brother has arranged for you to be put in solitary for the next few days as a simple precautionary measure. We'll be investigating your story, and if it's any comfort, I think we can safely promise a re-opening of your case.'

The desert seemed endless, unbroken, implacable. Ellen had lost count of the hours she'd spent being jostled, choked, jolted and buffeted as Joktan headed west, his rutted sand-tyres kicking up thick clouds of dust. They were like ants on a giant pool table, she thought, and for some reason the analogy depressed her for it emphasized how precarious their position had become. Joktan had spared her life, it was true, but the knowledge she carried in her head made her a dangerous and threatening liability; the Americans would have to kill her if they wanted their monstrous conspiracy to succeed. From time to time, she glanced nervously in the driving mirror, but to her relief, the horizon remained tranquil and clear.

After a while, the country began to change in slow, subtle ways. The foothills flattened out, turning into a vast pancake of land where Joktan was obliged to reduce his speed to minimise the vibrations from the hard-packed sand-furrows. He plotted his route by a Swedish Silva jewelled-bearing compass fixed into the vehicle's dashboard, following balises erected by the Hazelhoff Expedition of 1962. The balises looked black against the quiltwork of the desert sand. Soon, they were rolling toward a line of distant foothills.

'Is this the frontier road?' Ellen asked.

Joktan seemed amused. 'Calling it a road is a euphemism,' he said.

'What would you call it then?'

'It's a Class 'C' route, illegal to anyone without an official permit. You can see why.'

'Shouldn't we stay away from the markers? We're leaving a trail a blind man could follow.'

'Don't worry. Soon we'll be into the mountains and after that, there *is* only one way. This is it.'

The wind, surprisingly cool, lashed their vehicle in steady, persistent gusts, and after a while Ellen saw the craggy ramparts of the peaks ahead. They drank copiously, saturating their bodies with moisture, while Joktan checked the tyres, deflating them to absorb the bumps and abrasions.

The track began to climb, and soon they were winding their way through a baffling complexity of gullies. To Ellen, each new canyon looked indistinguishable from the rest, but Joktan drove confidently along the uneven roadway. The sun dipped, and veils of shadow began to gather in the valleys. Night soon, Ellen thought. What then?

Her worries were solved when they spotted the pale columns of cooking fires ahead. Ellen saw a cluster of nomadic tents and the shadowy outlines of people. Bundles of food hung in the trees, out of reach of hungry predators. At a crude well, flanked by hewn-logs, a group of young women were drawing water and pouring it into massive jars.

'Bedouin,' Joktan exclaimed with quiet satisfaction. 'They're camping at Shaiba, gathering the salt.'

'Will they help us?'

'Depends. If they're Bait Kabir, they'll probably regard me as an enemy. On the other hand, if they're Bani bu Saar, they'll feel bound to offer us desert hospitality.'

Some of the larger tents were made of leather, with grass mats stretched over wooden frames. In front of these, the men sat cross-legged, watching their approach in sombre silence. They looked fierce and primitive, and Ellen felt her stomach muscles quiver. Children ran toward them, yodelling a shrill, discordant welcome.

Joktan said: 'We're in luck. These are people of the Rualik. It's unusual to find them this far north.' He nodded toward a wall of small brown bricks. 'That's salt. They drain it out of the earth and press it into those moulds to dry. In a few days, it'll be solid enough to pack on to the backs of camels.'

'Will they harm us?'

'Of course not. Wait inside the truck while I talk to the elders. They will probably offer me tea, it's the desert custom. If they offer four rounds and then withdraw the pot, that means it's inconvenient for us to stay and we'll have to move on as quickly as possible. If, however, they offer three and no more, they'll be signifying that we are free to remain as their guests.'

'They look awfully ferocious to me,' Ellen said, eyeing the swarthy faces.

Joktan laughed. 'The Bedouin are proud, arrogant and warlike, but they're also the most hospitable people on earth.'

A party of children stood examining Ellen owlishly as Joktan approached the circle of warriors and went through the elaborate desert greeting. Ellen tried to look relaxed, which wasn't easy in the circumstances, she reflected. It was okay for Joktan, he knew the territory, but she was a tourist here, and she was tired, confused and frightened.

After a while, Joktan returned, shooing the children away. 'The Rualik have recognized me,' he told her. 'I've explained our predicament, and they've invited us to spend the night under their protection.'

'What about your friend Chesney?'

Joktan's teeth flashed in the darkness. 'The Rualik will take care of him,' he said.

Arnold 'Pappy' Chesney squinted through the windshield as their driver, Will Cronin, picked his way nervously across the mountain terrain. Their headlamps sent cones of light slicing through the gloom, but somehow the landscape seemed to lose perspective, making driving perilous in the extreme.

Chesney was filled with an almost feverish impatience. It had always been his greatest weakness, he knew, but he just couldn't help himself. Joktan's treachery had angered him deeply. You could never trust an Arab, he'd learned that in the Gulf War. Sooner or later, the bastards would always let you down. Moreover, Joktan was arrogant, refused to take orders, and worse still treated Chesney and his mercenaries with an air of barely concealed contempt. Chesney was looking forward to seeing how superior Joktan felt with a carbine pressed against his belly, but first they had to catch the bastard and there was an awful lot of space for a man and woman to lose themselves in.

Chesney's eyes, slitted against the gloom, spotted something in the hollow ahead. 'Cooking fires,' he exclaimed.

'Bedouin, probably,' Duru, their Arab guide, told him from the rear. 'They come to Shaiba to gather salt.'

'Didn't you say Joktan himself was a Bedu?'

'This is so,' Duru acknowledged gravely.

174

'Well, where else would the sonofabitch hide than among his own people?'

Duru looked troubled. He glanced at the little band of mercenaries and said: 'Major, it would be most unwise to approach these tribesmen fully armed. Like Joktan, their emotions are simple and direct. Take weapons into their camp, and they will regard you as an enemy.'

'They can regard us how the hell they like,' Chesney said, his eyes mocking. 'I think we're more than a match for a bunch of extras from *The Desert Song*.'

Only a handful of warriors were seated around the cooking fires as the two Land Rovers shuddered to a halt. The women and children had withdrawn discreetly out of sight. The Bedouin watched in silence as the seven mercenaries and their Arab guide moved warily into the firelight. Chesney spat on the ground, wiping his mouth with his tunic sleeve. 'Ask if anyone's passed this way in the last couple of hours,' he told Duru.

Duru spoke in Arabic, and the Rualik headman answered tersely.

'He says they've been camping here for the past three days. Before our arrival, they'd seen no one since leaving the Plain of Qamaiqam.'

'Tell him he's a lying bastard. Tell him we know damn well he's hiding Joktan somewhere in his encampment. Tell him either he turns him in or we'll tear his tents to ribbons. Translate that word for word. I want the sonofabitch to understand exactly what I'm saying.'

Fifty feet away, Joktan chuckled softly as he and Ellen watched the encounter from behind the folds of a Bedouin blanket.

'What's going on?' Ellen asked. Despite the chill, she felt sweat beading her cheeks and throat.

'Chesney's employing his diplomatic charm.'

'Will the Rualik betray us?'

'They'd sooner die.'

The Arabs' eyes flashed as Duru translated his message, but their expressions remained stony and impassive.

'Did you phrase it exactly like I said?' Chesney demanded when Duru had finished.

175

'Word for word, major. I promise.'

'And their answer?'

'They gave no answer.'

'Then I guess maybe it's time we kicked a little ass.' Chesney turned to his men. 'Spread out and search the encampment. Anyone tries to interfere, crack his skull with your carbines.'

The mercenaries were on the point of obeying when a series of clicks echoed in the darkness. Against the silence of the night, the sounds were alien and intimidating. Chesney felt a chill settle on his throat as robed figures rose from the surrounding rocks, covering them with old-fashioned rifles. The move was so sudden, so unexpected, that for a moment the Americans could only gape in astonishment. Chesney moistened his lips as he stared at the warriers confronting them. Several wore face-cloths so that only their eyes were visible; dark and expressionless, they glinted fiercely in the firelight.

Duru tugged at Chesney's sleeve. 'Major, I beseech you. Unless we withdraw at once, we will be in serious danger here.'

Chesney cursed under his breath. He'd ignored the training of a lifetime, underestimated the enemy. It had been stupid and unprofessional, and he had to struggle to keep his voice from trembling. 'Okay, back to the trucks, boys, slow and easy. I guess our ay-rab friends have caught us with our pants down.'

Nervously, the mercenaries backed toward their vehicles, watching the tribesmen with anxious faces. They piled on board, and the two Land Rovers swung back the way they had come, roaring out of the clearing in a thick cloud of dust.

Chesney pounded the dashboard, his face contorted with rage. 'That bastard's in there, I'm sure of it. Why else would they go to so much trouble to set up an ambush? They're protecting Joktan and the Conway woman both.'

'Why don't we hit the mothers from behind?' Cronin said.

Chesney rubbed his temple with his fingertip, trying to force himself to think. 'No, I don't want to engage in a firefight if we can help it – too many complications after-wards. My hunch is, Joktan will try to sneak out sometime before dawn. We'll bed down for the night and post sentries on the bluff above, where they can watch the Bedouin encampment.'

'And then?'

Chesney shrugged. 'Then we wait.'

Dinner was eaten in the open, in front of the central cooking fire. The tribesmen gathered around a huge metal plate with the women at their rear. The plate contained some kind of mealy substance, rather like porridge, scattered with pieces of chicken and lightly charred lamb. Leaning forward, the men plucked out mosels with their fingers.

Ellen eyed the substance dubiously, still shaking after the confrontation with Chesney and his men. 'What is that stuff?' she demanded.

'It's a cereal, one of the mainstays of the Bedu diet.'

'I'm not likely to find any sheeps' eyes buried in there, am I?'

'Unlikely. We may be honoured guests, but we're not that honoured.'

As Ellen reached for a piece of food, Joktan tapped her lightly on the wrist. 'It's bad manners for the women to eat first.'

'You're kidding me.'

'Women wait, that's the rule.'

'But I'm starving.'

'This isn't Manhattan, remember. Female emancipation is a little late in reaching the Bedu.'

Ellen looked at him incredulously, then glanced at the women hovering in the rear. Any idea she'd had that Joktan might be joking was instantly dispelled. 'I can't believe this.'

'Our hosts will make a few allowances in view of the fact that you are a westerner,' Joktan said, 'but for the sake of simple politeness, you really ought to follow tribal protocol.'

'But they're living in the Stone Age.'

'Speaking personally,' Joktan said, chewing happily on a chicken leg, 'I find their attitude remarkably civilized.'

177

Ellen glared at him. 'As an educated man, you ought to know better.'

'And as an educated lady, you ought to realize that in view of our circumstances, it might be prudent if we observed a few local customs. For example, the Bedu admire a woman who displays an appropriate degree of devotion. They would regard it as commendable if you were seen to be ... well ... pampering me.'

'What?'

'You might start by feeding me succulent morsels from the dinner plate, that sort of thing.'

Ellen was outraged. 'That's the most insulting thing I ever heard.'

'Careful. Some of these tribesmen might speak English, and they can be very ugly when their tempers are aroused.'

'You're doing this on purpose, damn you!'

Gritting her teeth, she plucked some food from the dinner bowl and jammed it fiercely between Joktan's lips. He grinned as he washed it down with a mouthful of water. 'Now you're getting the idea.'

By the time the men had finished their meal, Ellen was ravenous. She tore at the pieces of meat, cramming them into her mouth with handfuls of the mealy-thick porridge-like substance. The food tasted heavy and stodgy, but she tempered it with acrid black coffee which the Arabs served in small silver bowls.

Afterwards, her hunger satisfied, she sat gazing into the flames as the air around them chilled in the grip of the mountain night. One of the women brought her a blanket and she wrapped it around her shoulders, wriggling closer to the cooking fire.

'Cold?' Joktan asked.

'Freezing.'

'This is mountain country. Temperature always drops at night.'

She looked at him curiously. She knew he had been teasing her, and it was the first time since they'd met that she had seen Joktan display a sense of humour. Now however, his features were dark and sombre.

'How long can we stay here?' she asked.

178

'Few hours, no more. I want to move out before day-break.'

'What about Chesney and his men? They're bound to have sentries watching the encampment.'

Joktan picked up his dinner knife and examined it carefully for a moment. It was an elegant dagger crusted with silver moons. 'Get some sleep,' he told her. 'Don't worry about the sentries.'

Then he tucked the weapon into his waistband, and vanished into the gloom.

Chesney shivered in the chill dawn air as he started up the stony embankment. Cronin walked at his side, his cheeks hollow with shock. On the escarpment tip, the little group of mercenaries waited in silence, their faces unshaven in the brightening daylight.

Chesney felt stunned by the events of the past few hours. A terrible anger had started inside him, an anger born partly from frustration and partly from the awareness that he was being outsmarted at every turn.

When he reached the summit and saw the bodies of Werner and Massino, his anger developed into a smouldering rage. 'How long have they been like this?'

'Probably less'n an hour,' Cronin said. 'Blood hasn't dried yet.'

Chesney stared at the bloody corpses. He hadn't cared for Massino, but Tim Werner had been a good old boy; they'd fought together during the '91 Gulf War, and Werner had been steadfast to the core.

Duru, their Arab guide, regarded the bodies with superstitious dread. 'This is Joktan's work,' he whispered. 'He moves like the wind and vanishes into the night.'

'He's a slippery bastard all right,' Chesney said.

He spat on the ground, and jerked his head at the Land Rovers. 'Fetch the shovels, and let's get these boys buried before they smell up the entire valley.'

'Then what, Pappy' Cronin asked.

'Then we'll run that sonofabitch to earth.' Chesney's eyes looked murderous as he added: 'I'm going to take a personal pleasure in skinning his barbaric hide.'

179

Chapter Thirteen

The newspaper office bustled with activity. In the cramped little waiting room, Paul and Leila watched through a glass partition as typewriters clicked, word-processors hummed and young men and women bellowed deafeningly into their telephones. Why was it, Paul wondered, that an essential part of newspaper life seemed to involve operating in a state of perpetual confusion?

'Who is this man we've come to see?' Leila asked.

'His name's Harry Mullford. He works on the gossip page.'

'You certainly have a wide variety of friends.'

'Oh, Harry isn't a friend. He's what you might call an ancient adversary. As a matter of fact, he probably dislikes me more than anyone else alive. Harry wanted to marry Ellen − probably would have, if I hadn't shown up. He never forgave me for that. I guess there are some things a man never forgets.'

'Think he still cares about her?'

'I'm counting on it. Harry Mullford wouldn't raise a finger to help me, but he might do it for Ellen.'

Paul paused as the door opened and Mullford himself came into the room. He was a studious-looking man in a polo-necked sweater. When he saw Paul, his eyes flashed belligerently. 'I got your phone message. It sounded rather cryptic.'

'You know I wouldn't approach you if it wasn't important, Harry.' Paul indicated Leila. 'This is Miss Assad.'

Mullford nodded. 'Where's Ellen?'

'She's disappeared.'

'Disappeared? What does that mean?'

'It means I don't know where she is.'

'My God, have you been to the police?'

'It isn't as simple as that. Please listen to me for a moment, Harry, because I need your help. I realize that might sound a little presumptuous in the circumstances, but I happen to believe that Ellen's in great physical danger, and if you really care about her, you'll do as I say with no questions asked.'

'What the hell is this? Are you drunk or what? Where do you think you get off, coming here with a story like that?'

'Harry, I'm begging you. On my knees. Ellen's life may depend on this. You've got to believe me.'

Mullford examined Paul for a moment, impressed by his earnestness. Then he said: 'What do you want from me?'

Paul took out the photograph Grazzini had given him at San Quentin. 'This is a picture of a man Leon Snyder. He works for a company called Napier Oil. Back in 1991, during the Gulf War, he was operating behind Iraqi lines. Do you think you could check through your records and see if you can find any reference either to Snyder himself, or to Napier, or to any of the companies mentioned on this list.'

Mullford looked flabbergasted. 'For God's sake, what has the Gulf War to do with Ellen Conway?'

'Trust me, Harry. You promised.'

Mullford sighed. 'Okay, give me the bumf and I'll see what I can do.'

Mullford returned almost an hour later, carrying an enlargement taken from the newspaper files. His air of sullenness had vanished. Now he looked puzzled and intrigued. 'Won't you tell me what the hell is going on here?'

'If I could, I would,' Paul said. 'You've just got to trust me, Harry.'

Mullford dropped the picture on the waiting-room table. 'Well, I could find no reference to Snyder in the computer bank, but while I was combing through the picture file, this turned up.'

Paul leaned over to study the photograph carefully. It had been taken at the height of the Allied operations to liberate

Kuwait. It showed the Iraqi ruler, Sadaam Hussein, seated in his underground bunker with members of his personal staff. Paul's eyes widened as he examined the officer on Sadaam Hussein's right. There could be no mistaking the hawk-like features or the cruel, predatory mouth. The officer was Leon Snyder.

On 3 May Mossad Director Jacob Jabari was called to the office of the Israeli Prime Minister, Ariel Aronson. Aronson was a heavy-set man with snow-white hair whose humorous manner had been known to disconcert many of his political colleages. On this particular morning, however, his expression was grim and he wasted little time in getting down to business. 'We've had a report from our satellite people. Al Shisur's drawn up his forces on the Jordanian border. He'll be ready to move in a matter of hours.'

Jabari frowned. 'War?'

'What else? The man's insane. Does he think we're going to stand by and let him launch his attack without retaliation?'

'Have you protested to the Jordanian authorities?'

'Talking to Jordan's like talking to thin air. Nothing would please them more than to see al Shisur march right through to Jerusalem. They keep bleating about their access treaty, claiming the maniac has a legal right to cross Jordanian territory.'

'What are you going to do, Prime Minister?'

'What else can I do? Fight, naturally. However, I gave the Americans my word we wouldn't break the peace agreements, which means that unless I allow al Shisur the first punch, Israel will become the aggressor in the eyes of the world.'

Jabari pursed his lips, his eyes worried and reflective. He had told the premier nothing about his attempt to assassinate Joktan in the United States. The issue had seemed too sensitive to entrust to higher authority. Now it was clear he could keep the affair secret no longer. 'There *is* another matter you may not be aware of.'

'What's that?'

'We discovered, quite accidentally, that Salih Joktan had been spotted in San Francisco.' Jabari hesitated, knowing the effect his announcement would have. 'We sent in a team to eliminate him.'

Aronson looked thunderstruck. 'You did what?'

'We had to. We knew he was after the Talon Blue weapon system.'

'Why didn't you tell me this?'

'Would you have sanctioned the operation if I had?'

'Of course not. I'd have ordered you to notify the US authorities.'

'And then what? Joktan deported, flown back to Iraq to plan a new wave of terrorism? At least our way, the solution was permanent.'

'What solution? Is Joktan alive or dead?'

'Alive, regrettably,' Jabari admitted with a sigh. 'Only one of our people survived the encounter, and he's probably in the hands of the US authorities which means we have to assume that Joktan could have Talon Blue already in his possession.'

Aronson walked to the window and stared down at the buildings below. Never in his life had Jabari seen the Prime Minister so angry or determined. 'I'm calling an emergency session of the Defence Committee,' Aronson said. 'In the circumstances, I think we'll have to consider the possibility of launching an immediate pre-emptive strike against Iraq.'

At five pm the following evening, US President Lawrence Clayman spoke to the Israeli Prime Minister by telephone. The call had been Clayman's idea, though his suggestion had been welcomed by Secretary of State, Frank Hamilton. Both men sat in the Oval Office while the President urged Aronson to show restraint.

'In our experience, restraint is simply another word for appeasement,' Ariel Aronson said. 'Israel has learned over the years what to expect from her Arab neighbours. Despite the peace treaties, we've encountered a constant undercurrent of hostility.'

'Nobody's asking you to sit quietly and take it,' Clayman told him. 'By all means mobilize your troops, set up your defence positions. But for the sake of peace, for the sake of reason, wait till al Shisur shows his hand. There's still a chance we can negotiate.'

'Would you negotiate with a loaded pistol at your head, Mr President? Our intelligence sources suggest al Shisur may be in possession of a highly innovative US weapon system named Talon Blue.'

Clayman blinked. Placing his hand over the receiver, he spoke to the Secretary of State. 'What in God's name is Talon Blue?'

Hamilton shrugged. 'Search me.'

The President said: 'I'm sorry, Prime Minister, I don't quite follow. Are you suggesting the US administration has been supplying al Shisur with arms? Because if that is so, I must emphasize, sir, that there is no question of any military equipment being dispatched from this country to the Middle East.'

'I did not claim it was an official transaction,' Aronson replied. 'Nevertheless, we desperately need to know what it is we are up against. Can you tell me anything about the way Talon Blue functions?'

'Ariel, it's hard for me to admit this, but until a moment ago, I'd never heard the name Talon Blue in my life. However, I'll investigate, and if there is such a device, and if there's any evidence that it's fallen into the wrong hands, I'll call you back immediately. In the meantime, will you give me your word that Israel will not launch a pre-emptive strike?'

'I'm sorry, Mr President, but we must reserve the right to defend ourselves by any means necessary. Including nuclear missiles.'

'For God's sake, Ariel, at least wait a day or two! In the words of the old song, give peace a chance.'

'You might pass that message to al Shisur,' Aronson replied, and hung up the telephone.

The President outlined the details of his conversation to the Secretary of State, and both men contemplated the subject moodily.

'What *is* this Talon Blue?' Clayman said. 'Is it possible al Shisur really has managed to get his hands on some new Pentagon prototype?'

'Sounds unlikely, but I'll check it out, Larry. In the meantime, the UN General Secretary is flying out to the Mid-East in a last-ditch attempt to change al Shisur's mind.'

'That doesn't cheer me at all. We're not dealing with a rational man.'

'I know, it's a hell of a long shot,' Hamilton agreed. 'In the happy proverbial phrase, Larry, it looks as if the shit is about to hit the fan.'

Jo Marian Lee watched uneasily as Talon Blue was wheeled out of its hangar into the blinding sunlight. It looked grotesque on the concrete apron, its spindrel-like arms sprouting in every direction like some form of exotic plant. The workmen strained and panted as they eased it delicately into position, and Jo glanced at her watch. Ten fifty-five. The demonstration had been scheduled for eleven. Another few minutes and they would discover at last what they had been creating here. But Jo had something more worrying on her mind.

She drew Victor Conville gently aside. 'Vic, I've got to talk to you.'

'Yeah? What's wrong?'

'It's Ellen. She didn't get home last night. Her bed hasn't been slept in.'

'That's funny. She wasn't in the officers' club either.'

'I know. She went for a drive with Joktan.'

'Joktan?' Conville's eyes crinkled with amusement. 'That wily sunofabitch!'

'Don't be an idiot, it's not what you're thinking. She was trying to ferret out information, that's all. We think ... that is, Ellen and I *know* ... that this prototype business is nothing but a front. Something really weird is going on here.'

Conville looked amused. 'You're going to tell me about the army hiding in the desert?'

'I saw it with my own eyes.'

'So what? This is a military training area, isn't it?'

'It isn't only the army, dummy. There are no houses, no people, no sign of human habitation for almost a million miles.'

'Meaning?'

'Meaning that isn't Pheonix out there, and this isn't Arizona either.'

Conville was about to speak when they heard sounds of movement and turned to see a cavalcade of limousines approaching from the main gate, flanked on each side by motor-cycle patrolmen. The fleet was piloted front and rear by police cars with flashing lights. For the first time, Jo noticed army marksmen dotting the surrounding rooftops.

'Looks like our guest of honour is arriving,' Conville said.

As the convoy drew to a halt, men spilled into the sunlight, running to form a cordon around the central limousine. One of the vehicle's side windows opened and a man peered up at the bizarre contraption towering above them. Jo clutched at Victor Conville's sleeve. 'My God,' she whispered. 'It's Musallim al Shisur, the President of Iraq.'

'You're nuts. What would the Iraqi President be doing here?'

'I tell you, I've seen his picture on TV.'

A heavy humming sound started behind them, muffling the sound of Jo's voice, and she turned to look at Talon Blue which had begun almost imperceptibly to vibrate. There was no visible sign of movement, but along its generator, lights flashed and girders shuddered as the demonstration got under way.

For almost twenty minutes, they watched the machine steadily pulsating, then as suddenly as it had started, it ground to a halt. Without a word, the security guards climbed back into their limousines and started out across the desert floor.

'That's *it*?' Conville grunted with disappointment.

'Not quite. I think our transport's just arriving.'

With a muffled clatter, a mini-bus drew to a halt at the weapon site, and the three scientists scrambled on board. The driver, a bearded Iraqi in dark sunglasses, set off in the cavalcade's wake, and Jo narrowed her eyes against the heat-haze as she stared across the shimmering plain. After a while, she spotted a military convoy ahead, its vehicles scattered in disarray. As the mini-bus approached, she saw soldiers staggering about in mindless confusion. Many lay unconscious in the dust or sat on the ground, gazing dazedly into space. Others reeled and lurched among the stationary trucks. They looked comical, as if the entire division had drunk itself into a stupor.

Jo felt a numbness permeating her body. 'Dear God,' she whispered to Conville, 'are we responsible for *this*?'

All day, Major Arnold 'Pappy' Chesney had followed the line of painted *balizes* which marked the route to the Jordanian border, leaving the mountains behind and entering the awesome grid-iron of the open plain. He had no way of knowing if the tyre marks in the sand had been left by Joktan's vehicle or some earlier traveller who had chosen this gruelling route for reasons known only to himself, but Duru, their Arab guide, felt confident Joktan would follow the markers at least as far as the frontier line, and Chesney had to admit that Duru had been right on just about everything else so far.

Chesney's staying power was beginning to wear alarmingly thin. The Land Rover's vibrations had shaken his body to the core, and the endless hours of driving had dulled his brain into a torpor. He scarcely knew why he was doing this, forcing himself on beyond logic or reason. The woman had to be silenced, true, but they had contacts in Jordan who could accomplish the task just as skilfully, so why was he punishing himself? It was because of Joktan, he realized. He owed it to Massino and Werner. He owed it to himself. Nothing mattered except Joktan's death.

Already, the sun was beginning to set, and deep shadows lay across the shattered boulders littering both sides of the track.

'Pap,' said Tony Bowen from the rear. 'Can we stop for a minute? I need to piss.'

'Piss in your pants,' Chesney ordered curtly.

'In my pants, sir?' Bowen echoed. 'Yes, sir.'

No way, Chesney thought grimly, no way was he going to stop. Not until Joktan stopped, and the bastard seemed tireless, damn his greasy hide. The task of disposing of Joktan had taken on new significance during the past twenty-four hours. No longer was it a necessary, faintly unpleasant chore. Now it had become a sacred mission.

'Smoke,' Cronin said suddenly from the rear, and Chesney sat forward with a start.

He had been so engrossed in thought his attention had begun to waver. Now his senses quickened as he squinted through the dust-caked windshield.

They had entered a vast sea of rolling sand dunes, with feathery crests towering above them on every side. The setting sun cast shadows across the bulging slopes, and directly ahead, Chesney saw a willowy smudge curling skyward. A cooking stove.

Slamming his foot on the brake, he flagged down the second Land Rover. 'It's Joktan,' he said. 'Who else would be nosing around this miserable craphole?'

Waving at his men, he set off up an adjacent sand dune, sweat trickling down his stubbled cheeks. He was panting hard by the time he reached the summit. Directly below, he saw Joktan's Land Rover parked beside a patch of spindly acacia trees. A small pup tent had been erected at the vehicle's rear. The woman, Ellen Conway, was leaning over the paraffin stove, stirring something in a metal pot. There was no sign of Joktan himself.

'Where is he, Pap?' Bowen asked, climbing up to join Chesney.

'Inside the tent, I guess. Think you can pick 'em off from here?'

'In this light?' Bowen looked dubiously at the sky. 'Tricky, Pap. We ought to get a little bit closer.'

Chesney studied the terrain below. At one side of their dune, a shallow ditch meandered for several hundred feet before blending into the flatness of the open plain. It offered only moderate cover, but Chesney calculated it would take his mercenaries to within fifty or sixty yards of their target. 'We'll use that ditch as an approach route,' he whispered.

He slithered down the slope, followed by his men, and wriggled into the slender defile. Dust oozed into his shirt and camel thorn tore at his bedraggled clothing as he wormed, belly-flat, along the rubble-strewn bottom. The air was beginning to cool with the onset of evening, but Chesney's skin felt feverish with excitement. He tried to judge the distance, fixing his gaze on the shallow dirt wall, then he signalled his men to a halt and raised his head cautiously above the ditch-rim. He saw Joktan's Land Rover barely fifty yards distant. There was still no sign of Joktan himself.

As Chesney watched, the woman made her way casually to the driving seat and with no sign of haste, slid behind the wheel and started up the engine. He blinked in puzzlement, then cursed savagely under his breath as he realized her intention.

He swung up his rifle, clawing at the safety catch, but with a thunderous roar, the Land Rover burst into life and sped off across the open plain. Chesney opened fire, watching the tracer bullets arc eerily into the twilight. His men joined in, their carbines creating a deafening barrage which seemed to echo inside Chesney's head. The pup-tent disintegrated under the blistering rifle fire, its tattered canvas fluttering in the wind. A sudden iciness clutched at Chesney's stomach as he realized there was still no sign of Joktan. 'Sweet suffering Jesus,' he whispered hoarsely. 'The Land Rovers.'

He rose to his feet and began to run, his men galloping along in his wake. He couldn't believe how easily he'd been fooled. He'd fallen prey to the oldest enemy of all, his own emotions.

He was halfway up the sand dune when a deafening explosion split the air, and Chesney groaned as he watched a column of flame shoot into the sky. A second explosion followed the first, reverberating across the dappled slopes.

Chesney reached the summit and stood staring down at the blazing Land Rovers, his men gathering around him. In a hollow, the two vehicles were engulfed in flame.

'How'd he do that, Pap?' Bowen whispered.

Chesney said: 'He used the woman as bait, then crept back and fired our fuel tanks, the bastard!'

'It is typical of Joktan,' Duru exclaimed.

Chesney didn't answer. Stranded in the desert without food, water or transportation, he knew their chances of survival would be alarmingly slim.

He was contemplating the hopelessness of their position when something flashed among the sand dunes ahead. Chesney blinked as he saw the top of Duru's skull lifting off, not in a solid mass, but in tiny pieces, fragments of brain and bone erupting in a grotesque and bloody halo. Chesney felt a chill of horror as a shotgun blast echoed deafeningly in his ears, then his men leapt for cover, firing wildly at the spot from which the shot had come.

Chapter Fourteen

Joktan kept his head low as the bullets whistled above him. The place he had chosen was perfect for ambush. A wedge of sand formed a protective barrier between himself and his American attackers; in addition, a sharp decline at the rear offered a useful slope along which he could crawl to effect an encircling movement. His assault had been carefully planned; now it was time to execute phase two.

He drew back, inching down the slope, turning deftly to the right as he wriggled through the shifting sand. The shotgun felt slippery in his fingers, but the cooling air offered a salve against his fevered cheeks.

He smiled to himself as he listened to the pandemonium above. The mercenaries had gone crazy; they were ejecting cartridges and chambering new ones, laying down a continuous field of fire. The din was deafening, but for all its sound and fury, the impassioned broadside was achieving little.

The sand dunes rose around Joktan like the contours of a rumpled quilt. They blended into the darkness, their shadowy slopes textureless, as if by some strange and magical process, the earth had been drained of density. He spotted a slender 'V' slithering between two inclines, and turned along it, holding the shotgun in front of his chest, his body moving with the zig-zag fluidity of an attacking snake. He could hear somebody shouting among the dune crests ahead; it was Chesney's voice, ordering his men to hold their fire.

The barrage died away, leaving a silence that seemed

ringingly clear. Joktan drew to a halt, raising his head cautiously above the dune rim. He could see the mercenaries almost within touching distance, muttering and cursing as they reloaded their smoking carbines.

Joktan didn't hesitate. He drew a bead on the nearest target, sucked in his breath and gently squeezed the shotgun trigger.

Chesney jumped as the blast rang out. He saw Darley roll over in the sand and lie twitching convulsively. The shot had been close, incredibly close, yet there was no sign of Joktan himself, and no sign of where the attack had come from.

'Jesus,' Campbell muttered, staring down at Darley's disintegrated skull. Darley gave one last twitch before relaxing into the glassy torpor of death.

'Move,' Chesney croaked. 'The bastard's got our position marked.'

Without waiting to see if the others obeyed, he slithered desperately through the sand, his powerful body, so graceful when erect, floundering like an inelegant lizard. Chesney didn't scare easily, but something about the circumstances of the past few hours had totally unnerved him. Maybe Duru was right. Maybe Joktan *was* some kind of supernatural being, able to dissolve and materialize at will. How could they fight a spectre, for Chrissake?

He drew to a halt, sweating in the darkness, and the others waited for him to issue a command. The silence gathered around them, heavy and oppressive. Now what? Chesney wondered. He had to think, sort out the chaos raging in his mind. Four of his men dead, and both Land Rovers ruined. If they got out of this alive, it would be a miracle.

'Listen,' Campbell whispered.

Somewhere at their rear, a faint swishing sound drifted through the night. Campbell's eyes held Chesney's wildly. 'It's him.'

The swishing intensified for a moment, then abruptly faded. 'How far back, d'you think?' Chesney whispered.

'Twenty feet, thirty.'

'Maybe we can lay an ambush.' Chesney examined the surrounding terrain. A solitary boulder rose out of the gloom.

'That looks a good spot. Somebody'll have to stay behind while the rest sucker him forward.'

No one answered for a moment. God knew, he didn't blame them, Chesney thought, staring at their blank, terrified faces.

It was Cronin who broke the silence. 'I'll do it,' he offered at last.

'Nobody's forcing you, son.'

'Don't worry. I'll pick him off as he wriggles by.'

Chesney slapped him lightly on the shoulder. 'Good boy. Just bullet the sonofabitch and be done with it.' He jerked his head at the others. 'Make plenty of noise and let's see if we can divert the bastard's attention.'

They wormed on through the smothering sand, Chesney in the lead, his breath wheezing painfully. The dunes seemed interminable, gathering around them in a bewildering array. From time to time, Chesney had the uncomfortable feeling that the world and everything in it had been swamped by a monstrous ocean of sand.

A shot rang out, splitting the night like a thunderclap, and Chesney signalled his followers to a halt. Campbell and Bowen grinned in triumph. 'Bullseye,' Campbell said.

Chesney shook his head, his eyes sombre. 'That was a shotgun blast. Cronin was carrying a carbine.'

The smiles faded from his companions' lips, and they watched nervously as Chesney checked the firing mechanism on his carbine.

'What are you going to do, Pap?' Bowen asked.

'What I should have done in the beginning. Nail him myself.'

'Alone?' Bowen's eyes were incredulous.

'You got a better idea?'

The thought of going up against Joktan didn't appeal to Chesney one little bit, but he was the one who'd created this mess and he couldn't ignore the responsibility any longer. 'Soon as I finish the job,' he said, 'we'll find a way out've here.'

'Supposing you don't finish the job, Pap? Supposing Joktan finishes you?'

'Then, good buddy, you are on your own.'

193

Chesney gave them a cheerful wink, and began wriggling back the way they had come. He moved confidently and with purpose, but as the shadows gathered around him, his sense of bravado started to flounder. Don't crap out, he told himself angrily. Joktan's only a man, like any other man, and all it takes it a little patience and know-how.

His eyes scoured the darkness ahead, watching for any sign of movement which might signify the presence of life, his brain registering the minutest details; camel scrub to the left, shadow cluster directly in front, furrows on the slope above. Nothing was too small to escape his attention. Given the choice, he reflected, he would have opted for a more fitting arena. There was nothing to see goddamnit, nothing but endless hummocks of sand. Chesney preferred the jungle for night work. At least in the jungle you could use the foliage, use the terrain.

His body felt weakened by the interminable crawling. It wasn't natural for a man to wriggle along the ground like a rodent. He picked his way up a shifting incline, a detour of sorts, and a perilous one at that – he was running a serious risk of positioning himself against the skyline – but if he succeeded in reaching the summit, he would gain an advantage against his antagonist.

Suddenly, a shot rang out, its retort muffled and indistinct. It was followed by a deafening fusilade of rifle fire, then as abruptly as it had begun, the volley died away.

Chesney rose to his feet, his heart hammering against his ribcage. 'Sam, did you get him?' he bellowed.

No answer. A curious silence filled the land. What kind of stupid game were the bastards playing, for God's sake?

He charged madly through the suffocating darkness. The sand dunes fell away, and in a shallow hollow, framed by camel scrub, he saw the bodies of Campbell and Bowen staring at the stars.

Slaver dribbled across Chesney's stubbled chin as he scanned the curtain of gloom ahead. The shadows seemed to blend, taking on form and substance like a demonic monster bent on his destruction. This was no physical enemy he was confronting. Men, he could understand. Men, he knew how to deal with. But Joktan was a devil dredged from the bowels of hell.

Whimpering, Chesney began to run. The sand plucked at his ankles, dragging him backwards, but with a passion forged by hysteria, he blundered on into the desert night.

It was dawn when Chesney opened his eyes. He could see his hand framed against the sky, the fingers sticking up disjointedly. He was lying face down on a stony plain, but he had no idea how long he had been there. He had run crazily through the night, leaving the sand dunes behind and reaching the flatness of the open tableland. Somewhere he had dropped his carbine, but Chesney's mind had no recollection of that. His body had lost its sense of volition, as if the nerves connecting his brain to his torso had been knocked out of alignment.

He sensed a presence somewhere at his rear, and turned his head to see Joktan watching him from barely five feet away. Joktan was sitting cross-legged in the sand, the shotgun resting across his folded knees. His face was expressionless and his eyes were fixed upon Chesney with an icy calm. Chesney hadn't heard him approach, which was something of a miracle since he'd heard every other damn' thing for the past seven hours — snakes slithering, lizards scampering, bugs scuffling — but Joktan, as Chesney had learned to his cost, could move like the light.

He felt no alarm at the Iraqi's presence. He had gone beyond such emotions, and now his only reaction was a feeling of simple curiosity. For almost twenty minutes the two men stared at each other, then Chesney heard the sound of a vehicle approaching and saw Joktan's Land Rover careering toward them in a thick cloud of dust. Without a word, Joktan rose to his feet and Chesney felt terror gripping his heart as he realized the Arab's intention.

'No,' he croaked.

But Joktan ignored him, walking toward the battered Land Rover as it slithered to a halt. The wind plucked at his hair and peppered his beard stubble with sand grains.

'Joktan, you bastard. You can't just abandon me here.'

He slid into the passenger seat. There was no expression on his face.

'At least finish me off,' Chesney shouted. 'Don't leave me to linger slowly in the middle of the desert. It isn't human.'

Without a word, Joktan threw his shotgun into the dust. Chesney lay for a long time, watching the Land Rover's dust-cloud as it roared off across the desert sand, then he grunted deep in his throat, dragged himself toward the waiting firearm and placed its barrel painfully between his lips.

Gus McKlelland examined the photograph his brother Paul had given him. 'I still don't get it,' he grunted.

'What's not to get?'

'It doesn't make sense, for Chrissake.'

'I know it doesn't make sense. If that's Leon Snyder, security chief of Napier Oil, what was he doing in Sadaam Hussein's bunker during the 1991 Gulf War?'

'Are you telling me Napier had some connection with Sadaam Hussein?'

'Not just Napier. The entire cartel. Eleven companies, Gus. Collectively, those boys could buy and sell the US government.'

Gus shook his head wonderingly and flopped into the sofa, his plump face creased in thought. Paul and Leila watched his reaction.

Leila said earnestly: 'Mr McKlelland, one of the reasons behind the 1991 Gulf War was the Kuwaiti government's insistence on over-producing oil. That's what induced Sadaam Hussein to invade in the first place. Kuwait was keeping the world oil prices artificially low.'

'So?'

'So isn't it just possible that the interests of Iraq and the interests of the American oil cartel temporarily coincided?'

'What are you handing me here? American oil companies collaborating with their country's enemy to get the oil market rising again?'

'For Christ's sake, Gus,' Paul snapped, 'we don't know what we're handing you. All we do know is that this man, Leon Snyder, was photographed in February 1991 in the bunker of Sadaam Hussein. Now isn't that grounds for some kind of investigation?'

'How do you know the picture isn't a fake?'

'Because Grazzini's been locked up in San Quentin for the past three years. I don't see how he could possibly have faked it, even if he'd wanted to.'

Gus sniffed, the sound creating a resonance on the warm afternoon air. 'You did say Snyder was ex-CIA?'

'According to Grazzini.'

'Well, if that's true, and if there really is some involvement between Iraq and Napier, it's a pretty good bet Snyder will have used his old intelligence contacts to set up the liaison.'

'So?'

'I was wondering what projects he worked on at CIA. Maybe we should check them out.'

'How?' Paul asked.

'I've got a friend named Allan Hooper who retired from Langley about three years ago. He's now running a ski school near Salt Lake City. He always said to pick up the phone if I ever needed anything.'

Paul grinned. 'Gus, you're a marvel.'

'That's what I keep telling you,' he said modestly. 'You may have inherited the looks in the family, but I'm the one who inherited the brains.'

'Think we're beginning to get someplace?' Paul asked as he and Leila drove through the wooded countryside. They saw patches of ice forming disparate patterns across the surface of a mountain lake, but only the faintest traces lingered on the summits themselves, for most had melted with the spring.

Leila shrugged. 'Depends on this Mr Hooper, I guess.'

Paul glanced at her, his eyes softening. 'I'd never have gotten this far without you, Leila, I reckon you know that.'

'Don't make a big deal of it. We have mutual interests at heart, that's all.'

'Why do you always act so tough?'

She smiled thinly. 'You wouldn't understand the meaning of that word.'

'Know something? You're different to Ellen in every conceivable way, and yet we get along like a house on fire. Don't you find that strange?'

'What's strange about it?'

'Me. Usually, I find it hard talking to people, always have. But with you, I can say anything — tell you anything — and somehow you always understand.'

She looked amused. 'Is that supposed to be sweet-talk?'

'Of course not.'

'We're together for one reason only, because we've got a job to do. Remember that.'

'I wasn't getting romantic,' Paul said. 'Just trying to loosen things up a bit, that's all.'

'I'm never loose,' Leila told him flatly. 'One of the first things you learn about me is, I'm never loose.'

They turned a bend and spotted a ski-slope ahead, its incline protected from the sunlight by a craggy overhang. Here, the snow had lingered, forming a canopy which blended into the encircling cliffs.

The hillside was dotted with gaily clad skiers. At the side of the road, a large timber-built chalet offered hamburgers, hotdogs and rope-tow tickets. Flowers fluttered from miniature window boxes.

'It's like Switzerland,' Leila exclaimed.

They left the car in the parking lot, and climbed the stairway to the chalet office. A young man in a thick-knit jumper looked up as they entered.

'Is Mr Hooper in?' Paul inquired.

'Who's asking?'

'My name's McKlelland. Paul McKlelland.'

'Ah, yes, Mr McKlelland. Mr Hooper is expecting you. Will you come this way, please?'

Allan Hooper was a short man with a barrel chest and a balding head. He was somewhere in his mid-fifties, and despite his excess flab and his plump cheeks, he looked tanned and fit.

He led them out to the restaurant terrace. 'On dull days, this is the quietest spot around,' he explained, examining Paul curiously. 'You don't look a bit like Gus.'

'I'm the handsome member of the family.'

198

Hooper chuckled. 'I guess you're right. Gus may be a terrific guy, but let's face it, nobody's about to offer him a Hollywood contract.'

Leila broke in, getting straight down to business. 'Mr Hooper, is it true you used to work for CIA?'

'Twenty-seven years,' Hooper confirmed. 'But skiing was always my big passion.' He motioned ironically at his girth. 'You wouldn't think it to look at me now, but I used to be pretty good.'

'It's a nice spot you've got here,' Paul said.

'Sure. Six rope-tows in the winter months. Course, at this time of year, with snow conditions deteriorating, we're only operating two.'

Paul pulled out a chair and seated himself at one of the tables. 'Mr Hooper, during your years in the intelligence service, do you ever remember meeting a man named Leon Snyder?'

Hooper thought for a moment, then shook his head. 'The name isn't familiar. We may have run into each other, but Langley's a big place.'

Leila opened her purse and took out the photograph Grazzini had given them. She handed it to Hooper. 'That's Snyder.'

Hooper's eyes flickered. 'Sure, I remember this guy. Only we knew him as Wilfred Ferriday.'

'He's changed his identity?'

'If he's calling himself Snyder, I guess he must have.'

'Mr Hooper,' Leila said. 'Can you recall what Snyder worked on?'

'Sure. He was with one of those specialized departments, very clandestine.'

'Espionage?'

'More in the nature of scientific research. Snyder's speciality was psychotronic warfare.'

'What's that?' Paul asked.

'Russia started it back in the sixties when they bombarded the US Embassy in Moscow with microwave radiation. At first, our people thought they were trying to eavesdrop on our electronic communications, but then we began to suspect they had something more sinister in mind − an attempt to

199

disorientate Embassy employees by affecting their nervous tissues.'

'Is that possible?'

'Well, we knew the relation between low-level microwaves and psychological damage had already been investigated by top Russian scientists, so the United States decided it was time to deal itself into the game. We created a special department, Ferriday's – or should I say Snyder's – to examine the effects of electromagnetic impulses on human behaviour.'

'How?' Leila asked.

'The findings were mostly kept secret. I know they constructed a fleet of psychotronic generators. One rumour circulating at the time was that powerful and uncontrollable emotions – like seizure and paralysis – had been induced psychotronically.'

'At what kind of distance?' Paul wondered.

'At that time, three or four hundred kilometres. Of course, by now, assuming the experiments are still in progress, their methods should be far more sophisticated.'

'How come we've never heard about this before?' Leila demanded.

'Well, there've been reams of stuff published over the years, but nobody's taken it seriously. Nobody, that is, except the Pentagon. In 1981, they set up a budget of six million dollars to beat the Russians at their own game.'

'How would the weapon system work?' Leila asked.

'Simple. By using what's called a photonic barrier modulator, electromagnetic impulses can be beamed at enemy troops with repetition rates of from ten to twenty Hz. These cycles are psycho and biologically active, and by keeping up the pressure, scientists can induce behavioural changes, disrupting concentration, creating headaches, and most important of all, promoting complete mental disorientation. The attack would be difficult to guard against since it penetrates all known forms of insulation, and by causing widespread dizziness and confusion, leaves its victims virtually unable to defend themselves.'

'How long do the effects last?'

'Anything from several hours to a matter of days. Even

then, there's no guarantee that the casualties will recover completely. It's always been recognized that some kind of permanent damage is possible.'

Leila moved to the verandah and stood staring out at the ski slopes beyond, a terrible emptiness settling in her stomach. 'Such a device could alter the whole nature of modern warfare.'

'Sure it could. All you'd need do would be bombard the enemy with psychotronic impulses, then send in your troops and take over his positions without firing a shot. Of course, what we're talking about is strictly in the experimental stage. You'd have to perfect the system first.'

Leila turned to look at him. 'Mr Hooper, have you ever heard of a weapon named Talon Blue?'

General Abu Bakhit welcomed Gabriel Hausner, the UN General Secretary, on the steps of al Shisur's presidental palace. In deference to his guest, Bakhit had exchanged his military uniform for a western business suit, and his manner was convivial as he guided Hausner through the maze of corridors, accompanied by the inevitable entourage of plain-clothed security guards. The two men had met on a number of occasions, and Bakhit regarded the New Zealand diplomat as something of a personal friend. 'The President has arranged a meal in your honour,' he said. 'Nothing elaborate, you understand – just a modest luncheon so that you can talk together informally.'

'I'm obliged to the President,' Hausner replied. 'Let's hope we can reach some mutual accord, and remove the spectre of war from this unhappy region.'

Bakhit lowered his voice. 'I must warn you,' he whispered, 'you may find al Shisur a little strange tonight.'

'Strange?' Hausner echoed.

'I mean there are times he doesn't appear to be himself. It's a common affliction among men of destiny. The demands of state sometimes produce curious and unusual delusions.'

'What kind of delusions?'

'Oh, nothing extraordinary, but you must appreciate that President al Shisur has been under considerable strain lately. It would hardly be natural if his manner – his personality –

did not reflect that fact. He welcomes you both as a diplomat and a friend, but please do not be surprised by anything you see.'

Bakhit ushered Hausner into a sumptuously furnished chamber where in place of a table, cushions had been laid around a selection of dishes arranged Bedu-style on the carpeted floor. Musallim al Shisur liked to be reminded of his humbler beginnings.

Al Shisur himself was standing in the centre of the room. He made no attempt to approach his guest, but waited in the manner of a royal personage receiving a commoner. He was, however, smiling as the two men shook hands.

'*As-salaam alaikum,*' he said.

Hausner completed the greeting. '*Wa alaikum as-salaam.* It's good to see you again, Mr President. I hope, for the sake of the Middle East — for the sake of the entire world — our discussion produces positive results.'

Al Shisur stepped back as a servant entered, carrying a small silver bowl filled with scented water. Without a word, he carefully washed his hands. Hausner looked at General Bakhit, frowning.

'The President has an inherent horror of germs,' Bakhit explained. 'He prefers to keep human contact to the minimum. It is no reflection on you, Mr Secretary, but the practice of shaking hands is one western custom he would be happy to abolish.'

The three men took their places around the dining area, and Hausner waited politely for al Shisur to begin. The Arab leader leaned forward, plucking the cover from the central dish. Hausner saw steam rising from the barbecued lamb, delicately flavoured with prunes.

'I asked my chefs to prepare this especially.' Al Shisur had been educated at Cambridge, and spoke fluent English. 'I remember how much you enjoyed it during your last visit here.'

Hausner cleared his throat. 'Mr President, you have always been a more than gracious host. However, bearing in mind that time is swiftly running out, wouldn't we be well advised to commence our discussion without delay?'

'By all means. What precisely do you wish to discuss?'

Hausner looked nonplussed. 'Why, naturally, your designs upon Israel.'

'Is that all?' al Shisur said. He seemed amused.

'Mr President, unless I can prevail upon you to display some level of restraint, war between your two countries would seem to be inevitable.'

'My dear fellow,' al Shisur told him languidly, 'do please relax and enjoy your meal. In diplomatic terms, I'm afraid your visit here is a little late. You see, the war you speak of has already begun.'

President Lawrence Clayman heard the telephone ringing and switched on the bedside lamp. Beside him his wife Mildred stirred restlessly in her sleep. Putting on his spectacles, Clayman lifted the receiver.

'Larry?' He recognized the Secretary of State's voice. 'It's started. Our satellite pictures show al Shisur's forces crossing the Jordanian frontier and heading pell-mell for Israel.'

Clayman swore softly, all traces of sleep vanishing from his head. He threw back the bedclothes and reached for his nightrobe. 'What time is it, Frank?'

'Four o'clock in the morning,' Hamilton said.

'I'll meet you in the Oval Office in three minutes.'

The Secretary of State was waiting with the Chairman of the Joint Chiefs of Staff, Major General Nathan Kincaid, when President Clayman arrived. Clayman waved them inside, and drew the drapes across the bevelled, green-tinted windows. 'When did it happen?'

'About two am,' Hamilton said. 'I would have called you earlier, but we had to check it out.'

'It's definite then?'

'No question, Larry. It looks like the real McCoy.'

Clayman moved behind his writing desk, his eyes weary in the pre-dawn morning. 'What time will it be in Amman?'

Hamilton calculated swiftly. 'Almost midday.'

Clayman reached for the telephone. 'I'm going to call the Jordanian Prime Minister.'

It took several minutes for the call to be punched through. The Jordanian premier had just returned from a government

203

meeting and his voice, when it came on the line, was guarded. 'Mr President?'

Briefly, Clayman outlined the US satellite readings.

'We are already aware of al Shisur's movements,' the Prime Minister said. 'As a precautionary measure, our own armed forces have been placed on full alert.'

'You have to stop him, Prime Minister. Al Shisur has violated Jordanian territory.'

He heard the Prime Minister sigh. 'Unfortunately, sir, in practical terms there is little we can do. Al Shisur has full rights of passage under the 1998 Harasis Agreement. As long as he commits no act of aggression against Jordanian interests, he is free to proceed anywhere he chooses.'

For almost twenty minutes, President Clayman tried gamely to persuade the Jordanian premier to change his mind, but the Prime Minister remained adamant. In the end, Clayman hung up the receiver and conceded defeat.

He looked at Hamilton and Kincaid tiredly. 'How long before al Shisur's army reaches the Israeli frontier?'

The Chairman of the Joint Chiefs of Staff said: 'At the rate he's going, he'll be there within twenty-four hours. That's maximum.'

Clayman picked up the telephone and jangled the receiver rest. 'I guess I'd better warn Tel Aviv.'

When Jacob Jabari arrived at the Israeli Ministry of Defence, he found the building swarming with people. In the dusty hall, uniformed officers scurried from room to room. Everywhere there was a sense of movement and urgency.

Jabari stopped a man who was pouring out a string of commands to a flustered subordinate. 'What the hell is going on here?'

The officer's eyes were blazing. 'Haven't you heard the news? It's official. Al Shisur's crossed the Jordanian border. Israel is now at war.'

Ellen was silent as they drove across the endless pancake of land. She had spoken little since Joktan's disposal of the hapless mercenaries. It had been a terrible experience, and she'd hated her own role in the affair, despite the fact that

204

her survival had depended upon it. Joktan's ruthlessness had shocked her deeply. She'd recognized from the beginning the almost animal-like wildness in the man, but back there at the sand dunes he had behaved like a primitive beast. He hadn't told her the details, thank God, but his callous indifference had convinced her he was capable of anything. Well, what did she expect? The man was a savage, pure and simple. Beneath his veneer of sophistication, there were centuries of conditioning just aching to get out.

She drummed her fingers lightly on the door. 'Was it necessary?' she asked at last.

Joktan looked surprised. It was the first time she'd spoken in several hours. 'Was what necessary?'

'Killing those men. You did kill them, didn't you?'

'It was them or us.'

'That's a lie. We could have driven off after you'd destroyed their vehicles. That would have been the civilized thing to do.'

'Civilized?' He smiled thinly. 'You call it civilized to abandon people in the middle of the desert?'

'Are you telling me that what you did was a merciful act?'

Joktan shrugged. Sand flecks clung to his beard stubble, giving his face a strangely orange hue; he looked grotesque, Ellen thought, with his scowling eyes and wild, windblown hair.

'They were hundreds of miles from the nearest habitation,' he said. 'They had no transport. Their death was inevitable. I wonder what your choice would be in similar circumstances? Swift and painless from a shotgun or rifle, or slow and lingering from the sun and thirst.'

Ellen frowned, staring through the windshield at the plain ahead. Could it be true? Had Joktan been acting not out of anger, not out of malice, but according to some code of reasoning that was as old as the desert itself? She had to admit that his reply carried a certain degree of logic, and if it was so then Joktan could hardly be called an animal. On the contrary, he was a rare and compassionate human being.

'I'm sorry,' she said at length. 'I guess I misunderstood.

205

You risked everything to take on those men. You were very brave.'

'Not brave. Practical.'

'I realize too that I owe you my life. If you hadn't spared me . . .' She looked down at her hands. 'And I had the temerity to call you uncivilized.'

Joktan chuckled. 'That's because you are an American. Fortunately, being westernized myself, I appreciate how the Infidel think.'

'Salih?' she said after a while.

'Yes?'

'You do realize that in spite of what happened, I'll do anything in my power to stop Musallim al Shisur?'

'I am no admirer of al Shisur.'

'Then why go on with this ridiculous charade?'

'I've given my word, that's why.'

'For God's sake, thousands of people, maybe millions, will be slaughtered and mutilated. What's your word in the face of that?'

'My word is what I live by,' he told her quietly.

An angry retort sprang to Ellen's lips but she swallowed it back, sighing resignedly. There was little point in arguing, she realized. Joktan was right when he said she would never understand the Arab soul.

She sat for a while, watching the countryside unfolding, then her senses quickened as, squinting into the heat haze, she saw buildings rippling in front of her. Something was out there, trailers, outhouses, clapboard dwellings. 'Look,' she exclaimed.

Joktan nodded. 'It's an oil camp. They're dotted all over this area.'

'Will there be people there?'

'At this time of day, unlikely. The camps operate on a satellite basis, a central accommodation unit servicing a cluster of outlying rigs. Most of the men will be at work. They'll probably have a watchman looking after things, but the place should be largely deserted, at least until nightfall.'

They found the watchman in a tiny office, surrounded by crates of empty beer bottles. He was a rawboned Norwegian in his early fifties who seemed not only surprised to see them, but profoundly impressed that they had crossed the desert by such an unorthodox route. Ellen asked him if there was any chance of a shower.

'I'll give you the key to trailer 22,' the man said. 'It's empty at the moment, so you shouldn't be disturbed. Don't forget to turn off the water though. It's a precious commodity here in the desert, and we can't afford to waste it.'

The trailer was large and spacious, and despite its outer appearance, luxuriously appointed. In the tiny bathroom, Ellen fumbled excitedly among the row of body oils, lotions and shampoos. 'It'll be heaven to feel clean again.'

'It goes against the Bedu tradition,' Joktan told her gravely, motioning at the shower cubicle, 'but as they say in the west − ladies first.'

Joktan came out of the shower, rubbing his hair with a towel. He was naked to the waist, his tanned body lithe and muscular − a complex man, Ellen thought, examining him silently from the trailer bunk, difficult to comprehend. She owed him her life, but it was more than gratitude that was prompting what she was feeling now. It was something she couldn't quite put a name to, something overwhelming. She couldn't care about a person she'd only known for a matter of days, could she, even if it had been a pretty intense relationship? Not truly care? Or maybe she could. Maybe it happened like that. A thunderclap, the French called it. Could her emotions really be so transitory that she'd forgotten almost everything else, including Paul McKlelland? But then she'd never felt about Paul the way she felt about Joktan. He fired her senses, made her spirits vibrant and alive, so why should she deny that? Was it nobler, in the long run, to ruin all their lives for the sake of some outdated and misguided loyalty?

She watched him drying his hair in front of the mirror, his powerful muscles rippling. He had found a razor in the bathroom and had used it to shave away his beard stubble. Now he paused, studying his reflection critically. 'How do I look?'

'Great.'

'Not like a bandit, eh?' He waved his hand at the mirror.

'Is that a bandit's face? Of course not. It is an honest face. A face to inspire confidence and trust. A face any mother would consider her daughter safe with.'

Ellen rose, and stood beside him. 'I think it's a beautiful face.'

His eyes softened as he looked down at her. 'Despite the fact that I'll always be a Bedu at heart?'

'But at least a Bedu who appreciates how the Infidel think.'

Tenderly, he cradled her cheek with his palm. She stared at him in silence for a moment, then taking his hand, brushed it with her lips and pressed it gently against her breast. When Joktan kissed her, it was like the releasing of some long-deferred need. Her head swam and a fiery tingling started in her lower abdomen. She felt his fingers fumbling with her clothing and in a frenzy of emotion began to help him, tearing urgently at the straps and fasteners. The air-conditioner cooled her naked skin as her body emerged into the filtered sunlight, and she pressed herself against him, forgetting everything in the madness of the moment. The world seemed to tilt, losing clarity and focus, and her limbs trembled with emotion as they collapsed on the bed and went through the exquisite ritual of love.

Chapter Fifteen

A light rain cast drops of moisture across the Blazer windshield as Leila drove down the steep mountain roadway. She could see pine trees descending into the valley below. Paul had been unusually quiet since leaving the ski chalet, but Leila knew what he was thinking. Now that they'd discovered Talon Blue's capability, there was little to keep her here any longer. She could telephone her findings to her superiors in Tel Aviv and catch the next plane back to the Middle East.

Curiously, though, she didn't feel like leaving. It was the damndest thing, but the more she tried to figure out reasons for her reluctance, the more she kept coming back to Paul. And yet, Paul McKlelland wasn't her type at all. In fact, if she came right down to it, she didn't really have a type in the normal, accepted sense. Human relations, intimate relations, were anathema to her, and always had been. So why should she give a damn what happened to Paul McKlelland? But he seemed to have wormed himself under her skin. The way he'd gone after his fiancee, knowing in his heart their relationship was over yet still putting his life on the line, she had to admire that. She liked him. He was a nice man. She couldn't bear to abandon him now.

'What's your next move?' she asked casually.

Paul shrugged. 'I need proof. Something conclusive.'

'Can't your brother help?'

'Maybe. But when you kill a chicken, maybe it's best to start at the head.'

'Napier's headquarters in Muna City?'

'Right.'

Leila was silent for a moment. 'I'm coming with you,' she said.

Paul looked surprised. 'Why? You've got what you wanted. You know what Talon Blue is, what it does. Now you can go back to Israel and get on with the war.'

'I can't leave you to tackle Napier alone. You'll get yourself killed.'

'Don't worry about me.'

'We started this together and we'll finish it together. I'll have to call my people in Tel Aviv, but after that ...' She glanced at him sideways. 'We're still a team, McKlelland.'

His face broke into a smile. Paul didn't smile very often, Leila reflected, but when he did he was almost handsome.

She spotted a diversion sign in the road ahead and eased her foot on the brake, slowing her speed. 'Looks like we're being sidetracked.'

She followed the arrow to the left, bumping along an unpaved cart-trail which dipped through the curtain of pine woods. The route plunged sharply, carving a ragged tear through the bristling foliage. Suddenly, the mountain seemed to open up and they found themselves lurching along the rim of a yawning precipice. Paul glanced over the edge at the forest below. 'Hell of a way to divert traffic.'

Leila didn't answer. The road was narrow, and she had to use all her concentration to keep the Blazer on an even keel. She was acutely conscious of the chasm on their left.

'The workgang must have moved in pretty damn' quick,' Paul said. 'That sign wasn't there when we drove up.'

'What workgang? I didn't see any workgang.'

A tremor of uneasiness passed through Paul. 'You're right. No cop in his right mind would direct automobiles along a track like this.'

Leila's muscles tightened as she glanced in the rearview mirror and spotted a giant truck lumbering down the road behind. It looked immense, its elevated cab towering above them like a monstrous predator intent upon its prey. 'Somebody's on our tail.'

Paul twisted in his seat. 'Jesus, look at the size of that thing.'

Leila was about to answer when, with a spine-jerking thud, the massive truck rammed them from behind, driving the Blazer jerkily forward. Leila's words dissolved into a strangled scream.

'He's trying to force us over the edge,' Paul snapped. 'That truck probably belongs to Napier Oil.'

Leila's cheeks blanched as the giant vehicle rammed them again, pushing the Blazer perilously forward. Her palms felt sweaty gripping the wheel.

'You'll have to outrun him, Leila.' Paul's voice was surprisingly calm as he eyed the track ahead.

'On this gradient? You're crazy.'

'If you don't, he'll bulldoze us over.'

'My God.' Leila glanced in the mirror, moistening the inside of her mouth with her tongue. The truck was hurtling along crazily at their rear. The road unfolded, dipping down the tumbling mountainside, the trees flitting by a dizzy blur. A terrible sickness started in her stomach as she clung to the driving wheel in a desperate attempt to negotiate the twisting bends. Their wheels slithered on the uneven surface, kicking up clouds of dust.

'Faster,' Paul said. 'He's gaining.'

'If I go any faster, we'll sail over the edge.'

'We'll do that anyhow if the bastard rams us again.'

Leila felt sweat trickling between her breasts as she pumped the gas pedal. Branches scraped along the Blazer's hull, and her stomach chilled as she saw the road steepen into a terrifying descent, looping sharply to the left. We'll never make it, she thought. She jammed her foot frantically on the brake, but with a deafening screech, the Blazer skidded out of control. 'We're going,' she screamed.

'Jump,' Paul shouted.

Leila saw the precipice hurtling toward them and tore desperately at her seat harness. Her fingers found the door and she dived sideways through the opening. The world spun in her vision, merging into a bewildering hotch-potch of sky, trees and earth. Then her shoulder hit the ground and she was tumbling inelegantly down the steep sandy bank. She came to a halt at the cliff edge, and watched the Blazer sail into the air and plummet into the abyss below.

Paul lay directly in front of her, his cheeks smeared with dirt. 'You okay?'

'I think so.'

A bullet pierced the air above their heads, and they saw men spilling from the truck on the road above.

'They're shooting at us!' Leila exclaimed.

'Jesus!'

Paul leapt to his feet and seized her wrist, sprinting madly toward the nearby timber. He knew nothing mattered but the skimpy line of cover ahead. They had to reach it if they wanted to survive.

Then his heart missed a beat as he saw figures sliding down the slope in front and dragged Leila to a halt, his head swimming with desperation.

'We're trapped,' she moaned, filling her lungs with air.

'We could go down there.' Paul nodded at the precipice rim.

'You're crazy.'

'We don't have any choice, Leila.'

'It's straight down, for God's sake. We'll be committing suicide.'

'We're committing suicide if we stay where we are. I don't know about you, but I'd rather take my chances with the cliff.'

Paul moved to the edge and peered warily over. He could see a narrow channel leading between craggy buttresses. Easing himself into its groove, he began working his body downwards on the seat of his pants. Leila gritted her teeth and followed, guiding her progress with her flattened palms.

At the bottom, a jagged flake descended diagonally across the fractured slabs, and Paul paused on its rim to give Leila a helping hand. Then, moving as rapidly as they dared, they started down their perilous escape route.

Snyder came to a halt on the clifftop, shaking his head in wonder.

'Where are they?' Gronk gasped, trotting up to join him.

'Down there.' Snyder jerked his head at the gaping abyss.

'It's a sheer drop, for Chrissake!'

'I guess desperate people will try anything.'

212

'What happens now, Leon? We can't follow them down that.'

'Somebody has to.'

Snyder looked at his men, gathered along the clifftop. They were gazing into the emptiness below. 'Any of you ever climbed before?'

Charlie Machshalko said: 'I've done some scrambling in the Adirondacks. I'll give it a try, Leon.'

'Me too,' Tony Brady echoed.

'It'll be dangerous,' Snyder warned.

'Mainly, it's just a question of nerve,' Machschalko said.

Snyder studied them closely for a moment, then nodded. 'Okay. Just take it easy and don't get rattled. Remember you haven't got a train to catch.'

The others watched in silence as Brady and Machschalko took off their overcoats and inched their way cautiously down the slender groove.

Paul drew to a halt, examining the cliff-face. Directly below, their channel vanished into a series of rocky bulges. Here, the gradient was almost perpendicular. It looked an unwelcoming route, and Leila's cheeks blanched as she followed his gaze. 'We'll never make it.'

Paul spotted a narrow crack winding its way across the fractured surface. 'We can get down there.'

'A fly couldn't do it,' Leila protested, examining the hairline fissure.

'A fly wouldn't have to. Come on, it's down or out, win or lose.'

Paul reached the crack and turned himself delicately around until he was facing the precipice wall. He thrust his fingers into the tiny aperture, and using it as a support, lowered his feet cautiously down. His toes scoured the wall, seeking out projections, but the slab seemed smooth and featureless. Sweat streamed into his eyes and he saw Leila watching anxiously from above as he slipped his fingers further down the crack, lowering himself like a sack of flour.

There was no sign of their pursuers. A jutting roof shut off the precipice's upper reaches blotting out the sky, and

Paul felt grateful for that, since it diminished to some extent the terrible sense of exposure he was feeling, and fixing his gaze on the meandering fracture, he worked his way steadily earthwards, trying to shut his mind to the void beneath.

Slowly, agonizingly, ignoring the gaping vacuum, ignoring the wind ruffling his hair and clothing, he negotiated the slab and came to a rest on the ledge below.

Brady felt his momentum quickening, and jammed his feet desperately against the parallel walls. The cliff scraped at his pants, and he saw Machshalko crouched on the jagged flake, watching him with alarm. 'Hang on, Tony,' Machshalko yelled.

Brady landed on the flake with a muffled thud, grimacing as a jolt of pain lanced through his lower body. He had fallen heavily on his handgun. He pulled the weapon out, and delicately massaged his bruised flesh. 'Damn pistol nearly took my side away.'

'You'll be okay,' Machshalko told him brusquely.

He glanced down the cliff-face where on one side the flake descended in a diagonal line; on the other, a series of limestone ripples formed a precarious stepladder to the rocks below. 'Maybe we should split up,' he suggested. 'You follow the ledge, and I'll head this way.'

'That's perpendicular, for Chrissake.'

'I know it. But if I can get alongside McKlelland, maybe I can pick him off from a distance.'

'Charlie, you'll be taking a hell of a risk.'

'I didn't say I liked the idea, but it's worth a try.'

Brady watched Machshalko lowering himself warily down the limestone, then dusted his clothing and continued alone.

Leila looked down from the slender rim. She could see Paul crouching on the ledge below. Between them lay the appalling bulge with its almost indiscernible access crack. A terrible fear gathered inside her. 'I can't do it,' she shouted.

She saw Paul's lips twisting in exasperation. 'You've got to, goddamnit!'

'I can't, I tell you.'

'There's no other way.'

'I'm going back. They can't hang around that clifftop for ever.'

'You little fool! Just push your fingers into the niche and ease yourself down. There's nothing to it.'

Leila hesitated, eyeing the buttress uncertainly. She choked back a sob, and clenching her teeth, turned her body until it faced the cliff. The crack was sandy to the touch, and filled with pieces of gravel which rolled over her hands, peppering her face and hair. Her feet scuffled against the craggy surface, sliding and scraping as delicately, fearfully, she lowered her body down the rock wall. Her entire weight was suspended from her fingertips. It seemed a perilous manoeuvre.

'Move your right hand further down the crack,' Paul shouted from below.

'I can't,' she croaked.

'Of course you can. Transfer your balance to the other arm. Do it in stages, right hand, left hand. You'll get the hang of it.'

Leila's teeth were chattering. 'I can't move.'

'Do it, damnnit! If you hang like that, your muscles will cramp up.'

Leila swallowed. Closing her eyes, she edged her hand delicately down the fissure, and finding a hold, gripped it fiercely. Then she brought the other hand down to join it, lowering her body an inch or two. Again, she scraped at the cliff wall with her toes. The crack meandered to the right, running horizontally for a foot or two, and Leila worked her way along it, ignoring the dust wafting into her face. She shifted her balance from side to side, pausing where the crack dropped vertically to the ledge below. I'll never make it, she thought. She let her fingers slip down the ragged funnel, and finding a point where the crack filtered to the left, grasped it fiercely, letting her body slide deftly downwards.

'You're doing great,' Paul shouted.

Leila was filled with a dangerous sense of instability. Bile spurted into her mouth, and she swallowed it back with a conscious effort. Mustn't cough up. Mind cool, senses alert.

215

Ping.

The sound was strangely metallic, and glancing up, she saw a piece of rock fly from the cliff above her head. Almost simultaneously, the echo of a shot drifted across the craggy buttress to her left. Panic seized her as she squinted into the wind. Framed against the skyline, a man was lining her up coolly in his pistol sight. 'Paul,' she screamed.

He had seen the intruder too. Picking up a rock, he hurled it in the gunman's direction and the missile caught the man on the shoulder, neatly deflecting his aim. For a moment, their attacker clawed at the cliff-face, struggling for balance, then Leila's stomach gave a little quiver as he peeled from his stance and plummetted vertically into the void below.

Brady froze in his tracks as he watched Machshalko hurtling downwards. Machshalko turned and twisted as if his body, in its final moments of existence, was offering a last violent protest against the ending of his life. Framed against the valley floor, his desperate antics looked strangely comical. Brady watched mesmerized as Machshalko struck a jagged projection and catapaulted outwards, plunging the final two hundred feet. A terrible nausea started inside Brady, and he leaned against the rock, filling his lungs with air. His features were murderous as he pulled open his jacket and drew out his Walther automatic.

Leila felt her fingers loosening. 'I'm coming off,' she gasped.

'Hang on, for God's sake!' Paul shouted.

'I can't.'

Leila began sliding helplessly, the rock wall skidding by in front of her face. She heard Paul's cry of alarm as she gathered speed and tumbled over the ledge, rolling helplessly down the precipitous incline. Her fingers closed on a jagged projection, bringing her to a halt halfway down the slope with a jutting roof looming beneath her. Her lip was bleeding where she had caught it against the rock.

On the ledge above, Paul was taking off his jacket. He leant down, lowering the garment carefully. 'Grab hold,' he called. 'I'll try and pull you up.'

Leila looked at the jacket fluttering above her head. If she switched her grip, she could reach it easily, but terror seemed to have immobilized her senses. 'I can't move.'

'You've got to. Reach, Leila.'

She moistened her lips with her tongue, willing strength into her nerveless limbs. Gritting her teeth, she loosened her right hand and lunged across the limestone wall. She seized the jacket and transferred her weight in one jerky motion, clutching the garment fiercely with both fists. Paul's features strained as he struggled to hold her. He dug his heels into the rocky ledge, but he was overbalancing rapidly and she could see the weight of her body dragging him off. With a muffled moan, he toppled forward, skidding down the slanting incline, and Leila found herself falling again.

They reached the precipice and slid over its rim, the valley opening up beneath them. A slender pinnacle jutted out from the cliff-edge, and with a muffled rustling sound, the jacket zipped taut across its roof, bringing them both to a halt dangling on either side.

Leila clung to the flimsy material, almost demented. She heard Paul speaking from behind the outcrop. 'Are you okay?'

'Just,' she croaked.

'We've got to get on to solid ground.'

Leila looked desperately around. Beneath the overhang, she saw a slender ledge curling around the buttress at their left. It was almost within jumping distance, but without some kind of momentum, she knew she would never reach it. 'Paul? Got anything you can hold on to?'

Slight pause. 'Yeah. There's a small spur here.'

'Grab it, and ease the jacket upwards. I need some slack. If I give myself a little acceleration, maybe I can reach the mantelshelf.'

After a slight pause, the jacket slithered over the pinnacle summit, lowering her still further down the cliff face. Leila began swinging gently from side to side, working her body in a rhythmic, pendulum-like motion. She held her breath, judging her timing. Now, she thought, releasing her grip. The wind ripped at her face and hair, then she gave a sob of relief as her feet landed on the rocky platform.

'Leila?' Paul shouted from behind the spur.

'It's okay. Come on over the top.'

217

There was a muffled scuffling sound as Paul climbed over the pinnacle and lowered himself carefully down the other side, swinging the jacket toward her with his free hand. Reaching out, Leila caught it and braced herself against the cliff wall. 'Jump,' she said.

Paul's cheeks were pale as he measured the distance. He took a deep breath, gripping the garment tightly in his fist, then releasing his hold, swung himself desperately under the jutting roof. Leila pulled the jacket toward her, dragging him forward with all her strength. He missed the platform and slithered over the edge, but with Leila hauling from above, he managed to drag himself, panting, over the mantelshelf lip and collapse in a huddle at Leila's feet.

Narrowing his eyes, Brady spotted Paul and Leila on the platform below. They were in almost perfect view, apart from the overhang which slightly obscured his line of fire. Brady's palms were sweaty as he levelled the pistol, steadying the weapon with both hands. He would kill McKlelland first, the girl second. The girl was easier and less important, and at this range he couldn't miss. Gently, Brady squeezed the trigger.

Nothing happened.

Puzzled, he tried again.

No reaction.

He examined the weapon and discovered to his dismay that the firing mechanism had been damaged during his fall at the clifftop. Swearing under his breath, he laid the pistol against the rock, and pulled up his trouser leg. Taped to his calf was a slender stiletto. Brady drew the weapon from its leather sheath and began working his way cautiously toward the rubble-strewn mantelshelf.

'How're you feeling?' Paul asked, sprawled at Leila's side.

'Whacked.'

'We nearly didn't make it back there.'

'Who says we're making it now?'

'Don't worry, another two hundred feet should do it.'

'I've got news for you, coach. Two hundred or twenty thousand, I couldn't move another step.'

218

Paul said: 'Sshhhh!' and leaned up from the cliff wall, cocking his head to one side.

'What is it?'

'Could've sworn I heard something.'

Leila strained her ears above the murmur of the wind. Then a spasm clutched at her insides as she saw a man moving along the shelf toward them, wielding a vicious knife. 'Paul,' she screamed.

He swung round, startled, and Leila watched horrified as the intruder launched himself into a spectacular leap. He sailed through the sir, one arm forward, the other tucked expertly into his side. Paul took the full weight of the assault, and crashed backwards against the rockface. They struggled for balance on their precarious perch, wriggling and twisting in a welter of thrashing limbs. Leila saw the knife-blade flash as Paul seized his opponent's incoming wrist and hung on with all his strength. It was clear to Leila that he was no match for his powerful assailant who was hurling him around the mantelshelf like a sackful of grain. Paul's skull crashed against the overhang and a trickle of blood ran from his hairline as he tried desperately to keep from toppling over the edge.

I must do something, Leila thought. She picked up a rock and inched forward, bringing it down on the intruder's neck. The man staggered against the cliff-face, but with an extraordinary display of will, recovered his balance almost at once and seized Paul by the throat. His knuckles showed white at the skin, and Paul's eyes bulged as his features contracted into a grotesque grimace. Dear God, Leila thought. She swung the boulder a second time, driving it as hard as she could against the base of their attacker's skull. The man wheeled in a slow semi-circle, his hands clutching a gaping wound in his head. Leila planted her foot in the small of his back and drove outward with all her strength, closing her eyes as the knifeman vanished over the rim with a startled cry.

Paul collapsed to the ground, panting hoarsely, and Leila gathered him into her arms, pressing his face against her breasts. She could feel his body shivering.

'That's the second time you've saved my life,' he managed at last.

Tears coursed down Leila's cheeks as, sick with tension, she held him in a feverish embrace. Paul reached out, frowning, and touched the moisture with his fingertips. 'I've never seen you cry before.'

She shook her head, struggling to regain control. 'I must be getting old, I guess.'

'Don't apologise. I kind've like it.'

He climbed to his feet, and gently massaging his throat, began to explore the far end of the platform as Leila dried her eyes. He returned after a moment, his face glowing with triumph. 'We're down. There's a narrow goat track zig-zagging all the way to the valley floor. We can follow it easy.'

With a whimper of relief, she took his hand and began the final stage of their perilous descent.

Snyder lowered his fieldglasses, muttering softly, 'It's McKlelland and the girl. They made it to the bottom.'

'I don't believe it,' Gronk said with a trace of wonder. 'The bastard's unkillable.'

'Nobody's unkillable. He's clever, that's all.' Snyder thought for a moment. 'Maybe we should take a leaf out of McKlelland's book. Ever play football, Sam?'

'Football? No.'

'In football, there's only one surefire way to win.'

'What's that?'

Snyder slipped the binoculars into their leather case and winked knowingly. 'You've got to work out your opponent's strategy before he even thinks of it.'

Chapter Sixteen

Yermi Ze'ev's body tingled with excitement as he climbed into the aircraft cockpit. Dark-haired, twenty-one years old, Yermi was one of Israel's most youthful fighter pilots, having just completed his basic training at Hatzerim Air Base. This was the first time in his life, however, that he had carried out a systems check as a prelude to genuine action and his stomach clenched at the thought. Two years he had spent learning the tricks of his trade − formation flying, intercepts, mock sorties and surface bombing exercises − but this time the attack would be for real. The news of the advancing Iraqi army had electrified the squadron, and Yermi was one of the first to take to the air.

He attached the ejector risers to his parachute harness, plugged in his G-suit fittings and blew up the air bladders to prevent blood draining into his lower body at supersonic speeds. He checked his radio leads and instrument panel, then pulled on his oxygen mask and flying helmet. He closed his bubble canopy and started up the air-conditioning to protect himself from the scorching sun. His engine was screeching so loudly he found it almost impossible to think.

The runway ahead teemed with activity as, one by one, the squadron of Python B-5s roared noisily into the sky. Yermi gave the thumbs-up signal to the ground crews, indicating he was ready to go. Body tense, he pushed the throttle forward, his afterburn fumes forming a fiery spiral as he thundered along the runway. His speed on the HUD or 'Heads Up Display' was 150 knots. He pulled back smoothly on the stick until the flight path marker was above the horizon, and soared gracefully into the sky.

the radio boomed in his ear, giving him his flight course co-ordinates, and he entered them into his navigational system then slotted into formation and started the long flight to Iraq. Yermi's air speed was 180 knots as he crossed the Jordanian frontier, the desert wastes forming a dizzy blur beneath his fuselage. He could see the rest of the squadron clearly, spread out in line-abreast formation, following the contours of the land. They had agreed to maintain radio silence until the enemy forces had been left behind.

The heat from the baking sand shimmered upwards, creating myriad air pockets which danced the planes around, and Yermi's cruise speed crept up to 214 knots, his fuel burn 74 pounds a minute.

He saw a light flashing on the radar detection device, and glancing out of his canopy, spotted a dark stain spreading across the orange sand – the approaching Iraqi army. A tightening sensation started in his diaphragm as he looked down at the endless convoy of tanks creeping insect-like across the open desert. His left hand gripped the throttle and his right moved instinctively to the three-way switch which controlled his heat-seeking missiles. Then a voice crackled in his ear. It was Cohen, the squadron commander, breaking radio silence. 'I know what you're thinking, Sunshine, but forget it.'

Yermi spoke into the microphone attached to his helmet strap. 'We could drop our calling card as a welcoming gesture.'

'No dice. You may need those missiles before we're through.'

Yermi looked down longingly at the enemy armour. He longed to peel out of formation and swoop in to the attack, but first they had to knock out the enemy's air support. Their targets lay in Iraq.

With a sigh of frustration, Yermi tucked in behind the squadron and continued his journey eastward.

Ellen heard the roar of engines and opened her eyes, blinking. She was lying on the trailer bed, Joktan's arm draped around

222

her. He was fast asleep, his face pressed against her naked shoulder.

She held her breath, listening hard. The noise was growing louder. Easing gently from Joktan's grasp, she slid from the bed and tugged on her shirt and woollen jumper. Reaching for her jeans, she pulled back the drapes and peered through the dusty window. Beyond the oil camp, the desert, for as far as Ellen could see, was crawling with vehicles — tanks, trucks, armoured personnel carriers. Dust kicked up by their wheels formed an orange haze blotting out the sun.

Ellen finished dressing and shook Joktan awake. He sat up, running his fingers through his thick dark hair. 'It's started,' Ellen told him.

Joktan padded naked to the trailer window, the filtered sun casting ripples across his muscular back. Without a word, he began to dress.

'What happens now?' Ellen asked.

'We must give ourselves up.'

'Just like that?'

'Of course, like that.'

'You're crazy.'

'Do not worry. They are unlikely to carry out summary executions this early in the campaign.'

'Don't joke. That's the enemy out there, for Pete's sake.'

'Your enemy, not mine,' he reminded her mildly.

As they emerged into the sunlight, Ellen saw soldiers in scout cars exploring the oil camp interior. One of the vehicles pulled to a halt at their trailer door, and an officer blinked as he recognized Joktan. 'Colonel.' He climbed from the passenger seat and saluted.

'Who is in command here?' Joktan inquired in a soft voice.

'Lieutenant General Jabr al Auf.'

'Of the 16th Armoured Division?'

'Yes, colonel.'

'Take me to him at once.'

The officer ordered two of his soldiers to make room for their passengers, and with the driver sounding his horn, they sped along the lines of advancing armour.

223

Ellen saw a trailer ahead, drawn by a pug-nosed half-track. The officer waved the trailer to a halt, pulled up alongside, and ushered Ellen and Joktan on board. The trailer's interior was divided into three compartments, each section visible to the others through sound-proofed glass partitions. One was clearly the reception area. To the right lay what appeared to be the Division Commander's office. On the left was a cramped but functional conference room. As Ellen and Joktan arrived, a council of war was clearly in progress. Ellen saw a group of officers gathered around a tiny map table. One, a bull-headed man with a general's star, was addressing the gathering in slow, measured tones, pausing from time to time to indicate targets on the chart in front of him.

The officer who had brought them tapped lightly on the door and stepped into the room, leaning over to speak into the general's ear. He glanced at Ellen and Joktan through the glass partition and said something to the officer who returned and waved them to the vacant chairs. 'The general asks that you wait here until the conference is over. He will not keep you long.'

Ellen sat down as the man saluted and left the trailer. She leaned back against the shuddering hull. 'It's war, Salih. Hundreds, maybe thousands, of people are going to die to satisfy one man's incredible conceit. Nobody's behind al Shisur, not even the Iraqi people.'

'Stop worrying about al Shisur and start worrying about us,' he said. 'They will know by now that I helped you escape.'

Ellen frowned. 'What will they do?'

'That depends on how benevolent General al Auf is feeling today.'

She was silent for a moment. 'You don't regret it, do you, Salih?'

'Regret it?'

'I mean, what happened.'

He said: 'There are many things I regret about my life, but that isn't one of them.'

'I never thought it could be like this. I always thought ... well, I thought you had to know somebody for ages before you could feel the way I do now.'

224

'How is that?'

'Changed. As if I've gone through some kind of metamorphis.' She looked at him. 'Do you feel any different, Salih?'

'Not so you'd notice.'

'That's okay. I feel different enough for both of us. For the first time in my life – the very first time – I know exactly who I am and where I'm going.'

'You're a lucky girl.'

'Do you love me, Salih?'

'Love?'

'I mean, do you love me enough to put a stop to all this?'

Joktan was about to answer when a series of scrapings in the adjoining room told them the meeting next door was beginning to break up. The officers filed from the trailer, pulling on their berets and kepis. After a moment, General al Auf motioned Ellen and Joktan into his office and lit a cigarette, examining them thoughtfully. His face carried a natural intelligence which drew attention from his peasant-like features. Despite his hooked nose and shaven skull, Ellen thought there was something kindly in the general's appearance. 'When they told me what you had done,' al Auf said at length, 'I didn't believe them. Salih Joktan, the wolf of the desert, turning his back on everything holy to help an Infidel, an unbeliever.'

'You forget that I too am a Christian,' Joktan answered.

'A regrettable accident,' al Auf said.

'Does it make me expendable, along with the others?'

The general sighed, pouring himself a glass of water. 'It was the Americans who insisted the scientists must be killed, Salih. We ourselves would not stoop to such barbarism.'

'Where are they?' Ellen demanded, filled with sudden alarm. 'What have you done to my colleagues?'

'They're quite safe for the moment, Miss Conway. Until the Israeli army has been subdued, someone has to maintain the weapon system.'

'And afterwards?'

'Do not concern yourself with afterwards. Many people

225

will die during the next forty-eight hours. Only Allah can say who will survive and who will not.'

'What about us?' Joktan inquired.

'The woman must join her companions. We may need her skills in the battle ahead. You, Salih, will remain with me here. I shall radio Baghdad for instructions.'

Al Auf spoke into his intercom and after a moment, a soldier appeared at the trailer door. 'You will accompany this man to the prison vehicle,' General al Auf told Ellen. 'If anything happens to Talon Blue, you may be called upon to carry out emergency repairs.'

A hollow emptiness gathered in Ellen's stomach. There was something so final in the general's statement. She felt as if she was being parceled up for the slaughter-house.

As if Joktan guessed what she was thinking, he gently squeezed her hand. 'Don't be afraid.'

'I'm not afraid.' She forced a smile. 'Good luck, Salih. I'm sorry it had to end like this.'

Rising on her toes, she kissed him lightly on the lips and followed the soldier out to the advancing convoy. The man motioned her onto his motorcycle and they rode swiftly along the phalanx of slowly moving vehicles. She saw an armoured truck ahead, its doors sealed with metal bars. Her escort waved the driver to a halt and spoke to him briefly in Arabic, then the man unlocked the vehicle rear and waved Ellen inside.

There was little light, apart from the filtered sunshine penetrating the wire-bracketed window slits. Ellen smelled the fetid stench of sweating bodies and discerned a line of figures seated along the prison van's hull. She recognized Michael Wagner, Victor Conville and Jo Marian Lee.

'We thought you were dead,' Jo cried, hugging Ellen warmly.

As the truck started to move again, the others gathered around her, plying Ellen with questions; quickly, she out-lined the events of the past few hours.

'Joktan helped you?' Jo echoed when Ellen had finished.

'Saved my life.'

'I can't believe it.'

226

'Everything you told me was the truth,' Victor Conville admitted. 'I feel such a fool.'

'That's a hell of a confession coming from you, Victor. Anyhow, tell me what's happening here.'

'We survive as long as Talon Blue survives, it's that simple. To go on breathing, we keep it operating. They've built a special transport trailer at the centre of the convoy.'

'Can it be got at?'

Michael Wagner looked dubious. 'Unlikely. It's heavily guarded with armed troops.'

'Listen, it's up to us,' Ellen whispered. 'If al Shisur manages to knock out the Israeli army, we all know the other Arab nations will fall in behind him. Old passions run deep in the Arab soul, and despite the fact that al Shisur is universally hated among his own people, he can ignite an Islamic *Jihad* that will set the whole world ablaze.' She stared at them intently in the semi-darkness. She was filled with purpose and determination. 'Whatever it takes, whatever it costs, we've got to disable Talon Blue.'

The INS and radar screen indicated the target sixteen miles ahead, and Yermi Ze'ev cross-checked visually through his plexiglass canopy as the buildings of Baghdad rose against the skyline. His left hand gripped the throttle, his right moving back to flick the chaff switch. The chaff, ejected every twenty seconds, would form a decoy, drawing off any heat-seeking missiles fired at them from the ground during the critical period they were attacking their target.

Yermi's nerves were almost at breaking point. They were closing in fast, the squadron still in perfect formation. His eyes scanned the HUD, and he turned his search-radar from stand-by to 'on'. No one attempted to break radio silence. They were too low over enemy territory to risk alerting Iraqi artillery.

Yermi's speed shot up to 650 mph, and Iraq's sandy hills streaked by on each side of the cockpit canopy. The target was only fifty seconds away as he eased down to a hundred feet. He could see the airfield visually now, about two miles distant. He checked the radar warning receiver with a quick sideways glance – no sign of missile units operating in the area – then lowering the nose, he rolled, bringing the engine out of afterburner. There was a vertical line on the screen display, and Cohen slotted alongside him in tight formation as they moved in coolly for the kill.

Yermi called up the air-to-ground mode in the centre of the HUD, locked the FLIR/Optics sensor on to the target and rested his thumb on the bomb-release button.

Orange tracer bullets streaked into the air, blending spectacularly with the blazing sun. Yermi watched the airfield approach, lined up his flight-path marker vertically with the diamond in his HUD and started his vital pull-up. He was conscious of artillery fire from the ground below, but his entire attention was absorbed in the flickering readings on the HUD. His screen said seven seconds. The marker came into target position, and Yermi pressed his thumb on the release button, picking off two MK-82s.

He hit afterburner, easing his stick to starboard and pulling 4-Gs as he banked dizzily eastwards. The balloon-like bladders in his G-suit automatically inflated to prevent the blood draining from his brain. In the rearview mirror, he saw his bombs bursting in clusters of orange and white.

Cohen joined him on his climb for altitude, and at four thousand feet, Yermi began to whoop and holler. His body felt elated as he soared out of danger and started the long flight home.

The atmosphere in the conference room was electrifying. The Israeli Prime Minister listened in silence as his military advisers outlined the details of the initial air attacks. His pre-emptive strike had proved devastatingly effective, more so than any of them had dared envisage. Flying low under Iraqi radar, the Israeli air force had carried out over 200 sorties in less than seven hours.

'According to initial reports,' said Military Intelligence

Commander Rafael Hur, 'over 350 Iraqi combat aircraft have been destroyed on the ground. That includes their entire range of BI-14 bombers, at least 70 per cent of their Python B-5s, and most of their Sukhoi Su-7s. In addition, 89 transport aircraft and helicopters have also been wiped out.'

'Has there been any Iraqi response?' a minister asked from the other side of the room.

Hur said: 'The Iraqis strafed our oil refineries on Haifa Bay, and launched a bombing attack on the town of Mahra, but their squadrons were intercepted by our flighter planes, and we estimate that most of their assault force has now been eliminated.'

'No sign of nuclear strikes?' another man asked.

'Nothing so far. Our silo crews are on full alert, ready to retaliate the minute we pick up evidence of incoming missiles, but the Iraqis appear to be concentrating on conventional warfare.'

'What about our own losses?' Prime Minister Aronson asked softly.

'According to my last report, 14 Israeli aircraft are missing in action.'

'Fourteen.' Aronson nipped the bridge of his nose with his fingertips. He had taken a risk in ordering the aerial assault. He could have waited for UN intervention in the forlorn hope that the Iraqi advance might be halted by last minute diplomacy, but Musallim al Shisur's intransigence had convinced Aronson that only the most decisive action would save Israel from a crushing defeat. Now he had to live with the consequences.

Hur recognized the Prime Minister's dilemma. 'Men die in every war,' he said, softening his voice. 'There is no way to eliminate casualties. The only thing we can do is measure our losses against our successes. After seven hours of fighting, 440 enemy aircraft have been destroyed on the ground, and a further 28 shot down in aerial dogfights. At this rate, al Shisur will be stripped of air support before he reaches the Jordanian frontier.'

'*Baruch Hashem*,' Aronson said softly in Hebrew. 'Let us pray that our victories continue.'

Excerpt from CBS Television News

'Throughout the night, Israeli planes have been attacking military targets in Iraq in the most devastating aerial offensive since the Gulf War of 1991. Operations have been carried out against air defence units, communications centres, airfields, and defence headquarters. Three of Musallim al Shisur's nuclear reactors have been destroyed, and our correspondent in Baghdad says the Israeli air armada has now pounded Iraqi defences to the point of paralysis. According to Israeli Defence Minister Brin Lavon, Israeli losses have been few, and sources in Tel Aviv say the returning aircraft are now preparing to carpet bomb Iraqi armoured divisions approaching the Jordanian frontier . . .'

Yermi Ze'cv was the first to spot the enemy B-5. He was starting to move out of the line-abreast position when he was stunned to see a bandit blip nosing on to the radar scanner at ten o'clock high. The radio filled with chatter as the Israeli squadron broke electronic silence, bellowing warnings into their helmet microphones.

'Bandit north about fifteen degrees.'

'Affirmative Eli, affirmative.'

'Speed 350, altitude 20,000.'

Yermi picked up the bandit visually and pulled his jet in an 8-G turn to meet the attacker. The bandit turned tight in an attempt to lock on to Yermi's tail. He glanced at the tactical display to determine the bandit's direction, and called up the air-to-air mode on the HUD, trying to lock his FLIR/Optics sensor on to the target.

As the Iraqi pilot started his turn, Yermi swung starboard in the same direction, rolling his wings to eighty degrees of bank, and pulling 7-Gs. He watched the bandit move into the gun-cross, and switched the knob beneath the navigational instruments from Position One to Position Two.

Yermi's heart beat wildly as the digital radar screen flashed out the words: 'Target Acquired.'

'Master Arm On,' he shouted into his radio mask. 'Have tone, have tone.'

His right hand clutched the control stick as a missile lock indication appeared in the left Multi-Functional Display. Sucking in his breath, he pressed the number two fire button on his joystick. There was a sudden whooshing sensation and the aircraft trembled violently, then the bandit seemed to buckle outwards, erupting across the sky in a great mushroom of crimson flame.

A wave of elation swept Yermi as he shouted: 'Good kill, good kill,' and pulling out of his attack pattern, slotted neatly back into position.

The rest of the flight continued without incident. So tight was the squadron formation that Yermi could clearly see the two pilots on either side, and from time to time, they signalled each other through their plexiglass canopies. Yermi knew his companions were as spiritually exhilarated and as emotionally drained as he was. Combat did that to a man. The long hours of tension, the concentration, the furious bursts of energy when the target swung into alignment – they all took an inevitable toll.

The squadron kept their homeward flight high to cut down on fuel, and as the airfield came into view, it was a simple process to drop out of the clouds. Yermi felt his wheels touch down and pulled back the throttle, taxi-ing into position. The ground crews were dancing with delight as he opened his canopy bubble and clambered stiffly from the cockpit. Not a single aircraft had been lost, and already the mechanics, clad in oily coveralls, were opening up the hatches to commence refuelling. Yermi saw the diesel wagons lumbering towards them across the sunbaked blacktop.

Cohen grinned at him wildly as he took off his helmet, running his fingers through his stubbled hair. Something seemed to burst inside Yermi and he yelled out loud. Then like a pair of demented schoolboys, the two men began leaping about the sundrenched runway, pounding each other's shoulders in a frenzy of elation and relief.

President Clayman sat in the Oval Office and listened in silence to the briefing given by the Chairman of the Joint

Chiefs of Staff, Major General Nathan Kincaid. 'The Iraqi losses appear to be devastating,' Kincaid said. 'Their air force has been effectively wiped out, and what's left is in total disarray. After a night of concentrated sorties, the Israelis have gained virtual control of the air. Now their pilots can devote themselves to providing combat support for the Israeli ground formations.'

'Has the damage been officially confirmed?' the President asked.

'No word yet from our people in Baghdad. I guess the communications there have been pretty well decimated, so most of our information comes direct from Tel Aviv. However, our satellites do seem to confirm the Israeli claims. There's evidence of extensive damage to all Iraqi air bases, and many of their command posts can be seen burning vigorously.'

'Any sign of nuclear involvement?'

'Apparently not, Larry. The Iraqis are keeping their assault strictly conventional, and Israel seems to be responding accordingly.'

'What about the Iraqi army approaching the Israeli frontier?'

Kincaid said: 'At 0500 hours this morning, they launched a barrage of artillery fire from positions along the Jordan River. A softening-up process, it would seem. The main impetus of the attack appears to centre on the Hebron-Jerusalem road. It looks as though the Iraqis intend using the surrounding hills as a jumping off point for Beersheba and the Negev.'

'Without air support, that sounds a dangerous proposition.'

'Most military commanders would agree with you, Mr President. However, since both Jerusalem and Tel Aviv are being shelled by long-range Iraqi guns, it does suggest that al Shisur is preparing for a determined thrust into the Israeli heartland.'

'What are the Israelis doing?'

'From our satellite pictures, it looks as though their 10th Mechanized Brigade is moving into the area of Halil Atarit to seize the mountain ridge and control the Judean Hills overlooking the descent to Jericho. The 7th Armoured

Brigade is also advancing between the mountain spurs and Hassi Saar.'

Clayman was silent for a moment as he considered Kincaid's information. His eyes looked tired in the early morning. Throughout the night he had been woken continually with up-to-the-minute reports on the Middle East ground and air battle. 'The emergency meeting of the UN Security Council has just broken up,' Clayman said. 'They've passed a resolution calling on Israel and Iraq to cease hostilities immediately and settle their differences by peaceful means.'

'That's unlikely to have much influence on Musallim al Shisur,' General Kincaid replied.

'I agree. However, with most of his air force destroyed, he must appreciate the delicacy of his situation. He can't hope to complete his advance without effective air support.'

'You think he'll be more amenable?'

'It's worth a try,' Clayman said. 'He saw what happened to his hero Sadaam Hussein. Now, after only a few hours of fighting, he finds himself in exactly the same position. Al Shisur knows his country's on the brink of full-scale revolution. The Iraqi people are bitterly opposed to his warlike policies. Maybe he'll realize the time has finally come for compromise.' He picked up the telephone. 'Let's see if we can set up a dialogue with Baghdad.'

Israeli Military Intelligence Commander Lieutenant General Rafael Hur took off his cap as he entered the Prime Minister's office. The Prime Minister's secretary, Mona Boyer, raised a finger to her lips. Hur could see Aronson, fully-clothed, lying on a bunk behind a row of filing cabinets. 'He's still asleep?'

'He's exhausted,' Boyer said. 'He's been up most of the night, talking by radio to commanders in the field. I've given orders that he's not to be disturbed.'

'You'll have to break them,' General Hur said. 'We need decisions which can only come from the top.'

Boyer looked across at the sleeping Prime Minister. 'He's been dozing like that for less than an hour. He's not a young man, you know. If he keeps this up, sooner or later he's bound to crack.'

'Don't worry about Ariel Aronson. Old he may be, but delicate he's not. Get some coffee, and make it strong.'

Aronson's eyes fluttered as General Hur shook him by the shoulder. 'I'm sorry to wake you, Prime Minister, but we've reached a critical point in the battle for the Jordan River. Our commanders report that we now have total supremacy in the air. All major Iraqi bases have been destroyed, and their communication links are effectively cut off.'

Aronson swung his feet from the bunk, and sat for a moment, staring at the floor. When he looked up at Hur, his eyes were rimmed with red. 'Pull back all squadrons,' he ordered. 'Tell Levin to change tactics and concentrate his attacks on the enemy ground forces approaching the border.'

When General Abu Bakhit arrived at the Baghdad Palace, he found Musallim al Shisur's military advisers gathered in an ante-room adjoining the President's private quarters. Bakhit looked at them inquiringly as he took off his beret. 'What's happening?'

Silently, General Sadr handed him a piece of paper. It was a situation report from the commanders in the field. As Bakhit read it, his expression darkened. 'Has anyone told the President?'

Sadr shook his head and Bakhit regarded the officers with contempt. 'How are we supposed to fight a war if our own advisers fail to communicate with their head of state?'

'It's impossible to communicate,' General Sadr said. 'The President is like an ostrich with its head tucked firmly in the sand. We warned him what would happen if he attempted this advance without air support, but he believes he's receiving messages from God. Who knows what will happen when he learns the truth?'

'Well, he'll have to learn it sooner or later,' Bakhit said.

He pushed his way through the sombre throng, knocked lightly on the door, and entered al Shisur's private chambers. The room, though modernised, had been furnished in the style of an Arabian Nights palace. Exotic tapestries and billowing drapes adorned the walls and the high-domed ceiling.

The President himself was standing at the open window, gazing into the courtyard below. He was dressed Arab-style in gold-trimmed robes and a jewel-encrusted head-dress.

'Excellency?' Bakhit said.

Al Shisur looked at him. 'I saw a hawk today, Abu. It flew on to the Palace spires. It alighted once on each tip in turn, then flew away. It has to be a sign, don't you think?'

'A sign, Excellency?'

'Clearly the hawk represents the elusive bird of destiny. Had it alighted only once, the omen would hardly have been promising, but to land three times, Abu, that can signify only one thing. Victory.'

'The news, I'm afraid, is not good,' Bakhit warned.

'Give it to me,' al Shisur ordered.

Bakhit said: 'Most of our air force has been demolished during the last few hours of Israeli air strikes.'

A faint breeze ruffled al Shisur's beard. He was gazing into the courtyard again. He might have been contemplating the menu for dinner.

Bakhit continued: 'Enemy air attacks have forced our troops to slow their advance east of the River Jordan. The route is strewn with tanks from our 16th Armoured Brigade which has fallen victim to Israeli carpet bombing. I regret to inform you, Excellency, that our army is now left without air support for the fighting ahead.'

Somewhere outside, they heard a bell clanging. Traffic rumbled on the hot morning air. Al Shisur toyed absently with his *keffiyah*. 'The Israelis will be flushed with success,' he said. 'Everything is proceeding as I planned.'

'Excellency?' General Bakhit was puzzled.

'I need the enemy to be off his guard, Abu. That element is critical to my campaign. It's true their air force is formidable, but wars can't be won from the air alone. In the final analysis, it is always the ground troops who carry the day.'

Bakhit placed his report gently on the window-sill. He said: 'With respect, Excellency, though we are within a stone's throw of the Israeli frontier, it is inconceivable that our squadrons can continue to advance as long as the enemy holds air supremacy. We are faced with little alternative but to retreat.'

Al Shisur looked mildly amused. 'You disappoint me, Abu. I thought that you, of all people, would appreciate my strategy. There will be no retreat. Not one mile, not one inch. We are going to drive the Israelis into the sea.'

'And how is that to be accomplished?' Bakhit asked.

Al Shisur turned to look at him, the sunlight from the open window giving life to his eyes, accentuating the madness nestling in the small, dilated pupils. 'You will pass the order to our military commanders in the field that Talon Blue is to be engaged immediately.'

Chapter Seventeen

The whine was faint at first, growing steadily louder. Ellen held her breath, counting the seconds before the missile struck. 'Down,' she bellowed.

They dived to the deck and she clenched her teeth, waiting for the impact. There was a moment in which time stood still, then they heard a tumultuous explosion as something struck the prison truck roof. Suddenly, they were rolling over and over. It was like being inside a washing machine, Ellen thought, her body tumbling from wall to wall. The others were spinning around her, hitting the sides of the truck with loud metallic clangs. Ellen's shoulder struck the bulkhead as the stricken vehicle went on cartwheeling, its panels creaking under the strain.

She struggled desperately to keep her mind alert, holding on to her senses with an effort. They were still intact, thank God, the missile hadn't penetrated their armoured plating and the damn' truck had to stop rolling sometime. A wall split open with a deafening pop, letting in a deluge of sunlight, then the wagon rattled to a halt and lay on its side with its wheels still spinning.

For a long moment, the four occupants remained quite still. Ellen breathed deeply, filling her lungs with air. Somehow, the realization that she was still alive did little to restore her shattered wits. Her body was aching in every limb, and there was a throbbing pain in her left temple that seemed to radiate through her entire skull. She rolled on to her stomach and looked at the others. Jo's face was severely bruised, and Victor Conville was bleeding heavily from a cut above his left eyebrow. There was no sign of life from Michael Wagner. Ellen rose to her knees and slithered toward him.

Wagner was lying on his side, his glazed eyes staring at the vehicle's hull. He was clearly dead. Ellen stifled a sob. She'd scarcely known Wagner – a few desultory chats, a drink or two at the officers' club hardly constituted a meaningful relationship – nevertheless, the sight of his frozen features shocked her to the core.

'Mike's neck's broken,' she told the others.

'Jesus,' Conville muttered.

Ellen eyed the aperture in the upper bulkhead. She would think about Wagner later, when there was time to reflect and ruminate. Right now, she could hear the roar of explosions as the air raid continued. 'Maybe this is our chance to hit that weapon system,' she said.

Jo looked at her wonderingly. 'You want to go out into that madhouse?'

'It isn't a question of "wanting to", Jo. We *have* to. There's nobody else.' She turned to Conville. 'Are you with me, Victor?'

'All the way,' he answered, mopping blood from his forehead. Ellen nodded in approval. Maybe she'd been wrong about Conville. Exasperating, he might be, but he was solid as a rock when the need was there.

'Okay, it's every man for himself. Anyone falls, forget it.'

'Right,' Conville said.

Ellen peered out at the havoc the Israeli air attack had created. The entire convoy had ground to a halt, and everywhere she looked, great columns of smoke were belching from the blazing wreckage. Dust, kicked up by the missile blasts, formed an orange haze blotting out the sun. Many of the tanks were using their anti-aircraft guns, and the sound of their barrage added deafeningly to the din.

'Where *is* Talon Blue?' Ellen asked.

'Column centre,' Conville told her.

'Okay, let's go.'

She struggled through the jagged opening and charged along the lines of embattled vehicles, Jo and Conville running swiftly in her wake. Smoke swirled into her eyes

238

and her head rang with the plaintive wail of the incoming shells. There were tanks everywhere, and great mushroom bursts of flame that scattered earth in all directions. She tried to ignore the mindless bedlam which surrounded her, concentrating instead on keeping her legs moving when every part of her psyche screamed for refuge and shelter.

A soldier spotted her and shouted something in Arabic, lunging forward to clutch at her arm. She pulled to one side but his fingers seized her woollen jumper, tearing the sleeve from wrist to elbow.

Conville leapt out of the fumes, attacking the man in a flurry of whirling fists. The Iraqi went down, but almost instantly another group of figures appeared at Victor's rear. 'Keep going,' he shouted, his face contorted in the shell blasts. 'I'll hold the bastards back.'

There was no time to consider or reflect. With Jo at her heels, Ellen tore on through the smoke and flame.

Inside the general's trailer, Joktan watched al Auf reading the transcripts of radio messages from command headquarters in Baghdad. Outside, the noise of the air raid was deafening.

Since Ellen's departure, Joktan had remained largely silent. He was not a garrulous man by nature, and had used the interlude to work out his best plan of action. First, he had to rescue Ellen. He couldn't allow her to be assassinated. Next, he had to find some way out of this charnel house. It wouldn't be easy in the circumstances, but Joktan knew that escape was Ellen's only hope of survival.

'We've had word from General Bakhit,' al Auf told him. 'He wants you returned to Baghdad immediately.'

'How?' Joktan asked.

'There's a desert airstrip at a small village named Habab. It's about eight miles inside the border. Bakhit has arranged for a plane to pick you up there. You are to be flown at once to the Presidential Palace.'

'And then?'

Al Auf's features softened. 'Bakhit is a compassionate man, and he's always regarded you as one of his sons. So long as the President doesn't interfere, I would say your chances of survival are relatively strong.'

The general was sympathetic, and Joktan appreciated that. Nevertheless, despite the man's mildness, Joktan sensed his underlying disapproval. 'You think I was wrong to do what I did, general?'

'Foolish, Salih, that's all.'

'I would do it again,' Joktan told him flatly.

'You never fail to surprise me,' al Auf said. 'I see, after all, you are a sentimentalist at heart.'

'If sentimentality means being opposed to this war, then I plead guilty. Destroying lives without reason diminishes the soul.'

General al Auf pursed his lips, as if Joktan had put his finger on an inescapable truth. 'I have no love for al Shisur,' he admitted. 'However, I am a soldier, and as long as Abu Bakhit supports the President, I shall continue to do my duty.'

'How much longer must people go on dying because soldiers insist on doing their duty?'

The trailer door burst open and a infantryman appeared on the threshold, snapping to attention. His helmet was gone, and his combat jacket was covered with dust.

'What is it?' the general demanded.

'The prison truck has been demolished,' the man announced. 'One of the Americans is dead, the others have disappeared. We searched the wreckage, but found nothing.'

Joktan's senses reeled, and he saw the room beginning to spin. He leapt to his feet, thrusting the soldier rudely aside. Al Auf's voice echoed in his ears as he plunged through the door and sprinted along the line of stationary tanks. There was no thought in him now, only a blind, impassioned madness. He saw the armour snarled to a standstill, and the terrified troops crouching beneath the metal canopies. He saw the smoke belching across the smouldering bomb craters, and the orange dust forming a hazy blur that blended into the sky with no dividing line. If anything happened to Ellen, he thought, he would never forgive himself.

He reached the prison truck as medics were lifting a bloodstained corpse through a hole in the vehicle's side. To Joktan's relief, he realized the body was that of a man.

He turned back, battling his way through the milling, bewildered troops. He found a second body sprawled in the dust, and recognized Victor Conville. His sculpted features had been shattered by a bullet, probably whilst trying to escape.

'Grab your rifles and follow me,' Joktan bellowed at a group of soldiers huddling for protection under the canopy of a T-54, and without waiting to see if they obeyed, he galloped into the whirling smoke.

A terrible weariness had gathered in Ellen's limbs. It wasn't simply the run, she told herself, she could do that any day. This was fear, cold and debilitating. She knew what she had to do, but her nerves were stretched to breaking point.

She saw a trio of corpses on the ground, infantrymen hit by pieces of shrapnel. Their bodies lay in clumsy disarray, hand-grenades studding their bloodstained combat-jackets.

Ellen dropped to her knees, panting heavily, and steeling herself against the ugly wounds, began plucking the grenades from the soldiers' tunics and thrusting them down the front of her sweater. Jo did the same.

She flinched as an Israeli fighter screeched overhead. 'Can't be much further, dammit.'

'I think we found it,' Jo told her, nodding into the fumes.

Squinting, Ellen saw a huge ten-wheeler vehicle directly ahead, its elongated rear covered by a tarpaulin shroud. It towered against the sky, its massive cargo wreathed by curling smoke. Talon Blue.

The tension inside Ellen reached a crescendo. They still had to break through the security cordon of troops squatting around the vehicle's rim.

'Think they'd shoot?' she asked, waving at the soldiers who were flinching nervously with each successive explosion.

'They look like homicidal maniacs to me.'

'Then we'll just have to get rid of them.'

'How?' Jo queried.

Ellen plucked one the hand-grenades from inside her jumper and looked at it dubiously. 'Any idea how this thing works?'

'You just hook your finger into the metal ring, and pull.'

'Ever tossed one before?'

'Are you kidding?'

'How long before the detonator goes off?'

'Half a minute, twenty seconds. Maybe less.'

Ellen took a deep breath. 'Okay, hang on to your underpants.'

To her surprise, the pin came out easily, and with a nervous twitch, she rolled the grenade along the ground. Muscles tense, they crouched behind a stationary tank while Ellen counted the seconds under her breath. For a long moment, nothing happened, then they heard a loud bang, and peering out, saw soldiers leaping from the conveyor and scrambling desperately for cover.

'We've done it.'

They sprinted across the open ground and ducked beneath the heavy tarpaulin, shadows gathering around them as the massive shroud flopped into place. Ellen peered up at the giant framework and felt her muscles tighten. Talon Blue looked demoniacal, its blossoming tendrils forming a complex canopy which sprouted in every direction. 'Will you look at this thing,' she whispered. 'What in God's name have we constructed here?'

'How we gonna spike it?' Jo asked.

'We'll use the grenades.'

'Think they'll be powerful enough?'

'They worked out there, didn't they? What the hell, they're all we've got.'

Girders criss-crossed the weapon structure from base to summit, and Ellen began to climb, picking her way up the complex latticework, testing each step as she moved from rung to rung. She could feel the coldness of the hand-grenades pressing against her naked skin. Jo followed breathlessly in her wake, her feet making little clopping sounds on the metal bars.

It was an easy ascent, and Ellen felt grateful for that. Plenty of holds to choose from, and no sense of exposure, thanks to the gloom, but she was shivering nevertheless. Not out of cold, she realized – it was breathlessly hot beneath

242

the heavy tarpaulin – no, her trembling came from fear. She was petrified out of her wits. The secret was to stop thinking, to shut off the mind and ignore the vagaries of the imagination, to concentrate instead on the physical things, like the metal rivets crusted with dust, the iron cross-braces with their aluminum coating, the bristling antennae and delicate sensor rods.

Her fingers felt numb from the constant groping. Probably tension, she thought. Scared, you noticed things like that. Derring-do was never my style, she told herself. I wanted a little excitement, sure, but when this is over I'll settle happily for the quiet life in Santa Clara.

She reached the generator's bevelled underbelly and paused to run her hand along the metal casing. A wire bracket secured it to the central support mast. Pulling the grenades from under her jumper, she began wedging them against the crossbar. 'Give me yours,' she snapped at Jo.

Jo fumbled in her anorak pockets, passing the deadly little objects delicately upwards. 'How d'you figure on setting 'em off?'

'Easy.'

Ellen peeled off her jumper and began to untwine the woollen strands. She twisted them together to form a slender line which she tied to the ring of the nearest hand-grenade. Then she began to ease down the pylon, unravelling the jumper as she went, creating a precarious umbilical cord. 'If I can play this out long enough, maybe we can detonate the grenades from the deck below.'

'By that time, the war'll be over.'

'You got a better idea?' Ellen snapped.

It was a slow and agonizing business, and from time to time, the strands came apart in Ellen's fingers, but frowning with concentration, she knotted the pieces patiently together and carried on with her tortuous, painstaking task.

When Joktan reached the Talon Blue trailer, he found troops uncoupling the damaged driving cab. A replacement vehicle stood waiting nearby.

Joktan examined the smoking wreckage. 'What happened?'

243

'Air strike,' a soldier said. 'The cab suffered a direct hit.'

Something about the damage bothered Joktan. Most of the impact appeared to have been beneath the chassis; the vehicle's roof and passenger cabin were relatively untouched.

He saw a piece of shrapnel lying in the dust, and picked it up. 'Hand grenade,' he said, showing his find to the soldier. 'This attack was carried out from the ground.'

'But that's impossible,' the man protested. 'The conveyor is heavily guarded.'

Joktan raised his voice, addressing the soldiers at large. 'Search the trailer, check it over from stem to stern. If you spot any saboteurs, hold your fire. We need to capture these people alive.'

Joktan wore no markings on his jumpsuit, but he exuded an air of authority that was impossible to ignore. The soldiers obeyed without a word.

Sweat gathered on Ellen's body as she worked her way feverishly down the metal framework. Unravelling the jumper and twisting the strands into a serviceable line was proving a slow and meticulous task. Several times, she was tempted to abandon it completely, but some inner streak of stubbornness kept her going. She played out the line section by section, its braided threads pitifully slender, dangerously brittle.

Jo hissed warningly from below, 'Ellen? Somebody's coming.'

Ellen felt her heartbeat quicken. 'Soldiers?'

'That's what it sounds like.'

'Well, I can't pull the firing pin yet. We'll go up with the grenades.'

'How much longer do you need?'

'Maybe another five minutes.'

'Okay, I'll see if I can keep them occupied.'

The tarpaulin canopy was thrust rudely aside, and Ellen's heart hammered as she saw troops framed in the sunlit opening. A cry rose from the intruders as they spotted Jo wriggling through the metal lattice-work. They'd taken the bait, thank God, but Ellen knew Jo couldn't distract them for long. Fingers numb, she tried desperately to speed up her progress. Crazy, she'd been, thinking she could get away with this. It would be only a matter of time before the troops looked up and saw her clinging to the scaffolding.

Below, Jo had worked her way behind a line of rubberized condensors, and Ellen heard the Iraqis chattering as they formed a two-pronged pincer movement to cut her off. Jo was leading them a fine old dance, twisting and backtracking, and Ellen was grateful for that since every second she remained at large added a few more inches to the detonating line.

The Iraqis were scattered all over the truck now, their voices ragged and excited as they scrambled among the network of girders, homing in on their quarry. Suddenly, a shot rang out. The sound was mind-jolting in the stifling enclosure and Ellen gave an involuntary gasp. Looking down, she saw Jo peel from the scaffolding and drop to the deck with a muffled thud. The soldiers froze into a silent tableau, and Ellen stared in horror at a crimson stain spreading across Jo's anorak. Dear God, she thought, her heart pounding.

Suddenly, Joktan appeared and knelt at Jo's side. He pressed his fingers against her carotid artery, his dark face flushed with anger, then rising to his feet, hit the soldier responsible savagely between the eyes.

As the man crashed backwards, Ellen saw the troops lining her up in their rifle sights. Joktan's voice, calm and authoritative, rose through the mêlée. 'Ellen, come down.'

She didn't answer. Jo's death seemed to have immobilized her senses. Anguish seared her chest, hurting so badly she wanted to cry out. She was still too close to the handgrenades to pull the firing pin with safety, but if she didn't act now, she knew the moment would be lost forever.

'Ellen.' Joktan spoke again. 'These men are like children, excitable and impulsive. Unless you come down, they will certainly kill you.'

She took a deep breath, her body shivering violently. Then gripping the line with both hands, she clenched her teeth and tugged as hard as she could. With a gentle swishing sound, the makeshift rope flopped into her face. Tears sprang to her eyes as she realized the wool had snapped several inches below the spot where the hand-grenades lay hidden.

Joktan climbed up the pylon and seized her from behind, waving at the troops. 'Check the scaffolding,' he ordered. 'See what she's got up there and dismantle it as carefully as you can.'

Then speaking soothingly into her ear, he guided her, still weeping, down the complex, shuddering framework.

The cabin stood on a clifftop, surrounded by trees. Its timbered roof was sagging in places, and its broken windows had been patched with old Coca-Cola boards. There was no sign of smoke from its metal chimney.

Paul and Leila studied it wearily. 'Forest look-out station,' Paul said. 'They probably only man the place during the fire-risk season.'

They had been walking for hours, shuffling and stumbling across the wood-cluttered hilltops, the country endlessly repeating itself. Now, footsore and exhausted, they examined the cabin like pilgrims catching their first glimpse of the Promised Land.

'Hey, there?' Paul called. 'Anyone at home?'

No answer.

Leila tried the door. 'It's locked.'

'Maybe it'll jimmie.' Paul examined the keyhole appraisingly. 'Got a nail-file?'

'Nail-file? I think so.'

Paul knelt down, tinkering at the lock with expert precision. After moment, there was a muffled click and the door swung slowly inwards.

The cabin was small and musty, its floor and windows coated with a thin layer of dust. A narrow bunk stood in the corner; beside it was an emergency radio.

'Looks like we can call for help,' Paul said.

'Think it'll work?'

'Let's see what happens when I slot the batteries into place.'

He pushed them in and switched on the radio. Instantly, the set began to hum. 'Bingo.'

Pressing his thumb on the 'Transmit' button, he spoke into the microphone. The receiver crackled, and after a

246

moment they heard a voice emerging through the static. 'This is Dodgeville One calling Sawtooth Seven. Do you copy? Over.'

Paul gave the acknowledgement signal.

'Who are you?' the voice demanded. 'What are you doing up there?'

'Hikers. Got lost in the forest. Our food's gone, and we're in really big trouble unless you can get us out of here.'

'Take it easy, pal. You'll find plenty of eats stashed in the cellar. How'd you get into such a mess?'

'Lost our compass. Backpacks too. We been stumbling around for hours, trying to find a way out.'

'Well, it'll be nightfall soon. I guess you better sit tight and wait for morning. I'll get one of my boys to pick you up first thing. However, I'll have to ask you to pay for any food you eat. Cabin has to be fully stocked, and I got budgets to account for.'

Paul promised that he would, and they discovered the food cache stored below ground to keep it cool during the summer heat. The fare looked far from appetising – canned beans, canned chilli and canned peaches – but they were grateful for anything which might stem the hunger pangs cramping their stomachs.

Paul gathered some wood and lit the stove, then as darkness fell they cooked their modest supper and ate it at the cabin table. By the time they'd finished, a profound lassitude had gathered in Paul's body. His thoughts blended into a mindless reverie that had no shape or meaning.

'Tired?' Leila asked as he leaned back in his chair, staring out sleepily at the stars.

'Yeah. Been quite a day.'

'I guess we're lucky to be alive.'

'That wasn't luck. That was you.'

'Don't exaggerate.'

'I'm not exaggerating.'

His eyes softened as he looked at her. He hardly knew this woman, he reflected, yet in some strange way he felt closer to her than to anyone else in his entire life. Including Ellen. 'You're quite a girl,' he said.

'I'm not sure how to take that. We're business partners,

247

remember. What I did was for purely selfish reasons.'

'That's a lie. The first time maybe. But this afternoon, on the cliff-face, that was different. That was for me.'

Leila looked embarrassed. She rose to her feet and began gathering the empty plates. Paul watched her in silence for a moment, noting the way she avoided his eyes. She was beautiful, he thought. Even with her hair tangled and her clothes dishevelled, she was beautiful. A man would have to be crazy not to see it.

'Leila?'

'Yes?'

'I'm glad you came along on this trip.'

'Sure.'

'I mean it. Not because you saved my life. Not because you helped me track down Snyder, but because it gave me a chance to really get to know you.'

'You're screwballed.'

'I never felt more serious in my life.'

He reached out, pulling her toward him, pressing his face against her stomach. Leila hesitated a moment, then slowly, tenderly, ran her fingers through his hair. She took his face in both hands and kissed him gently on the mouth. When she tried to pull back, he seized her in his arms, fastening his lips against hers. She sensed the urgency in his body as he worked his hands beneath her shirt, seizing her small firm breasts. Her nipples puckered at his touch and she closed her eyes, letting him cover her throat with kisses. She heard the sound of his breathing, like an animal in some strange ecstatic rapture. Then her skin shivered and she was caught in the grip of a fierce sexual awareness. This was no simulated passion, she knew. Her limbs were aflame, her head swooning. She groaned deep in her throat as Paul picked her up as lightly as a feather and carried her over to the empty bed.

Leila heard the sound of a truck arriving and found a battered Datsun at the cabin door. A man in the uniform of a forest ranger smiled at her amiably. 'Hi, I'm Johnny Haber. You the folks who got themselves into trouble here?'

'That's right. Thanks for coming.'

'No problem. We'd have picked you up last night except

that it's a bumpy ride over Chateau Mountain.' He looked around. 'Where's your partner?'

'I'll go and fetch him,' Leila said.

She moved off through the trees, following a narrow track leading to the clifftop. Something had happened to Leila during the past few hours, something she couldn't explain, even to herself. After all, she was no vestel virgin, she'd had her share of men — more than her share, if the truth were known. But never — never once — had she felt the way she'd felt last night. Curiously and inexplicably, Paul had touched some chord within her and now, against logic, against reason, she felt inescapably changed.

Was this all it came down to then? No big mystery, just the right combination of hormones, and suddenly the world became a brighter and sunnier place? All her life she'd been missing out on that one essential element and hadn't even realized it. It was crazy. But what was even crazier, little short of mind-blowing in fact, was the question of what she was going to do now?

She found Paul standing on the clifftop, staring across the forest below. He did not turn as Leila approached, and a faint breeze ruffled his hair, curling it back from his forehead. Sunlight glinted on his wire-rimmed spectacles.

'Truck's here,' she told him.

'Yeah, I heard.'

Something in his voice made her frown. It was toneless, flat, filled with indecision. She studied him closely. 'You okay?'

'Sure.'

'You're not . . . angry or anything?'

'Why should I be angry?'

'I don't know. Maybe you're sorry about last night.'

He shook his head. 'I'm confused, that's all.'

'Confused?'

'I don't know who I am any more. Last week, everything seemed cut and dried. I was in love with Ellen. Now . . .' He shrugged.

Leila was silent for a moment. She'd been so wrapped up in her own problems, she hadn't even paused to consider Paul's. Now she sensed the crisis bubbling inside him.

249

'Nobody can help the way they feel,' she said. 'It isn't something you plan, like a business or a career. Human emotions happen whether you like them or not.'

'But I'm not the kind of man who does things impulsively,' he told her. 'I thought there was nobody in the world I cared about as much as Ellen. Yet here I am, a few days later, discovering I was wrong. That takes a bit of getting used to.'

Right, Leila thought, for me as well as you. You can't turn your back on a lifetime of conditioning and pretend it never happened.

She reached out and gently took his hand. 'Let's not keep the officer waiting,' she said.

Chapter Eighteen

'Your plane is ready now, colonel,' the soldier said, snapping to attention at the door of the general's trailer.

Joktan rose to his feet and looked at al Auf. 'I would like to take the woman with me.'

Surprised, the general glanced at Ellen through the glass partition. Her tattered jumper had been replaced by a borrowed Iraqi combat jacket, and she was staring moodily at the floor, hands clasped, head bowed. 'Why, Salih?' al Auf asked.

'She is in great danger here.'

'You think she will be safe if you take her to Baghdad?'

'At least she'll have a sporting chance.'

General al Auf said: 'I'm sorry, it's impossible.'

'For what reason?'

'Because she's the only American left alive. If anything goes wrong with Talon Blue, I'll need her to carry out repairs.'

'She's already tried to disable the thing once. Allow her anywhere near that weapon system, and she'll do her damnedest to put it out of action.'

Al Auf pursed his lips thoughtfully. He took his flak-jacket from the wall and pulled it on, his brutish face sober and reflective. 'I believe you are right,' he said at last. 'The woman is more of a liability than an asset.'

'You know I'm right, general. As long as she remains with the column, Talon Blue can never be completely safe.'

'Very well, take her with you. I wish you luck with the authorities in Baghdad.'

Al Auf moved to the trailer door, strapping on his helmet,

and Joktan stepped aside to let him by. His face was calm, his eyes grateful. 'I wish you luck too, general, with your little American toy.'

The Iraqi soldiers watched with awe as the giant generator was wheeled into position. Mechanics raced to undo the fastenings, rolling back the sheets to reveal the weapon's skeletal framework. It towered above the convoy like a grotesque microbe.

General al Auf eyed the contraption uneasily. Over to the west, he could hear the solid crump-crump of artillery fire as Iraqi guns engaged the Israeli aircraft. It seemed hard to believe that this weird monstrosity could turn the tide in the battle ahead.

'What happens if the enemy planes put a missile down the weapon's throat?' Colonel Turkia inquired, standing at al Auf's side.

'Hopefully, our Zionist friends will be far more interested in knocking out our armour than in wasting precious warheads on what looks like a giant washing machine.'

One of the mechanics ran up to al Auf and saluted. 'Talon Blue is now ready, general,' he said.

Al Auf drummed his fingers lightly on his map-holder and stared out at the distant sand. 'Well,' he said, 'shall we see what our magical device is capable of?'

The lights framing Talon Blue's generator were blinking on and off as Ellen rattled by in the open scout car. A terrible depression had taken hold of her. It wasn't simply the memory of Jo's death, though that in itself had been traumatizing enough, but the realization that everything they'd attempted, the loss of Jo, Conville and Wagner, even her own arrest had been little more than a protest hurled against the wind filled her with bitterness and dismay. The madness, she knew, was only just beginning.

Their driver pulled to a halt on the desert airstrip, and Joktan helped her into the waiting plane. Over west, they heard the muffled crump-crump of heavy explosions.

'We must hurry, colonel,' the pilot said as they squeezed

into the tiny flight cabin. 'There is another air raid commencing.'

Ellen examined the clouds through the porthole window, but she saw no sign of the approaching planes. The pilot lowered his flaps and ran the engine up to full power. Then he started along the runway, and lifted gracefully into the sky.

Yermi Ze'er felt his fighter shuddering as he pushed his throttle forward into afterburn. His air speed read 350 knots. At 6000 feet, he back-pressured the control handle, maintaining formation on the squadron's left wing. Despite the danger, he was relaxed and rested after several hours of sleep. A ripple of excitement passed through his body as he spotted the enemy forces below. They were spread across the desert like a swarm of approaching ants, and Yermi smiled wolfishly as he pressed his finger on the radio switch. 'Charlie Two, Charlie Two, target directly ahead, distance seven miles.'

'Affirmative, Charlie Two,' a voice crackled. 'Moving into attack formation now.'

Yermi checked his HUD as the aircraft in the squadron's centre went into mid-afterburn, zooming up to 10,000 feet to form a protective canopy against any Iraqi fighters which might have escaped the previous night's bombing. He turned his search from 'stand-by' to 'on'. He could see the enemy armour clearly now, the metallic vehicles spread out in fanlike formation. Yermi gave a low whistle of approval. The Iraqi commander was taking no chances on bunched-up missile hits. He had scattered his forces across an expansive area, making them difficult to pinpoint, difficult to attack. Clever, clever, Yermi thought.

He was five miles from the target now. Time to ease up. He back-pressured the control handle, banking steeply into the sun, then he checked his radar warning receiver for indications of SAMs or Triple A before going into a plummetting dive. Five thousand feet. Four thousand. Three-thousand-five-hundred. He could see the ground streaking up to meet him, and held his breath, resting his thumb on the bomb release button. The altimeter needle was spinning wildly, like a rotating top. He glimpsed the tanks directly beneath, their armoured plating camouflaged to blend into the desert terrain. Their squat turrets were fitted with circular radar dishes which could seek out and lock on to attacking fighters, but Yermi knew the accuracy of the vehicles' 23-mm guns was questionable when firing at aircraft flying at speeds of more than 300 knots.

He frowned as he spotted an airstrip on the desert below. A plane was soaring into the sky, its pilot, conscious of the incoming attack, battling desperately for altitude. Yermi checked his bomb sight and saw the depth blip centring on the lifting machine. With a grunt, he pressed his release button, and almost by reflex, hit afterburn, pulling his stick into a screeching ascent.

In the rearview mirror, he saw the plane's nose-cone erupt in a fiery pumpkin and elation filled him as he banked the Python and headed east, looking eagerly for a second target.

Ellen could scarcely breathe as the cockpit filled with smoke. The pilot was sprawled across the instrument panel with most of his head gone, and flames were licking around the splintered windshield. The plane itself was plunging like a doomed pigeon.

'Are you all right?' Joktan shouted above the roar of the slipstream.

Ellen didn't bother to answer. They were only seconds away from hitting the desert floor. She had to get the aircraft under control.

Desperately, she tore at her seatbelt and pushed the pilot's body roughly to one side. Taking his place, she struggled to life the fuselage nose. Her stomach chilled as she worked the control stick, willing the aircraft to respond. She could see the ground streaking towards her and held on with all her strength, her fingers slippery, drained of sensation. Slowly, laboriously, the stricken jet straightened, and Ellen banked to starboard, swinging the craft into a sharp U-turn. The wind pounded her face as she watched the desert zipping by below.

'I didn't realize you could fly a plane,' Joktan bellowed.

The tank convoy swung into view, and like a grotesque radio beacon they saw Talon Blue rising directly in their path. Its metal casing blotted out the sun and Ellen felt a shiver of anticipation. She knew what she had to do. It was like a fever burning inside her. She didn't question her motives, didn't pause to consider, even for a moment, the possible consequences to Joktan and herself. All she understood, all she thought about, was that by some miracle, she'd been given a second chance.

The tower dipped and swayed as she steered the aircraft toward it. She felt no fear, only an ice-cold certainty. Everything seemed to be happening in slow motion, as if she had reached a point where the world hung motionless in time and space. She watched the tower expanding, spreading across the sky like a mythical monster welcoming them into its embrace. She could see lights flashing around its generator as she guided the aircraft in. At the last moment, Joktan realized her intention. 'No,' he shouted.

He flung himself across the controls, shouldering Ellen aside, but she hung on grimly as tracer bullets arced into the air from the tank column below. Something exploded on the starboard bulkhead and she tumbled backwards, a paralysing numbness settling in her upper body. When she tried to move, her limbs seemed drained of energy.

Talon Blue reared up to confront them as Joktan battled to raise their angle of approach. With an ear-splitting screech, the plane clipped the pylon's summit and careered across the sky in a blinding torrent of smoke and flame.

Standing in his tank turret, General al Auf watched the blazing aircraft hit Talon Blue's tip and richochet skyward, spewing out pieces of dissolving fuselage. To the general's surprise, the weapon's pylons continued to vibrate, but he knew it would be a miracle if, after such a devastating impact, the device was completely unharmed. 'Bring me an assessment of the damage,' he snapped at his aide, Major Aricha.

The major hurried away as al Auf scanned the sky

worriedly with his field-glasses. The Israeli planes had withdrawn, but if the weapon system had been immobilized, al Auf knew his convoy would be doomed.

'Talon Blue is still operating,' the major announced, hurrying back a few minutes later. 'Parts of the super-structure have been destroyed, but as far as we can tell, the emissions themselves appear to be continuing. However ...' He hesitated. 'We have no way of knowing if they will still have the desired effect.'

Al Auf studied the smoke-ridden horizon. 'Let us pray that they do,' he said.

Joktan struggled to bring the jet under control. The doomed machine was losing power by the second and he could see the desert streaking by in a bewildering blur. It had all happened so quickly, too quickly for his stunned brain to assimilate. First the Israeli attack, then Ellen's suicidal assault, and now here he was, poised at the controls of an aircraft he had no idea how to operate.

Ellen lay on the deck, her jacket drenched with blood. Her eyes looked glazed − shock probably, Joktan thought, but shock alone wouldn't diffuse the life-force so − he knew it had to be something else, something he didn't dare put a name to.

'How do I land this thing?' he shouted. 'I have to get us down. Somewhere. Anywhere. We're going to disintegrate.'

She blinked up at him, and he saw her lips move, the words reaching him faintly above the roar of the slipstream. 'Reduce power to fifty per-cent.'

'It's already reduced. We're limping along like a crippled mule.'

'Then go into the NAB mode on the HUD. That's the heads-up display screen in front of you.'

Joktan examined the control panel and swiftly obeyed. The HUD screen responded with new readings, a left-right line-up, and an up-down line-up. 'What happens now?'

'Drop the gear with the A key and the flaps with the D key, and hold speed at 150 knots.'

Joktan did so, feeling the aircraft trembling beneath him. The desert changed texture, swelling and undulating as it zipped by below. It would take a miracle, Joktan knew, to put down their blazing machine on such an uneven surface.

'Line up the vertical ILS line with the vertical lines of the gun-cross,' Ellen said. 'That'll give you a guide path. Keep the marker slightly below the horizon, and adjust the position of the horizontal ILS pitch-bar to hold it centred on the gun-cross lines. Don't let the marker drift. Now extend the speed brakes, and pull back gently on the stick to slow your descent.'

Joktan watched the ground coming up fast and clenched his teeth, bracing himself for the impact. The aircraft was bucking and lunging like a frightened beast, and he clung desperately to the controls, fighting to keep on an even keel.

A terrible shudder ran through the fuselage as they hit the ground and skidded forwards at a stupefying rate, scattering wreckage in every direction. Joktan was plucked from his seat and hurled across the deck. His head clipped the ceiling beam, and he blinked confusedly at the bulkhead. Then his vision blurred, and his body relaxed into peaceful oblivion.

General al Auf stood studying the terrain through his high-powered field-glasses. It had been over an hour since the last Israeli air attack, and though many of his vehicles were still blazing, the skies remained encouragingly clear. Moreover, there was no sign of activity along the Israeli defence lines.

He glanced up at Talon Blue, which was still pulsing its electronic emissions into the fume-tinged atmosphere. Was it possible the crazy contraption had really worked?

'See anything?' Colonel Turkia inquired, joining him in the tank turret.

'Sand,' General al Auf told him.

'It's quiet. They could be drawing us into a trap.'

'On the other hand, that monstrosity might actually have done its job.'

'Only one way to find out, general.'

Al Auf agreed, but he eyed the smoke-blackened horizon worriedly. Once they crossed the Jordan River, retreat would be hazardous in the extreme, but they could be wasting critical minutes by not pressing their advantage. Al Auf came to an unwilling decision. 'Order all tank units forward,' he snapped crisply. 'Platoons of infantry will precede them to clear the enemy trenches and defence positions.'

Lieutenant Ibrahim Jaffe sat in the Israeli bunker, sewing a button on his camouflage shirt. From time to time, he paused to take a sip from the plastic glass in front of him. The glass contained home-made wine which Corporal Rish had brought from his cellar in Tel Aviv. Though it was strictly forbidden to drink alcohol so close to the front, the presence of seven soldiers, plus a mangy dog which Private Becker had found wandering about the wasteland outside, had turned the bunker's cramped living quarters into an airless oven, and Lieutenant Jaffe found the wine offered a welcome respite from the suffocating atmosphere.

'What's happening out there?' Sergeant Goldberg said, glancing up at the concrete ceiling. 'Why's it so quiet, all of a sudden?'

Lieutenant Jaffe finished his sewing, nipping the thread with his teeth. He tested the button for firmness before draping the shirt over a nearby chair. 'They're taking a rest, that's all. Even fly boys need a break once in a while. Besides, planes have to be refuelled.'

He paused as dimly in the darkness they heard a low, metallic rumbling sound which rose on the air, swelling and intensifiying until it filled the entire bunker. The sweating troops looked up, holding their breaths. 'What the hell is that?' Corporal Rish whispered.

Jaffe reached for his combat shirt and pulled it on. 'Wait here. I'll check it out.'

The air was warm as Jaffe picked his way through the tangle of low sandy foothills. He could smell the odour of diesel fumes on the scented air. To the west, the line of military emplacements guarding the approach roads to Jerusalem studded the summits like tombstones. Smoke columns whirled across the river, forming a wispy veil which hung over the land in a feathery mantle.

Jaffe wriggled to the nearest hill and took out his field-glasses. The rumbling sound was growing stronger now. He swivelled his lens to focus, and whistled softly through tightly clenched teeth. Directly in front, armoured tanks flooded the

258

landscape for as far as Jaffe could see. Like a vast metallic carpet, the great convoy was advancing slowly toward him, kicking up a haze of choking red dust. It was like watching the earth systematically skinning itself. 'Dear God in Heaven,' he whispered under his breath.

The others looked at him questioningly as he scrambled back to the concrete bunker. 'They're moving in,' Jaffe exclaimed. 'The entire bloody Iraqi army. They're heading directly for Jerusalem.' His hand was trembling as he picked up the telephone. 'This time I think we've got 'em.'

Private Amair Kalut of the Iraqi 3rd Infantry felt dangerously exposed as he padded in front of the convoy of tanks, gripping his rifle across his chest. Madness, it seemed, to move like lemmings into the teeth of the enemy guns. Rumours claimed the Israeli forces had already been neutralized by Musallim al Shisur's new secret weapon, but Amair had little faith in rumours, and even less in the President himself. Amair Kalut hated his country's leader. He regarded the man as a dangerous, psychotic maniac with his death squads and interrogation camps, and Amair was not alone. Most of the soldiers he had spoken to, those brave enough to express their feelings, had little stomach for this war. They remembered the excesses of Sadaam Hussein, the terrible suffering of the early nineties and the internal upheaval which had followed. Now it was all beginning again, and all to satisfy one man's demented ambition.

The odour of diesel fumes hung in Amair's nostrils, mingling with the dust which had clogged there during the day. He could scarcely see the sun for the smoke fumes which hung like a veil over the entire landscape, but its filtered heat beat down on his combat shirt like the hammer of Allah.

Something moved on the ridge ahead, and Amair squinted to see through the orange haze. A line of tanks had gathered along the rim. Israelis. As Amair watched, more tanks appeared, spreading out to form a cordon of iron across the Iraqis' path. Soon, the entire horizon was bristling with armour.

Amair saw puffs of smoke belching from the 20-mm guns, heard the screech of the incoming shells.

Peerrrrsshhhhoooooom! with a thunderous explosion, a
vehicle directly to Amair's rear erupted in a blinding
mushroom of smoke and flame, sending pieces of white-
hot metal whistling into the sky. Perrrdoooom, perrrdoooom.
The earth shuddered as the deadly shells landed among the
advancing army.

Amair and his companions were caught in a frenzy of
panic. The explosions were almost continuous now, blending
into a perpetual roll which swelled and ebbed according to
the proximity of the blasts, and smoke and dust blotted out
the entire world until Amair was conscious only of the few
bare feet over which they moved. Pieces of shrapnel whipped
through the air, ripping the infantrymen to shreds. From
time to time, Amair's stunned ears caught the deafening
whumph-whumph of their own guns opening up, but most
of the bedlam seemed to evolve from incoming enemy fire.
He whimpered under his breath as he dropped to a crouch,
his body shaking. The earth shuddered violently, and he saw
a man's skull splinter into a million pieces, hurling bone and
brain fragments in every direction.

'We must get out of here,' Mahsin Shuas shouted, his
words almost obliterated by the din.

Amair needed no second invitation. Hurling his rifle into
the dust, he followed Mahsin blindly through the choking
maelstrom.

Joktan opened his eyes, blinking in the sunlight. A terrible
pain throbbed at the back of his skull, and when he ran his
fingers through his hair, they came away wet with blood.

Cautiously, he eased himself up. His body was stiff, and
every movement was excruciating. The aircraft, what was
left of it, still smouldered around him. Most of the roof
had gone, and pieces of burnt-out wreckage were scattered
around the outlying area. A deep furrow in the earth marked
their crazed momentum.

Joktan heard sounds of movement, and squinting through
the ruptured fuselage, saw the Iraqi army in full retreat.
Tanks and armoured personnel carriers were clattering painfully back the way they had come, kicking up spiralling
clouds of dust. Infantry troops, those without transport,

shuffled along in listless disarray, their faces haggard with misery and defeat.

Joktan watched them for a moment, then a spasm of alarm knotted in his chest. Where in God's name was Ellen? He rolled on to his knees and began scrambling through the smoking wreckage. He found her at last, half buried by sand. Her eyes were closed, but when he pressed his fingers against her throat, he felt a faint, rhythmic pulse-beat. He opened her combat jacket and examined the wound beneath her left breast. It looked ragged and ugly, the flesh rimmed with blue at the edges. Joktan took out his handkerchief, and bunched it over the hole in an effort to stem the bleeding. Then he rose to his feet, lifted her tenderly into his arms, and set off toward the column of exhausted, retreating soldiers.

Chapter Nineteen

Paul, seated in his rented car, studied the oil refinery from behind a line of plane trees. Twin high-wire fences, several feet apart, surrounded the main enclosure, with watchtowers placed at strategic points around the perimeter. An electronically operated gate, reinforced with steel bars, controlled the main entrance where a large sign read: NAPIER OIL INCORPORATED. He could see armed guards patrolling the yard inside.

'They certainly don't roll out the welcome mat,' Leila said. 'It's like a military fortress.'

He nodded. His decision to penetrate Napier's security was beginning to look more dubious by the minute. 'It'd take an army to get in there. Let's head into town and ask around a bit. The locals should know what the score is.'

They found a tavern on the edge of Muna City with a bar that was pleasantly cool after the stifling heat of the Californian noon. The lights had been dimmed, and a handful of customers sat on high stools at the counter; others were scattered around the alcoved tables at the tavern's rear.

The bartender was a medium-sized man with a long, doleful face. Paul studied him shrewdly as he ordered drinks. Something in the man's manner suggested he had an incurable nosy streak. And who better to approach, Paul reflected, than the local bartender?

Keeping his voice casual, he said: 'Kind've quiet in here, isn't it?'

'Quiet? Sure. It's only twelve o'clock.'

'I figured lunchtimes would be bustling. I mean, with an oil refinery just along the road.'

'Napier?' The man laughed, wiping the counter with a damp cloth. 'As far as Muna City's concerned, Napier might as well be in a different universe.'

'Its staff don't drink in your bar?' Leila said.

'Its staff don't drink anywhere, period. They sit in that compound and never come out.'

'How about the locals?' Paul queried.

'What locals?'

'The ones the company employs.'

'The company don't employ locals. It ships in outsiders and puts them up in its own special barracks. Christ knows what they do all day.'

Paul glanced at Leila, sipping his drink. 'Expensive, isn't it, importing workers like that?'

'Listen, that's no ordinary refinery out there.'

'No?'

'In fact, some of us figure it ain't a refinery at all. Hey, Frank?'

The bartender raised his voice, calling to a group of people seated around one of the tables. A man rose to his feet and strolled toward the counter. He was thickset and bearded. He looked at Paul and Leila curiously.

'I was just telling these folks about Napier,' the bartender said.

The man grinned, popping a pretzel into his mouth. 'You mean our local Alcatraz?'

'Frank's a paramedic,' the bartender explained. 'Last summer, there was an accident along the road, one of those heavy oil wagons tumbled into a ditch. Frank had to go out with the ambulance and bring in the driver. Tell 'em what happened, Frank.'

He shrugged, seeming to enjoy the sudden attention. 'By the time we got there,' he said, 'the wreckage had been split wide open. That truck wasn't carrying oil at all. It was carrying water.'

'Water?' Paul echoed.

'Right. The stuff was running into the ditch, fresh as a mountain stream. That tanker never carried oil in its life.'

263

'That's weird.'

'It gets weirder. Later on, I had to take the driver's personal effects out to the refinery, and they let me into their admin office. Those big storage tanks you see through the fence-wire, they're phonies.'

'How could you tell?' Leila asked.

'Too clean. There's not a smear of crude on their intake pipes. Anyone who's been around an oil refinery knows damn' well how the stuff congeals on the inlet valves.'

'Why would they go to so much trouble to build a refinery that doesn't refine?' Paul demanded.

'Cover,' the man told him calmly.

'Cover?'

'Everyone in Muna City knows that Napier Oil is a CIA set-up.'

'You're kidding me.'

The man shook his head, tossing another pretzel into his mouth. 'Covert operations,' he said, winking broadly.

'What kind of covert operations would they be conducting in the middle of California, for Chrissake?'

'Beats me, cowboy.'

Paul sipped at his beer, thinking hard. He'd wasted days chasing around the countryside when all the time the real answers had been right here in Muna City. A refinery that didn't refine, workers who sat in their complex and never came out, tankers which carried water instead of oil. Clearly, something unorthodox was going on, but if he wanted to discover Napier's secret, he still had to penetrate the security cordon.

'Anybody ever get inside the place?'

'Willard Conley does,' the bartender said.

'Who's Willard Conley?'

'He's our local baker. He delivers bread to Napier every morning except Sunday.'

'Well,' Paul said, draining his beer, 'I guess the man to talk to must be Willard Conley.'

'I don't like it,' Willard Conley protested. 'I don't like it at all.'

'What's not to like?' Paul asked innocently.

'Napier's one of my best customers, for Chrissake.'

'Well, you appreciate a joke, don't you, Mr Conley?'

'A joke, yes. But I don't even know you people.'

Paul took out his wallet and peeled off several banknotes. Like Leila, he was dressed in baker's coveralls with the message CONLEY'S FOR THE FINEST BREAD IN TOWN inscribed over the breast pocket. He pushed several large-denomination bills down the front of Conley's jacket.

'Like I explained,' Paul said, 'it's Leon's birthday and we want to give him a little surprise. As soon as we've finished, we'll return the uniforms and you keep the money. Is it a deal?'

Conley looked slightly mollified. 'I just hope you know what you're doing,' he said.

'Trust us, Mr Conley, trust us.'

Paul glanced at Leila and climbed into the delivery truck. It had taken him nearly an hour to persuade Conley to co-operate and already he could see the man was wavering. They couldn't afford to delay things any longer. He engaged gear and pulled out of the baker's yard, Conley watching worriedly from his office door. Paul gave him a wave and swung on to the highway, joining the mainstream of traffic.

'Think we convinced him?' Leila asked.

'Hell, no. But I guess the money did the trick.'

'What happens now?'

Paul was silent for a moment, watching the road ahead, then he said: 'First, I'm going to drop you off at the next service station.'

'Are you nuts?'

'You're not coming, Leila.'

'Like hell I'm not!'

'It's too dangerous. I'll handle this alone.'

'Forget it,' she snapped angrily.

'I don't want anything happening to you, that's all.'

'But it's okay if it happens to you, right? Listen, we started this together and we finish it together. I'm coming, and that's final.'

Paul's heart sank as he heard the intransigence in her voice. He'd been hoping to talk her out of it, but it was clear she had no intention of quitting. For Paul, a subtle change had taken place in their relationship. Whereas before she'd been a resourceful ally and a comforting companion, he now discovered that he really cared about her, and couldn't bear the thought of seeing her hurt. But Leila was like a tiger when her mind was made up. Nothing in the world, he realized, would induce her to back down.

He spotted the refinery entrance ahead and pulled off the highway, drawing to a halt at the main gate. The guard, a muscular-looking young man in dark sunglasses, examined him curiously. 'What happened to Willard?'

'Willard can't make it today. We're the new delivery team.'

'Hold on a minute. I'd better check.'

Paul waited in silence as the man stepped into his guard-hut and punched out a number on the telephone. He spoke briefly into the mouthpiece, then pressed the electronic device which slid back the barrier with a gentle purr. 'It's okay,' the man told them. 'You'll find the cookhouse at the far end of the admin block.'

Paul thanked him and steered the truck through the entrance gate, his heart thumping wildly against his ribcage. 'We're in,' he breathed.

They cruised among the complex sprawl of metal towers and clapboard buildings, passing the Medical Section and Fire Station, and tracing a railroad track where container boxcars stood waiting to be unloaded. Large notices gave warning of restricted areas. 'Sleepy little place,' Paul observed.

'Too sleepy,' Leila said. 'That paramedic was right. Those storage tanks look almost brand-new.'

'Everything here came right off the assembly line. Let's park and take a closer look.'

He pulled to a halt in a narrow alley, and switched off the engine, his stomach tense as he tried the door of the nearmost building. It opened easily at his touch. Inside, rows of heavy equipment covered the floor as far as he could see. He motioned at Leila, and taking her arm, steered her cautiously across the narrow hallway.

In the security office, the two guards, Kroopes and Aikman, had just started their morning shift when Aikman noticed

266

a red light flashing on the surveillance panel. He pressed a button, and one of the video screens flickered into life. 'Hey, Freddie, look. We got intruders in Warehouse Three.'

Kroopes joined him at the control desk. 'How the hell'd they get in there?'

'Christ knows. We'd better sound the alarm.'

'Wait.' Kroopes caught his wrist. 'Hadn't we oughtta check this out first? Could be legitimate.'

'No way. Warehouse Three's a restricted area. Nobody enters without electronic ID.'

'Let's play it safe, Jerry. First we check, then we scramble, okay?'

Aikman looked surprised. He paused for a moment with his hand on the alarm bell, then he shrugged and reached for his gunbelt dangling over the nearby chair. 'Okay, anything you say, coach.'

Snyder sat at his desk, watching Paul and Leila on the video screen. An aide brought him a coffee, placing it on the blotting pad in front of him. 'Is it them?' the aide asked curiously.

'Who else would have the balls to bulldoze their way through the security check?'

'How could you be sure they'd come, Mr Snyder?'

'Logic. This was the only place left.'

'Want me to send somebody out to pick them up?'

'No.' Snyder leaned back in his chair and sipped at his coffee, his features casual and relaxed. 'I'm curious,' he said. 'I want to see how far they get first.'

Paul heard voices and seized Leila's arm, pulling her behind a piece of heavy machinery. Footsteps echoed at the far end of the building as a group of businessmen walked up the central aisle. They drew to a halt at a service elevator where one of the men slipped an ID card into an electronic slot. A light switched on, and with a gentle purr, the elevator rose slowly up from the basement.

Paul looked at Leila as the men descended to the floor below. 'Something's down there.'

'Yes, but you need a special ID just to operate the winch.'

'Maybe we can find a stairway.'

'Dressed like this, we'll stand out a mile.'

Paul saw a door leading off to the left. A sign above it said: LOCKER ROOM AND SHOWERS.

'This way.' He clutched at Leila's wrist.

The room was crammed with metal cabinets. A line of shower stalls stood at the rear, and hard hats and coveralls hung from the bare brick walls. Paul began unbuttoning his baker's tunic. 'Switch clothes,' he said. 'It'll make us less conspicuous.'

Three minutes later, clad in helmets and boiler suits, they headed toward the doorway.

'Somebody's coming,' Leila exclaimed.

Paul drew back, and they watched in silence as a young man carrying a leather briefcase made his way to the elevator and slipped his ID card into the control slot.

'Maybe this is our chance,' Paul whispered.

He picked up a small length of piping and handed it to Leila, then he selected another piece for himself and walked brazenly towards the elevator with Leila following in his wake. The man glanced at them, displaying no surprise at the sight of two workers carrying pieces of refinery equipment.

Inside the moving car, the man examined them curiously. He was tanned and fit-looking, with brown eyes and regular features. 'New around here?' he asked.

'Right,' Paul said. 'We got in yesterday.'

'Yeah? Where from?' The man's hair had been trimmed very short, giving him a youthful, almost college-boy air.

'Up north,' Paul said. 'Seattle.'

The man looked puzzled, and a hint of suspicion entered his eyes. 'Seattle? What the hell were you doing in Seattle?'

'Personal business,' Paul said desperately. 'My aunt got sick.'

'Your aunt? Are you nuts?' The man nodded at the equipment in their hands, his amicable air vanishing. 'Where the hell are you going with that stuff anyhow?'

'We're taking it down to the basement.'

'Refinery gear?' The man looked incredulous.

'It's a special consignment. Rush job.'

'Bullshit.'

It was clear that their cover had been blown. The man looked hostile as he pulled back his jacket, revealing a pistol in a leather holster. Paul froze against the car wall, staring at their confronter with a sickly expression. His brain appeared to have gone into neutral.

Then Leila, without hesitation, drove her metal piping savagely into the stranger's testicles and he doubled forward, the air exploding from his lungs.

'Grab his piece,' she snapped.

Paul fumbled for the man's automatic as the elevator lurched to a halt and the gates slid open with a muffled purr. A group of people stood facing them in the doorway, brandishing pistols and submachine-guns. At their centre was Leon Snyder. 'Mr McKlelland,' Snyder said, and his small, predatory eyes reminded Paul of a striking snake, 'I was beginning to fear you might never get here.'

Iraqi infantryman Amair Kalut heard the shriek of an incoming shell and threw himself on the ground, covering his head with both arms. He felt the earth shuddering against his chest, showering him with pieces of arid topsoil.

Amair was shivering all over with terror and exhaustion. Their retreat had not been the dignified withdrawal the Brigade commanders had promised but a panic-stricken rout, with the scattered Iraqi army – troops and armour alike – trying to distance themselves from the relentless fury of the Israeli shells. Never in his life had Amair known anything like it. The ground was littered with the charred skeletons of burnt-out tanks, and ravaged corpses lay everywhere.

It was a vision from hell, Amair thought, dragging himself to his feet. He longed to find some secluded corner where he could lie down and ease his aching limbs, but the thought of the pursuing army forced him doggedly on. There were no platoons or companies any more; the entire battalion had disintegrated, with men staggering aimlessly among the wreckage, looking for refuge and succour.

Through the twisting smoke tendrils, Amair saw Mahsin Shuas crouching over a figure in the dust and recognized the wounded man as Murur Kashmiri, a grocer's son from An Najaf on the southern Euphrates. Murur was moaning and gripping his knee with both hands.

'What happened?' Amair asked, squatting down on his haunches.

'Shrapnel,' Mashin said.

Murur rolled up his pants leg to display a ragged hole in the front of his shin. Surprisingly, the wound was scarcely bleeding, but Amair could see tiny bone splinters protruding through the purple flesh. It was clear the limb had been fractured.

'You will never walk on that,' Amair said. 'We must get you to an ambulance.' He motioned at Mahsin. 'Let's see if we can lift him on to his feet.'

Murur whimpered as they dragged him upright, hooking his arms across their shoulders. He bent his knee, holding the foot delicately off the ground.

'We'll never find an ambulance in this,' Mahsin said, looking at Amair sweatily.

Amair peered with dismay through the swirling smoke. He realized Mahsin was right. In such confusion, their chances of spotting a red crescent were practically non-existent. Nevertheless, they couldn't leave Murur here. 'Perhaps we can flag a ride on one of the tanks?'

'He needs treatment, brother. Unless that wound is dressed, his leg will become infected. And you know what that means.'

Amair did know. He had a feeling Murur had already lost the leg, but he was careful to keep his voice light-hearted as he said: 'We'll get it fixed as soon as we find a place to rest.'

They staggered on through the dust and flame, supporting Murur precariously between them. Every few seconds, low-flying planes strafed them from the air, and they heard the whine of incoming shells and saw the flash of explosions among the escaping tank columns.

Amair had no idea how long they had been walking when he spotted a scattering of buildings through the smoke. 'A village,' he said.

As they approached, they realized to their dismay that most of the houses had been shattered by artillery fire. Their roofs had gone and their walls had crumbled into rubble, but at least they offered a temporary haven in which to dress Murur's wound and replenish their fading strength. Painfully, they staggered across the fallen masonary and lowered Murur into the debris of the nearest building. There was no sign of the village's inhabitants.

Murur's face was pallid with pain, and his eyes, in their sweat-grimed mask, looked yellowish as he moaned softly under his breath. Mahsin rolled up Murur's trouser leg and examined the wound. 'Ankle's swollen. I think the flesh could be infected.'

He took off his haversack, fumbling inside for his first-aid kit. 'We will never last till nightfall unless we find water. Our bodies need liquid, and Murur's wound has to be cleaned.'

'There must be a well somewhere,' Amair said. 'Give me your canteen, and I'll see what I can do.'

Amair slung the canteen over his shoulder and shut his mind to the deafening explosions as he picked his way through the shambles of the ruined village. He ducked instinctively as he heard a piercing, high-powered screech. There was a trail of smoke, and the building in which Mahsin and Murur had taken refuge erupted outwards in a blinding flash of flame.

Amair stared horror-stricken at the spot where barely a minute ago they had been examining Murur's leg. Mewing deep in his throat, he staggered back and began burrowing desperately through the rubble.

He found his companions' bodies ripped into a grotesque assortment of unrecognizable fragments. Tears streamed down his cheeks and he drew back in revulsion as he stared at the ragged pieces of blue-veined flesh. Then he wiped his fingers on his tunic, picked up Mahsin's rifle and shuffled back to rejoin the retreating troops.

Joktan walked in a daze, clutching Ellen against him. The roar of aircraft was almost incessant now as Israeli planes strafed the retreating convoy. Joktan ignored the machine-gunfire, stumbling on blindly into the smoke. At one point, he flagged a lift on a passing half-track, but the vehicle struck an unexploded shell which damaged its caterpillar tread and he was forced to begin walking again.

He scarcely knew what he was doing any more. The numbness in his head had stupefied his senses. He was conscious only that Ellen was dying, might be dead already, for all he knew, though why it mattered with all the slaughter around him was beyond his understanding. Mindless, it had been, to gamble everything on a crazed flight across the Iraqi desert. He was a mature man, 'well seasoned', as they said in the Rub al Najar, so what had possessed him to turn his back on everything sacred and holy? You couldn't account for it in any rational sense, you couldn't explain, even to yourself, the way the mind worked. The woman had brought something special to his life, a sense of meaning he had thought long forgotten. He couldn't define that in logical terms, but there was nothing in the world more important to him at this moment than Ellen Conway's survival.

Ellen lay motionless in his arms, her cheeks smeared with dirt, her hair swishing gently against his thighs. He noticed that her eyes were open. 'Salih?' she whispered.

'Try not to talk,' he told her.

She blinked, struggling hard to concentrate. Her eyes were dull, not glassy exactly, but filled with a curious incomprehension. 'What happened to the plane?'

'We landed in pieces. But at least we're still alive.'

She was silent for a moment. Then she said: 'My chest hurts.'

'Shrapnel. I'm taking you to an ambulance.'

For the first time, Ellen became aware of the shuffling, demoralized men. She peered at them curiously, her long hair brushing against Joktan's legs. 'Where are they going, all these people?'

'Back to Iraq.'

'Are they in retreat?'

'I'm afraid so.'

'Oh Salih. Talon Blue didn't work. Can you ever forgive me?'

272

'You did what you had to,' Joktan said.

He didn't want to talk, nor to hear Ellen talk, only to concentrate on maintaining his momentum. Left foot, right foot, Ellen's weight dragging remorselessly at his shoulders.

'Am I going to die, Salih?' she asked after a moment.

'Not if I can help it.'

'I can't feel my legs any more. That's the way dying happens, isn't it? Starts at the feet and moves upwards.'

'I won't let you die,' he said.

'Oh Salih, even you can't stop the inevitable.'

For a time, Ellen spoke in riddles, and Joktan realized she was hallucinating. She rambled on about Mackhead, about her lover Paul, and about someone named Tilly Johnson. Her words made little sense. After a while, she lapsed into unconsciousness, and Joktan walked for another hour before he saw, directly ahead, a stationary ambulance with a red crescent on its hull. Its crew stood at the vehicle's rear, watching the lines of retreating troops, and Joktan stumbled toward them. 'I have an injured woman here.'

A medic glanced at Ellen briefly, and motioned Joktan to carry her inside. Two wounded casualties lay on the metal stretchers and Joktan laid Ellen gently on the spare bunk while the medic undid her jacket, removed Joktan's bloodsoaked handkerchief, and examined the gaping wound. 'How did it happen?'

'Shrapnel, I think.'

'Been unconscious for long?'

'She keeps coming to, then drifting off again.'

The man grunted, and carefully cleaned the wound. 'It is not good, brother,' he said at length. 'She needs hospital treatment quickly, and you can see the state we're in. Our fuel tank is punctured.'

'I'll find a vehicle somewhere,' Joktan promised.

'That won't help. The shrapnel is too close to her heart. If she remains with the column, the jostling could kill her.'

A terrible frustration blazed inside Joktan. Outside, they heard voices clamouring as a scout car pulled to a halt at their vehicle's rear. The four soldiers inside were gesturing excitedly at the eastern sky.

'Paratroopers,' one of the men said as Joktan and the medic emerged from the truck.

Joktan saw tiny umbrellas framed against the smoke. Dipping and swaying, they descended gracefully along the line of distant mountains, their canopies shimmering in the sunlight.

'Israelis?' the medic asked.

The soldier nodded. 'Looks like they're going to attack our southern flank.'

'For the love of Allah, can't they see the state we're in?'

Joktan's breathing quickened as a wild idea formed in his mind. It was dangerous in the extreme – in his own case, probably suicidal – but with a little audacity, he might yet save Ellen's life.

He looked at the pistol strapped to the medic's waist. The man was engrossed in conversation, discussing the enemy parachute drops. Joktan plucked the weapon from its leather holster and aimed it at the driver's head. 'Get out of the car,' he ordered.

The man looked at him. 'What are you doing?'

'Get out, I said.'

'Have you gone crazy, man?'

Joktan drew back the hammer with a muffled click. 'You have four seconds to live, brother.'

The driver glanced at his three companions, and without a word they scrambled hurriedly to the ground.

Joktan spoke to the medics over his shoulder. 'Put the woman in the vehicle rear.'

'You can't take this car,' the driver protested. 'It belongs to Colonel Barazani.'

'Do as I say,' Joktan commanded cooly.

Without a word, the medics laid Ellen in the back seat of the scout car and two minutes later, Joktan was driving furiously toward the jagged ramparts of the distant hills.

Prime Minister Ariel Aronson sat in his office and listened in silence as the Chief of Military Intelligence outlined the events on the outskirts of Jerusalem. 'Elements of the Iraqi 15th Armoured Brigade attempted to move along the Jericho road,' he said, 'but after series of successful sorties, our air force managed to turn them back. Shortly after three pm, Talman's paratroopers, preceded by artillery fire, attacked the southern flank of the enemy convoy. Bowen threw in his second battalion on the western sector, together with tanks from the Jerusalem Brigade.'

'What about enemy communications?'

'All destroyed,' Hur confirmed. 'According to General Brill, the Iraqi army is retreating in disarray.'

'So Jerusalem is safe?'

'Yes, Prime Minister. The area has been effectively cleared, and Israeli troops control the entire west bank.'

'Where are the Iraqis now?'

'Following tracks through the Judean Desert.'

'Let's keep them moving,' Aronson said.

'That order has already been given,' Hur assured him. 'There is however, one small problem.'

'What's that?'

'The Jordanian government has protested against Israeli forces using its territory as a battlefield.'

'To hell with Jordan. The Iraqis started this war, and by God, I intend to make sure they never start another. Contact all commanders in the field. Present my compliments and tell them they must press this fight to the finish.'

'I'll see to it at once, Prime Minister,' Rafael Hur said.

'The Iraqis are done for,' the US Secretary of State declared. 'They're being pushed back relentlessly across the Judean Desert. Israeli tanks have encircled al Shisur's forces and shut off their reconnaissance battalions. According to our satellite pictures, the armoured battle is continuing at close quarters.'

'It'll be a slaughterhouse,' President Clayman breathed.

'Al Shisur brought it upon himself, Mr President,' said General Kincaid, Chairman of the Joint Chiefs of Staff.

'Wrong. He brought it upon the Iraqi people. They didn't want this war, nobody did. This is what happens when psychopaths get into power.' Clayman looked at the Secretary of State. 'Any sign of nuclear deployment?'

'None, happily. The Israelis are carrying out their attacks

275

on conventional lines. I understand General Wyatt's brigade is opening up the Bir-Halu Road and engaging Iraqi forces from the high ground near Mukesa. They're sending small armoured units into the valley to draw the enemy fire, then smashing their positions with air strikes. The Iraqis are attempting to withdraw in a disciplined manner, but they're being harassed from above and engaged intermittently by parachute units attacking from the west and south.'

'It'll be a massacre,' President Clayman said. 'Senseless, stupid and futile.'

'Can't you call Ariel Aronson?' the Secretary of Defence suggested. 'Ask him to pull back his men and allow the Iraqis to retreat without further loss of life?'

'You think Aronson will listen?'

'He's a civilized man. It's worth a try, Larry.'

'He's also a highly intransigent man. He won't rest until the Iraqi army has either been obliterated, or Musallim al Shisur has surrendered.'

'If Aronson pursues the enemy into Iraq, we'll have a hell of a tricky situation on our hands,' General Kincaid put in. 'The Arab nations will never stand by and allow such a thing to happen. Can't you try talking to al Shisur direct, Larry?'

'Speaking frankly, I'd rather talk to the devil. Apart from having scorned every attempt at a peace initiative, al Shisur's credibility has been shot to hell. Even with his secret police behind him, how long can he survive after such a humilating defeat? No, if it's a ceasefire we want, we'll have to approach somebody new.'

'There's Abu Bakhit,' Kincaid said. 'He's head of the armed forces, and an extremely powerful man in Baghdad. He's also something of a hero among the Iraqi people. I have it on good authority that Bakhit disapproves of al Shisur. He's said to be a reasonable and compassionate man. It's just possible that, faced with the present chaos, he might move against al Shisur to save his country further unnecessary suffering.'

President Clayman thought for a moment, folding his hands on the table. Sunlight from the open window cast pastel slivers across his sleek grey hair. Outside, they heard the hollow tones of a distant megaphone – a speaker addressing a protest meeting against the Iraqi invasion. Clayman reached for the telephone. 'Let's see if I can contact General Bakhit,' he said.

Chapter Twenty

The sun shimmered in Amair Kalut's eyes. He could see the horizon blending into the sky in a dazzling haze. They had left the rolling hillocks behind, and now the plain stretched flat as a pancake in every direction. Amair had no idea how long he had been walking. Hours had passed since the tank columns had left the struggling bands of infantry behind, and this thankfully had led to an easing of the aerial bombardment as the Israeli planes, tempted by more substantial targets to the east, continued to harry the armoured divisions in front. Only occasionally would a returning enemy fighter swoop low to strafe the lines of demoralized troops. The ground was scattered with rifles, helmets, and pieces of discarded equipment as the exhausted soldiers, drained of strength, devoid of hope, moved like zombies across the endless wasteland.

Amair dwelled mostly in his mind. He was scarcely conscious of the horrors surrounding him — the smouldering tanks, the blackened corpses — only the torturing pangs of thirst kept him in touch with any semblance of reality. He had emptied his canteen several hours earlier, and now his body craved moisture.

He saw something gleaming in the sand ahead, a tiny lake, and with a strangled cry, staggered toward it. Dropping to his knees, he was about to plunge his head into the rippling water when a sergeant in a ragged combat jacket seized him by the scruff of the neck. 'Don't be a fool. Do you want to poison yourself?'

'I must drink,' Amair croaked.

'Drink that, and you'll be dead by nightfall. Look.'

For the first time, Amair noticed corpses floating on the murky surface. Shredded by artillery fire, their entrails undulating among the reeds like exotic sea anemone.

'Here,' the sergeant said, uncoupling his canteen and pushing it into Amair's hand. 'One swallow, no more. I need that to get me to the frontier.'

The liquid had a metallic taste but Amair didn't care. He closed his eyes, savouring its coolness. Then he returned the canteen gratefully, dragged himself to his feet and stumbled resolutely in the sergeant's wake.

The building stood in a flat saucer of land, flanked by a cluster of spindly acacia trees. Amair lay on the bluff as Sergeant Arad studied the windows through a pair of powerful binoculars. To the east, they heard the distant rumble of the retreating tank convoys and the incessant thunder of heavy explosions. The Israeli attacks had been unremitting.

Sweaty groups of infantry crouched in the hollow, their faces haggard and weary. Amair caught the whiff of their body odour as he lay face down in the dust, and with it came the inescapable redolence of fear, an elusive aroma that was dangerously contagious. The troops had been separated from the main brigade, and now, like waifs on the edge of a storm, were beating their path painfully eastward.

Sergeant Arad grunted as he examined the building blocking their way. Its earthen walls had been expertly sandbagged. 'There is no sign of movement,' he said.

'Perhaps the building is deserted,' Corporal Shakhbut suggested.

'And perhaps not. Paratroopers have been seen dropping into this area. We should send someone in to take a closer look.'

'Send in men as bait?' the corporal echoed. 'That is of such barbarity that I cannot think of it. If we are to die, then let us die together.'

'Why die at all when a little foresight could guarantee our safety?'

'It will waste too much time. I am sure the building is deserted.'

279

'I pray you are right, brother,' Sergeant Arad said with a sigh.

He waved at the men behind and they moved forward in single file, the sergeant in the lead. Ahead, Amair saw the gentle folds of the beckoning foothills.

When they reached the limit of their cover, the sergeant studied the building again, a light wind ruffling his hair. Splodges of sweat traced the spine of his speckled combat jacket.

He signalled brusquely, and they scrambled into the sunlight. The scorched walls looked like the ramparts of some ancient fortress, and sweat swam into Amair's eyes as he moved toward it. A small turret dominated the roof's southernmost corner, sand-coloured and rimmed with observation slits. A crude ladder had been propped against its rear.

Amair heard a soft, almost undiscernible plopping sound, and before his astonished gaze, a tree was uprooted and tossed across the ground. A second later, the blast hit him with the impact of a sledgehammer, spraying the troops with white-hot shrapnel.

Someone shouted: 'Mortars.'

Spurts of orange flame lanced from the building's windows, and the earth shuddered as a second shell landed in their midst. Amair's skin felt torn and bloody. Behind him, a man was shrieking like a wounded animal.

In a tumult of smoke and flame, he saw the sergeant cupping his hands to his mouth. 'Back,' the sergeant bellowed, motioning with his arm. 'Get back.'

A soldier was ripped in two in front of Amair's eyes. Another hung halfway up a tree, yelling insanely as the Iraqi infantrymen began their perilous retreat. Waves of burning air hit Amair in an almost continuous barrage. Wrapped in the stench of cordite, he felt as if he was being flayed alive, every nerve, every sinew laid hideously bare. A piece of shrapnel caught him in the lower abdomen and he spun wildly, clutching a gaping hole where his stomach should be. He collapsed to the ground, shuddering violently, pieces of smouldering earth showering all around him. There, on the rubble-strewn hillslope with half his body blown away, Amair Kalut laid his cheek against the bloodsoaked sand and quietly died.

Joktan stopped the scout car, eyeing the line of hills ahead. There was no sign of human presence, no sign of anything at all apart from a few clumps of camel thorn clinging tenaciously to the barren topsoil.

Joktan was puzzled. This was the area in which the paratroopers had landed, he felt certain, yet even the dust appeared undisturbed.

He turned to look at Ellen in the rear. She was sprawled unconscious on the leather seat, her cheeks hollow and waxen in the sunlight. Worriedly, Joktan felt her forehead. It was feverish to the touch.

He scanned the hillslopes again. The Israelis had to be somewhere nearby. As if in confirmation, a shot rang out, kicking up dust near the scout car's wheel.

Joktan rose from the driving seat, cupping his hands to his mouth. 'I am unarmed,' he shouted in English.

There was a moment in which nothing happened, and Joktan held his breath, shutting his mind to the overwhelming barrage of heat, then a voice yelled: 'What do you want?'

'I have casualty here. A woman.'

Another pause. Heat waves shimmered off the sunbaked rock, but there was no sign of movement, no sign of life. At one point, the earth sloped into a steep 'V' formed by a dried-up riverbed. High above, Joktan saw an eagle wheeling on the wind. Ragged cliffs cast dark shadows across the orange sand.

'Get out of the car and place your hands on your head,' the voice ordered at last.

As Joktan obeyed, a group of Israelis came out of a gully toward him, machine guns at the ready. They carried heavy field packs, and their faces were daubed to blend in with the terrain.

They gathered around Joktan, examining him curiously. 'Who are you?' their officer demanded.

'That is not important. I have an injured woman in the car. She's an American. She needs help.'

281

One of the soldiers was staring at Joktan incredulously, his lips writhing as if he couldn't believe his eyes. He swallowed several times and exclaimed in a hoarse voice: 'It's Joktan.'

The officer frowned, examining Joktan with a new intensity, his moustache rippling in the wind. 'You're out of your mind.'

'It's Joktan, I tell you. I'd recognize him anywhere.'

'He's right,' another man said. 'It *is* Joktan.'

The officer's features froze. He seized a machine gun from the nearmost soldier and pushed it roughly against Joktan's chest. 'Both hands on the car, you murderous bastard.'

Joktan placed his palms on the vehicle's hood while the Israelis searched him. The officer kept prodding him with the machine gun, as if anxious to provoke a reaction. Joktan said with a sigh: 'I'm not going to resist, you fool.'

'Where are your friends?' the officer demanded.

'I have no friends. I came alone.'

'You're lying. It's some kind of trick.'

'It's no trick. You have my word.'

'Why would Joktan give himself up without a fight?'

'This is why,' Joktan said, lifting Ellen from the scout car.

The officer hesitated, his dark eyes registering the pallor of Ellen's cheeks, the bloodstained dressing taped to her lower chest. Her skin looked almost transparent in the sunlight.

He spat on the ground and turned to his radio operator. 'Gabriel, get me comms. Let's see if we can whistle up some transport here.'

Thirty minutes later, Joktan sat in a helicopter with Ellen cradled in his lap and watched the hills flitting by in a dizzy blur.

The cell was small and cramped, its only light a single wire-bracketed lamp in the centre of the ceiling. There was a narrow bunk, a tiny washbasin, and a minuscule lavatory set into the wall.

Paul lay staring into the semi-darkness, filled with weariness, confusion and defeat. He felt bad about Leila. He had led her into a trap. She shouldn't even have been here;

her job had been over, but she had stayed behind because that was the kind of girl she was. He could never forgive himself for his carelessness and stupidity.

He heard footsteps in the passageway outside, then the door creaked open and a man came into the cell, carrying a coffee jug and two paper cups. The man was big, and because of the low ceiling, he looked even bigger. His face was deeply tanned, and in the semi-darkness his white hair gleamed like a misty halo. It was Leon Snyder.

Paul eased himself onto his elbows, examining the newcomer curiously. Snyder was smiling as he sat on the tiny stool. 'How're you feeling?'

Paul ignored the question. 'Where's Leila?'

'She's in the debriefing room, being interrogated.' Snyder made a placatory gesture as he noticed the alarm in Paul's eyes. 'Don't worry, son, she's being questioned, that's all. It's part of the routine.'

'What routine? CIA?'

Snyder filled the paper cups with coffee. 'Let's say an amalgamation of certain government departments. Napier Oil is our cover. Of course, in all other respects Napier is a legitimate organization.'

His expression was relaxed and friendly, but there was something sinister in his hawk-like features as if to him emotions and attitudes were merely pieces in some complex and intricate chess-game.

'What d'you mean, government departments?' Paul demanded. 'Are you trying to tell me that you work for the US government?'

'Sure.'

'Liar.'

Snyder chuckled. 'You're upset.'

'You bet I'm upset. You tried to kill me, you bastard!'

'That was unfortunate. And regrettable.'

'Who are you anyhow? Snyder? Ferriday? How many aliases do you operate under?'

Snyder leaned back against the wall, his snowy hair framing the aquiline fierceness of his brick-red face. Seeing him so close, Paul was conscious for the first time of the man's powerful physical magnetism. 'If you want the truth, my

283

real name is Frank de Tabley, but Snyder's the one I'm using at the moment.'

He handed Paul a paper cup, and examined him in silence for a moment. 'You're quite a character, Mr McKlelland. Rarely have I encountered a man of such tenacity.'

Paul ignored the compliment. 'Are you really CIA?'

'Of course.'

'Then will you tell me what you were doing in Sadaam Hussein's bunker in the 1991 Gulf War?'

Snyder looked amused. 'Son, you continue to surprise me. How did you know about that?'

'Never mind how. Answer the question.'

Snyder sipped his coffee. There was a slipperiness about him that made Paul's senses crawl, but for whatever reason, he appeared to be in an expansive mood. 'Very well, it's true,' he admitted. 'My friendship with Sadaam Hussein was one of my most celebrated achievements.'

'We were at war, Snyder. You were fraternizing with the enemy.'

'A fraternization which proved very useful. You see, in 1991 Sadaam created a human shield, deploying western hostages around his strategic installations. I managed to persuade him to let them go.'

'How?'

'Bluff, like everything else. Most intelligence work involves bluff. The Allied commander in the Gulf War bluffed the Iraqis into believing he was about to launch a ground offensive. The Iraqis fell for my bluff too.'

'What are you, Snyder? Some kind of agent provocateur?'

'Bravo, Mr McKlelland. You're a clever man. Yes, indeed, back in 1990 we knew Sadaam Hussein was already planning to attack Israel. We also knew he would soon have nuclear capability. We couldn't afford a nuclear war breaking out in the Middle East, so we offered him an alternative.

'What alternative?'

'Top secret US military equipment.'

'You're kidding me.'

Snyder shook his head. 'When Sadaam Hussein invaded Kuwait, he believed he had in his possession a weapon capable of setting the air aflame. He even boasted about it to the western press. As events proved, he was miserably incorrect. But he gave us a perfect opportunity for cutting him down to size.'

'Under the auspices of the United Nations.'

'Exactly.'

'I can't believe this.'

'Believe what you like. It happens to be true.'

'And you did it all with the approval of the US government?'

'The government? Of course not.'

'But you said ...'

Snyder waved his hand dismissively. 'Governments change and fluctuate. Only principles are important.'

'What are you talking about?'

'I'm talking about this wonderful country of ours, Mr McKlelland. Somebody has to protect it. Somebody has to ensure that the institutions our forefathers struggled so hard to create are kept safe and inviolate.'

'I thought we had a Constitution for that.'

'Constitutions, like everything else, are open to interpretation.'

'Let's get this straight. Are you claiming that our security services have taken it upon themselves to operate independently of the United States government?'

'Let's say a group of concerned and dedicated people *inside* the security services, people who love this country and will do anything in their power to protect its interests both at home and abroad. Devoted patriots, if you like.'

'So within the CIA, within the fabric of the intelligence machine is an elite core of professionals making their own decisions and carrying out their own operations?'

'That's about the size of it,' Snyder said.

Paul considered for a moment. Snyder was too assured, too smug to be lying.

'Does the President know?'

'The President?' Snyder chuckled. 'Believe me, Mr McKlelland, Presidents are dangerous people. They meddle with the intelligence services, mishandle them, abuse them, then put the blame on the very men they've corrupted. Look at the CIA purges of the seventies. Look at Bush's indecision

285

in 1991. We were within marching distance of Baghdad, and he called a cease-fire with victory in his grasp. He let the situation suppurate and fester. Those of us who remember those days have learned never to place our trust in Presidents. We've taken it upon ourselves to look after our country's interests in any manner we consider necessary. No, Mr McKlelland, decisions regarding the welfare of the United States can not, I'm afraid, be left in the hands of Presidents.'

Snyder's voice was flat and calm, as if he believed the validity of his statement to be beyond contradiction.

Paul said: 'Is that why you supplied Musallim al Shisur with Talon Blue? So he would have the capacity to bring Israel to its knees?'

'Al Shisur is a difficult man. In psychological terms, he's probably certifiably insane. Unfortunately, he presents a serious threat not only to Mid-East stability, but also to the oil supplies of the industrial world. Somebody has to stop him.'

'How?'

'Same way we stopped Sadaam Hussein.'

Paul sat quite still, absorbing the implication of Snyder's words. Somewhere outside, he heard a sentry whistling. 'Bluff?'

'That's right.'

Paul felt his senses quickening. 'Talon Blue is a bluff?'

'Of course, Mr McKlelland. Let me explain the situation. For years now, al Shisur has deliberately violated the arms limitation agreements. We know for a fact he's been secretly building up an arsenal of nuclear weapons. At the moment, that arsenal is crude and primitive, certainly no match for Israel's, but according to our intelligence sources, within eighteen months – two years at the outside – the situation will change dramatically. War, a terrible war, Mr McKlelland, has been inevitable for some time. Al Shisur has to be stopped, but the problem lies in how to do it. We can't send in troops at the drop of a hat. The Arab nations are very sensitive about US intervention, even under the UN flag, and the American people will be far from happy about entering a conflict which promises to be many

286

times bloodier than the one against Sadaam Hussein. So we decided to force al Shisur's hand.'

'The bio-gas.'

'Bullseye, Mr McKlelland. Yes, we used bio-gas. We knew Israel had been experimenting with the stuff for years, as has India, of course. Unfortunately, their efforts have proved only moderately successful. Bio-gas is too impracticable to become a real substitute for oil. However, we persuaded Musallim al Shisur, by showing him documents, letters and photographs, that Israeli scientists had made a dramatic breakthrough in their energy research and within a year would make the use of oil obsolete in the industrial world. Al Shisur realized he couldn't wait for the updating of his nuclear arsenal. He had to move fast.'

'That's when you offered him Talon Blue?'

'Exactly. We have to give him something to take the place of atomic missiles, and our scientists had been developing Talon Blue for years, ever since the Russians started their research into psychotronic warfare.'

'Does it work?'

'Talon Blue?' Snyder smiled thinly. 'It's a piece of expensive junk. We spent millions on the thing before we discovered that. We did manage to produce a headache or two, but nothing of any substance. Talon Blue is like a child's toy, good for games and little else.'

'But al Shisur wouldn't attack Israel without some kind of proof.'

'We gave him proof. We carried out seven controlled demonstrations, and al Shisur was present at every one. The results were ... devastating.' Snyders face creased into a grin.

'But how ...'

'The Iraqis used their own troops as guinea pigs. We introduced drugs into their water supply. Nobody dreamed of checking. Even if they had, it's unlikely they'd have noticed anything. The substances we used were the most sophisticated on the market, and al Shisur was delighted with the results.'

'You mean, you deliberately started a war to further your own political interests?'

'Correction, Mr McKlelland. The war was inevitable. We simply hurried it along a little. Al Shisur has gone into battle, confident that his amazing new weapon will suppress his enemy's ability to fight. He's about to discover that he's made a terrible mistake. Israel will humiliate him before the eyes of the world, and he'll become an outcast not only among his own people, but also among the countries of the Arab alliance. All that will have been achieved without the deployment of a single American troop.'

'And the President is unaware of this?'

'Everyone, son, not merely the President. There are certain areas which heads of state should never be allowed to enter. It's a sad fact, but true, that idealists have little place in politics. In the words of Adam West, it's always the good men who do the most harm in this world.'

Paul leaned back against the wall. Knowledge could be a painful thing, he thought. The audacity of the plan was breathtaking. Its strength lay in its very simplicity. Snyder had played him like a fish on a line, he and Leila both. And yet he didn't even feel angry, that was the strangest part. 'I suppose I should consider myself privileged. For the first time in my life, I know something the US government doesn't know.'

Snyder drained his coffee and crumpled the cup in his palm. 'That, son, is the most unfortunate part of all.'

'Meaning you now have to silence me?'

'It isn't easy playing God. Sometimes you're forced to do unpleasant things. If there was any way of avoiding this I would, but your existence threatens the whole operation.'

'What will you do, blow out my brains?'

'No. Bullet-ridden corpses have a habit of raising question marks. We'll drop you out of a helicopter somewhere over the Pacific. It's a little trick I learned back in Vietnam. If anyone should recover your body, it'll look like a simple drowning accident.'

'And Leila?'

'You go together, I'm afraid. It's a lousy shame, but there's no alternative.'

Snyder rose to his feet. Now that his confession was over, some of the fire had drained from his features and he seemed filled with a strange and elusive guilt. 'I admire you, Mr McKlelland, I want you to know that. You've proved a clever and formidable adversary. I wish it didn't have to end this way.'

He went out of the cell, locking the door carefully behind him.

The hospital corridor was shiny and new. Joktan watched the nurses bustling by, their hard heels clattering on the polished floor. His wrists were handcuffed, and armed soldiers guarded him on either side.

Something had happened to Joktan during the past few hours, something he could scarcely explain, even to himself. He had heard of experiments in which the entire psychological make-up of human beings could be altered by passing an electrical charge through the brain, and his experience in the desert seemed like that. In a curious way, he felt as if the patterns of his consciousness had taken a new and indefinable turn.

Since they'd wheeled Ellen into the operating theatre, there had been no word from the medical staff, and Joktan's anxiety was beginning to approach breaking point. He was their enemy, true, but in the name of humanity surely they would tell him if anything had gone wrong? Patience, he thought. The wound had been bad. The surgeons wouldn't be able to rush things.

A man came strolling along the corridor, staring down at Joktan curiously, and he met the gaze in silence. The stranger was tall and dark-skinned with fierce-looking eyes and thick wiry hair. 'You know who I am?'

Joktan nodded. 'Jacob Jabari. Head of Mossad.'

Jabari seemed pleased with the acknowledgement. He sat down in the adjoining chair and brushed an imaginary dust speck from his thigh. He had the air of a man who was trying hard to conceal his emotions. 'Cigarette?' he asked, fumbling in his pocket.

Joktan took one, and leaned forward to accept Jabari's light. There was no animosity in the Israeli's gaze; he looked merely curious, like a fisherman examining the teeth of a landed shark. 'How long has the woman been in?'

'Over an hour,' Joktan told him.

'Any news?'

'Nothing so far.'

Jabari drew hard on his cigarette, blowing a stream of smoke toward the ceiling. The draught from the air-conditioner ruffled his wiry hair. 'Colonel ...'

'Don't call me colonel,' Joktan said. 'I am Bedu now.'

'Here in Israel you will always be Colonel Joktan. You're a prize catch, colonel. They will want to put you on show.'

'Public trial?'

'Naturally.'

'Will they execute me?'

'I doubt that. They'd like to, of course. A lot of people, including me, believe you deserve it. But you sacrificed yourself to save the American woman, which should make you something of a celebrity in the United States. Israel will wish to appear magnanimous. I imagine you'll be sent to prison.'

'For a Bedu, that is worse than dying.'

'Nothing is worse than dying, colonel, believe me.'

Victory had muted Jabari's hatred, so that now he regarded Joktan more as a trophy than as an enemy. Tonight he would celebrate, but for the moment, he wanted to revel in Joktan's physical presence.

A doctor appeared in the corridor and Joktan's muscles tensed. He rose to his feet, a terrible numbness creeping through his lower limbs. The doctor gave him a reassuring nod. 'She's out of danger,' he said, and Joktan felt a flood of relief.

'Is she conscious yet?'

'Just.'

'May I see her?'

'She needs rest.'

Joktan raised his arms, displaying the handcuffs. 'This could be the last chance I'll get.'

The doctor smiled. 'Very well. Just for a moment.'

Ellen was lying motionless when Joktan entered the bedroom. A video screen monitored her heartbeat. The reading looked steady and even.

Joktan moved to the bed, and saw her eyes flicker

with recognition. They fixed on his face, puzzled at first, then growing sharper and clearer as her senses returned. 'Salih?'

He reached down and gently squeezed her hand. The hours of tension had left him feeling vulnerable and raw, and now he could think of nothing to say. 'How do you feel?' he managed at last.

Her lips twisted into a painful smile. 'Like somebody punched me in the ribs.'

'Doctor says you're going to be all right.'

'What about you, Salih? They've been chasing you for years.'

'Everything comes to he who waits,' he smiled.

'Oh, Salih, will they execute you?'

'Probably not. Prison, I imagine.'

'You'll never stand it. You belong in the desert.'

He realized that this was probably the last time in his life he would ever look at her, and felt a sudden flash of pain. His brain seemed bruised, as if he had driven it beyond the boundaries of human capacity.

'Was it worth it, Salih? Giving up your freedom to save me?'

'More than anything in the world,' he said gently.

He remembered the sweet curve of her spine and her soft breasts when he had been locked in a madness too strong to control, and he felt a sinking sensation in the pit of his stomach. She carried an air of sensuality that had never failed to excite him.

'What will you do now?' he asked curiously.

'Home, I guess. Back to the United States. I've made up my mind I'm going to finish with Paul. It won't be pleasant, but it has to be done. After that, I'll make a new beginning.'

'Well, I wish you luck.'

'You too, Salih. Thank you for my life.'

The doctor appeared in the doorway. He looked apologetic. 'You must leave now, colonel. The lady needs rest.'

'Am I permitted to kiss her?'

'Of course.'

Joktan leaned over, pressing his lips against Ellen's. She

slid her arm around his neck, and he felt her fingers kneading his thick dark hair. 'Goodbye, darling,' she whispered hoarsely.

Her cheeks were glistening as he followed the doctor out through the door.

The roar of the helicopter echoed in Paul's ears. He lay on the deck, with Leila at his side, their hands and feet securely manacled.

The huge machine rattled as it sped steadily westward. In the open hatch, Snyder's henchmen sat staring down at the ocean below, their husky physiques accentuated by padded overclothing.

'How far d'you figure they'll take us?' Paul asked, raising his voice above the clamour of the rotor blades.

'They'll clear the coastal area,' Leila answered. 'Too many boats.'

Paul smelled the nearness of her body and felt a sharp, almost physical pain. He was so concerned about Leila, he didn't even feel frightened any more. He couldn't account for that, the way he could care for another human being more than he cared about himself, and of all the things he regretted, the one he hated most was the thought of the countless hours and days they'd wasted.

He looked at her face, partly obscured by shadow. 'Are you scared?' he shouted.

'I was yesterday, but not any longer. I always knew there was a pretty fair chance we wouldn't come out of this alive.'

'I've been so stupid, so mixed-up,' he told her. 'I couldn't see the truth when it was staring me in the face. I thought I loved Ellen, but I was wrong. It was you, Leila. Right from the beginning. It was always you.'

Her eyes sparkled in the semi-darkness. 'You really mean that?'

'I wouldn't say it if I didn't.'

'I think you're beginning to grow on me too.'

'Well, I'm glad we didn't find out about it when it was too late.' He hesitated. 'Listen, ever follow baseball?

'Baseball? No.'

'There's an old baseball saying. It isn't over till it's over.'

'I have a feeling we're about to disprove that,' Leila told him frankly.

Paul's muscles tensed as two of the men came towards him from the helicopter hatch. 'I think it's time for my bath.'

They picked him up, and carried him, kicking and struggling, to the cabin doorway. A terrible nausea started inside him as he felt the slipstream buffeting his face. He could see the ocean far below, its shimmering expanse forming an endless, breathless curtain. Even at that height, his eyes picked out the wispy foam-crests of the distant whitetops.

'Take off the bracelets,' a man said. 'This is supposed to look like a boating accident.'

Paul heard a muffled click as his wrists and ankles were released. He lashed out with his feet, trying desperately to force his way back into the cabin interior, but his powerful captors seized him in a brutal embrace, lifting him bodily into the air. His stomach fluttered as he was pitched headlong through the open hatch.

He felt the wind pounding his cheeks and his senses dissolved as his velocity quickened. He saw the whitecaps streaking up to meet him and clenched his teeth, bracing himself for the impact. His heels drove into the foam-tossed waves and he plummeted down, down, down into the ocean's chilly depths. Then his head broke the surface, and he sucked desperately at the air. He saw Leila falling about fifty feet to his left, her body turning in a graceful somersault as she entered the water with a tumultuous splash.

Paul shook the moisture from his eyes, rolled on to his stomach and began swimming determinedly towards her.

When Abu Bakhit knocked on the door, Musallim al Shisur was seated alone in the centre of the room. He had abandoned his Arab robes for the full-dress uniform of an Iraqi general, and the spotless tunic, bristling with medal ribbons, looked faintly incongruous beneath his flabby, self-indulgent face.

The air was heavy with incense and somewhere a tape was

playing. Bakhit recognized the music. It was a Kurdish folk-song from the northern mountains.

The President did not look up as General Bakhit approached. His eyes were cloudy with thought.

'Excellency?' Bakhit said.

For the first time, the President noticed his presence and stared at Bakhit in puzzlement, as if trying to remember his visitor's identity.

'I bring bad news, Excellency,' Bakhit told him.

'What news?' al Shisur demanded.

'The Iraqi army is in full retreat.'

'Retreat? That's impossible.'

'I assure you, Excellency, my sources are unimpeachable.'

'Have you been in touch with General al Auf?'

'Our communication lines have been destroyed, you already know that.'

'So what you're saying is mere conjecture?'

'Not conjecture, Excellency. I'm afraid it is a simple statement of fact.'

Al Shisur waved his arm wearily. 'Why am I surrounded by defeatists? Even you, Abu, a man I trusted like a brother, have turned against me.'

'I was never with you,' Bakhit told him quietly.

Al Shisur frowned. He drew himself out of the arm-chair and stared intently into Bakhit's face. 'Never?' he breathed.

Bakhit's features were heavy with contempt. 'You have turned my country into a butcher's yard with your madness. You've suppressed the people, destroyed the fabric of our society, made a mockery of our laws and institutions. And now, against everything sane and holy, you have plunged us into a futile, unwinnable war.'

'Not unwinnable. Never unwinnable. It is my destiny to drive the forces of Zion out of the Holy Land. What about Talon Blue?'

General Bakhit said drily: 'It seems that your precious weapon didn't work.'

'Impossible. I saw it in operation with my own eyes.'

'Nevertheless, it failed to stem the Israeli counter-attack, and our troops are now being harassed both from the land

and from the air. Unless a cease-fire can be negotiated, the enemy forces will hound them all the way to Baghdad.'

'Cease-fire?' Al Shisur looked incredulous. 'How can we negotiate a cease-fire?'

'We can make a formal declaration of surrender, accept the UN resolutions, and renounce all claims on Israeli territory. The Americans have agreed to act as a go-between.'

'Nonsense. We still have our nuclear missiles. It isn't too late to obliterate Jerusalem and Tel Aviv.'

Bakhit's eyes glittered with loathing. 'I have done many things for you in the past, but I will never permit you to drive my country to suicide.'

Al Shisur filled his lungs with air. Turning, he walked to the window and pulled back the shades to look down at the courtyard outside. The fading sun cast pinkish ribbons across his bloated cheeks. 'All I ever wanted was justice for the Arab people,' he said.

'All you ever wanted was glory and immortality for Musallim al Shisur.'

An air of sadness came into al Shisur's eyes. 'You believe my motives were purely selfish, Abu?'

'You've destroyed our nation, Excellency. You've plunged us into an humiliating conflict, and now we are forced to abase ourselves, not only before Israel, but before the entire world.'

'You realize, of course, that to do such a thing would make my position as President untenable?'

'I do.'

'Where am I to go, Abu? Which country will accept me? I am an outsider among the members of the Arab alliance. If we sue for peace, how can I face the future with honour and dignity?'

'There is only one way,' General Bakhit said.

Unbuckling the leather holster at his hip, he took out his pistol and placed it on the table next to al Shisur's wrist. '*Allah Akbar*,' he said.

Al Shisur looked at him, frowning, as General Bakhit bowed and quietly left the room.

Rufo Pompeyo of the fishing boat *Dalmacia*, forty-eight

hours out of La Bufadore, was dozing in his cabin when his first mate, Augusto Licurgo, appeared in the open doorway.

'We have a strange fish in our nets, *mi capitan.* I think you had better come aloft.'

Puzzled, Pompeyo followed Licurgo up the narrow companionway. In the hazy moonlight, he saw the Mexican fishermen hauling something over the vessel's rail. As they lowered it gingerly to the deck, he realized the shapeless bundle was a drenched and bedraggled human being. A second followed almost immediately, water spewing from its sodden clothing. They lay side by side, their pale faces turned towards the sky.

'Are they still alive?' Pompeyo exclaimed.

'By the grace of God,' his first mate said. 'From the condition of their skin, they must have been in the water for at least twelve hours.'

'A miracle. How could they possibly have survived?'

'They used this.' Licurgo held up a dripping plaid shirt. 'They tied it into a ball and filled it with air like a football bladder. It helped to keep them afloat.'

Pompeyo examined the unconscious forms curiously. The sea was a treasure-house of mysteries, he reflected; despite all his years as a fisherman, it never failed to surprise him. He noticed that one of the casualties was a girl and came to a swift decision. 'They are shivering. Wrap them in blankets and carry them below. I shall radio the hospital at La Bufadore and return immediately to port.

President Clayman opened his eyes as he heard a tap at the office door. 'Who is it?'

'Mr President?' It was a Secret Serviceman's voice. 'You asked me to wake you, sir.'

'Ah, yes, thank you. Tell the others I'll be right there.'

Clayman rose to his feet, rubbing his face with his fingertips. He went into the tiny bathroom which adjoined the Oval Office and bathed his face with cold water. Drying his cheeks, he examined himself critically in the wall mirror. He was beginning to look his age, he thought. The uncertainty of the past few days hadn't done much to improve his appearance or his disposition.

296

Clayman combed his hair, fastened his necktie, then crossed the corridor to the conference room where most of his advisers had already assembled. They rose to their feet as Clayman entered, but he motioned them back to their seats and took his place at the head of the table. 'I've been speaking to the Israeli Prime Minister,' he announced without preamble. 'At present, the Iraqi army is heading for its homeland under heavy attack from Israeli ground and air forces. Musallim al Shisur's military might appears to have been effectively smashed.'

'Wouldn't this be an appropriate time for the Israelis to back off?' asked the National Security Adviser.

'Of course. Ariel Aronson knows that if he pursues al Shisur's army into the heart of Iraq, he'll be placing at risk our entire Mid-East peace initiative. The arms limitation agreements, the new territories – they'll all be thrown into jeopardy. Aronson's willing to listen to reason, but only on one condition. He want al Shisur replaced as the head of government in Iraq.'

For a moment, silence hung over the table, then General Kincaid said. 'How are we supposed to arrange that?'

'We can't arrange it, Nathan, that's the whole point. Whatever happens, the United States mustn't be seen to interfere in Arab affairs. If al Shisur is to be overthrown, it will have to be carried out by the Iraqi people themselves. I've been on the telephone to General Abu Bakhit, commander-in-chief of the Iraqi armed forces, and I found him, I must say, a perceptive and intelligent man. He recognized the Iraqi predicament immediately, and is going to talk to al Shisur himself. If al Shisur can be persuaded to step down, maybe we can look forward to a true and lasting peace in the Middle East.'

'Al Shisur's never listened to reason before. What makes you so sure he'll do so now?'

'Sadly, I am not sure,' President Clayman admitted, 'but for the people of Iraq, the alternative means anarchy, disintegration and continued suffering. I am putting my faith in the one man who seems to have a comprehensive understanding of what this crisis is all about. Everything, gentlemen, now depends on General Abu Bakhit.'

297

At that moment, the phone rang on the mahogany cabinet, and one of the Secret Servicemen moved across to answer it. He spoke for a moment, then raised the receiver respectfully. 'Mr President?' he said. 'You have a message from Baghdad.'